Passion
and
Death
in
Tuscany

Passion
and
Death
in
Tuscany

At
the
Edge
of
Time

RALPH O. STONE

To order additional copies of this book, contact:
Xlibris Corporation
1-888-7-XLIBRIS
www.Xlibris.com
Orders@Xlibris.com

Contents

Chapter One 9

Chapter Two 34

Chapter Three 70

Chapter Four 115

Chapter Five 155

Chapter Six 195

Chapter Seven 234

Chapter Eight 281

Epilogue 320

To Marga Stone, my wife, I dedicate this book for her help and advice but moreover for downloading confusing floppy disks. And to Helen Cosby Lewy for excellent criticism and many corrections of my Italian spelling and grammar.

Chapter One

With only his bony knees protruding stork-like from the soothing hot water, Al Praitt lay dozing in the extra long, old Italian tub. For several minutes he pondered a good, catchy first line for his new book. How about, "Courage, honesty and truth are virtues, but who needs virtue if you're handsome, charming and sophisticated?"

Now somewhat pleased with his paradigm, Al chuckled, "Those words are the best bit of sophistry I could imagine to describe George Crawford Van Dyke, Ph.D., English professor and fraud. And that introduction is perfect for the twenty-five thousand words I've produced in the last three weeks.

Then slowly, he moved to a sitting position and, now motivated by his plans for a festive evening of celebration, he stepped agilely from the copperplated heirloom tub. Almost mechanically, he dried his six-foot frame. Then, facing the large mirror for a few minutes, he seemed transfixed by the amount of matted brown hair on his chest and head. Then like a skilled cosmetician, he carefully examined the set of crow's feet between his left eye and ear. "Well, that's not too bad for an old geezer who somehow manages to attract too many sexy young women."

Finally satisfied with his self-examination, he quickly finished his daily shaving ritual, and with a splash of lotion was ready to dress for the evening. But suddenly, music from the living room flooded the bedroom. A velvety smooth bass sang: "In Italy, six-hundred and forty. Then in Germany, one-thousand and twenty." Now Al's rusty baritone joined Ezio Pinza's glorious basso, "One hundred in France and in Turkey, ninety-one but in Espana, one thousand and three and some you see are country girls, others contessas, et cetera." Al was completely engrossed in the silky, textured bass–Leporella's aria to Donna Elvira from Don Giovanni.

Exuberant, Al called out,"Oh, you devil, Pinza. You are the very personification of that greatest of all womanizers, Don Giovanni. And how the women everywhere loved you! What a way to make a living!"

The music suddenly stopped and Al quickly resumed his plans for the evening. In the bedroom, he slipped on his favorite silk boxing shorts and V-neck undershirt. From the nearby armoire, he selected a beige wool shirt, gray tweed slacks and a wool tie.

Glancing into a large nearby mirror, he approved his evening dress. "Mozart's birthday with a bottle of champagne, good food and be back here by nine-thirty. Shall I drive?" He weighed the decision, then pulled back the window curtain and peered into the dimly-lit courtyard. Light, feathery snowflakes drifted in the darkened night.

Al turned from the window, "Well, that's that! I walk. On with my heavy shoes and topcoat."

Again he surveyed himself in the mirror. His rutty-brown hair resembled a small haystack. With several rigorous strokes from his pocket comb, he looked presentable but he concluded, "I must wear my scotch plaid cap."

Nearly ready to leave, he completed his inventory: wallet, handkerchief, house key, flashlight. Okay, let's go!

Then as an afterthought, he remembered the thermostat which he reduced to 20c and left the corner lamp glowing.

From the open door, he surveyed the freezing early evening, then closed the door tightly, locked it, and pocketed the key. With the flashlight, he probed the slippery staircase and carefully descended to the small enclosed patio which divided the rectangular area between his quarters and the ancient masonry complex that had been another living area for working members of the extended family.

He glanced around the frozen garden and the massive oak gate which for six hundred years had been the guardian entrance to the large farmhouse entrance. Then, gripping the large, iron bolt with both hands, he slid it sideways enough to free the small interior door which opened directly into the driveway.

Again he paused, his light cutting a clear pathway to the road, left to Montefiorale and right to Greve, now lost below in the overcast night. His first steps were cautious feelers, then confident of his footing, he stepped quickly along the sloping ancient road. Automatically his flashlight revealed each pothole, rut and icy surface. The silence was broken by the crackling shards of ice, each a staccato warning to Al's forward motion. Nevertheless, he carefully avoided the larger frozen potholes which his flashlight exposed.

Soon the ancient road reached the steep descending slope perhaps only a hundred meters vertically above the frigid fog-bound village of Greve. Now the smooth surfaces became a series of slightly banked switch backs and a dangerous hazard to foot traffic and quite impossible by car.

Al felt challenged by the icy descent. Each pothole, rut and icy surface became a threat. Like a gymnast, he constantly shifted his weight as he maneuvered his body and feet to retain a perilous balance. These swift responses reminded him of a skilled skier attacking each turn on a slalom course—one event he had never successfully challenged.

Then as he continued his automatic body motions, he remembered his bouts as an amateur welterweight—bobbing, ducking, side-stepping, weaving, erratic motions to confuse his opponent and leaving an opening for rapid jabs followed by a smashing right hook and knockout.

Soon Al could see the dim outline of a large brick building but the road suddenly switched to his left and Al was barely able to retain his balance by touching the ice with both hands while maneuvering his body against a small snow bank. "Damn!" he muttered, "almost a crash landing just when I thought I had it made."

Now on level ground, relatively free of snow and ice, he quickly covered the short distance to the large triangular Piazza Giovanni da Verrazano named for the great Italian navigator-explorer from Greve. For many New Yorkers, they could boast that their Verrazano-Narrows Bridge was the longest bridge in the world, some sixty feet longer than San Francisco's Golden Gate Bridge, which held the record only to be surpassed by first the New York Verrazano-

Narrows and then by the Hull Bridge in Britain, which was 1410 meters long, thus surpassing the New York span by twelve meters and the San Francisco span by thirty meters. But for Al and most native San Franciscans, their bridge was not only the highest, but certainly the most beautiful.

But for Greve's proud denizens, and for frequent tourists, the Verranzo's long, sloping tapering square was unequaled by any other. Paved with cobblestone, it's aged worn surface was smooth and attractive for every purpose. And it's irregular dimensions, some 125 meters at its lower base, which slowly narrowed after some 80 meters to its eastern end, next to a small church and then exited to a small street. Here in the Verrazano, for the shopper's convenience, most of the commercial shops, stores, offices and restaurants are protected by a twelve-foot wide arcade.

And every Wednesday, Greve's great square is quickly transformed from a modest but proud commercial center into a crowded community of shoppers by the hundreds and bands of bargain hunters, all searching the square now lined with wagons, carts and trucks all displaying shoes, cloths, and household goods. Shoppers compete for food–fish, bakery delights, meat, fruit, vegetables, almost everything anyone might want or need–including small collections of bad paintings, trophies and plain junk. The entire scene forms a rich tapestry of rural Tuscany.

Al, like most of the curious and bold, always arrived early for the Wednesday market day for they knew that Thursday the great square and it's many shops would be empty and closed.

Now on this cold Monday evening, the square was empty and dimly lit. Al rapidly crossed at the widest point which led to the intersection of A-22, the entrance to the Chianti country and a small crossroad leading to the small bridge over Greve's lazy stream. At this junction of the square was that town's only bank on one side and an attractive art shop on the other. And across A-22 was Greve's largest food store–The Coop. Before turning into A-22 and the nearby Ristorante Moro, Al glanced at the glaring lights of Cinema Boito and the nearby police station, neither building was known to Al who hastened his pace toward the red neon sign some 150 meters distant. For Al, Trattoria Mora would be more romantic if named after Boheme's Cafe Mumus.

Now as the cold air ripped his face, Al rapidly approached the brightly-lit cafe, a long wooden, rectangular building, perhaps twenty meters or more and almost an equal measure at its opposite ends. The area was well lit by evenly-placed square windows which faced a row of ten or fifteen late-model sedans, all parked on each side of the entrance.

Two large doors opened into a small vestibule which served as a cloak room and protective entrance to the cafe. Here were a collection of expensive heavy coats and scarves neatly hanging from wooden pegs to which Al deposited his own.

As Al pushed hard against the heavy door, blasts of warm air and young voices cheered him. Once inside, he paused as the many voices fell silent and all eyes seemed to note his presence. He smiled and turned as the sound of the cheerful ambience radiated throughout the long-narrow dining area.

Having dined here six or seven times, Al quickly seated himself at one of the several empty tables which, with the kitchen and bar at opposite ends, was separated from the larger dining and dancing room by a two-meter high divider. This larger and more attractive section was often crowded during the summer season.

Against the wall facing Al was a smaller dining area with identical sturdy, heavy tables which extended from the entrance vestibule to the corner kitchen area.

Next to this crowded kitchen were tables near the small busy serving area and opposite the waiter's station. All of the young people were crowded together at small square tables which complicated service and reasonable communications for everybody. And the waiter's problems were complicated by the frequent table changes and noise of the boisterous diners who stood gesticulating and laughing as only young Italian or Greek students communicate: with hand, arm, body and head movements.

Al was amused and entertained by this young crowd quite different from student or adult scenes in Berkeley. Immediately he was transformed from a retiring professor and writer to an interested and fascinated witness to youth celebrating life, a scene he had forgotten since leaving Berkeley a few years earlier.

Now Al directed his attention towards two young couples opposite and slightly to his right. Quite obviously , they had been watching Al in his prolonged observation of the exuberant youth. They smiled as Al made eye contact which signaled a shared communication of age and youth.

Moments had passed and yet the hustling waiters were still prisoners of the loud hungry diners. So Al now directed his attention to a quieter area on his left which included a small bar with two stools and a dessert kitchen still silent and an adjacent office and cashier's register. Except for the bartender who also catered sweets, the only attendant was a well-dressed gentleman who obviously owned or managed the trattoria.

For a few more relaxing moments, Al luxuriated in the warmth and radiating joy of the long room. But suddenly his reverie was broken by a short, stocky waiter who handed Al a well-worn, two-paged menu while offering a cheerful, "Buona sera, signore."

Al smiled and replied, "Si, grazie" as the waiter turned momentarily toward the other couples who were still dining and talking. All studied the lista del pranzo and from previous readings, quickly decided on soupa, ensalata verde, costoletta and dolce. But first, the champagne and antipasto.

Minutes later, the waiter returned, "Signore, mi scuse e pronto?

Al looked cautiously and replied, "Si por favore, ma ora vorrei un bottiglie champagne.

"Bene," the waiter replied, "vino spumante e forse Martini-Rossi spumante?

"Si," but Al was concerned what the waiter might bring.

Seconds later, the waiter was back with the champagne in an ice bucket and a champagne glass. As he carefully served the champagne, he asked, "Scusi, Signore Professor, okay?"

Al glanced at the bottle and a small plate of antipasto. "Molto bene. Cameriere, grazie."

Quickly the waiter opened the bottle and poured a small quantity for approval.

Al eased the glass to his mouth, and felt the wine bubbles tickle his palate, "Molto bene e grazie."

As the waiter moved to leave, Al asked "Por favore, cameriere, vorrei soupa, insalata verde, costoletta, pane e dolce, okay?"

As the waiter scribbled the order and asked "Quando?"

"Non presto, forse vente minuti."

Now Al was quite ecstatic and poured his glass almost full. For seconds he stared, then lifted his glass high, "Happy Birthday, Wolfgang!" The nearest couple was watching Al's celebration and sat in bemused attention.

Al took several sips and in elation lifted his glass and added, "And a

Happy Birthday to me!" The astonished nearby couple smiled a note of approval and also lifted their wine glasses and nodded, "saluti, signore!"

Al continued to sip the champagne and nibble the snacks. Quietly he was radiant, an epiphany, caressing, comforting experience which he only remembered from the first days of his marriage to Joan.

Slowly the nearest couple approached his table and in an English-French accent said, "Good evening, sir. You seem to be celebrating, yes?"

Al was momentarily startled, but quietly replied, "Indeed I am, sir. Yes, today is Mozart's birthday and by coincidence it's also my birthday."

The French couple were amused, but friendly. "So you honor Wolfgang Amadeus Mozart and yourself. That's wonderful and thank you for sharing your birthday."

Al beamed quickly, "Thank you, but won't you please sit down and share this wine with me?"

The couple also smiled warmly, "That's very nice and we would like to honor you and Mozart, but we must return to Florence."

Al extended his hand which the husband squeezed politely as did his pretty wife. "We are the Bechets and we live in Paris. I am sorry that we cannot stay for a while, but we must return to Paris tomorrow. Good night." And they were gone with waves and smiles.

Al returned to his wine and antipasto and within minutes, his waiter returned and quickly placed the soup nearby, asking, "E buono, Professore?"

"Si. Grazie, Dino."

Hearing his name, the waiter smiled and moved quickly to the crowd of young people, several of whom were loudly demand their bills. "Dino, por favor, mi conti presto!"

Within minutes, only three or four couples remained from the large group and these diners showed no sign of leaving.

Now as Al savored his bean soup, Dino appeared with the mixed green salad and the veal cutlet and a steaming dish of penne and ricotta.

"Okay, Professore?" Dino asked.

"Yes, very good and thank you, Dino."

Al mulled over his dinner and relaxed in the comfort of the cafe. Then having finished the meal, suddenly Dino returned with a chocolate sundae.

"Here, Professore, ice cream and chocolate."

For a second, Al was speechless. "Dino, this is wonderful. The best chocolate sundae I have ever tasted."

Dino, amused by Al's exuberance, smiled broadly and added, "Buon
appetito."

For several more minutes, Al sat quietly absorbed in the soft laughter from
the five couples still dining. But suddenly the heavy front door swung wide
open and two handsome young men and their stunningly beautiful young
women barged into the room. Having scanned the area, they now took the
heavy tables that had been occupied by the foreign couple. The young men
quickly pushed the tables together, which allowed the couples to face the
surprised American.

Immediately, Dino arrived to interrupt the chatter in English and Italian.
As they laughed and argued about the drinks, Al was immediately absorbed
and focused on the two beautiful women.

One was a striking brunette, tall, sensual and athletic in motion and
elegant in style. Her companion, a strawberry blonde, moved aggressively,
smiling and projecting her beauty, strength and health, which from their
height and body language, signaled pleasure and sex. But the sleek brunette, equally tall, was in sharp contrast with her friend. From her head of
dense, silken raven hair, hanging carelessly in small waves, the brunette's
finely molded face and dark eyes suggested discipline, passion and courage, and her board shoulders and firm breasts could have indicated swim-
mer or pianist.

Both women were clothed in baby-blue, skin-tight stretch ski pants which
clearly outlined their strong, athletic bodies in form and beauty. And each wore
seemingly braless tops, concealed by beige turtleneck cashmere sweaters over
which they wore off-white silk down jackets. They appeared to be in their early
twenties and obviously were good friends.

Following trivial discussions with the two men about food and drinks,
their orders were taken. As the two men whispered and laughed, the women
welcomed the change to gossip and size up the noisy crowd. Then Dawn, the
blonde, nudged Lucia, and both women stole glances at the American who
felt trapped by their beauty and beguiling flirtation. Now both women subtly
curious, suddenly arose and quickly confronted the surprised American.

"Pardon us, sir, but aren't you one of the American Professors on the

Stanford staff?" Both women flashed radiant smiles which seemed to reassure the embarrassed Al Praitt.

Surprised and pleased, Al welcomed their question. "No, I'm afraid not, but would that I were since you both seem to be students at Stanford's campus in Florence."

Then the blonde first introduced herself. "My name is Dawn Knight and I am a student, but my very good friend, Lucia Conde, is not a classmate, but we do share a small apartment. At this point, Lucia flashed a broad smile and asked, "If I'm not too blunt, we were wondering what you might be doing in Greve? And your champagne has also made us curious."

Al was delighted. "Well, I am or was a professor until recently, but now I'm here for a few months to relax and finish a short novel. As for the champagne, yes, I'm celebrating–drinking wine to two good men–one very famous, obviously not the man you see, but more importantly the man you don't see but often hear and appreciate. Certainly Austria's greatest composer, Wolfgang Amadeus Mozart whose birthday I am celebrating, together with mine, which is our only connection. Of course, I love his music and listened to his Don Giovanni before leaving my house tonight."

At this point, both women laughed uproariously, "Don Giovanni? You? How wonderful!"

"No, no! I mean Ezio Pinza singing the role of Leporello in Don Giovanni, particularly his catalogue aria to Donna Elvira–absolutely wonderful and very funny."

At this, Dawn and Lucia laughed, "Yes, we both know and love that opera. Who knows, professor, maybe you are a Don Giovanni?"

"I'm afraid that would be impossible. I haven't the voice, the looks or the ambition for that role."

At this point, the two male escorts became impatient and called Lucia and Dawn by name. Startled, the two women whispered, "Ciao" and retreated to their positions beside Benito and Carlo. Both men were obviously agitated and jealous and insulted the women with crude remarks. Apparently Lucia was able to ease the tension with sincere apologies and Dawn's excuse, "I thought that he was a professor from Stanford which he was until recently."

"You mean Stanford in Florence or in California?"

"No, in California. He's here writing a book."

Before further cross-examination by the jealous males, Dino returned with a small bottle of grappa and a bottle of white wine and a large plate of antipasto. Without speaking, Dino set out glasses before each person for possible requests. Then in a final motion, he deftly slid the platter of antipasto toward the women and softly offered, "Buon apppetito."

The food and wine temporarily assuaged the male tempers as both couples sensing the tension drank and ate in quiet desperation. But only Benito drank the grappa, which he tossed down in repeated gulps while reaching for cheese and salami. Within minutes, most of the food had disappeared while Lucia and Dawn slowly sipped wine as Carlo continued to gulp down the remaining grappa.

Having completed the light supper, both men again expressed some degree of anger and jealously. "That was a stupid mistake," Carlo blurted followed by Benito's accusation, "You're rotten women!" At this, both women laughed sarcastically, "And you're both crazy!"

Before the issue could explode, Carlo grabbed Dawn's arm and announced,"We're leaving! We promised to visit my parents for a few minutes. I called them and they want to meet Dawn!" Before Lucia or Benito could protest, Dawn and Carlo were edging towards the door. "We'll be back in a half-hour. His parents live nearby."

For a few minutes, Lucia and Benito sat quietly, then to reduce the tension, Lucia gently took Benito's left hand. For the now-drunken Benito, her hand was an amorous signal which he seized with a pull and an affectionate kiss on her right ear. Lucia reacted with alarm as her entire body stiffened.

"Benito, please. Stop!"

But her plea to stop only encouraged Benito to press his advantage and pull her towards him.

For seconds they struggled, but now the grappa had affected Benito's balance and as Lucia struggled to rise, Benito fell sideways. Quickly she freed herself and escaped around the table which prevented her assailant from grabbing her.

The notice and disturbance had aroused not only Al's attention, but also that of the four other diners and Dino and three other waiters. Everybody stood in shocked surprise as Benito staggered to his feet.

"Bitch!" Benito bellowed, "Let's go! Now!"

Realizing her peril, Lucia fled to Al's table. As Benito shouted obscenities, Al stepped in front of Lucia and whispered, "I won't let him touch you!"

For a few seconds, Benito continued to curse, then suddenly lunged forward in an aggressive effort to attack Al.

Quickly Al stepped forward just as his drunken assailant swung his right arm in a wild unbalanced attack. As Al side-stepped the lunging Benito, he gently kicked his attacker on his backside.

Off balance, Benito fell forward on his chest as his head struck hard against the table leg. There Benito lay motionless, his head dripping blood on the table leg and the floor.

Suddenly the stunned silence was broken by a woman's scream, "He's dead!"

"He's not dead. He's only drunk and unconscious," a waiter exclaimed.

For several seconds, the small crowd stood staring at the motionless Benito. Then Al, taking Lucia's arm, stepped over the stricken body and asked the visibly-shaken Lucia to join him at a nearby table. She was very happy to seat herself hard against Al's protective body as the small crowd, still shocked, returned to their tables.

With Benito still lying motionless, Dino knelt over him and examined his head which continued to ooze droplets of blood. Dino arose and soon returned with a small bucket of water which he rapidly poured over the wound and all over Benito's head. Dino stared at the motionless body as did Al and Lucia and everybody else in the cafe.

Slowly Benito moved his head and struggled to stand, but only again to fall backwards. Again, Dino came forward with a large soiled cloth, wiped Benito's wound, which appeared to be a small cut and bruise. Having regained almost full consciousness, Benito sat on the floor staring at Dino.

"Who attacked me?" Benito asked.

"Everybody!" Dino exploded. "And you're a rotten bastard!"

Before Benito could stand, a large, powerful policeman appeared. Towering over the stricken Benito, he spoke directly to the injured, but still belligerent drunk, "Don't try to escape!" Without further comment, he lifted Benito to a standing position, then threw him over his shoulder and shouted to the cafe manager and Dino, "He won't bother anybody, but he will sober up in jail and be charged with drunken behavior in a public place."

Then the policeman struggled out of the cafe, joined by the manager.

At the parked police car, the policeman opened the door and threw Benito into the locked compartment and drove away.

Back in the cafe, Al and Lucia sat close together before Dino and the manager, joined by only four other diners, formed a small circle.

First the manager apologized profusely for the violent event, promising that he would personally file an additional complaint against Benito for failure to pay his bill.

As everybody peppered both Al and Lucia about their feelings, their fears, others offered sympathetic words of encouragement. Then the last couple who had already paid Dino thanked him and left.

Alone Al and Lucia sat close together sharing their sudden mutual attraction. But Al, somewhat embarrassed and uneasy with the close body contact with Lucia, asked her quietly if she would mind if he sat opposite her. She readily agreed, adding that she wanted to have eye contact with her hero and her friend.

Facing each other, Al called to Dino who was cleaning up the mess on the nearby floor.

"Yes, Professore, may I help you?"

"Please, if you don't mind, maybe Miss Conde would like to share some champagne with me. Would you, dear lady?"

Lucia was not only surprised, but very pleased to share a bottle of champagne with her handsome protector, and Dino was also pleased to be a small part of this victory celebration.

Minutes later, he appeared and with a magnum of Martini & Rossi, which surprised and pleased Lucia and Al. Then quickly producing three glasses, he completed the triumphant ritual. Dino quickly filled each glass as Al touched Lucia's and Dino's glasses. "To Dino, the referee, doctor and champion." Quickly, Lucia translated Al's remarks which brought smiles to Dino's handsome face, who again touched each glass and added, "To America and the Professore!"

Slowly Dino returned to the bar and conversed briefly with the manager.

In the now-deserted dining room, Al and Lucia sat silently facing each other. Quietly with only a trace of a smile, Lucia faced Al who struggled to retain a rising sexual glow.

And Lucia suddenly responding to Al's amorous transmission welcomed the strange and wonderful glow of passion.

Neither stricken victim spoke then, each realizing an embarrassing tinge of excitement, and laughed almost simultaneously.

"What were you thinking, Lucia?"

"Oh, well, I was thinking how charming and wonderful you are."

Al blushed and added, "Lucia, you are a remarkably beautiful woman and you cause me to wish that I were young again."

Lucia was enchanted with Al's confession, weighing each word as a hint for affection and romance.

"Well," Lucia whispered, "You are a very handsome and attractive man and I'm glad that you aren't younger because then you couldn't project your courage and maturity. And I must confess, you do remind me of my father who would now be about your age. How my mother and I loved him!"

For several seconds, a quiet sadness lingered before Al broke the silence. "You spoke sadly of the past, Lucia. I hope my outspoken confessional doesn't trouble you."

Again Lucia paused and offered a slight smile, then replied, "No, quite the contrary. Your strength gives me courage. But, well, about twelve years ago, my father died in a terrible accident. Then after my mother had recovered from a prolonged period of suffering, she married a handsome Italian businessman, and for about three years our lives were restored only suddenly to be smashed again."

Slowly tears formed and dropped on Al's outstretched hands.

For seconds neither spoke. Then slowly, Al lifted Lucia's hands and kissed them. "Forgive me, dear Lucia, I shouldn't have asked about your family."

"Oh, no," Lucia softly replied. "How should we get to know each other if we can't share each other's lives?"

"Of course," Al offered. "And I do hope that we may share our pasts and perhaps our plans for the future. And, by that, I mean a friendship."

The sadness suddenly dissipated as Lucia added, "Yes, of course, friendship."

"I mean that," Al suggested. "A friendship, a real friendship."

Encouraged by the tones of voice and the warmth of their smiles, they agreed that they had too much in common to forget this evening.

"It has been quite the most unusual and exciting evening I've ever experienced," Al volunteered, which Lucia answered with a smile as she appeared confused.

"Oh, Al, it's late. Dawn should have returned." Then, glancing at her watch, "It's almost ten. She left two hours ago! What could have happened?"

Surprised by her outspoken fear, Al cautiously replied, "Do you know where she went, Lucia?"

"Yes. She said she was going with Carlo to meet his parents and that she wouldn't be gone long. My problem is that she and Carlo have the car which is the only way I have to return to our apartment in Florence."

Nervously, Al glanced at his watch, then volunteered, "I'm terribly sorry, Lucia, if Dawn and Carlo don't return soon, maybe I could get my car and drive you back tonight."

Then, as an afterthought, Al replied to himself, "Damn! even if I do get back to the house, the road's too dangerous to risk driving."

Lucia understood Al's message and concern, "Well, maybe Dawn and Carlo will return soon."

But even before Al could respond, the cloak room door opened wide allowing a gust of cold wind accompanied by a handsome stranger to appear. For several seconds, the fur-clad man stood transfixed at the open door.

As the stranger stared at Al and Lucia, she whispered, "Oh, my God! It's him."

The icy silence was quickly dissipated by Dino who greeted the stranger while simultaneously jerking the door closed. "I'm sorry, sir, but our dining room is closed and we will be closing the entire cafe when all guests leave."

"Well, I understand, but perhaps I could warm up with some brandy and whatever else you might have."

Dino nodded, "Yes, we will be glad to serve you brandy and I'll find a plate of antipasto. Please seat yourself."

The stranger politely thanked Dino and quickly thrust some bills into Dino's hand. Then he took the same seat and table that the departing four-some had occupied almost two hours earlier.

Lucia appeared shocked as she gripped Al's warm hands. Quietly she informed Al who the stranger was.

"Well," Al offered, "I believe your good friends will be here soon and you shall be on your way back to Florence." Then he whispered, "Don't worry, Lucia, I'll get a taxi and we'll leave."

Now Lucia squeezed Al's arm, then turning her head, she whispered in his ear, "Darling, now I'm frightened. That man over there is my hated stepfather.

The same man who accidently killed my mother and my little brother and later raped me."

For seconds Al sat in shocked surprise, then whispered, "Shall we leave?" Maybe we could go to the hotel and get a taxi or maybe a room for you?"

Again they sat quietly as Al tactfully sneaked glances at Lucia's stepfather and now Al's bitter enemy.

Finally Lucia suggested, "No, dear man, maybe we should wait a few more minutes while you pay the bill. As you do, I will pretend that I am going to the ladies rest room where there is an unofficial exit door just beyond the toilets. I'll slip out that way and hide behind some large trees just in front of the clinic. Then when Michele, my ex-stepfather, goes looking for me, as I'm certain he will, you get out fast and join me behind those trees."

For seconds, Al weighed Lucia's plan, then whispered, "Good. I'll call Dino and pay the bill. Then, you go out the back door, but wait for a few minutes and listen for any loud or unexpected talk or noise. Then you silently slip out and I'll join you about the same time. But stay hidden behind those trees!"

Agreed and confident, Lucia and Al talked softly. Then, to confuse Michele, who quite obviously was straining to hear the couple's words, they raised their voices slightly. "Well, if Dawn and Carlo don't return soon, I think we should walk over to the parent's house and demand that they drive us back to Florence without further delay."

"Absolutely, Uncle George," Lucia spoke in a loud, clear voice. Dawn's got to get her act together right now!"

Carefully they continued to appear agitated while watching Michele's reaction. He strained to listen, checked his watch and stared hard at Lucia and Al.

Suddenly Lucia stood, then paused, "I'm going to the rest room, but I'll be back in a few minutes." Bending low, she whispered, "when you leave, please bring my white jacket. It's here on the bench. Okay? Please take care of Dino for me." With that, she swept around the room divider near the kitchen. Al could hardly hear her snow boots as she almost skated around the corner.

Instantly, Michele projected himself to Al's table. "May I talk to you, sir?" Seated, Michele quickly identified himself and asked, "I'm quite surprised to see that young lady with you."

"Why?" Al bristled.

"Simply because I was Miss Conde's legal guardian until she became a liar and a petty criminal."

"Miss Conde, a criminal?" Al blurted.

"Yes. I allowed her to work in my shop, but she repeatedly stole money and jewelry and cheated my customers so, of course, I dismissed her. She's a liar and a thief so be careful. Mr.. . . ?

"My name is Allan A. Praitt, and I'm here for a short time, but your report about Miss Conde greatly disturbs me. I just met her here tonight with her friends and she's been waiting for them to return. She must return to Florence tonight.

"Well, don't expect her to return, sir. She's a very devious and unbelievable young woman. I know because I was her stepfather for several years."

Al quietly bristled at Michele's vicious lies while thinking, "And you raped her."

Now Michele suddenly stood. "Did she say where she was going now?"

"Mr. Leone, Miss Lucia will probably return soon, as she mentioned the ladies' room."

With that, Leone walked rapidly around the divider while Al quickly settled their bill with Dino, who, alarmed by Leone's rude behavior, thanked the professor profusely.

Quickly Al pulled on his top coat while concealing Lucia's white jacket, then out of the dimly-lit cafe, Al ran across the street towards the tall, dark trees. From behind the largest of the Sycamore trees, there was Lucia.

At once Lucia was encased in his powerful arms as Al explained that Michele had gone looking for her. Confident, but quiet, they listened for sounds from the nearby cafe. Then suddenly the silence was broken. The roar of an engine and the lights of an accelerating car illuminated the shadows behind the trees. Al and Lucia laughed as Michele's black Mercedes sped away.

"Great!" Al laughed. "The bastard's gone! Now let's return to the square and the hotel on the corner."

In less than a minute, they had rounded the intersection and were approaching the hotel when they heard Leone's Mercedes approaching. Quickly, they concealed themselves behind a wall and listened.

In less than a minute, the engine's roar signaled Michele's departure as the relieved couple entered the hotel and waited. Finally a graying clerk appeared who humbly asked, "Have you been waiting long? I heard a noise, but couldn't get here sooner."

"No," Al replied, "but we would like to call a taxi, if you don't mind." When the old man appeared confused, Lucia quickly translated Al's question.

"Well, dear Al, the clerk says there isn't any taxi here at this hour. And when I asked him about a room, he smiled and said that all of the rooms were taken."

"So, what do we do now?" Lucia asked.

"Before we try walking back to my house, where do you think Leone has gone?"

"I don't know. He might drive towards Panzano, but I doubt it because he knows that my grandfather has told everybody that Leone is a thief and a liar. And my grandfather, who always carries a pistol, has promised to kill him on sight. So I don't think Michele will visit Panzano soon."

"And I don't think he will try the steep road to Montefiorale. When I walked down the hill from my house, which is less than a mile from here, I almost fell several times where the road becomes a few steep series of switch backs."

"Well, my handsome hero, what do you suggest?"

"We really don't have any choice, darling girl, but to climb up the icy road."

"Fortunately, I've a flashlight, so maybe the climb won't be too hard."

Soon the steep trek began, past the dark side of the hotel and soon a hard left over the crusty ice, now frozen much harder than almost four hours earlier.

Quickly Lucia and Al linked their gloved hands and began the slow ascent. With Al's bright light selecting the best footing and their linked hands providing additional strength and stability, they seemed to move upward much easier than Al thought possible. After quickly negotiating the first switch back, they paused. "Darling," Al caressed the word with affection, "Are you okay?" And Lucia responded with equal affection, "I couldn't feel better."

As they easily climbed each switch back, their confidence grew and their fears dissipated into puffs of frozen breath. Soon they completed the slalom-like track and quickly moved toward the distant lights. Slowing, Al pointed with his free hand, "There, darling, the lights are my house."

Now they moved faster, still holding themselves together, a single entity which soon became the first link in a long chain that neither person could imagine.

Finally at the great gate, Al gently freed his left hand, and with both hands he slid the large bolt which released the small door from the rest of the ancient oak entrance. As the small inner door swung open, it's rusty hinges protested.

Again, taking Lucia's hand, Al pulled her close to him as he lifted his right foot to clear the bottom framed entrance which was a mortised connection between two jambs and the lintel. This exterior door, some five by three feet, allowed easy passage for only one person at a time, a necessary defensive device for times of attack.

Soon the couple stood briefly in the small interior court now seen more clearly by the exterior light which illuminated the entire area and the stairway which lead to the small upper deck and the large front door.

Again Al and Lucia linked hands in an affectionate grip. At the door, Al fumbled for the key before inserting the large bronze key and felt the bolt withdraw. With an easy push, the door opened silently as a rush of warm air engulfed the pair.

They quickly entered after Al pushed the door firmly closed. Again, he inserted the key and felt the bolt slide into place.

Finally they were home, warm and secure. In the warm living room, Lucia glanced around the ancient room, some fifteen by twenty feet. At the space opposite the fireplace, a modern, six-foot convertible sofa dominated the room. Opposite the front door was a large, hot water radiator which radiated warm air and was one of eight similar devices in each of the rooms in the large ancient house-fortress.

And the heavy oak floor was covered by a large Chinese blue rug whose center was dominated by a magnificent large ferocious dragon and four small but similar dragons, all guarding each corner.

To complete the calm ambience of this major room, several steel engravings depicting scenes from the Middle Ages were spaced in appropriate places.

Lucia was almost stunned by the room's comfort and beauty. "It's very unusual, Al. I would have never imagined that such an ancient and forbidding stone structure could have been so radically transformed."

"Nor I either," then adding, "but that's what money, taste and imagination has done by my Italian friend, Arturo Fagiolo, with whom I am exchanging houses for this half-year. He has my house in Berkeley, which isn't as grand as this, but certainly as comfortable and much more accessible. Each of our houses has advantages and shortcomings, but I'm comfortable and satisfied and Arturo writes that he is, too. But he does have a small grand piano in the front bedroom which I don't have. But I do have an excellent music center with a complete hi-fi system for tapes, CD's and other recordings. It's really everything I need for my music needs. So, while I can't play an instrument, I am able to listen to the greatest music from the world's greatest composers."

"Lucia, although I suppose it's just as late for you as it is for me, why don't you rest on this large sofa while I put on a CD from Arturo's large hi-fi library in this adjoining room—the speakers are concealed in this living room."

At this point, Lucia followed Al into the large combination kitchen and dining room with a small pantry, sink and larder cleverly inset into the outside wall. With a small, but expandable oak dinner table and four matching oak chairs, Lucia was impressed. "Your friend has good taste and practical sense. It's a wonderful room."

"Now" Al offered, "I would like to propose a mild but cheerful libation." And with that, he removed a bottle of French champagne from the refrigerator and two appropriate glasses.

"What a lovely good night surprise," Lucia almost purred. As Al carefully poured the wine into each glass, Lucia added, "and I have a little surprise for you, Mr. Birthday Man, but I'll wait for the appropriate time."

Al was almost giddy with excitement and could hardly control his hand as he gave the glass to Lucia.

"Now, Professor Praitt," Lucia solemnly intoned, "a toast to Wolfgang Mozart, to you, Mr. Praitt and last and least, to myself, also a birthday celebrant. Exactly twenty-one years ago, I was born in Verona, Italy."

For seconds, Al was speechless. Then, raising his glass, "Birthday greetings to the most beautiful woman in the world." Then each celebrant touched glasses and drank.

"Darling girl, why didn't you tell me and your friend Dawn at the cafe?"

"Oh, Al, I considered it for a second and then decided that it wasn't the time or place and might have suggested that I was intruding in what had been your private celebration."

"On the contrary," Al offered. "It would have added a more important dimension to my rather exaggerated sense of self-importance. But now, here, I can celebrate your birthday, which is much more appropriate than back in that noisy trattoria."

"Now, let's take our glasses and wine to the more comfortable living room where we can discuss sleeping arrangements for the night."

At the word sleeping arrangement, Lucia inwardly flinched, "What is he saying? What is he thinking? No, no, he can't mean that–that he wants me to sleep with him?"

Al noticed the frown on Lucia's face and instantly recognized her apprehension triggered by "sleeping arrangement."

"Lucia, please forgive me. I should have said bedroom selection. I should have realized that my thoughtless phrase could be misunderstood, and I'm very sorry."

"Don't apologize, Al, please. I'm not embarrassed and I fully understand what you meant. It just sounded uncharacteristic of you. Now, as you have three bedrooms, we each have a choice, right?" The champagne had a rapid effect on Lucia's emotions.

"Well," Al intoned ceremoniously, "we have one large bedroom just off the living room, and a small bedroom in the front section, which is next to the bedroom with the small baby grand. And there's a large tower bedroom which is reached by the steep spiral staircase. The bed is small but the room offers a spectacular view."

"Darling lady, we shall inspect each room, and you shall have your choice. Each is comfortable and one quite larger than the other. Shall I escort you on your tour?"

The quick tour ended as Lucia declared, "That's easy, Al. Obviously the larger room is yours because all of your books, bed and furniture are there."

"No, No," Al protested. "That doesn't make any difference. Why don't you use my room. I'll quickly change the sheets. Besides, the bathroom is nearby to the right of the entrance and beyond the sofa. I forgot to mention that when we came in."

For a minute, they teased and pretended to argue, but soon Lucia had her way and chose the smaller front bedroom.

The issue was settled as were questions about the bathroom. Towels and blankets and a final word about morning arousal, breakfast and departure.

With Al's questions settled, each faced the other in an unspoken, but embarrassed good night. Finally Lucia grabbed Al and kissed him softly on the cheek.

"Good night you wonderful, brave man," and with that, she quickly disappeared into the front bedroom.

Al watched her go, turned and stepped into his bedroom, softly closed the door and moments later, he was snug under the comforter. Then he turned off the bedside lamp and soon relaxed into a wonderful sleep.

Sometime after seven, Al slowly awakened from a deep and refreshing sleep. As he stared at the first rays of sunshine, he heard sounds from a piano which he thought must be from the radio which sometimes automatically came alive simply because Al had forgotten to turn off the timer which he occasionally set to arouse himself or to induce slumber after a day of strenuous writing.

Now he opened his door and a rapid series of notes rising to a crescendo filled his ears. He listened intently to the music which was familiar and beautiful. "It's got to be Beethoven!" He listened closely, marveling at the pianist's technique. Then it came to him. The Moonlight Sonata, yes. That's it. The Presto, the third and final movement.

As he continued to listen, praising the pianist's skill, it suddenly came to him, but who could it be? This must be the radio, but it couldn't be from the speakers in the living room.

"Well," he thought, "I don't remember Lucia mentioning music or the piano." But she must be playing. Minutes later, the explosion of notes ended.

Hastily, Al put on his bathrobe, slipped on his slippers and almost ran to the closed door of the piano room. He knocked and Lucia answered, "Come in." There she sat upright on the piano stool, her fingers still on the keys.

"I'm sorry. Did I disturb you?"

"Did you ever, dear friend!. I couldn't believe that beautiful music was coming from here. I thought it must have come from the radio, which I sometimes have turned to a music station. But it was you playing Beethoven's so-called Moonlight Sonata No. 14, Opus 27, No. 2. And that final cascade of notes had to be the Presto Agitato, right?"

"Exactly. I know you must be crazy about music because of your outspo-ken love of Mozart."

"Really" Lucia asked, "but you must also love Beethoven's music, all of those sonatas, trios, quartets, concertos, symphonies, songs, one opera and a mass and probably many other pieces that I've never heard about."

"But, Lucia, you never mentioned that you are a very gifted pianist."

"Well, you flatter me. Would that I were a gifted pianist. But I do hope to become one. After all, I've been playing since I was four years old."

Overcome with emotion, Al reached over and kissed her hand and then her forehead. "Well, darling friend, if you aren't great yet, then either the critics haven't heard you or you haven't given the critics a chance."

"No, Al, I wish that were true, but they have heard me, and they have written complementary criticism about me, but with a few reservations. But I still have a long way to go. Okay, good friend and music lover, I've stimulated your musical appetite. Now, why don't I prepare breakfast for the both of us?"

"I've got a better plan. Why don't I do what I can while you play. I'll fix breakfast, juice, scrambled eggs, toast, coffee. How does that sound?"

"Your plan plays well with me, and I accept."

"What would you like? More Beethoven? Maybe Chopin, Liszt or Schumann or maybe some favorite like Schubert or possibly—he's really quite marvelous. So what's your favorite?"

"I don't really know. I like almost everybody but for now, maybe Chopin. A romance or a nocturne."

"All right, Mr. Chef, while I pound the piano, you whip us up some breakfast."

As he backed out of the small piano studio, Al made certain the door was wide open, then he offered, "I should have something ready in fifteen or twenty minutes."

Soon Al had expertly put together a breakfast of orange juice, scrambled eggs, toast and coffee. With eggs and toast in the oven, Al was ready. Stepping into the living room, he caught the last few notes of Chopin's Raindrop pre-lude. "Damn, why don't you stop and listen?" Now he called, "Lucia! Alicia de la Rosa."

"Oh, Al, I smell something awfully good! And you flatter me. Alicia de la Rosa. How I wish it! She's one of the very best. I had hopes that she would take me if only for a few lessons. But she heard me play and she gave me courage without accepting my pleas. Then she added, 'You don't need any help anyway.'"

Al seated Lucia at the table and accepted the large glass of fresh squeezed orange juice. Soon Al poured her coffee and quickly presented the toast and scrambled eggs.

Before plunging her poised fork into the scrambled eggs, Lucia beamed, "You are really something, Mr. Praitt, like my father who was a great cook, writer, father and hero. I couldn't have been luckier. Two wonderful parents who spoiled me rotten while giving me love and courage. Everything they had, they shared."

Al sat listening, then asked, "Lucia? Or could it be Lucy? I like the name Lucia, but it sounds so formal. I realize that it is Italian, but what do your friends call you?"

"You're right, most of them call me Lucy, but darling man, you may call me anything you like. But may I continue to call you Al?"

"Of course, please call me Al. I've always hated Allan."

Lucia's comments eased Al's embarrassment and together they relaxed into a polite dialogue of music and books while finishing breakfast.

After another pause, Lucia asked Al, "We've talked a lot about me, but I would like to know more about you. About the only facts I know about you are, you were married but your wife died, you are a published writer, and you have grown children.

"That's right, dear lady. I suppose that I should fill in the blanks: What I've done, what I was, what I hope for. As we get to know each other, I'll try to answer and explain, but for now, I've got an important one for you."

"Yes?"

"How do I get you back to Florence and when? I've got a car and the road is probably clear now, which will allow me to share your companionship a bit longer."

Lucia was silent for seconds. "I've got a better idea. I'll call Dawn, who should be at our apartment waiting to hear from me. Then I'll catch a bus in Greve, okay?"

Al considered that a reasonable solution, but now wishing to prolong her companionship, he suggested that he should drive her home.

After some discussion, Lucia accepted and Al immediately decided to warm up the Fiat sedan which has been included in the house exchange.

Lucia volunteered to clean up the kitchen while Al hurried out. Beside the house, the Fiat appeared ready. But to warm up the engine, Al soon realized that that old car wouldn't start. He twisted the key in the ignition, but he soon realized that probably the battery was dead.

He knew something about Enrico, the tenant who shared the house that shared the addition to Benedetto's. Already he had a few awkward exchanges with his friendly neighbor. So now, Al approached the house and was relieved to see that Enrico was trying to start his own car.

Hearing Al's footsteps, Enrico, who was a mechanic, turned and greeted Al, "Buon giorno, professore! Come sta?"

"Not so good," Enrico. "La mia macchine e rotto."

"Rotto? Not start?" The mechanic asked. Al realized that Enrico knew more English than he knew Italian.

"Okay, I look now!"

While the mechanic tinkered with the engine, Al turned on the ignition. "Stop, signore, battery dead. Must charge."

Suddenly Enrico returned with a gauge and battery cables which he skillfully attached to the worn battery terminals. For a minute, he studied the needle in the gauge while repositioning each cable.

Satisfied that the mechanic had completed the test, Lucia questioned him and listened to his immediate reply which she translated to Al, "He says the battery is old and very weak, but that he will try charging it for a couple of hours."

"Please tell him that I will gladly pay for his service and that if the battery should be replaced, please do so. If he could get the car started in an hour, I'll drive you back to Florence."

"Also tell him if he can't get the car started now, go ahead and put a battery in now."

Minutes later, Lucia explained, today is Sunday and all of the shops are closed, but he would be glad to install a new battery tomorrow."

"Yes. That's fine with me, but now I'm afraid you'll have to take the bus back to Florence."

With the issue settled to buy a new battery, Al shook hands with Enrico and then escorted Lucia back to the house.

Al was nervous and disappointed that he couldn't share his companionship longer.

With a degree of finality, he suggested a telephone call to Dawn, adding, "After the call, I'll accompany you to the bus station. It comes directly into the square but we should call the bus office and ask for today's schedule."

Soon Lucia was talking rapidly with Dawn and punctuated with gusts of laughter, she soon hung up. Then Lucia saw the nearby phone book, found the bus line's number and called.

Again a short reply, "Al, the bus runs only every other hour on Sundays. And will arrive in thirty-five minutes. Can we make that one?

"Sure we can. You have nothing to carry but the clothes you're wearing. I'll get my light jacket and we'll slide down the hill."

Minutes later they were on the narrow road, now free of ice and water. The walk down was unlike the condition twelve hours earlier. As they descended, both struggled for words, but Lucia made certain that each had the other's phone number.

Soon they reached the square and found the bus station was nothing more than a bus counter next to the cashier's office, which was a combination pharmacy and soft drink counter.

Al wanted to buy the ticket, but Lucia would have none of that. "After all, dear friend, you put me up, fed me and above all, you protected me. Now I hope you won't forget me because I know that I can't forget you. You made me believe in myself and you're—you've made me feel like a woman again."

Minutes later, the bus arrived early. They stared at the bus and driver who reappeared after seconds in the office. Quickly the driver started the engine while signaling Lucia to enter. They clutched each other in a final kiss, then Lucia struggled aboard the bus.

As the large green bus backed slowly, Al frantically searched the windows for one last glimpse of Lucia. Finally their eyes met as the bus accelerated forward and abruptly turned into the intersection.

Chapter Two

After the bus left, for a few seconds Al felt emotionally drained. "What am I doing? Falling in love with a beautiful young woman? Yes, and so talented and charming."

He quickly left the square, passed the hotel and strode rapidly along the narrow street which soon became the steep road past his house which ended at ancient Montfiorale.

His mind began to review the conflicting series of events from the past twenty-four hours. Why should I continue this relationship? It was just a bizarre evening which fortunately ended without any serious problems. What's in it for her or for me? She's hardly more than a young woman and I'm old enough to be her grandfather. She's only twenty—really twenty-one yesterday and I'm an old—well, a not-so-old sixty-seven. But she's forty-six years younger, which is impossible. Why should I become involved? Of course I'm flattered by her affection and I'm excited, but why should I encourage her and become her surrogate father and clandestine lover. Incestuous!

The silent monologue raged on, a maelstrom of ideas, values, morality and responsibility, "But am I really responsible for her? Maybe not. She is twenty-one!"

Now his pace slowed as his soliloquy became philosophical, "Yes, you are responsible for her. Who else is there? Her parents are dead. From your behavior last night and your attitude, you have told her that you feel responsible. Certainly that's the way you responded twice last night. True, but what else could I or any other male do when she demanded my protection?

Behave like a coward and allow that drunken bully to literally haul her out? Of course not! So did you do the moral thing? You must obey the moral obligation you had, not once but twice. Really you should be congratulating yourself and you really reacted morally and properly with that bastard stepfather—Michele Leone, a real S.O.B. if I ever saw one!

Don't sell yourself short. You've won her confidence and affection—probably love." Then in a serendipitous flash, Al reacted. "Of course it's all existential and however tragic, I am at the edge of time."

Suddenly his reverie was broken by a hearty, "Buon giorno, Professore!" Al had reached the front gate and there was the car and the mechanic. "Si, buon giorno, Enrico," Al exclaimed.

"Tumoro, Professore, I take battery. Start car, OK?"

"Oh, si, and grazie, Enrico!"

They shook hands and Al opened the gate. Suddenly he felt both relieved and pleased. As Al had never had a mechanical aptitude, he hated all mechanical problems. Now with the car "fixed" he could get back to work.

Once back in the house, he cleared and washed the breakfast dishes, glanced cautiously around the scene and decided to remake the bed still fragrant with Lucia's perfume.

With the bed remade, Al turned to leave as his eye caught the reflection of a string of pearls on the floor. As he picked them up, he tried to remember whether Lucia was wearing them last night. His mind was blank. Too much action and excitement, he thought, then he paused, "But she was wearing them when we drank the champagne here. So either she took them off last night or they must have fallen at some point when she wasn't aware."

Again Al floated on clouds of euphoria, then glancing at his watch he realized that it was now almost one. His inner alarm was shrill as Al almost jumped to his feet. The self-discipline which began deep in his childhood and almost reached a peak of rigidity in the Army Air Corp guided him through a difficult first marriage and became his inner light and strength through years of academic drudgery and achievement.

His sense of determination and control reasserted itself. "Oh, relax a bit. You've had two good days. True, but I must finish the book and the sooner I do, the better I'll feel."

From a desk drawer, he first removed ninety-three pages of a typed text secured in a heavy black binder. Then he removed the cover from the electric typewriter and plugged the cord into the outlet. Almost mechanically he inserted a sheet, then stopped and read the last five pages of the text from the binder. Satisfied that his story was moving easily, he thought, "Okay, so you've satirically described the vanity and arrogance of the worst man in the English department or anybody you've ever known. And you've described him as an aggressive, but equally successful womanizer."

Now how are you going to resolve these seeming conflicts between the faculty code of ethics and this man's wanton behavior? Who would believe that the University would grant tenure and some recognition to such a charlatan and ass? You explain that he was a Phi Beta Kappa, was and still is a very handsome man with a charming and attractive wife and two small children. But he is a seducer and has had affairs with countless coeds, two or possibly several women, married or single young career instructors, and not the least or probably the last—wives of current professors. Would anybody ever believe such a mocking story of academic life?

For a minute or two Al stopped and laughed. That won't be difficult because we have that very real role model in the body and conduct of George Crawford Van Dyke. True, and many staffers do or strongly suspect that Van Dyke accurately fits your description. So how do I conceal his identity while simultaneously satisfying and denigrating this handsome no good?

Again Al was deep in "cognitive creation"–a phrase Van Dyke frequently used to flatter colleagues and creative writing students. So I changed his name to St. John Gainsworth, A.B. and M.A. from Harvard and a Ph.D. from Oxford. He is fluent in French, Italian and Spanish and has published three books about love and the Latin personality.

With several honors and achievements, Professor Gainsworth will hardly be recognized as the ego-maniac, philandering Van Dyke.

Now to thrust the satire further, you introduce the beautiful Maria d'Este as an Italian student of Gainsworth. This girl-woman student is the only daughter of a fabulously rich Italian family from Rome. The girl, Maria, falls madly in love with Gainsworth, who repeatedly seduces her and falls hopelessly in love with her.

Although the girl knows that St. John Gainsworth is married, she accepts him because he convinces her that he will soon divorce his wife for infidelity with several businessmen over a period of fifteen years, and neither of his small children are his "flesh and blood."

Of course Maria not only believes it but demands that she and St. John confront the woman and expose her shameful behavior to the media.

Now here's the dangerous and risky point, how can he and Maria bring this off without destroying his career? To remove himself and Maria from the scene and lend credit to Maria's story, he will obtain a sabbatical to teach at the University of Rome for the next academic year. There he will hire an Italian friend who is also a notorious womanizer to fabricate a series of letters between St. John's wife and several Italian businessmen who are known for their frequent bed-hopping activities. With letters and paid fraudulent documents, St. John will divorce his wife, Jerry, who will retain custody of the girls, and St. John will magnificently reward her with a settlement of the family house and an annual income of thirty-five thousand dollars.

Having successfully completed these complicated deceptions, St. John and Maria d'Este will marry and St. John will retire from U.C. and live happily ever after in Italy on Maria's family's money.

For the next two days, Al studied the story and the plot. Could he bring it off as an academic opera buffo—possibly a parody on Gilbert and Sullivan or a satire on academia. But would it sell like hot cakes and soon be transformed into a Hollywood blockbuster?

And the real St. John Gainsworth, aka Van Dyke, could continue on his merry bed-hopping marathon.

While reflecting on his planned satirical adventures, the phone rang, suddenly thrusting Al into reality.

"Hello, Al Praitt speaking.

"Professor Praitt? This is Dawn Knight. I met you last Monday night at that cafe in Greve, remember?"

"Indeed I do, Miss Knight. How could I ever forget that interesting and exciting evening. And I certainly would like to see you again and also Miss Lucia Conde, but under more favorable circumstances. Oh, indeed I haven't forgotten nor will I for any time soon. I am glad you called because I would like to see you again under more pleasant conditions."

"Thank you, Professor, and the reason I called is that Lucia and I would like to see you as soon as possible."

From her warm and enthusiastic tone, Al concluded that the urgency in her voice suggested more than a short friendly exchange.

"Yes, Dawn. I'd be pleased to accept your invitation whenever you and Lucia have some free time from your busy schedules. Just let me know a bit in advance. But now, if Lucia is there, I would like to talk with her."

"Oh, yes, she's right here, and I know that she wants to talk with you. Just a minute, okay? Here she is."

For a few seconds, the phone was silent before Lucia answered. "Hello, Professor. How are you? I've been wanting to call you, and I would have later today if Dawn hadn't beaten me to the phone. But I had hoped that you would break the ice, 'Professor.'" Al detected a slight suggestion of sarcasm, but more probably sadness in her otherwise soft tones.

"Well, yes," Al almost stuttered, "I should have called and indeed I would have if for no other reason than to ask you about the pearl necklace which I found on the floor of your bedroom."

A ripple of laughter followed and Lucia replied, "Yes, those are my pearls and I must have dropped them before I went to bed, or maybe I subconsciously dropped them for extenuating reasons. But now that you have them, you must return them."

Each person now played the cat and mouse game until Al exclaimed, "Lucia, you've teased me long enough. May I come tomorrow? Now it's too late, but tomorrow would be perfect, but first I must know what time would be convenient for you?"

"Just a minute, please. I'll ask Dawn. Al—Professor—dear friend, Dawn and I would like to have you join us here for lunch, say one-thirty or two, the Italian colazione."

"That sounds fine to me, but how do I find your place? I'm only fairly knowledgeable about Florence."

"Well, Al, our place is across the river in a hilly area near the Pitti, but I think to avoid problems, I'll meet you at the Ponte Vecchio, the old bridge with shops on each side and is closed to car traffic. At this point there is a one-way street with a stop light. We could meet about one. You will be driving the old Fiat? Okay? Yes, I'll be waiting at the bridge and direct you to a nearby parking lot."

"Great," Al interjected. "Now what would you like me to bring? Wine? Cheese? Fruit? Cake?"

"Don't bring anything. We have all we need for a good meal but if you insist, we wouldn't object to some sparkling wine."

"Wonderful," Al concluded. "So tomorrow, Thursday, we meet and eat and dance in the street."

"What did you say, professor? What do we do in the street?"

"I'm sorry, Lucia. I couldn't resist a chance to pun and rhyme. I do it all the time."

"Al, you are funny! Okay, tomorrow at one-thirty. Bye."

Still bathing in the glow of their phone camaraderie, Al felt reluctant to resume writing. Twice he sat at the typewriter and couldn't produce a word. Then suddenly his mind erupted. *How could I have forgotten the reason for the book, and therefore the reasons for my being here? The winery! Yes, the winery!*

"Which reminds me, why haven't I had a letter from at least one of my three kids? After all, I expect two of them, Steven and Allan, and maybe Virginia, to be involved in my efforts to establish a family winery–Les Caves de Bacchus, and our motto, 'Wine for drinking'.

Now if I can clear twenty-five thousand from the book and maybe more from the film rights that should be enough to get the business started. And my retirement salary plus a loan against the house, if necessary, should provide operating expenses for two or three years. But an important part of the enterprise is to get distribution in major stores and, equally important if not more so, would be our wine name on the wine list of important restaurants. That's the real key. If we could get into Chez Panisse, Fleur d'Lys and into the major hotel dining rooms, and maybe if we could make some outstanding Cab or Chard or a really outstanding Pinot and pick up a few ribbons in competitions, then we would be in a strong position to expand and make some real money."

For several minutes, Al relived his experiences in wine making and his plan to rescue his sons from aimlessly drifting between part-time jobs, drugs and unemployment. His sons, Stephen, 32, and Allan, 29, after graduation from Cal seemed reasonably well-established. Neither had married but each had several live-in girlfriends which was a socially-acceptable substitute for marriage. But neither Al nor his wife accepted that code without some family conflicts. And while their only daughter, Virginia, at thirty-four, the Praitts only successful sibling, was often caught in arguments between her doting father and critical mother who usually favored both sons.

That Joan should favor "her boys" could be easily understood by her father's affectionate favoritism for "Ginny" at the expense of her brothers.

Usually the Praitt family conflicts were settled without serious recriminations until "Ginny" got pregnant. About five weeks after her graduation from Berkeley High, Virginia confessed to her father that she had missed two periods. Weeping profusely and obviously very frightened, she explained that after graduation, she had "partied" with her boyfriend that night. Al consoled her and promised her that if she wanted to have an abortion, he could probably arrange it as soon as possible. She readily consented, to which Al cautioned, "Please, darling, don't tell your mother or your brothers. This will be our secret."

Although Joan never knew about Virginia's abortion, she sensed that something had drawn her daughter closer to her father. But this brief fling with promiscuity became a "red light against unprotected and impulsive" sex which served Virginia well. She knew that both parents and her brothers had strong and occasionally over-active libidos—a common problem in Berkeley and the entire Bay Area.

Virginia fully cemented her father's affection and support when she graduated Phi Beta Kappa from Cal and was immediately offered scholarships from all the major law schools. She never regretted her demanding studies at Boalt, but after two years as law clerk for Justice Brennan, she abruptly resigned.

Both parents were shocked with Virginia's sudden and unexpected decision. She returned to Berkeley and explained that after almost six years of law, she was disillusioned and "burned out."

Her snap statement was, "Now I'm going to Hawaii for a month's vacation and when I return I should hope to know what I want or hope to do."

And she did. In great expectation, both parents celebrated her return and her announcement. "Now don't be too disappointed, but I must do something which isn't technical or as dry as law, but something which is both gratifying and productive."

Then raising her wine glass, "Here's to teaching and social work, but

probably something of each." Both parents congratulated her and agreed that
she would be successful in either or both professions.

Al was very proud of Virginia, but somewhat surprised when only a
year later she confided to him that she wanted to marry, raise babies and be
a good wife. Then quietly adding, "I've found the right man for a husband
and father. I met my fiance," she said, raising her left hand and displaying
a diamond set in a ring of several small emeralds. "He's a practicing lawyer
with a small law firm which handles divorces, child custody and a wide
range of social problems. As you might expect, the firm isn't rolling in
money, but it is a decent living and a very satisfactory practice for the three
partners who have been teachers and social workers, but decided they
could be more effective as lawyers."

Al and Joan were pleased with their daughter's decision, which reflected
their social attitudes and values that had formed a strong bond for their marriage. No topic, whether it was crime, politics, religion or stupidity escaped the
dinner table discussions, which had become a family institution since the children were in grade school.

The following morning was clear and sunny and Al decided a short walk
would be "good medicine." At the road, he decided to investigate the developed area nearby on the road to Montefiorale. Soon he arrived at a small
cemetery which was enclosed by a high, white-washed brick wall on three
sides, while the entrance was secured by a sturdy wrought iron fence with a
locked gate.

From the entrance, Al could see several rows of well-maintained graves
and headstones, and behind a high wall of vaults which identified each space by
a placard and container for flowers. Al concluded that the vaults must contain .
the remains of some of Greve's illustrious citizens and the small, neat cemetery
clearly reflected the Italian's attitude towards death.

As Al had not had his morning coffee or breakfast, he quickly returned to
his ancient fortress, but stopped to greet Enrico who smiled and mentioned
the car and battery.

For a moment Al was flustered, then, realizing that Enrico was politely
asking for payment, he blurted out, "Quanto, signore?"

Enrico smiled, "Non troppo, vente dollari e cosi dieci milla lira per piacere
trenta mila lira tutto.

For a second, Al was embarrassed, then Enrico gave him a small printed statement with the battery listed at 20,000 lira and labor at 10,000. Quickly Al opened his wallet and gave him a 20,000 lire and a ten and five thousand lira notes.

Enrico smiled, "Grazie e troppo!"

But Al smiled, "Non trappo!"

Again they shook hands and Al hurried into his house.

As it was now almost ten o'clock, Al gulped down orange juice, coffee and toast. Then rubbing his stubble, again he showered and shaved. Now he surveyed his limited wardrobe, selected woolen slacks and a shirt similar to his Monday night attire and was almost ready to leave. But his watch brought him up short. "It's only ten forty."

For the next hour, he seemed unable to occupy himself with anything except what he might say to Lucia and Dawn. His mind couldn't focus on any particular problem or topic which might be of interest to either young woman. For the first time in many years, he had to admit, "Damn, I'm confused. Well, hell, I'll wing it. Why try to plan a conversation? The women will make things interesting so why try to control the situation?"

About eleven-thirty, Al checked the thermostat, again, put on his heavy overcoat and locked the front door behind him. Quickly he bounded down the stairs and out the small front gate. There was the Fiat with keys in an envelope on the driver's side. He waited for a few seconds, inserted the key in the ignition and the engine greeted him with a roar of approval.

Relieved, he sat almost a minute listening to the engine slow to an idle. As this was the first time he had driven since a few days before the big freeze, he cautiously moved forward and slowly turned onto the narrow road which, now free of ice, revealed its ugly potholes and broken paving. Keeping the car in first gear, he cautiously maneuvered the small sedan safely through each switchback. At the small intersection connecting the narrow one-way street and the square, he stopped and instead of continuing another hundred meters to the main road to Florence, he suddenly remembered that he hadn't checked his mail for over a week.

Back again to the square and a small building identified by the small gilded sign, "Ufficio Postale," he stopped. At the only open window, Al was greeted with a smile, "Buon giorno, Professore, ecco sua posta."

Al thanked the middle-aged woman in her black smock. Returning to the car, Al glanced through the several envelopes noting one from his publisher and one from his daughter. Carelessly ripping open each envelope, he opened the one from his publisher. "Mr. Praitt–Al. As we haven't heard from you since January 14, we hope your book is progressing satisfactorily. Your deadline, I hesitate to remind you, is May 15."

"Don't sweat it, Gordon. The typed manuscript will be there long before deadline."

Next, putting aside several other letters, Al quickly read Virginia's note. "Dad, etc., etc., Oh, yes, in closing, I'm pregnant and our bambino is due sometime in July. Love V."

"Well," Al concluded, "all's well that ends well."

Carefully he backed the car into the square. At the intersection, he turned cautiously onto Road 222 which was Tuscany's principal highway to Florence. As he had driven this road on three or four previous occasions, he knew that the road through Impruneta was a better access to Florence and the Arno. Although the traffic was heavier by this route, he admired the large complex of industrial and residential life–a virtual cornucopia of muscle and brains which was the life blood of the area.

Following the signs which directed traffic in both directions around the city, Al sneaked the car cautiously into the bumper-to-bumper traffic. Bearing left, Al slowed to a stop where a polizia di circolazione, one in handsome uniform, directed the noon concentration of cars, motorcycles and small trucks, all determined to bully their way through.

Having survived the traffic crunch, Al now realized that he probably could not find any direct street along the Arno. But as all of the cars and busses were pushing toward the Piazza della Republica, Al worked his way through narrow alley-ways and one-way streets.

Finally almost directly in front of him was the Ponte Vecchio. He stopped as the one-way traffic demanded and there at the bridge intersection was Lucia. He watched, studied each car then tapped his horn which brought an excited response from Lucia. Agilely she dodged the threatening traffic and almost leaped into the car. Greetings exchanged, she gave directions, "Follow the traffic along the river and at the next bridge, turn right and we can avoid most of the noon traffic."

On the southwest side of the Arno, Al found a parking area and stopped. There, relieved of the tension, they smiled affectionately and Lucia with map in hand pointed to the detailed network of streets to her apartment.

"Would you like me to drive, Al? I know the area quite well."

"Say no more, dear friend. Please take the wheel before I dump us into the river."

"You couldn't do that but you could easily become tangled in this spaghetti-like system we call viale, vicole, strada–avenue, alley, street."

With Lucia at the wheel, Al suddenly knew what Italian driving was like. She whipped the Fiat through the turns and up and around hills faster than the Fiat had ever experienced. Al was shaken, but impressed with Lucia's experience and skill. Suddenly, at a small driveway, the car slowly ascended and parked beside a small building.

"Here we are safe and sound, Professore. This is my apartment building. So welcome to your new home away from home. I rent out the smaller apartment while the larger has more space and provides separate bedrooms for Dawn and me. But we share one bath which by design allows a shower for guests."

Before Al could fully recover from Lucia's driving mastery, there was Dawn waving and smiling.

"Welcome to our Italian version of heaven, Professor."

With Al sandwiched between the two women, they ushered him around the garage door to a flight of stairs which took them to the second floor apartment. The heavy front door opened into a small foyer and hall closet. From there the apartment divided into a living room with a large window facing the expanse of Florence.

Now the two stopped, allowing Al to marvel at the scene, "What a marvelous view," Al almost gushed.

"Not bad for a couple of innocent country girls," Dawn teased. "But this is only the beginning. From here, we move to the dining room and then into the kitchen." And from that other kitchen door is a short hallway which leads to our bedrooms with the connecting bath and a small half bath for guests."

Dawn concluded, "And that is a short Cook's tour of Casa della donna. I love it and I think I'll find an Italian lover and stay here with Lucia, if she doesn't object too much."

"Okay, everybody," Lucia suggested, "let's have something to drink and then enjoy my version of a small but excellent Italian meal."

At the mention of a drink, Al suddenly remembered the champagne jammed into a small area behind the back seats of the Fiat. "Oh, I did remember some wine," Al said apologetically, "I'll get it."

"No, we're not going to allow you to escape now. I'll get the wine," Dawn commanded.

Al continued to marvel at the design and comfort of the apartment as Lucia quickly spread several dishes of cheese, salami, small artichoke hearts and asparagus spears. "How does that look, Pop?" Lucia whispered.

For a second, Al was confused but smiled.

Now Lucia squeezed his arm. I can't call you Professor anymore. That's too formal. And I don't think we're quite ready for darling or sweetheart, but maybe 'Pops' will be acceptable for now."

"Yes," Al nodded. "'Pops' is fine or you could say 'Lucky.' That was a term I was known by when I was flying many years ago. I'll explain how I acquired that nickname sometime when we're talking about history."

Suddenly Dawn popped into the room. "I found your treasure, Al. You really had it safely hidden. I'll put it in the fridge which should save the bubbly for us and not the floor."

For the next half-hour, they joked, teased and laughed as they raved about Lucia's antipasto.

"Now we have serious gormandizing awaiting us, right?" Dawn asked.

Lucia disappeared into the kitchen only to return with a large platter of steak and mounds of gnocchi. "We'll have the salad after the main course. I know that the Americans serve the salad first, but most Italian's don't. Now for a chianti classico."

The two women looked askance at Al. "You are the invited guest, Signore Praitt, but we would be honored if you cut the steak. I realize this is a burden, but you are appointed senior and Lord and deserve to cut this large piece of Florentine beef. Will you, dear man?"

Al was pleased as he was surprised by the large steak. "Before I begin this ritual slaughter," Al laughed, "I know by its size that this must be a Florentine steer."

Lucia became momentarily serious. "I realize that Florentine beef is virtually unknown in the States, but it is principally grown only in Tuscany. It's a large, white animal which is highly prized by the Florentines for its flavor, texture and tenderness. Not that I'm an expert on beef, but as an Italian-American who was brought up on American steak, which is good, I do prefer Florentine beef. I'm sorry to sound chauvinistic, so before I make a complete idiot of myself, let's all take a bite and see how it compares with Kansas beef, considered the best in America."

With that injunction, Al raised the large carving knife and holding the huge slab of broiled beef with a fork in his left hand, he deftly carved three large steaks leaving at least half the rare meat on the platter.

"I know that this beef must be all or more than you said, Lucia. This knife sliced it like it was butter. Okay, we each have about an equal portion. Now maybe you'll add some gnocchi to each plate, Dawn, and we can begin what promises to be the great Italo-American pig-out!"

For a few seconds, the three chewed silently in almost ritual silence. Then, everybody smiled.

"Wonderfully tender," Dawn gushed.

"And equally tender and tasty," Al added, "but it's more than tasty. It has a subtle smell and taste that is quite different from any other beef I've eaten."

"Your criticism is what the so-called connoisseurs say about Florentine beef," Lucia offered, "but let's just eat and enjoy it for our own tastes and not get too carried away because if the gnocchi is up to par, it's as wonderful as the beef. Really good gnocchi is very hard to find, but even more difficult to make."

Now the pleasures of food and drink became somehow related to other sensory pleasures.

"As much as I enjoy food, which is only too obvious," Dawn began, "I also love poetry, romance novels and of course music, particularly classical and good popular which doesn't include rock 'n roll. But my favorite sensory pleasure—I'll let you guess."

Both Lucia and Al smiled and almost laughed.

"I haven't an idea what you are suggesting, Dawn, but I might guess sitting with a loved one at a sunset or maybe nude bathing in a cool mountain stream."

Dawn smiled, "You're partly right, but what is really your greatest pleasure, Lucy?"

After a long, studied pause, Lucia answered "For me, that's quite easy.

Music, particularly the piano and the violin and the human voice, perhaps in reverse order."

Al nodded, "For all your skill and beauty at the piano, why do you place the voice as your first choice?"

"Of course, I love to play the piano and it gives me great pleasure, but consider the human voice, male and female, and the several registers, tones, moods and subtleties which only voices can produce. No other instrument can begin to express the beauty, feeling, joy and tragedy of life. Great voices like Callas, Marian Anderson, Renata Tabaldi, Flagstadt and many past and present greats, Caruso, Gigli, Corelli, Bjorling and now Pavorotti and Domingo. The list is almost endless. Fantastic voices which bring us to tears, laughter, fear and excitement. The piano can't do that, but it can suggest some of these emotions as can both the violin and cello. But no other instrument can equal the human voice."

Al and Dawn weighed Lucia's strong emotional beliefs before Al added, "Of course, I agree with you, Lucia. I, too, enjoy the human voice in all it's strength and beauty, songs, operas and choruses, but I also like orchestra with symphonies, quartets and the many combinations which constitute both serious and interesting popular music."

Before Al could pontificate further, Dawn laughed, "You two long hairs! Sure music is great, so is painting, sculpture and ballet, but more importantly, you have mentioned the theatre where voices are enhanced by body language, maybe the very best of the arts."

Al and Lucia sat silently somewhat confused by Dawn's rising emotions. Then Dawn asked, "You do agree, don't you?"

Lucia and Al nodded, hopping Dawn wouldn't embarrass them, but Dawn was ready to spring the trap.

"So maybe, we're just a bunch of stuffy, long hairs who like to talk about the arts and wax long and eloquently about our passions. But aren't we neglecting something much more fundamental and personal, exalting and beautiful? I could add many other adjectives and adverbs." Dawn paused, expecting a comment.

Now Al and Lucia knew that Dawn had either baited a trap or was ready to tease them with additional questions.

"Okay, if you two are either too uptight, embarrassed or fearful of mentioning God's greatest gift to mankind and all forms of interesting behavior, I'll say it!" Dawn laughed.

"Sex. Good, old-fashioned love-making. Seduction. Fornication. To put it bluntly, fucking. F.U.C.K." Dawn exploded.

Al and Lucia exchanged embarrassed grins, then Lucia, looking somewhat nervous replied, "Well, I can't speak about sex with any authority because my experience was not what I would, would—well it didn't compare with what I witnessed or knew about from my parents, and later what I read from books or saw in films. But I'm glad that you speak from experience, Dawn."

Throughout Dawn's amusing monologue, Al was embarrassed but only because he sensed how serious, how visibly flushed and near tears Lucia appeared. He recalled how frightened she was when her stepfather suddenly walked into the Trattoria Moro. Yet she seems quite open to my feelings.

"Well, Dawn, you sure know how to bring a discussion about art, beauty and love to its ultimate conclusion. Not that I'm trying to smother what might or could be an intimate discussion of sex, but I am enjoying this dinner too much to discuss any activity which interferes with my appetite."

With that comment, they resumed eating and extravagant remarks, gesticulating with forks and knives, an attention-breaking ritual which relieved abused feelings. Adding to their dining camaraderie, they joked and teased each other with a rich exchange of jokes and bawdy limericks.

Then as Dawn and Al were topping each other's scatological humor, Lucia collected the empty plates, rinsed them and carefully placed them in the washer. As the two jokesters continued their banter, Lucia produced the champagne and handed it to Al.

She smiled as Dawn raised her glass in a mock toast, "To our handsome wine steward for his charm and his skill. May he forever fill our hearts and our glasses with champagne."

Quickly Al accepted the cold champagne, wrapped the bottle in a napkin and expertly removed the wire and foil. Then very cautiously withdrew the cork with only a slight pop. Quickly he filled each glass to three-quarters and then offered, "To good health, fortune, friendship and love."

After another round of champagne, Lucia produced a large plate of tiramisu, the only dessert which is enjoyed by almost all Italians and most Americans who have tasted it.

The glamorous cake was a three-layered combination of small finger-like cookies soaked in strong coffee and brandy, then smothered in Mascarpone, heavy butter-like cream, then topped with more cream and chocolate flakes. "There are many kinds of tiramisu, but this one is my baker's favorite."

Al, who had never tasted such a cake almost gushed after his first taste. "Lucia, did you make this cake?"

"No. As I said, my baker did. It's beyond my limited skills and I don't think many housewives make it. Anyway, it really is my favorite desert, as it probably is for many Italians."

Again the trio lapsed into tidbits of trivia until both women confronted Al and tactfully suggested that he might reveal himself.

"Now, Professor. Mr. Handsome mystery man. We hardly know you while you've listened to us verbally reveal an earful of our petty lives." Dawn managed to combine coquettish charm with an insinuating smile.

For seconds, Al was embarrassed but managed an acceptable reply, "Of course, why not? The basics are simple. I'm a retired professor of English from U.C. Berkeley and I'm a widower. My wife, Joan, died almost five years ago. I have three children. My oldest is Virginia, aged thirty-three, recently married and now pregnant. And I have two sons, Stephen, aged thirty-one and Allan, who is twenty-eight. Neither son is married and for many reasons don't seem interested in marriage or steady employment." He paused noting how Dawn and Lucia reacted to his remarks about his children.

Lucia asked immediately, "Al, you seem to be somewhat concerned about your kids. Are you?"

"Not my daughter, who not only is very pretty like her mother, but she's very smart with degrees in law and social welfare which she shares with an equally bright and handsome husband. As for my sons, they have B.A.'s from Berkeley, but like many others who grew up in the sixties and seventies, neither of them was terribly excited about working or taking life seriously."

Dawn interrupted, "I can understand that perfectly. A great many people of our age simply don't believe in the system, which they see as an unscrupulous collection of corporations, politicians and generals who can't be trusted. I agree that attitude is an over simplification of a very complex problem which can only be understood and corrected by the people. But I believe," she added, "if we don't like it and want to change it, it's our responsibility and generally everybody's to become involved."

Al registered surprise while Lucia nodded her head, then offered, "You seem to agree."

"I couldn't agree more, but without boring you with my opinion about methods or solutions which we may talk about later as we see each other, I'll continue my brief autobiography."

"As you may know, or maybe you don't know, on Mozart's birthday, which I was celebrating along with my own last week, I quietly reached a ripe sixty-seven, which is a good age."

Before he could continue, both Dawn and Lucia jumped in, "I can't believe that you're sixty-seven! You're kidding! You don't look sixty. You don't even have gray hair or any wrinkles!"

"You're very generous, very kind and, of course, I'm flattered and pleased. And I don't feel like sixty-seven, particularly with you beautiful and charming women. Maybe since I met you, I've shed fifteen years. Would that I could. And I don't really feel much over fifty. I do most of the athletic exercises I did at that age. Maybe I'm just lucky, but the truth is, for whatever reason, I never looked my age. When I was fifteen, I could get into movies for a kid's price. I wasn't very big and I had almost no beard. Then in my early twenties, I filled out and grew over six inches in height. But even at twenty-three, I only weighed one-hundred and sixty, and was about 6 feet and was sometimes asked to produce my driver's license when sitting at a bar."

"How lucky for you Al! But how did women our age relate?"

"That's a good question, and in some cases women seemed not very interested, but what really surprised me were several I met who were in their thirties who really came on pretty strong."

"Of course! Why not! You were a young hunk and didn't know it. Women love that!"

Al only grinned. "Well, don't think that I didn't appreciate their charms. Still I didn't push my luck, if for no other reason than I was naive. But by thirty, I had a fair number of experiences and had only recently gotten out of the Air Force after almost five years. By 1947 I was almost finished with Cal. For all of the promiscuity during the war years, I didn't know many Cal coeds who were sexually active. No, they were still like their mothers and probably their grandmothers from a much stricter period. When compared with women in the thirties and early forties, you and Dawn and virtually every young female of your age are much more honest and open about their sexuality than at any time of which I am aware, particularly in our heritage of a powerfully brutal and bigoted puritanism.

"Right on, Pops!" Dawn laughed.

For a second or two, Al only grinned while evaluating Dawn's first usage of "Pops."

"While we're talking about generational differences and cultural attitudes without sounding too pedantic, I'd like to point out a few of the cultural and behavioral differences that were taboo and often illegal that existed when I was a teenager in the twenties and thirties and continued after the war. And in some places, these strict codes still exist."

Both women were now completely captivated by Al's unexpected candor.

"The moral code demanded that all girls should remain virgins until marriage. And the dress code almost demanded that all females should be clothed and protected and never wear anything sexy. This code thus protected their virginity with heavy corsets and girdles. Corsets were undergarments which covered their bodies from breasts to crotches and were laced tightly from the back and occasionally from the front. And girdles, which replaced corsets in the late thirties, were elastic sheathes which stretched from below the breasts and almost to the crotch, thus protecting the female treasury from wandering and aggressive hands. And to protect their sacred mecca below, a tight pair of step-in panties could be attached to the corset or girdle thus sealing the wearer in a mummy-tight enclosure."

Now both women were almost exploding in laughter with Al's serious description.

"How do you happen to know so much about women's underwear, Mr. Professor?" Lucia giggled.

"I saw my mother's, my aunt's, and pictures in the papers. Women's underclothes–brassieres, panties, corsets–were not forbidden to inquiring males."

"But as these large protective devices became intolerable for the wearer, the girdle replaced the corset. It was less costly, easier to get into and pretty much served the same purpose for more comfort and less cost.

Most women, particularly younger ones, quickly bought the strong, elastic sheaths which didn't reach to the breasts but tightly enclosed the torso from the stomach to the crotch, and some offered attachable panty bands connecting the from and back of the girdle to prevent the sheath from moving upwards."

Dawn was particularly amused and outspoken, "Pops, you were a close observer, seems to me."

"Not by choice, Dawn. But every male, unless he was blind and asexual knew about girdles, and for two or more decades girdles were the form-fitting garment of choice. I suppose they were an effective device for holding the tummy in and maybe offering support to the hips, which sometimes begin to sag."

"Sir, if your story wasn't so funny, I'd think you were some kind of nut, but I know you're not. Maybe you're a cultural research sociologist."

"Thank you, Dawn. I'm not, but my own frustrating experiences with female clothing frequently delayed or thwarted my diligence and ambitions. Do I make myself clear?"

"Indeed you do," both women chorused.

"Shall I express the male's frustrations with the girdle to the full impact it had on a male's ego as well as his fingers and hands?"

Both women exploded in laughter. "You really are a good raconteur! Yes, give us a detailed account of the male's attack on the woman's girdle as it struggles to protect it's wearer's virginity."

Having gotten into his story-telling mode, Al was secretly very pleased that both women were enjoying this routine, which Al had used with male friends when discussing their unsuccessful efforts with women.

"If you insist ladies, I'll be brief and to the point." Al feigned a serious demeanor.

"During the prolonged period of the girdle—which seemed an eternity to many of my friends of other years—although petting and serious necking were a frequent activity on dates, many old horny males knew that unless his aging amorata was willing or able to take off her girdle, further pleadings were bound to fail unless he could reach Mecca, and by skillful digital titillation arouse her to such dizzying heights of passion as to throw off her armor and be seduced."

By now, the women were howling with laughter.

"Al, you're a born storyteller and comic. Don't stop!"

"Okay, but my simple description of the average male's efforts at conquest are really painful and grim."

"Okay, Professor, we're ready for your indictment of our sisters and mothers. Continue your tragic description of you frustrated males."

"Now, let's see. Oh, yes. Now, the poor male, thoroughly aroused from a prolonged period of hot-blooded kissing and teasing, is ready for the final assault. Since the aroused female has not demonstrably or determinedly said no, he continues his pursuit. Desperately he struggles to sneak his fingers under her girdle. Meeting no resistance, his tongue engages hers while his free hand and fingers massage her breasts.

"Convinced that she is capitulating to his caresses, he believes that she is relaxed and aroused. Slowly his fingers creep toward the holy place, but just as he senses that she is ready, suddenly she squeezes her thighs together so as to entrap his fingers between both legs, now locked tightly with his fingers crushed between her thighs and the girdle.

"Panic-stricken, the male winces in pain and groans, 'You're breaking my fingers!'"

"I'm terribly sorry," she mocks, "but if you promise to remove your fingers, I'll unlock my legs."

Both women were in tears of laughter.

"Al! Al! You're fibbing. Neither of us ever did anything like that."

"Well, ladies, if you were of the girdle generation, you probably would have accepted that moral dictum without question and refused to go all the way. I'm certain that your mothers used this defensive strategy many times."

Everybody was laughing and not seemingly embarrassed by Al's calculated humor. Dawn was apparently moved more than Lucia, whose slight grimace seemed to register something less than full acceptance.

As the laughter dwindled, Al seized the opportunity to relieve his anxiety and encourage Lucia and Dawn to reveal themselves.

"Now that I've exhausted my repertoire of stale humor, I would enjoy hearing any anecdotes about your lives. You are both fascinating women, but I hardly know either of you. I do know that Lucia loves music and is an accomplished pianist, but I know almost nothing about you, Dawn, except that you're studying here from Stanford."

For a moment or two both women smiled, which then encouraged Al to ask more about the Monday night party.

Dawn blushed and laughed, "I suppose that I do owe you an explanation. Lucy knows about my embarrassing disaster but without relating all of the ridiculous details, this is what happened so far as I remember or am willing to admit. Did I introduce you to Carlo, my date for the evening? He had convinced me that I should meet his parents who live in a small but beautiful house not far from the trattoria. So we go there and enter, but his parents aren't there. So I kid him about trying to set me up for something. 'No, no,' he replies. Then he adds in broken English, 'You no understand—is okay. Polis set don.'"

"So I sit down and he comes back with a drink. 'Salute,' he says. So we both sit there laughing and drinking and I fell asleep. Pretty soon I awoke and it's after midnight and I realized that I had left Lucy with that animal. I managed to get Carlo on his feet and drove the car back to the restaurant, which of course was closed. I was very upset with myself and damned angry at Carlo who got my message fast and drove me back home. And that's the honest truth. You do believe me, don't you Professor?"

Al only smiled. "Of course. As a matter of fact, your misfortune became my good fortune. I got to know Lucia under terrible circumstances which were soon transformed into a wonderful serendipitous event for me, and I would hope for Lucia, too. As the Bard would say, 'All's well that ends well.'

"So here we are trading secrets and I hope becoming good friends. But Dawn, that little episode doesn't tell me much about you. Although I have some small understanding of Lucia's troubled life, your biography remains a secret."

"How much of the who, what, where, when and how would you like, Mr. Writer?"

"Why don't you take me back to your Stanford days and then reveal how you got there and why. Just fill me in with some of the major facts. I've already observed that you are very clever, very intelligent and witty, which suggests that you and your family have been through some serious living. Am I right?"

Dawn smiled knowingly. "I think that you maybe flattering me a bit and giving my parents more than they deserve. But I appreciate your generous approval of my family.

"But before I offer some rather critical opinions of Stanford, perhaps you might be interested in my family tree, which however stately and strong it appears to be, its roots and trunk aren't entirely what a genealogical tree chart might reveal–not that we're just a bunch of scrub pines.

"I'm sure you recognize the names, Comstock, Huntington, Crocker and yes, Stanford. Big names and their wives too, particularly their first names. My mother, Joy Bubbles, and her mother, my maternal grandmother, Peaches Honey. And now we come to fathers. My dad was really an Italian. Richard Knight, aka Notte, Italian for 'night', from Fort Bragg, California."

"That's very interesting, Dawn." So your father was Cal's famous or infamous quarterback Dick Knight. I didn't know him personally, but everybody at Cal knew him in the early sixties."

"I'll bet they did, Professor, and all about him, too, and my mother, too! I love them dearly, but they were a pair–meant for each other!"

Both Al and Lucia smiled in polite surprise, but before either could ask their leading questions, Dawn continued, "Shall I shock or enlighten you more?

"Before I shock you with revelations about my father and mother, I should reveal an even more interesting couple, my maternal grandparents. Peaches Honey Crocker and Oskar 'Whiskey' Crocker, both noted for their libertine ways in and out of beds and bars–theirs and others."

Now both Lucia and Al laughed softly which concealed their surprise and embarrassment.

"I'll tell you the real shocker about them which my grandmother only revealed to me once several years ago when she was drunk and angry about her husband's latest 'prank' which she refused to tell me. But the shocking revelation was about Oskar's occasional visits to Sally Stanford's famous brothel."

Now both Dawn and Al looked as shocked as they were delighted. "You mean the Sally Stanford? The famous whore and madam," Al asked.

"Right! The one and only! What happened was that both Oskar and Peaches were making the rounds with their good friend, Herb Caen. So Oskar proposes to visit Sally Stanford's place and Peaches demands to go along.

"Well they get to the glamorous large apartment and after a drink with the madam, Oskar picks a beauty and vanishes. Minutes later, a handsome old gent comes in and believing that Peaches is a working pro, grabs her by the arm and before Peaches can say anything, she's off to another bedroom."

Now both Al and Lucia are showing signs of disbelief.

"It's true or as true as Peaches would have me believe. Anyway, Peaches said she really loved her date who slipped her a hundred dollar bill and the compliment, 'Darling, you are the best women I've ever met in a bedroom.'

"So when they came out, Oskar, Sally and Herb, plus two whores, cheered and laughed. Herb promised never to reveal the story and Peaches slipped Sally the C note which seemed to suggest her way of saying she never screwed for money."

By now Lucia and Al were shaking their heads in disbelief.

"Well, Dawn," Al offered, "you certainly have some sporty relatives and good Stanford alums."

"Not Oskar. I think he claimed Harvard or maybe Yale. But yes, Peaches was and is a Stanford alum. Unfortunately, Oskar was killed in a car accident not long after his party at Sally's.

"So that covers one part of my parental and family history."

"Very impressive," Al volunteered, "but before this revelation, you promised some information about your father and mother and your opinions about Stanford."

"Okay," Dawn offered, "I was born July 4, 1966 in the Haight-Ashbury. So I'm a real firecracker and claim Thomas Jefferson, our nation's second president, as my idealized relative, just as you, Al, claim Mozart.

"But to give real meaning to firecracker and celebrations, I'll add this about my birth and my mother Joy Bubbles and my father Dick Knight, aka, Notte. Both had only recently been graduated from Cal and Stanford and for a month or more had been celebrating while protesting the Vietnam War, which according to my father and mother was the most immoral and stupid war the military had ever allowed the politicians to drag them into.

"Well, here it was, early July and I wasn't due until the last week of the month. And although I was kicking up a storm, my behavior didn't stop mom and dad from drinking and smoking dope with all of their friends in the Haight-Ashbury.

"Mother told me later they had planned to get married shortly after getting pregnant, but her parents wanted a church wedding and neither Peaches nor Dick would stand for it—both of them were atheists and the mere mention of religion would send them into tirades. So they put off a Justice of the Peace wedding until after graduation and ultimately long after Monday July 6, which still would have made me legal had not all of their boozing and doping caused me to pop out about about three weeks early.

"Fortunately for me, I was healthy and not in any way impaired by my parents' month-long celebration. Now, about my given name Dawn Noon and my family name Knight, my parents explained to me were the number of times they screwed before I was born—three times daily!—they brag!"

Lucy and Al could hardly contain their embarrassed snickers. But they didn't make a comment.

"Now about Stanford and my opinion about the 'Farm.' I don't' hate it, but I do relish a healthy contempt for its righteous smugness and its condescending arrogance. Most of the student body and staff, particularly the Hoover phallic think-tank wizards, believe that they are chosen people and God's gift to education.

"So why am I there? Simply because my mother is an alum as were several of our relatives, all of whom were foisted on the farm because my great, great grandfather left some ten million in blue chip stocks to the school. Hidden in our family closet are the names of Sutro, Huntington, Castro, Crocker and other infamous thiefs and crooks.

"But on my father's side of the fence, you get only good old Italian names like Notte, Saleri and Benedetti. As I mentioned, my grandfather Giovanni Notte changed his name to Knight as did several other fisherman-farmers in or around Fort Bragg shortly after the turn of the century."

For a few seconds following Dawn's long and interesting monologue, Al finally broke the silence with a question about Dick Knight, Cal's famous or infamous quarterback.

"Your Dad really saved Cal's football season in the Big Game."

"Yes, I know. Who doesn't know about that play? In fact, I really don't care who won the game. But considering my feelings about Stanford and football in general, the so-called Big Game is usually not much about anything except getting drunk and getting laid by somebody you don't know."

Both Al and Lucia could hardly decide to laugh or blush, which was exactly the confusion Dawn enjoyed whenever somebody brought up a subject which she didn't like.

Realizing that she had insulted Lucia and Al, Dawn risked a giggle. "I'm sorry, gang. My bitchy self got the best of me. Of course, football is important to a lot of people and I do enjoy the game."

For several seconds, the trio lapsed into a nervous silence which Al interrupted with the suggestion that, "Maybe we should conclude this interesting session. If there's any coffee, I would appreciate a cup and as it's getting on toward four, I should be leaving soon. It gets dark shortly after five."

Both women almost automatically moved into action and minutes later all three were sipping coffee and discussing plans for another get-together. "Maybe," Al joked, "when we collect enough laughter and tears from these sessions, we can publish a book."

"Or," Dawn offered, "we could write a TV script for a comedy called, 'Fathers and Daughters.'"

"I like that idea," Al added, "but how could we make it racy without suggesting sex?"

"You're the writer, Professor, so use your imagination, but keep it clean," Dawn said with a hint of sarcasm.

"Before you leave, Pop, when would be a good time for you to return?" Lucia's voice suggested a note of urgency.

"Anytime you ladies would like, I'll be willing and ready."

For a few minutes, Dawn and Lucia discussed their schedules; classes for Dawn and for Lucia practice and coaching at the conservatory.

"How about next Saturday, Pop? And would you be willing to return here for another session of tall tales? After which we'll take you to our favorite restaurant. Oh, yes, do you have a telephone number?"

"Yes, I do and you have mine. Agreed, Al got his coat and asked, "Do I follow the same street I took—or you took, Lucia?"

"Yes, that would probably be the easiest way but not the shortest, but when you near the Ponte Vecchio bear to the right until you reach the river, then follow the river for about two miles which should bring you into one of the streets pointing to Impruneta."

Ceremonies over, both women guided him down the short stairway to his parked car. Here Al stopped. "Thank you both so much for a wonderful day," at which point he kissed Dawn on her cheek, and as he started to repeat the ritual with Lucia, she cautiously whispered "not on my cheek" and pressed her soft lips against his, adding, "I'll be waiting."

As Al slipped into the Fiat, both women offered him a cheery, "Drive safely!"

The return was relatively easy with Al missing only one turn which he almost immediately corrected at the next street. Before dark he reached Greve and a few minutes later parked the car near the stone wall adjacent to Enrico's house.

Back in the ancient fortress, Al noted how comfortable the building was. Slowly he surveyed the interior as if he were searching for something. His mind wandered and for the first time, Al couldn't collect his thoughts. "Pull yourself together, man! You've got a few things to do before turning in." That injunction seemed to arouse him. Then it dawned on him. Lucia! She's sneaking into your brain and maybe more than that! He luxuriated in that fantasy for several more minutes before deciding to read yesterday's Herald-Tribune. He had hardly settled into a soft chair when the phone rang. Again it rang as he reached the kitchen. "Hello" just as he pressed the phone close to his ear.

"Yes, this is Al Praitt."

In almost an whisper, Al instantly recognized Lucia's voice.

"I'm glad to hear your voice and know that you're back home safely. I was afraid you might have taken a wrong turn but I should have known better than that. Anyway I also wanted to thank you for being our guest."

Al was temporarily stunned. "I am really pleased that you called because I've been wandering around this empty house ever since I got back and I don't seem able to get any writing done."

Lucia was secretly pleased. "Well, maybe you are tired from our big day here. I'm tired too, but I've got a couple more hours of practice. So I'll let you go. Oh, yes, another small question. My pearls?

This jolted Al back to reality. "Your pearls!" How stupid of me! When I changed clothes, I forgot to put them in my jacket pocket. I'm terribly sorry, which gives me more reason for next Saturday's visit. Please forgive me. I don't usually forget important things."

The conversation drifted into an embarrassing almost teenager litany of trivia until Al whispered, "Thank you dear friend. Now you practice and I'll write."

To which Lucia whispered, "Sweet dreams" and hung up.

Al sat for several minutes. "Well," he thought. "I don't know who's got whom, but as much as I'd like the feeling, I must pull myself together."

Again he picked up the paper, turned off the kitchen light and slowly entered his bedroom. For some time he listlessly read the paper until finally, glancing at his watch, he noted it was after nine. He rose, turned off the living room light, then remembered his nightly ablutions. Done, he was soon back in bed and softly snoring.

For the next several days, Al couldn't seem to focus on his writing. It seemed silly, particularly so, Al conceded, because it was nothing more than readable trash. But as much as he struggled for words or ideas, he invariably wound up with a few ridiculous sentences which he ripped from the typewriter and angrily threw into the nearby wastebasket.

After pacing back and froth, Al decided to break his frustrations with music. Nearby, near a row of shelves was a radio and combination tape and CD player. Above and below the radio and player were rows of tapes all clearly identified by composer and music. Quite obviously Fagiolo loved music, symphonies, chamber music, opera, even some American jazz. Al was impressed and noted there were some of the same tapes and CDs he had in Berkeley, but few CDs, as the recording industry was slow to develop the market.

After several minutes in deliberation, he slowly selected a Beethoven quartet, Opus 18, No. 5. "That's a good beginning," he mused "then I can work my way through the early works and maybe understand Beethoven's development."

Having selected the tape, he made the proper adjustments, turned on a master switch and waited. Suddenly the room erupted in a volume of sound. Al groped for the volume control, reduced the sound, made other adjustments and sat down to listen. For several minutes, he was engrossed in the beauty, logic and structure of the quartet.

Now returning to his desk, he stared at the blank sheet in the typewriter. His mind was still following the music. Slowly he struggled with Beethoven and himself. How does this music relate to my book? He paused as if answering his own question. Why not include some serious music in George Gainsworth's rotten personality. Give the bastard some credit for his charm and personality—he loves good music! That's it! Particularly Beethoven with whom he can secretly compare himself–a little hard of hearing, and yes, crazy about women–and women crazy about him, too.

For a few minutes, Al sat quietly organizing the relationship between the anti-hero Gainsworth and Beethoven. This could be a marvelous spoof–the vain, egotistical professor and the world's greatest composer!

Satisfied with his ideas, Al's fingers rapidly reproduced his words as the carriage moved quickly from left to right. After several minutes Al stopped, scanned the typed text, noted several spelling errors and slowly resumed developing Gainsworth's personality.

Suddenly Al stopped typing and reflecting on Gainsworth's affected academic pretensions and recalled how he would strike a calculated academic pose in the classroom or at a cocktail party and slowly pronounce, "From my studies of Freud and Wilheim Reich and several musicologists, I am able to understand the creative agony of many important writers and musicians."

At this point, Al stopped typing, remembering with a laugh how Reich and his orgone box had become a ludicrous joke for many Berkeley students and faculty shortly after World War II, but became a serious movement among some psychologists and psychiatrists in California and New England.

Again Al began typing, "Creativity," Van Dyke would whisper, "cannot be understood except within the turmoil of the creative process whether that person be a Shakespeare, Einstein, Beethoven, Wagner or Gershwin or the great Mark Twain. Each and every human's sense of creativity is a product of the invisible force of orgon, a magnetic gas which stimulates one's genitals and makes possible the orgasm.

"Until Reich discovered orgon and was able to measure its force and importance, science was not able to understand creativity. But Reich's studies, which were first accepted by Freud and Einstein, had an enormous impact on psychology and psychiatry. But as important as Reich's studies were, there were scoffers and critics, particularly after Reich had invented his orgon box, a large rectangular container in which a person could be enclosed allowing trapped orgon to flow through a small circular hole. The person in the box then spread his or her legs wide as to allow the orgon to project directly onto the genitals. After a short period, one half hour or less, the person's genitals would accumulate massive quantities of orgon which were projected throughout the body in the form of creative and sexual energy."

At this point, Gainsworth would pause, scan his listeners and, lowering his voice, add, "Reich's discovery and research can only be compared with the work of a Galileo or an Einstein."

Now, certain that he had his audience trapped, Van Dyke, a.k.a, Gainsworth would continue, "But the force of the creative energy can only be completely understood by the frustrations of the Beethovens or the Wagners or Gershwins as a form of cognitive bipolar dissonance, as opposed to cognitive creative resonant harmonies." As his audience would always appear confused, Gains-Van Dyke would add, "Now allow orgon to guide you to creativity and great orgasms."

Having typed this errant nonsense, Al was delighted. His mind was now alert to the calculated pretensions and mannerisms of several colleagues who were skilled academic poseurs. Students weren't often fooled and openly ridiculed these teachers, but Al concluded, "I guess all of us so-called intellectual types are bull-shitters."

As the Beethoven quartet had ended, Al was pleased with his description of Gainsworth as a buffoon.

Noting that it was now one p.m., Al thought of lunch. Yes, soup, sandwich. Then back to this damned book!

In the kitchen, he noted that in addition to his well-stocked larder there was a variety of Italian salami, cheeses and soup. After some consideration, Al spotted a can of minestrone and selected one, read the contents, smelled the open can with approval and poured it into the waiting pot. With the flame on low, he quickly prepared a ham sandwich. Now for a beer, and lunch will be ready.

Having finished his lunch. Al lapsed into a reflective mood, his mind questioning the series of events since the January 27-meeting with the young women. The ugly scene and the threatening scene with the stepfather. Why did this happen? But immediately he dismissed the question as nothing more than another existential event which is all part of the excitement and challenge of daily life.

He glanced at the clock, almost one-thirty. "Maybe I should take a short walk. I certainly need some exercise." Through the bedroom window, he noted bright sunshine. "Good. Walk down to Greve, get the Herald-Tribune, pick up bread and groceries and pick up the mail. Guess I'd better take the car—of course that would be too much to carry."

Ready and dressed for the cold, he closed the heavy front door, locked it and descended the steps. Once outside, he was quietly pleased with the warm winter day.

After a few nervous coughs, the engine started as Al reflected on the scene. Satisfied, he quickly turned the Fiat around and slowly began the descent to Greve. At the junction he followed the narrow street into the square, which was a pleasing pictue of tranquility. Again he parked near the hotel and bus terminal which he now entered. Yes, they had a *Herald*. The young woman smiled as she handed Al the paper along with change from his five thousand lire note. "Grazie, Professore."

Back into the large now almost empty square, Al was pleased. Apparently she knows something about me and probably everybody has heard about the scene at Ristorante Moro. He walked slowly to the post office only to be disappointed with the sign, "Chiuso." Now he doubled back to the drogheria where without struggling in Italian, he pointed to bread, butter, eggs, and cereal. He asked about meat. The clerk, a cheerful heavy women, smiled, "Carne–meat, non di qui, not here" then pointed toward the square "qui presso, nearby."

Al quickly paid the bill and departed as the cheerful woman added, "Buon giorno, Professore!"

"Well," Al thought, "it sounds like everybody knows me." Entering the square at the intersection, he crossed the cobblestone area to a small shop displaying meat and a large stuffed boar's head. He entered and was greeted with a friendly, "Buon giorno, Professore!" To which Al replied, "Grazie, di voi," then pointing to a row of cut meats, he asked, "Steak?"

"Si, bistecca."

Speaking in garbled Italian and English, Al was able to buy a small quantity of beef steak and pork chops. He was vastly relieved with his purchases and offered a hearty, "Goodbye!"

Back in the car, he noticed a large, black Mercedes sedan parked nearby. As he started the engine, he suddenly remembered the black Mercedes from "that night. Yes, that's it–couldn't be any other. So Mr. Leone is around!"

Quickly but carefully, Al backed the car out, entered the intersection and was soon climbing the steep grade home.

Once back in the house, Al neatly arranged his food supplies while wondering about the reappearance of Leone. "Now that I know he's around, I'll be ready for him, but now he knows about me, but does he know where I live? Yes, he probably does," Al concluded.

Again at the typewriter, Al slowly typed but couldn't concentrate on his "potboiler." He reread the two pages from his morning's efforts and was somewhat surprised that only two hours earlier he had been speculating on the meaning of the Monday night birthday party blow out, ending with Lucia and Al escaping and Leone's search for them.

For several minutes, Al pondered the importance of Leone's presence. "Would it be too disturbing for Lucia if I mention that he's been in Greve again? Obviously, she's terrified by him. No, I better not risk it. Maybe I should alert Dawn, but make certain that she doesn't tell Lucia."

Having settled that question, Al suddenly remembered to bring Lucia's pearls. "I can't possibly forget them again," Al thought. "Wrap them in a handkerchief and put them in my overcoat pocket." And to make certain he didn't fail, he retrieved the pearls, wrapped them and carefully shoved them into the inside pocket of his heavy coat.

Returning to the typewriter, Al reread his last page and satisfied that his satirical description of Van Dyke would be humorous to academia and the reading public, he paused. After several minutes of frustration, Al conceded that he had run out of gas. "What in the hell is wrong with me? " Al muttered out loud. After several words and oaths about his frustrations, he paused. "Oh, hell! I give up! I can't pull it together now. Better get outside. Take a short walk."

Almost hurriedly, he pulled on a wool sweater and cap, took his nearby walking stick and quickly left the house. The air was crisp and clear but the sun cast a thin blanket of warmth which dispelled the frustrations that had paralyzed Al's creativity.

On the narrow road Al decided to walk toward Montefiorale, the ancient fortified village which overlooked much of the valley. For a few minutes he studied the magnificent panorama of hills beyond Greve and in the haze he could make out Panzano. He continued his walking and then stopped to admire a large new house which had been built on a acre or more of excavated level land. The house and its precise location suggested wealth and good taste. There were gardens and immaculately tiered flower beds hidden behind two smaller buildings with red tile roofs, which provided space for equipment and tools for the small, splendid estate. Curious, Al studied the house and having decided that nobody was around, crossed the wide driveway and reached the large parking area. Here he noted that land excavated for the house and garden area had been used to level the hillside for the parking area. Walking quickly around the large area, he was surprised by the steep slope which drifted toward a ravine.

His curiosity satisfied, Al returned to the road and headed for Montefiorale, now less than a mile away. As he continued on the gentle ascent, Al was pleased by the size of the church whose weathered brick surfaces dominated the village. Here the road divided, one fork leading to a parking area and the other to the church and the village.

From this view, Al was exalted and curious about the large cluster of old stones and brick buildings which dominated the hill top. A wide, brick, paved path framed the rows of flowers in this rectangular area. For a village, the church facade dominated much of the area. From there he crossed to an upper parking area which soon took him to a long row of ancient stone structures, now all remodeled into expensive town houses.

These buildings formed the segment of a semi-circular section which enclosed half the village. The other half was protected by a very high wall which terminated at the church. An inner row of residences and shops completed the circle.

The narrow stone street, once deeply rutted by wagon wheels, was testimony to its usage and antiquity. But now the rutted surface had been resurfaced but its narrow width limited the street to foot traffic, these conditions dictating the need and reason for the parking areas in the residential section. Quite obviously the handsome restored buildings were owned by rich Florentines who only returned to ancient Montefiorale when comfort and quiet demanded.

The presence of an attractive restaurant conveniently placed near the center of the outer ring of the residences clearly indicated the desire and need for a small classy trattoria. With it's extensive and expensive menu posted, Al studied the "lista del pranzo" and noted that his next dining experience must be here soon.

Glancing at his watch, Al was surprised that it was almost four o'clock and that he should be back before sunset. "Still," he reflected, "it's hardly a mile down to the house." As he hurried through the upper parking lot among the several expensive cars, he noticed a highly-polished black Mercedes 500. For seconds, he stood. "Could this be Leone's car?" As he started to leave, he touched the metal covering the engine. "It's cool so the car hasn't been driven in the last hour. Maybe Leone has a place here." Just before leaving, he jotted the license plate number F-T 765 on a small piece of paper.

Al was both exhilarated and apprehensive as he quickly strode back to his house. Again reflecting on his small adventure, he remembered walking past the upper parking lot which he recalled was almost empty of cars, not more than three, but was one of the three Leone's Mercedes? "How do I know this was the same Mercedes I've seen before?"

As he prepared his dinner, he reviewed what little he knew about Leone and decided that he should make discreet inquiries. For the next half hour, his thoughts jumped quickly from Lucia to Leone to Dawn and back to his "potboiler," and finally to his three children, then suddenly remembering that he had two letters from Virginia but nothing from Steve or Allan.

Although he had prepared an excellent steak dinner, Al hardly tasted the food as his mind struggled to assemble the many irregular pieces of this complicated mental jigsaw puzzle. Unable to discover any particular pattern to the names, faces, places, times, events and circumstances, he gave up.

Frustrated by his failure to produce any acceptable answers to his growing number of questions, Al muttered loud enough to shatter the silence, "Damn! Shit! Why can't I produce a few answers? I must be losing my mind!" Again a cold silence engulfed the room. "Okay," Al muttered, "I give up. Maybe Beethoven can provide some relief from my confusion."

Al began searching the long row of tape cassettes. "Ah ha!. Here it is! The Hammerklavier. Okay, Mr. Serkin, give it to me! This is what I need to dispel my gloom and confusion." Quickly he snapped the piano sonata into the player and slowly relaxed into the luxury of the large sofa.

He waited in expectation as the first series of chords struck his ears, da ta ta dum, and then repeated on a higher note, da ta ta dum dum. Hardly a spectacular introduction, Al conceded, nothing like the chordal introduction to the Pathetique sonata. Then sitting back he listened, lost in the complexities of the first movement and then a short, lively scherzo.

Anticipating the long mysterious and tragic Adagio whose repetitive questioning harmonies almost brought tears to Al's eyes, "What is Beethoven asking?" Al would question, "What is he saying? So is it his deafness, his tragic love affairs? His prolonged and bitter struggle for custody of his nephew, Karl? Probably all of these," Al concluded.

As the longest slow movement of any of Beethoven's thirty-two piano sonatas ended, Al treasured 106 the most and never tired of hearing it. "But," as he would gladly admit, "I love all of his thirty-two sonatas, particularly the late ones. All of these were written when he was almost totally deaf."

With the last ascending powerful chords abruptly ending the Sonata, Al was relieved because he believed Beethoven was again asserting his determination to survive the forces that fate somehow had released to destroy him.

For several minutes Al sat quietly sharing in the catharsis of Beethoven's music. All his doubts and questions, which only an hour ago had tortured him, were dispelled in the euphoria of the Hammerklavier. Slowly he rose from the sofa, turned off the tape deck and prepared for bed.

After almost nine hours of dreamless sleep, Al felt completely revived and soon was ready for the day. "So, it's Friday. Time to move the book to fast forward, write my children a few interesting notes and make plans for tomorrow's big day with my ladies."

By nine o'clock he was rapidly typing with only occasional short moments to reread and, where necessary, change a phrase or sentence. By noon, he had completed almost eleven pages. "Time for a sandwich and a beer," Al suggested.

Following his noon respite, he again confronted his typewriter and still his muse urged him on. The story literally flew out of the electric Olivetti with chapter seven ending on page 140. Al was intoxicated with his progress but cautiously told himself, "With a few corrections and rewrites, I'll have this tale of academic chicanery and satire ready for my agent by April." Buoyant and enthusiastic, Al stacked the typed pages together with the completed text and secured them in a folder. Then ceremoniously, he flicked off the typewriter switch and caressingly covered the typewriter. He was elated.

To celebrate the occasion, in the kitchen larder, he produced an unopened bottle of Italian brandy. The first sip warned him against further presumptuous celebratory drinking, but it failed to diminish his enthusiasm.

Now remembering his self-pledge to write his children, he uncovered the typewriter, inserted a page of airmail stationary and quickly produced a full page of his efforts: the Italians, his house, plus several questions about her health, husband and child. Within fifteen minutes the letter was completed, signed with affectionate wishes and placed in the addressed envelope. But the letters to Steve and Allan were somewhat awkward and stiff. He wanted to encourage them with positive questions but found his rhetoric stiff and almost patronizing. After a half hour of frustration, Al suddenly ripped the page from the machine, "Damn! Just write them a note about your experiences here, the food and wine, yes, and stress the wine with an enthusiastic tone of camaraderie about their joint venture in viticulture. Try to make your family relationship a strong force for success and fun."

After an hour of calculated fact, fantasy and hope, Al was relieved. "This should, I hope, encourage them to get their act together." He signed the letter Corragio! Ciao! Dad.

With the completion of his required writing, Al now sat down to prepare his agenda and plans for Saturday's get-together. "Let's see," Al considered, "I'm going to want to know more about both girls and their parents, relatives and lifestyles. Maybe they will want to know more about me which is dull and simple, a tough life, the Air Corps—but don't get too deep about that idiotic five years of frustration and stupidity. And don't get carried away with your thirty years at Cal. Let the girls ask the questions. But above everything else, I must find out as much as possible about Leone. Lucia must know far more than she's told. And Dawn, she probably knows something too. After all, the women have been living together for a couple of months at least."

Having completed his scribbled agenda, Al added—don't forget Lucia's pearls!

Suddenly Al noted that it was almost dark and he had completed his letters in the shadows. Abruptly he turned on the lights and was surprised how the room seem changed by the standing lamps. For several minutes he struggled with the radio in an effort to tune in the Armed Service Network. Failing to find the station, he turned to the tape deck and quickly found a tape of Rubenstein playing Chopin. "That should provide me with good dinner music."

In the kitchen, Al quickly prepared a couple of pork chops, potatoes and vegetables while frequently stopping to absorb the Chopin nocturne. After a half-hour of preparations, he was ready to eat, then he remembered the wine.

"Chianti! What else? Tuscany and wine are mighty fine!" Raising his glass, Al solemnly toasted, "To Tuscany and beautiful women." Between the food, the Chopin and thoughts of Lucia and Dawn, he was quietly happy.

A half hour later and Al was ready for dreamland.

Chapter Three

Rising early, Al shaved and showered and soon completed his morning ritual. Driven by nervous energy, he prepared breakfast and ate it rapidly while making a mental list of 'must do': "Dress casually, bring pearls, buy gift, buy wine." Then he compiled a time table: "Leave for Florence by ten, arrive at their apartment about eleven."

Satisfied with his preparations, Al quickly washed his breakfast dishes, made up his bed and then methodically dressed.

Before closing the heavy front door, he paused, surveyed the room, turned on the floor lamp and departed after making certain that the door was tightly locked.

Again the cold engine coughed and sputtered several times before Al was satisfied that it was warmed up. Confident that the Fiat wouldn't stall, Al slowly headed the small car toward the main road. There he slowly looked for any sign of traffic before cautiously descending to Greve.

Once in the town square, already alive and noisy with vendors and shoppers, Al found a parking place. At the small post office, he asked and was disappointed with the response, "Non posta." Quickly he joined the crowds of noisy shoppers. He was pleased and surprised by the variety of foods, products and goods prominently displayed. As buyers and sellers argued and bargained, Al joined in the excitement. At one stand he noticed a variety of trinkets, small brass animals, alabaster vases and dishes, and hand carved cats and dogs, none of which were priced.

Al realized that between his limited ability to speak and bargain in Italian and his almost equally limited knowledge of prices, he was indeed seriously handicapped. Nevertheless, he plunged excitedly into the noisy scene.

Picking up a brass cat, Al asked, "Quanto?" The smiling, attractive sales lady answered, "Non troppo!"

Again he asked, "Quanto? Quanto?"

Sensing Al's frustration, the woman answered in broken English, "fur yu, meester, leetul, geef me fiff dolar."

"No, I give you five thousand lire."

The bargaining continued rapidly as Al selected a small alabaster dish and a hand carved cat. Within minutes, Al completed the transaction and handed the smiling woman thirty thousand lire. Al was pleased that he had made a good deal while the sales lady could hardly conceal her delight as she carefully wrapped each piece.

As Al took his two packages, the small crowd, which had enjoyed the bargaining, laughed and cheered.

Once in the Fiat, Al glanced at his watch. Only five after ten, good! I should be in Florence about eleven and at their apartment soon after.

The traffic from Greve to Impruneta was relatively light but quickly increased as Al sought the circular road which would soon bring him next to the Arno. Now for reasons he didn't understand, he was approaching the river and a bridge.

Across the bridge, he slowed and by carefully selecting narrow streets, he soon ascended a small hill. Suddenly there was a wide, four-lane road which soon brought him to a large square. "Piazzale Michelangelo." Here he stopped to admire much of the panorama.

On this clear Saturday morning Giotto's Bell Tower stood tall against the massive Il Duomo which shared the horizon with Piazza Santa Croce, Palazzo Vecchio and nearby, the city's heart and life, Piazza della Republica. Al was intoxicated by the garden and beauty of this Florentine jewel.

Almost reluctantly, he returned to the wide Viale Galileo as it twisted around the descending road which circled the Boboli Gardens. Here Al began to recognize the small streets and a few landmarks which he had noted on his last visit. By luck or intuition he suddenly saw Lucia's and Dawn's apartment.

As he carefully parked his car, quickly both women descended on him. "Buon giorno! Benvenuto, Dottore. Come va?" These greetings were blessed by hugs and breasts pressed tightly against him from both sides. Embarrassed but pleased, Al deftly replied with a quick kiss for each woman.

"You darling man!" Dawn gushed. "You've arrived early!"

"But not too early," Lucia purred. "Now come. Avanti! We'll have some wine and begin where we left off last week. And we have some juicy lies to tease you with."

With Al in the middle, the two young women escorted their man to the apartment. Once inside, Al noted that the furniture had been rearranged with the sofa still against the left wall but now the small serving table had been placed opposite the sofa. A small elegant cloth covered the table top and three wine glasses, a carafe of red wine, a platter of thin crackers and a wedge of Gorgonzola suggested a session of sipping, eating and talking. A single chair faced the table and sofa.

Quickly Lucia and Dawn sat together and urged Al to sit facing them.

"Now Professor Praitt, we've again seated you as our guest of honor and we're ready to resume our question and answer game. But before we start, let's have some wine and cheese, and maybe we can trick you into a romantic confessional," Dawn winked and smiled at Al.

"I don't know whether this intimate format suggests a confessional or an examination. Maybe we should make some rules," Al suggested.

"But before we begin this inquisition," Lucia smiled, "let's have some brain food, and while we're eating let's each consider questions and answers which reveal or conceal our past, our present and maybe our future."

All agreed and for several minutes, they nibbled and sipped in an animated conversation.

"Now," Dawn suggested, "let's agree to a few rules. As it's now just after twelve, let's limit this session to one hour, okay?"

Everybody agreed and Al added, "Let's limit each question and answer to five minutes." Again, total agreement.

"And I suggest," Dawn added, "let's also agree that we may each ask only one question in each sequence of three. In that way, we can prevent Al from dominating our humble feminine lives."

"Good, Dawn, I like that because you two Lucrezia Borgias can't do me in."

For a few seconds, Lucia and Dawn appeared confused. "So you sly literary type," Dawn laughed, "you would compare us with a Roman femme fatale? Well, I've read a bit of Roman history and while I would like to compare you with Marc Anthony, maybe you're really a Caligula or a Nero."

"Wait a minute, you classical scholars, we're not here to insult or to praise each other, but simply to know each other better." Lucia seemed more offended than sarcastic, which both Dawn and Al acknowledged.

"Please excuse us, Lucia. I was just being silly." Al pleaded.

"Fine. Now when are we in our question and answer game?" Dawn asked.

"I think we seem to agree that each one is entitled to one question and one reply limited to five minutes in each round, right?"

"You got it, Al, but how about questions of our sex lives? Are they fair game?"

Quickly Lucia cut in. "I really don't think that personal questions or a discussion of our sex lives is acceptable or necessary."

Somewhat embarrassed, Al and Dawn nodded. "Let's agree that our purpose is to know and understand each other and perhaps understand ourselves."

Dawn and Lucia quickly agreed.

"Who wants to ask the first question?" Dawn asked.

"Since I'm something of a stranger to both of you," Al volunteered, "I'll try to answer any question either of you might wish to ask."

"Good," Dawn reacted quickly, "What are you doing here in Italy and why did you decide to come here rather than, say, England, where you wouldn't be handicapped with a language problem?"

"Well, rather than England, which I have visited several times in the past forty-two years, I chose Italy for several reasons. First, I have never been here and always wanted to visit this beautiful country and two, because an Italian professional friend suggested that we exchange houses for six months. So he gets my house in Berkeley for the spring semester while he's teaching at Cal. And I get a six-month paid vacation, which gives me time to complete my book and meet the deadline without the constant interference I would have in Berkeley."

Now Lucia was ready. "If it isn't too personal, what's your book about and why are you writing?"

Al sighed, "No, that's not too personal. I'm writing because I need the money. My book is a farce, a satire about a professor at Berkeley who no longer is there, so I don't have to worry about this character. Since I don't have the talent to write serious books, I earn extra income from my 'potboilers' which are probably the only genre that I can easily write. It must be part of my nasty sense of humor."

"I know that I've already asked my one question," Dawn interjected, "but would you allow me one small question about what you were doing in England forty-two years ago?"

"Okay," Al laughed. "I got a free trip to England forty-two years ago courtesy of the U.S. Army Air Corps."

Both girls laughed as Al added, "I was just trying to be cute. I was a flying officer sent first to England and soon to France."

Now Lucia was quick to ask, "What was it like? My father served in Italy in two or three places, but I know nothing about the war in France or Germany."

Al hesitated, "I'll try to brief. I was commissioned as a bombadier in 1942 and served as an instructor for B-17s for two years. But immediately after D-Day on June 6, 1944, all flying personnel who had not been in combat were sent either to the Pacific or to Europe. And I wound up in France not flying B-17s but B-26s and not as a bombadier, but as a navigator."

"And please," Dawn almost begged, "would you mind just giving us a bit more about your war experience?"

"Okay, if you insist," Al frowned. "In a few words, flying combat over Germany was about as close to heaven or hell as any flyer could ever suffer, as the Germans' belligerent behavior only caused us to blow up most of their towns, factories and railroads. Fortunately, after surviving forty-five missions I got a two-week vacation in England. Not only was that a life-saver, but now that my days in that flying coffin, the B-26, also known as the 'widow maker' were almost over, I was delighted.

"Still, because of Air Corps delays, I didn't get home for six months, which allowed me time to enroll for Cal's spring semester in 1946. I could add a great deal to my five-year career in the Air Corps, which is now called the Air Force. I learned a lot the hard way. And I learned just how bigoted, arrogant and inefficient the Air Force is, but they are probably no worse than the Army, Navy or Marines. Furthermore, all military organizations are quite similar whether they're German, Japanese or Russian."

"Wow!" Dawn exclaimed, "you really don't care much for the military, do you, Al?"

"I'm sorry. I shouldn't have blown my stack. There are a lot of good people in the services, but there are also those like General Patton and General MacArthur who believed they were gods."

Taking a deep breath, Al almost laughed, "Now it's my turn to ask a question."

Dawn and Lucia smiled, "Fire away, professor."

Smiling at Lucia, "I would like to ask you about your parents and what you are doing here in Florence?"

For a few seconds, Lucia seemed apprehensive. "Well," she paused as if she were struggling, "I can't give you a short happy answer. Not that my life has been a tragedy, mystery or comedy. I've had my ups and down as everybody has, so, well, let's see, maybe I should start at my beginning here in Italy."

For a few seconds, Lucia seemed frightened, then she slowly brightened and in a light voice began, "First of all, I was born in Italy, in Verona to be exact, where father was base commander. And as Al knows, I was born on the same day and month as he, which I think was lucky for both of us and for our patron saint of music Wolfgang Amadeus Mozart."

At this time, Al and Dawn ceremoniously arose and laughed, "three cheers for Lucia, Wolfgang and Al!"

Feigning embarrassment, Lucia laughed, "Thank you. Now do you want to hear my short life history?"

"As noted, I was born twenty-one years ago in Verona and blessed with the most loving parents anybody could ever have. My mother, Eleni, was part Greek, English and Egyptian, and was born in Alexandria. And her mother is my grandmother, Justine, who was lucky to have married my grandfather, Massimo."

"It's quite complicated how my parents and grandparents met and married and came to Italy. Shall I just skip that and return to the present?"

"No," Dawn added. "You've never mentioned this part of your life to me."

"Yes, continue, Lucia," Al said, "how did your grandparents meet?"

"I'll try to be brief but my family history is complicated and goes back to before World War II. My maternal grandfather, Justine's father, was a Greek-Egyptian businessman who had married Justine's beautiful English-French mother in Egypt a few years before the war started. Then in 1942 the Germans seized Greece and moved into Egypt where they combined with Rommel's African Army. My parents were desperate so they hired a small boat and sneaked back to Greece where my great-grandfather had many relatives, friends and a house in the mountains.

"For two or three years, Justine and her parents were safe as were many other Greek-Egyptians, but suddenly that changed as the Germans began a ruthless campaign to kill any Greeks who might be a threat to their small occupying force."

"And what happened?" Al asked.

"Well, there were bands of Greek guerrillas, communists and royalists who continued to attack, which resulted in the Germans killing fifty Greeks for every German. And that's how my great-grandfather and grandmother were killed. Fortunately, Justine was left with an old maiden aunt."

"Very interesting, Lucy, but how did Massimo come into this story?" Dawn asked.

"My grandfather, Massimo, was a German hostage in 1944 working as a longshoreman who had been sent to the Greek port of Volos where he helped load German transports. Just before the Germans began leaving Volos, Massimo met Justine, who had just run away from her old aunt, and Justine saw Massimo and asked him to help her escape to Italy.

"Massimo quickly agreed and gave her shelter in the small room he had near the docks. After about two months, an Italian freighter came into port and Massimo took her aboard as his wife. They finally reached Livorno, the port for Tuscany, the very port where Massimo had worked as a longshoreman and had won a small measure of fame and fortune several years before the war."

"Am I boring·you?" Lucia asked.

"No, no. This is fascinating. What else?"

"Massimo was born in Naples, and because he was almost six feet tall when he was only fourteen, his parents took him out of school and soon got him a job working on the docks. After a few years he ran away and came to Livorno where he soon got a job as a longshoreman."

"And what happened?" Dawn asked. "You mentioned his fame and fortune."

"This is very interesting and funny. In 1936 a huge Italian prize fighter named Primo Carnero had become the World Heavyweight Boxing Champion in a fixed fight. Well, he was training in Pisa and one day his manager offered about a hundred dollars to anybody who could last one round with the champion.

"Well, grandpa Massimo had done a lot of fighting as a stevedore so he quickly volunteered. In the ring somebody helped Massimo put on the large boxing gloves, then in the center of the ring Carnero and Massimo touched gloves. Immediately Carnero charged grandpa who stepped out of the way. Then when Carnero charged again, grandpa slugged him in the head and the champ dropped like a rock, out cold!"

"Really, Massimo knocked out the world champion?" Al hooted.

"Yes, he did and to this day, Massimo has the newspaper which printed the story.

"Then, Carnero's manager gave grandpa the money and told everybody that Massimo had a small pipe in his glove."

"What happened after that?"

"Massimo was only too happy to leave Livorno and moved to Panzano where he bought several acres of land with the money and that's where he and Justine have lived ever since. But now, Massimo is a rich man with two or three farms and the grocery stores, bakery and meat market in Panzano."

"How old is he?" Dawn asked.

"I'm not certain, but I think he's 86 and he still weighs at least 250 pounds and is at least six feet, six. Just about everybody in Tuscany knows him or has heard about him."

For a few seconds, nobody spoke, then Lucia added, "I've been talking for a long time, so I would like a break."

Quickly Dawn produced some cookies and soon Lucia offered some tea.

All agreed that Lucia's life was very special, but now it was Al's turn.

Somewhat reluctantly, Al agreed to answer questions.

Again, Dawn took the lead, "You told us why you're here, Al, and something about your war experiences, but you and your family are a mystery as indeed you are, too. Much as we like you and admire you, we can only guess about your values and what makes you tick. You've got five minutes to reveal the true Professor Al Praitt."

"Right," Al agreed, "but unless I talk very fast and skip many times, places, accidents, etc., you aren't going to get much more than my birth, family, education, etc. and the names, dates and places."

"That's okay, Professor, you're right. We don't need every petty detail. Just give us the important facts."

"Good. The facts are: I was born in Santa Barbara, California, on January 27, 1919 and I had a loving older sister and a worthless older brother and two smart younger sisters, all of whom were born in Santa Barbara.

My mother was a strict and loving parent as was my father who had served in the Marine Corps during the Spanish-American War. But in 1929 while Dad was working in Northern California, my mother suddenly died. He returned immediately and with help from relatives he took care of us until he hired housekeepers.

Soon my older sister graduated from the university, married and with her husband took care of us. Much later I saw my brother who had been in a circus, and then the Navy and finally had become a successful businessman and a drunk.

"Now if you ladies don't mind, I would like to skip over the ups and down which dominated my family for several years. I don't think we had it any worse than millions of other American families. As my mother's sudden death was a terrible tragedy for us in many ways, it was only a prelude to that far greater tragedy, the Great Depression, which gripped not only the United States, but most of the world from 1929 until World War II began in 1939."

Al slumped quietly in his chair as both women stared at the wall for a few minutes.

Finally pulling himself to an erect position, Al brightened, "I should have skipped that melancholy part. For all of the tragedy of the Great Depression, life went on. People continued to work whenever possible. But we were a leaderless people in effect. The President and the Congress did almost nothing to end the Depression. But in 1932 the people elected a new President, Franklin Delano Roosevelt."

"Wasn't he very controversial?" Dawn asked.

"Indeed he was, and his problems were compounded by the Republican Congress which refused to pass any of the bills and programs Roosevelt and the Democrats proposed."

"That's hardly new," Dawn laughed, "the Democrats and Republicans have been fighting each other since the cow jumped over the moon. And I should know because my father is a liberal Democrat and my mother is a rock-ribbed Republican, but hasn't a clue about politics. Fortunately, she almost never votes."

"This is very interesting, Al. As an Italian American and a musician, I know very little about history or politics. So tell us more about President Roosevelt and the great world wide depression."

Rising to the occasion, Al glowed, "Franklin Roosevelt was one of the most unusual Presidents we ever had. Born a patrician from a wealthy family, FDR, as he was often called, deserted his Republican relatives, and after holding a series of important appointed offices was elected President by a huge majority in 1932. Nevertheless, as I just said, the Republicans controlled Congress, blocked most of Roosevelt's programs, and if the Congress didn't, the Supreme Court did.

"Nevertheless in 1936, FDR was again re-elected by a landslide. Then as the threat of war became ominous, Roosevelt did everything possible to prepare us for action. But his political support began to wane as many Americans opposed FDR's effort to prepare. Nevertheless in the controversial election of 1940, Roosevelt barely won a plurality.

"Now Roosevelt did everything legally possible to help England fight the Germans. Then when the Japanese attacked us at Pearl Harbor on December 7, 1941, we were in the war. And at that point I volunteered to join the U.S. Army Air Corp, not that I was enthusiastic, but I knew that I would be drafted into the Infantry almost immediately. So on December 8th I was sworn into the Army Air Corp and on Tuesday, December 9th, I received notice that I must report for induction into the Army."

"I'm a bit confused," Dawn asked. "You volunteered, but were drafted? How did that work?"

"Two years before the war began, the Congress passed a law requiring all American males over 18 to register for military duty. Of course I did so. When the Japanese attacked on December 7th I knew that the exemption I had to attend college would immediately expire. So I volunteered for pilot training instead of waiting to be drafted into the Army and probably the Infantry."

By now, Lucia and Dawn appeared to lose interest, which Al noted. "This is a long story which I'll shorten and skip to that period in 1945 when I was in Paris after almost two weeks of R and R in England.

"By 1944 the war in Europe and the Pacific was going our way and Roosevelt had won an unprecedented fourth term. On April 12, as I was boarding a bus in Paris, I noticed a newspaper with the banner, 'Roosevelt est mort!' Standing on that crowded bus, I was overcome with emotion and began to weep. Several Parisians noticed me and patted me on the back.

"Quite honestly, Roosevelt's death gripped me like the passing of a close friend or a loving relative, and I believe that millions of Americans and our allies also felt that way. Unquestionably Franklin Roosevelt was the true leader of the free world."

For several minutes, nobody spoke until Dawn said softly, "That's a terribly tragic story and much more personal than I could imagine. Thank you for the courage and honesty to share it with us."

At this point, tears were filling Lucia's eyes. She looked away as she discretely dabbed her eyes and face with tissue.

Al broke the ice with a laugh, "Come on, ladies, let's have some more wine and then have that lunch that you promised me. I'm hungry."

For a few minutes the women busied themselves in the bedroom and reminded Al about the other half-bath just off the kitchen.

Soon they reassembled as Lucia took the lead, "There's a wonderful restaurant near, the Il Toro, and we have reservations for one-thirty. Andiamo!"

Having quickly walked near the Boboli Gardens, they soon entered Il Toro, clearly an elegant and expensive restaurant. The handsome head waiter welcomed them warmly while greeting Dawn and Lucia by name and Al as Professor.

Quickly Al realized that it would be expensive but readily accepted the fact that he could afford what he assumed would be his treat. At this point Lucia and Dawn, now beside the waiter, discretely whispered, "Signore, before you consider anything silly, not that you would, I would like you to know that this treat is on Dawn and me, preferably me because this is my favorite restaurant, which means that our friend's money is not acceptable here. At least, not now. Capisce?"

Al was momentarily at a loss for words, then with a smile, "Darlings, I wouldn't dare to protest and create a 'bruta figura.'"

"Well," Dawn laughed, "you are something else, no 'bruta figura.' Another three months here and you will be a card-carrying Italian."

Having been ceremoniously seated at a choice table by a small garden and waterfall, the beautiful trio slyly smiled as Lucia whispered, "We seem to be the center of attraction. Don't be annoyed, darlings, we Italians are like this."

A handsome waiter soon greeted them with a gracious smile, "Buon giorno, signore, signori. My name is Carlo," and in perfect English, he asked, "Is there anything special you would like? I believe Signora Conte likes fish and Florentine beef, but we have many other principal dishes we Italians enjoy. For instance veal, rabbit, quail, duck and other seafoods. While you are studying the menu, I'll bring a bottle of wine. Perhaps a '81 Chianti classico. Would that be acceptable, Signora Conde?"

"Well, that depends on what we want to order. As you know, I'll probably start with sea food, a shrimp or small fish dish. I'll wait for my guests to choose."

"Of course, Signora, I'll return in a few minutes."

After studying and admiring the many-paged elaborate menu, Lucia suggested, "Shall we put our collective choices together and ask our waiter to take it from there?"

"Good idea," Dawn volunteered, "let's each make a choice for soup, salad, entree, dessert and wine?"

Al agreed but continued, "If we each should order four or five dishes, we will end up with more than enough food for several days—and I don't think this place provides 'doggie bags.'"

Again Lucia asserted herself, "Do either of you wish soup? They have an excellent variety of zuppas as they do salads. Al, why don't you get us started?"

"That sounds good," Dawn added, "I'm thinking of an artichoke salad and swordfish—pisce spada with polenta and for dessert, tiramisu."

Lucia now asserted her gracious hostess role, "This restaurant has a magnificent kitchen and staff capable of preparing heavenly food, so I'm going to suggest their special vegetable salad, chicken cacciatore or rabbit and finally tiramisu."

Within seconds the waiter was standing behind Al, "I believe that you are probably ready to order, but before you do, would you mind if I bring a small delight from our chef? He would like to surprise you."

Al smiled, but also indicated surprise and confusion. Dawn turned to Lucia and quizzically suggested, "Do you know anything about this?"

With a Cheshire grin, Lucia asked, "How could I?"

Suddenly the Chef and Carlo appeared pushing a small ornate cart. At the table the chef carefully placed a large silver serving dish in the center of a perfect circle of delicate roses. From the silver dish he ceremoniously removed three beige mounds, each about the size of a half-orange and placed each on a silver plate. With his small slicer, he shaved tiny truffle flakes over each mound.

Then Carlo, not to be denied a role in this culinary ceremony, skillfully drizzled tiny droplets of clear liquid over each delicacy.

Together, the Chef and his head waiter stepped back, smiling and waiting for the trio's response. As they sat in suspense, Carlo tactfully slid each plate a bit closer to the silent trio.

"Per favore," the chef smiled. "Mangia!"

Al, without further hesitation, lifted his knife as both the chef and the waiter nodded approval. Quickly he removed an inch-sized wedge and put it in his mouth. For perhaps three seconds, his face hardly moved, then in a subtle expression of surprise and delight, Al projected sublime ecstasy. And before he could express further gustatory pleasure, both women were overcome with silent elation.

"It must be a blend of meats, maybe beef and lamb, spices and corn or grain." Dawn offered.

Lucia had finished a second wedge before again suggesting, "I'm hardly a gourmet or a skilled food critic, but I sense a variety of herbs and wine."

Now Al asserted himself, "I agree that this is very complex, surely butter or maybe cream which when blended with the juice of certain meats or vegetables interact chemically to produce exiting new tastes. Really, great chefs know these mysteries which they express in their culinary masterpieces that in their temporal way are equal to great paintings, sculptures and bronzes."

"My exact words, Big Daddy. I wish I could come up with them in my art class at Stanford," Dawn snickered.

"They're good!" Lucia added, "but while you two are gabbing, I'm finishing the most exciting food I've ever tasted."

As each supplicant reveled in an almost sinful celebration of gourmet exultation, suddenly Carlo appeared, "Did you enjoy our chef's surprise?"

"Carlo," Lucia offered, "I've never tasted anything as delicious and exciting in my life."

"Nor I," both Dawn and Al agreed.

"I don't suppose the chef would reveal the ingredients of his masterpiece?" Al asked.

"I'm afraid that you're right because nobody on the staff knows what the ingredients are or how the chef uses and combines them. The only fact that we know is that he bakes them and then allows me to slice the truffles sometimes or drizzle the sauce."

"Well, it's the greatest culinary surprise that I have ever experienced," Al added.

"You three Americans are only the second diners the chef has allowed to taste his specialty. He particularly wanted Dawn and Lucia because they have eaten here often and the chef not only admires their charm and beauty, but he knows they are highly intelligent and have excellent taste— in food and dress."

Al registered pleasure and surprise as both women smiled knowingly while adding a sincere, "Thank you, Carlo, and above all, please tell the chef that we thank him profoundly for allowing us the pleasure of his masterpiece."

"One other reason the chef asked you three to taste his dish is because he knows how critical most of his Italian customers are. Yes, on several occasions he's presented a new culinary dish only to have our regular customers insult him with their stupid comments. He's a very sensitive man. But you made his day with your facial expressions and few words. And he asked me to express his joy for your approval."

For a few minutes, the trio almost gloated in the pleasure of this experience.

Soon they returned to reality by ordering three dinners of one fish, etc. plate, one rabbit, one carbonara, salad, dessert, and two glasses of white wine and one of Chianti.

When they had completed their gourmet gluttony, the restaurant was almost empty.

Noting his watch, Al offered, "Ladies, it's after three and I should be considering my departure, particularly because you both have responsibilities much more important than mine."

"Oh, Al, don't flatter us," Dawn joked. "My courses are a joke. All I have to do is wiggle my ass to get an A but Lucy does have to practice. Right, Miss Lucia della Rosa?"

"Not quite right, Miss Centerfold." With that comment, Al winced. Lucia's tone and sarcasm suggested less harmony in their relationship than he had believed.

"But I expect you're right, Dawn. I've got to practice at least four hours every day and today I got in only two hours this morning. So, yes, I've some more hard work before dreamland."

Al felt more comfortable with Lucia's placatory apology which encouraged him to comment on their unfinished question and answer game. As they walked briskly past the Boboli Gardens, Al asked, "Would you ladies like to continue our game next weekend?"

"Of course. Why not?" both women answered simultaneously. "You've got a lot to explain, sir," Dawn laughed.

"Maybe," Al smiled "but Dawn, you've told us hardly anything, or maybe you shared your secrets with Lucia."

"Of course," Dawn joked, "we ladies haven't any secrets, have we Lucia?"

Cautiously Lucia added, "No, I don't suppose. Although I would guess that all of us have some really deep feelings that may be forever hidden."

At that, Al was emotionally shaken, but he said nothing.

Soon they reached the apartment. "Let's have some coffee and then we'll let you escape," Lucia sighed.

For a few seconds Al, in a fit of quiet, was tempted to reject their invitation. Then realizing that both women would be insulted, he joked. "Yes, I suppose we do need a proper ending to one of the most wonderful afternoons of my life."

Soon both Lucia and Dawn had coffee and cookies on the side table. After ten minutes of affectionate small talk, Al rose and fervently kissed a somewhat surprised Lucia. In return, Dawn deftly turned Al around and planted a large, wet smack on his mouth. The social code ended as Al quickly descended the stairs and, at the car, waived goodbyes. For two seconds, he returned their smiles, noting tears tracing Lucia's sad smile.

The return to Greve was uneventful as a fantasy of pleasure and sex constantly intruded on the demands of his muse. Without thinking, Al climbed the hill from Greve, parked the Fiat and trudged up the stairs. The empty house seemed more like a tomb than a work house.

As it now was after five, Al automatically turned on the lamp, then paused. Confused by the bright light, suddenly Al remembered that he had left that lamp on. For a few seconds he stared at the lamp, "Maybe I didn't leave it on. But, but how could the lamp have been turned off?" Dismissing the question, Al quickly moved from room to room carefully examining the furniture–a comprehensive inventory of each room and even the five-foot high armoire which he jerked open while stepping back as if he expected an intruder to pounce on him.

After five minutes of Sherlock Holmesian investigation, Al reluctantly concluded that his memory must have played a nasty joke on him. And to deny his suspicions he recalled two earlier embarrassing relapses–his demand that his bank had charged a hundred dollars to his account, only to have the manager produce a copy of his check. Then later, when he misplaced his favorite cap and accused Joan of losing it. "Well," Al concluded "either keep better track of your subconscious behavior or write notes to yourself."

Finally returning to his "potboiler," he sat paralyzed for thought, then remembering that he hadn't decided on a title, he felt relieved. "Okay, Al, how about 'Love and Lust in Academia'," or to be really silly, 'Love and Lust but Publish or Perish'? Not bad. That would go over big in academia. Maybe I'll use it."

Realizing that his title search was a silly distraction, he sat quietly. Finally, he laughed, "Of course it must be satire. Nothing else is possible for me." Then he slowly began to type, "Every college or university has its share of academic fakes and clowns, so I've concocted St. John Gainsworth as the real-life philandering George C. Van Dyke, who is professionally hoisted on his own petard after he beds, deflowers and then proposes marriage to a beautiful teenage exchange student whose parents are rich Italians.

"Would any wealthy Italian family allow their only daughter to marry a divorced, middle-aged, academic clown? Of course not! Damn! So I get the satire almost finished, only to realize I've created an impossible situation. Well, I must figure out an alternative for either the girl or the family. Maybe they're both phonies?"

Al quickly arose from the typewriter table, flipped off the switch and hurriedly covered the machine. "Hell, what to do? Play some music? Have a drink? Might was well. Maybe I can dream up an acceptable conclusion."

Almost in a trot he covered the short distance to the kitchen. Between anger and almost despair, he ransacked the wine and liquor cabinet. No luck! No brandy or booze. Only wines and liqueurs!

"Well," he paused, "I need bread and meat and maybe–I've got mail." Noting it was now after five, he quickly pulled on his top coat, checked his wallet and bounded down the stairs. Then remembering that he hadn't locked the door, he raced up the steps and made certain that the door was locked.

Fortunately the Fiat purred to a start and minutes later, Al parked in the almost empty great square. Relieved that most shops were still open, Al first stopped at the combination variety store and bus station. Quickly he found the brandy, the *Herald Tribune* and soft drinks. As the pretty, young clerk bagged his purchases, "Sum ting mor, Professore?" she smiled. Stunned, Al added, "Potato chips, ice cream, and a chocolate mix."

"Tank you, sir!" Al could have kissed her as he hurriedly departed.

At the post office, still open, Al asked "una lettera, signora?" "Si, Professore, Molte per lei."

With that smiling gesture, the mail clerk handed Al several letters and a small package. "Grazie!" Al managed a grin.

Now for meat and bread, Al remembered. Here is a meat market, but no bread. Entering the empty market a ringing "Buona sera, professore" greeted him. "Come sta?" To which Al could only smile and say "Grazie." With a few rudimentary gestures and fractured English and Italian, Al had a sausage, steak and chicken. Again he completed the departure ritual, now with two large bags of food into which Al added his mail and newspapers.

At his parked car, he dumped his bags and walked quickly to the panificio where again a plump smiling clerk quickly found him the whole wheat bread and suggested a cake, which Al added to his bag with the bread. Then in a parting gesture, the clerk whispered, "Professore ecco un focaccino!" Al was profuse in his thank you's as he nibbled on the sugar cookies and hurried to the car.

While depositing his bags to the back seat he noted a package which suddenly he realized were the gifts he purchased last Saturday–the brass cat and alabaster dish. Almost embarrassed, Al remembered that he hadn't mentioned either gift. "Good, a small thank you for last week."

Soon the Fiat easily climbed the hill and almost parked itself next to "his" house. By carefully rearranging his bags Al was barely able to bring his purchases to the door. Hastily he unlocked the door and soon had food and drink properly stored.

Next he poured a hearty glass of brandy, took the potato chips and plopped himself on the sofa with the mail. As he sipped the brandy and noted its smooth body and bouquet, he examined each letter–first Virginia's classic scrip, then a letter from each son, something from U.C. and finally a scribbled address which he recognized as Arturo Fagiolo's writing.

Carefully he opened his daughter's letter. "Dear Sweet Daddy," she opened with a loving account of her baby (Allan, of course) her husband, and life. At this point, the prose seemed constricted.

"Well, dad, I hate to mention this but both my brothers are in jail for drunk driving and resisting arrest. I've talked to them and they are terribly ashamed and depressed. But don't worry. Bob and I will have them out on bail in a day or two. Forty-eight hours in jail might be the best thing that could happen to them. Love, V.B."

For a few seconds Al mulled over his sons' problems, then dismissed further worries. "Yes, a couple of days in the jug might be just what they need." With that thought, the father opened each son's offering. Stephen's explanation was simple, "Too much booze, so I paid a fine and promised not to drive when drinking." Then he added, several silly quips, "No booze, no cops, nothing to lose. Our wine will thrive if we don't drink and drive."

Al scanned Allan's letter.

"We both get busted returning from a long weekend at Tahoe. Because I protested my sobriety, the CHP wrote us both up and tossed us in the can at Tracy. I wasn't legally drunk, only 0.7 which is close, but not legally drunk. I may file a complaint but because Steve was smashed, I got a ticket, too. But don't worry, if at our age we can't be responsible, something's wrong and it isn't you, Dad, or our mother. Bless her! I hope all goes well with your book and your plans for a winery are still alive, and well, both of your sons are taking U.C. Davis Extension classes in winemaking. We're counting on being partners in Cave de Bacchus. Love Al. P.S. Write soon!"

Al relaxed, satisfied with his children's explanations and affection. He mixed brandy and chips as he ripped open a letter from the English department. From the chairman, Al gloated, "As you may have heard, we are still strapped for money, but if you could help us with one of your classic humor seminars next fall, we would all be most appreciative. Think it over, Al, your kids could run the winery! Oh yes, one good laugh, that nut Van Dyke in Rhetoric finally got nailed. Some teenager claimed he had fondled her! Of course, he did, and many others. Anyway he's out pending a trial! Think about our offer for that seminar. Good luck. Dan."

"Well," Al mused, "so Van Dyke will soon be a goner just about the time my book comes out."

Again another sip of Martini and Rossi and Al scanned Fagiolo's letter. "Pleasant enough," Al considered, but why in the hell did he call the plumber for the water heater?" Then remembering the small package, he ripped it open only to reveal the colored birthday paper. Noting the card of a fat college prof in cap and gown sipping wine, Al laughed. But what's inside? Carefully he opened the smaller package which contained an Ah Soh cork puller, just what I need here! Then ripping the larger package open, there was a Gary Larson animal book, "Happy Birthday, Dad. We hope you get this package on time but if it's late, consider the usual excuses. Besides this cork puller will save you a lot of frustration and Gary Larson will remind you of Simon and Breezy who will meow and bark when we mention your name. Love, Ginny, Steve and Al."

For several seconds Al sat quietly smiling and wiping away the steady beads of tears.

After several more nips of brandy, Al put on a Debussy disk and as the familiar music and brandy soothed and comforted him, he yawned and drifted off to sleep.

For over an hour, he snored softly then suddenly awakened. "Wow," he uttered, "it must be almost ten" as he staggered to the other room, brushed his teeth, peed and popped into bed. "What a marvelous day!" was his last thought.

From his bed Al could see the morning sunshine which seemed strong enough to pull him almost magnetically toward the window. And in the distance he could hear the cacophony of the Sunday morning bells. "Okay, all you good Christians, this is your day. Make the most of it. Say your prayers, but don't confess all of your sins. The priest doesn't like long confessions."

Nevertheless, Al decided to begin the day with music as he slipped Mozart's Requiem into the CD player. For all his latent and seldom-spoken criticisms of religion, Al was an unabashed admirer of Mozart's Requiem. Rather than a mournful, stylized, Catholic religious celebration of a soul, Mozart's powerful Requiem seemed more like a celebration of life, joy and happiness, not only for Mozart for whom death was near, but for all humanity.

Stimulated by Mozart's music, Al now directed his energies to immediate demands—Sunday morning's breakfast and back to the "potboiler."

As he slowly ate and reflected on the Requiem, his mind began a philosophical debate between pleasure, morality and society. "So here I am trying to complete a satirical spoof about my friends, colleagues and the profession I practiced and venerated. And to compound my own hypocrisy, I'm doing it for money."

For several minutes, his mind struggled with contradictions, then suddenly he found an acceptable explanation.

Quickly he turned to his typewriter, which still was ready for his apologia and aphorism:

"Pomposity and arrogance are the concealed warts and wrinkles of not only academia, but are more pronounced in the great professions of the theater, in law and certainly in the high clergy. But in this latter profession," Al gloated, "their relationships with the deities lends them an aura few mortals would dare mock or criticize. So between town and gown, we petty people must tread lightly. Nevertheless with razor wit and sharp tongue, we may enjoy our sport."

Satisfied with his clever syllogism, Al returned to the immediate thrust of his humor. "Now that I've got George Van Dyke's-Gainsworth persona pretty much reduced to an intellectual fool, it's time I bring this 'potboiler' to a reasonable conclusion. So I got myself into a jam, but at least I don't have to worry about Van Dyke suing me now."

After several minutes of reflection, in a bolt of serendipity, Al had the answer. "Suppose Maria was faking her rich family history? Suppose she had been a part-time hooker in Rome and came to Berkeley to add a certain Berkeley University cachet to her credentials, and by sheer good luck had met St. John Gainsworth, aka Van Dyke while passing as a Cal student. Or she could say that she was visiting Cal and planned to enroll the next semester.

"Okay! But why does she go after Gainsworth-Van Dyke? Because she hears students talking about him. She sits in on several of his classes and then aggressively follows him while feeding him the line about her rich Italian family. And she expresses great interest in his theories about sex and creativity. Almost immediately she has him eating out of her hand and within a week she beds him and her sexual experience and tricks have Gainsworth hog-tied.

"After a few weeks of super-saturated sex, she cons her love to lend her three thousand dollars. Pledging her eternal love, she accepts an expensive engagement ring, cons Gainsworth into divorcing his wife, and then gets an additional two grand to arrange things with her rich parents. She promises to meet him at the Excelsior Hotel where he will meet her parents. Poor Gainsworth signs his property and salary away to his wife to obtain the divorce, then flies to Rome where he belatedly learns that he has been totally swindled."

"Beautiful," Al gloated. "Perfectly silly satire but it should sell well."

For the rest of the beautiful Sunday afternoon, Al's typewriter never stopped. As dinner time approached, Al had completed all of the major chapters, now numbering almost two hundred and fifty pages. "At this rate, with a few rewrites, I should have this baby ready for my agent by the middle of March."

As it was now almost six and the cheerful mid-February sun had slipped away, Al called it quits and soon was celebrating with brandy and crackers.

Suddenly the phone rang shaking Al from his euphoria. "Hello," he blurted. Instantly, Lucia's soft, almost caressing voice awakened and enchanted the aroused listener.

"I'm calling, dear friend, only to tell you how much I miss you. I know that sounds silly and maybe it is, but as much as I enjoy Dawn's company and friendship, your presence is necessary. I really need you, Al."

For a few seconds there was silence. Then suddenly Lucia, in an almost terrifying whisper cried, "Al! Al! Are you there?"

"Yes! Yes! Of course, darling! Your voice and your message, well, well, I'm, I'm. How can I express my surprise and delight? I feel much as you do here in this large, empty house. For all my writing conceits, you dominate my inner self as nothing has in a long time."

For several minutes Lucia and Al exchanged notes, ideas and hopes while trying to restrain their emotional excitement. Finally both sensing an embarrassing need for ending the conversation, simultaneously decided on an earlier time than the planned meeting.

"Darling, Lucia, instead of my meeting you and Dawn there next Saturday, why don't you come here Friday, stay over night and we'll have fun with Dawn Saturday, and maybe we all can visit your grandparents in Panzano."

"That would be perfect, you darling man. I'll leave my car so Dawn can drive up Saturday, and I'll take the bus, which will get me there about noon. Will that be okay?"

"Perfect. Wonderful, Lucia! I can hardly wait until Friday noon." And with a final loving goodbye, Lucia and Al sat quietly in a state of euphoria.

For the next two days Al arose early, and by nine his typewriter sounded like a Teletype. But periodically his mechanistic creativity and skill would cease as his mind drifted into a romantic reverie of an idealized scene of Lucia, her long, dark hair and strong features—the most beautiful woman I've ever seen. And almost slyly, with a tinge of embarrassment, he could see her breasts, firm and molded, slightly tilting upward—pale cones crowned with pink areolas with glorious firm nipples.

For Al, the book was completed, finished, over. Actually, he was to discover later, the text needed some rewriting, but he could still make his May 1st deadline, or so he believed.

Friday morning was given over to cleaning, planning and preparing. "Dinner here tonight, green salad with avocado, if the shop has one, peppers. Baked chicken and ice cream. Simple! But the peppers and avocado. Better get them before she arrives. Leave here by eleven. Fine. But tonight? I'll remake the bed in the upstairs bedroom, but what about tomorrow night when Dawn is here? Yes? No? Maybe? Suppose that she hints or suggests that she would like to share my bed?" Al smiled and almost blushed at the idea.

Before leaving, Al again checked his larder: wine, champagne, chicken, lettuce, fresh bread, eggs? "Better shop." With his list in hand, he thrust on his jacket and ceremoniously locked the door.

At the market there were only a few cars and shoppers. Again in the vegetable market Al added green onions and leeks to his package of artichokes and green peppers. Again the proprietor and his wife exchanged smiles and greetings while carefully selecting only the best produce for the Professore. Next at the poultry shop, Al was pleased with a plump hen and then on to the wine shop for white and red wine and champagne. For the chicken, the cheerful proprietor suggested a chardonay from Venito or Trento. Eager to complete the wine purchase, Al accepted the owner's selections with a sense of satisfaction and completion.

Next, in considerable inner turmoil, Al reached the bus station. Quickly the pretty young clerk greeted the Professore and Al reciprocated with a smile and question, "Ha leu, le giornale?" which the smiling clerk had in her hand. For a second, Al appeared in a quandary, then blurted out, "L'autobus di Firenze? In dieci minuti, Professore."

Al quickly settled into a nearby chair and opened the *Herald Tribune* as the bus stopped almost directly in front of the building. In seconds he was on the sidewalk and moments later Lucia descended into Al's extended hand. They exchanged friendly greetings, but were careful to control their feelings. Taking Lucia's bag, Al quickly whispered, "How wonderful! I couldn't be happier."

With that, Lucia squeezed Al's arm lightly, "You are very special!"

Within minutes they were in the Fiat and soon were ascending the hill. "Darling co-conspirator," Al almost gushed, "are you all right? And Dawn? She understood and didn't offer any innuendoes?"

"No, she took it okay. Although I felt she was a bit surprised. But I quickly soothed her feelings by inviting her to join us here tomorrow after her morning class. And I also suggested she join us to visit my grandparents in Panzano. Was that okay with you?"

"Perfect, Lucia. I like Dawn and I don't want her to feel neglected, but I did want to see you alone here with me."

"Of course. This is the way I wanted it and this is the way I planned it. Dawn may be my best girlfriend who has had far more experience with men than I have. Now I'm not going to allow her to come between us. You are the first male friend I've had in a long time and, well, I think we are made for each other, darling. Is 'darling' okay between us when nobody is present?"

"It's perfect until we are no longer embarrassed by what people think."

Minutes later, with the car parked in its usual place, Al produced his two large packages and reached for Lucia's bag.

"Darling man, you have your own bundles and I can easily carry my own bag. It's very light with not much more than my nightie and purse."

Together they ascended the stairs and quickly entered the warm, comfortable room. In a second, they were in each other's arms, kissing tenderly and enjoying the rising passion of their bodies.

"Before we go any farther, darling, I just want to clarify an embarrassing point that Dawn raised about the joy and experiences of sex, remember?"

"Yes. And I also saw the pain in your face as you sought to change the subject."

"It's true. I was a virgin until that bastard Leone raped me. But long before, when I was full in the bloom of adolescence, I thought a lot about sex and I even wrote a poem about my sexual fantasies. If you would like, I think I can still remember the lines. It goes like this:

> The demons of the night no longer screech at me
> Or send me groping for the wine to bring sweet sleep to me.
> Now, impatient for the night, I plan my dreams,
> Where there I know my love will always be.
> His loving eyes, his welcome lips,
> The excitement of his touch!
> His thighs so fair and strong.
> Agony! Elation! Exaltation!
> The demons of the night are gone!
> Vanish day! Welcome night!
> My love is waiting near for me.

For several seconds, they held each tightly, then Al whispered, "What a beautiful poem of love, and you were only thirteen! Darling, now I more fully understand the intensity of your passion."

"You really loved my fantasy? It was my secret until now."

"Thank you so very much, Lucia. Your poem reveals so much and is so important to me. And it forces me to reveal something about myself which I refused to admit or to explain when we were discussing our lives with Dawn."

"I don't understand what you're suggesting. Is it something important that I should know? And don't tell me you've had a gay past." Lucia laughed, but spoke softly and cautiously.

"Oh, no! Nothing like that. It's this. I guess I was fearful of a small but important fact. Now don't be alarmed darling, but the fact is, I was married before I ever met Joan. And what I believed was a loving woman and I had fallen completely in love. Her name was Betty, or Betsy as she preferred. It was a case of love almost at first sight. Then immediately, after our first date, we were in bed."

Somewhat relieved, Lucy asked, "Well, what was wrong with that? Were you teenagers?"

"Oh, no! I was twenty-three and she was twenty-one and it was only a month before the war started. But the day after Pearl Harbor I enlisted in the Army Air Corps. Then about two months after that I got a Dear Al letter telling me it was all off. No reason. No explanation. I was literally destroyed. Then about a year and a half later, I got a letter from her asking if I would like to see her again. Well I was very confused, not that I hadn't seen other women during that period. I was now a commissioned officer, a second lieutenant, awaiting orders to go overseas."

Lucia was intently curious, "What did you do?"

"First I thought about her, then as she had included a phone number, I called her and bang! She said she was living in Laguna Beach, was a registered nurse and physical therapist, and she would drive to Blythe, California where I was stationed the very next day."

"So you met her?"

"Yes, and she apologized profusely for breaking our unofficial engagement. Well, she was a very sexy, pretty woman and immediately I was hooked."

"Then what happened?" Lucy was obviously confused.

"She explained she was able to quit her job and would return in a few days and we could get married."

"And so that's what happened? You got married? But for how long?"

"Well for three years, including the year and a half I was in Europe. But during the time we were living together, she continued writing to an old boyfriend whom she planned to see, and I think she finally did see him. Well to make things short, I was in combat for nine months before the war ended, then for eight months I had administrative jobs. Then the Air Corps tried to keep me in the occupation army.

"Finally I got home in December of 1945. But only after a prolonged series of infuriating military mistakes, the stupid details of which kept me in Europe for another four months. By then, I was almost psychotic with rage."

"That's beyond belief, darling."

"Worse yet, within a couple of months after I got back I learned that Betsy had been having affairs with several men, that she had spent almost all of the five thousand dollars I sent her, and sold an almost new car I had bought just before I left."

"Darling, this is horrible. I understand why you didn't explain your early life."

"Well I was so angry and bitter I planned to kill myself and maybe her, too, but fortunately I was seeing a psychiatrist who managed to help me get my life together."

"So you got a divorce?" Lucy asked.

"Yes. Within a couple of months, and what helped save me was that I had enrolled at U.C. Berkeley. So between studying and meeting other people, I slowly put my life together and graduated in two years."

"Al, darling, thank you for telling me. I would never have imagined your miserable experience. But then later, you married Joan, you said?"

"Yes and Joan, bless her, she helped put my life together. But for a long time I was very bitter and didn't date a woman really until I met Joan. And a post script to that long horror story, from the beginning of the war until almost three years after the war ended, I rarely dated and rarely bedded a woman. I wanted to but somehow I couldn't get over the war and the additional misery for three years."

"But you're okay now, aren't you, darling?" Lucy was still apprehensive.

"Well what saved me was a psychiatrist, a different doctor who suggested that I write what happened, how I felt and what I hoped to do."

"And did you take his advice, darling?"

"Yes, I wrote a long, rambling story, almost a novel, full of self-pity and hatred. Then I threw it away and wrote a poem about it—not terribly long, a kind of allegorical but bitter poem, not a beautiful poem but a real tragic tale."

"Darling, you look tired and sad. May I hold you and love you? Your tragic story helps me to understand you and your occasional funny remarks."

Suddenly they were in a passionate embrace, even as tears welled and quietly washed away their agony.

"Now, my darling, we've wept for the past and we've suffered for reasons or forces we know not what or why. But now our suffering is over. Someone once said, 'love conquers all' and tonight we shall prove it!" Lucy was triumphant.

"But first we must satisfy our inner needs—food! I hunger for food but ache for love, and soon we'll feast until we're satiated."

Quickly a modest meal was prepared, eaten and enjoyed. Then, without a care, they kissed and stood naked beside their bed.

For almost a minute they held each tightly. Oblivious to everything but the rising passion of their bodies, carefully Lucia freed one hand and softly caressed his hairy chest and whispered, "You are so handsome, strong and athletic."

"You flatter me, sweetheart. I'm just an old geezer in good shape and still blessed with hair, which once was red and matched my temperament."

"Darling lover, please don't refer to yourself as an old geezer—whatever a geezer is. No, you are my handsome Adonis with beautiful hair decorating your head and body and your love king."

Embarrassed by her candid observation, Al gently kissed each pink nipple. "Oh, darling your body is so much more beautiful and exciting than mine. You are Venus with the glorious breasts firm and molded, twin peaks from heaven."

"I'm flattered but I'm not really satisfied with my breasts. They're okay, but not like Dawn's, which are large and firm and stand straight out. Mine thrust up which seems strange."

"But darling, beautiful Lucia, your breasts are ideal. Breasts which gently tilt upward are a gift from the gods, praised by the poets and immortalized by the great sculptors. True, very few women are so fortunate. I've only seen one other woman whose breasts were tilted and exciting, but yours are perfectly round and gracefully tilt full and firm all the way to your pink aureola, and from there to their consummate beauty, the nipple—that glorious provider of food, joy and love."

"Of food, joy and love?" Lucy laughed. "Food? Oh, you mean milk!"

"Yes, darling. I really have a fantasy about your breasts, but most men do, too."

"I don't quite understand this fantasy you men have about women's breasts."

"Well," Al stopped, "I suppose most males and females first admire and evaluate each other's face. And that is an important aspect of measuring the opposite sex. But for most males, if the female is young, he will automatically evaluate her breasts, and if they are adequate, well-formed, large, small or whatever, he will then check out her body, legs, etc."

"So you men really study we females rather closely? Well, we women also look you men over closely, too, but since you don't have breasts, we casually examine your anatomy, height, weight, fat, skinny, but most importantly, your personality, which for many women is the most-important first-qualifying test—more important than a handsome face."

Al was impressed. "So the handsome Don Juan doesn't score much if he has a poor personality?"

"Of course. What woman wants some jerk who has nothing but a handsome face?"

"I couldn't agree more," Al offered. "And men, too, are very concerned about the female personality. It counts a lot, but the precursor that really conveys the first message is the face and the tits."

Lucy giggled. "The tits—breasts! But what about our faces, eyes, noses, mouths, teeth, chin and yes, our hair?" We spend so much time and money trying to attract you men and now you tell me that men are primarily 'tit and ass' men. Is that really the way you guys are?"

"Well," Al concluded, "you've pretty much summoned up the average male's assessment skills. Oh sure, we give high points for brains, charm, personality and total physical beauty—that's pretty much the criteria for beauty contests."

For only a few minutes more did this joking dialogue continue. Then in surprise move, Al gently lifted Lucy onto the bed.

"Oh, you darling lover, you know what I want. Words are one thing, but action is on my mind."

"Of course, my sex-starved nymph, and what you need, you get."

Quickly they lay together, their bodies entwined and passionately assertive, unafraid and challenging. They teased and played, their tongues and their mouths hungry and ravenous. Slowly rising passion engulfed their bodies and spread rapidly from the throbbing love palace. Every nerve and muscle radiated passion and love—a beautiful duet of soft and sudden moans, groans and then sudden erotic eruptions, violent and sublime, slowly fading only to burst again in a final song of exultation and love.

Fortunately, their vocal explosions punctuated by slow, rhythmic contortions and spasms of pleasure were locked in the security and silence of the darkened ancient fortress.

They lay quietly, absorbed in each other's ecstasy. Finally Al whispered, I know you were practically a virgin, but how do you know so much about love-making?"

Lucia kissed him softly. "I learned from you, darling. You must be the world's greatest, except, well, I'm too embarrassed to offer my little secret."

Now aroused and rolling over from his back, Al tempted her with tender soft kisses. "Please tell me your secret."

"I'm still embarrassed about how I first learned the ABCs of sex." Again Lucia paused. "This was the beginning for me. My parents house was very large and their master bedroom was directly connected to my children's bedroom by a large dressing room-closet and bathroom. Often their doors were open, and as a small child I frequently became frightened or just wanted to sleep with them.

"And my parents always welcomed me and loved me. Well one night, after I had been asleep for what seemed a long time, I heard my mother crying and making strange sounds. I was frightened and when the sounds they were making became louder, I was almost terrified. So I suddenly rushed into their bedroom, which was light enough for me to see that their bodies were thrashing violently as they both groaned and mother cried, 'Darling! Darling! Darling!'

"At that point, I jumped on their bed, screaming 'Mama! Mama'. However frightened I may have been, both of my parents were even more shocked as both sat up clutching me and kissing me. 'Darling, baby! Mama and Daddy are okay. Please don't cry.'

"And my father kissed me and held me so tenderly. I stopped crying and asked, 'Mommy, Daddy, have bad dreams?' And with that question, both of my parents laughed, 'Yes, Lucia, we were having bad dreams.'

"That was the beginning, and after that they usually closed the connecting closet door, but even so, I could sometimes hear them making love. And as time passed, I asked them about their bad dreams. And they were both so wonderful and honest as they slowly explained sex to me. This was certainly the best sex education any child could ever have experienced. Over the next several years they told me about love making and reproduction so that well before puberty I understood most of the important things about sex.

"And my sex education was a natural process because we had a swimming pool and my parents always swam naked except when we had house guests or friends over for a swim and picnic.

I began to develop breasts and pubic hair when I was around ten, and by twelve I had started to menstruate. But because my parents had been so loving and truthful about sex, I was ready for adolescence.

"And I suppose," Lucia's voice softened into muted sobs, "my father's sudden and tragic death–Oh! How he and mother loved me, encouraged me, trusted me and made it possible for me to survive. I was an only child and to have daddy suddenly die, and only two or three weeks later both my grandfather and then my grandmother, for whom I was named, died of heart attacks. Maybe my grandfather's heart just stopped because he was much older than grandmother Lucia.

"But then to end everything, my Uncle Charles, dad's younger brother, was killed in some kind of air accident in Vietnam. He had been a pilot in the Air Force, as had been my father until he resigned his commission in protest of the Vietnam War. But I don't think that Uncle Charles was still in the Air Force at that time. I've heard some strange stories that Charles was killed when the private plane he was flying was accidentally shot down.

"And the final result of these deaths was that we all moved back to Italy. Then the last episode in the tragedy occurred just before my fourteenth birthday. My step-father Michelangelo Leone, whom you have met, had married my mother about a year and a half following our return. Soon after that she had a baby, so I was thrilled with a baby brother."

Now Al, shocked by the long story, asked, "Lucia, are you, are you all right?"

"Yes, I'm okay, but the worse is yet to come.

"Soon after baby Paulino's birth, the doctors discovered that he had a serious problem. On June 19th, 1980, when I was thirteen and studying at the Firenza Conservatory, Michele was driving mother and Paulino to a specialist in Bologna. Suddenly Michele's Mercedes struck a peasant's wagon which shouldn't have been on the autostrada. Both my mother and Paulino were killed instantly and Michele was seriously injured. He was in a hospital, first in Bologna and later in Firenza, after three months, he was able to return to his business."

Al was almost overcome with sympathy and love. For several minutes he cradled Lucia in his arms, wiping away the frequent trickle of tears.

Lucia kissed Al slowly, "Darling, Al, you are the most wonderful man and husband I could ever want, and because of this I must add one final sad–no tragic–footnote. After I had developed some kind of affection for Leone–and in all honesty, he had treated me with great understanding and affection, or so I believed, after mother and the baby's death, then on my fourteenth birthday, seven years ago, he gave me a wonderful birthday party at a marvelous restaurant for several of my best friends.

"After my friends had gone home, instead of returning to our large house in Fiesole, he drove me to his elegant art shop in Firenze. I asked him why he had gone to his shop and he said, 'Well, I had to pick up a few items in the store because early tomorrow, I must drive to Rome and I wanted to reassure you that everything will be done to take care of you in my absence. And I have a little birthday surprise for you in the shop.'

"As it was now well after ten, I was tired and annoyed. But he gave me a beautiful Gucci case, exactly the same as the one he sometimes carried. Then after the case, he took a bottle of French champagne from the small, built-in fridge in this elegant small apartment he had in the back of the shop. He filled the two champagne glasses and offered this toast, which I'll never forget, 'To my darling Lucia, my future and my joy.' Well, I almost fainted. But I drank and he quickly refilled my glass. By that time I was feeling rather dizzy and sick. I remember asking him if I could lie down and he said, 'Of course, why not.' And the last thing I remember was a wet, sloppy kiss on my lips.

"Sometime in the early morning, it must have been around six, I woke up feeling sick and terrible. I started to get up and noticed there was blood all over my dress and panties. I managed to get into a tiny bathroom and take off my clothes. My vaginal area was very sore and bloody and worse yet, I started to vomit.

"Soon I stopped vomiting and decided to try the small shower. The warm water soothed me and although I was still sick and weak, I felt a bit better, and I suddenly realized that I had been raped.

"After a few minutes, I just got a towel and sat there crying. But I knew that

I had to do something, so I began searching and ransacking the small apart-ment. I found another small closet with some women's clothes in it, and as I pulled at the drawers one concealed drawer suddenly popped open. Inside were several envelopes, papers and some American money.

"Sensing that these papers and large envelopes were important, I opened my Gucci bag only to discover that Michele had accidently switched bags. His bag included his passport, some official documents and large sums of American money. I stuffed everything into his bag then tried to phone my grandparents in Panzano.

"Fortunately they were home and I blurted out my story to my grand-mother who soothed me with loving words. And then my grandfather got on the phone and he tried desperately to help me, but the rage in his voice was clear. He said that he and Justine would leave immediately, but he would also phone the trauma center in Firenza, and with that he whis-pered his love and care and said that the police would soon be there as would he and grandmother.

"I had found some women's clothes and although they were too small, I had to wear something. Dressed, I looked around the small room which had a tiny kitchenette, really everything necessary–then I saw that the bed cover and sheets were saturated with my blood.

"And very soon, the police arrived and pounded on the front door. I quietly opened it and they asked me who I was. I told them and described what had happened. Fortunately, one of them was Dr. Valentine, whom I came to know and much admire for his medical skill and care.

"In my pain and nervous excitement, I forgot to mention the papers and money in the secret compartment. As the police were collecting the bloody sheets and blankets and my underwear, my grandparents arrived. As I wept profusely, they quietly caressed me as Dr. Valentine offered me advice.

"Within minutes, I was taken in a waiting police car, accompanied by my grandparents and the doctor. At the trauma center Dr. Valentine examined me, took several vaginal smears, and asked a surgical nurse to take additional bits of vaginal tissue and body fluids. With the examination complete, he strongly suggested that I should remain overnight and if no unexpected medical prob-lems developed I could leave with my grandparents the next day.

"For several hours my grandparents continued to sit with me as I lay in bed.

Then grandfather explained that grandmother Justine would stay while he consulted with the police.

"The next day, Dr. Valentine again visited me and assured me that except for some pain and severe psychological damage, I should recover without further physical damage, but that I should plan on help from a psychiatrist. And, in a final measure, he suggested that I schedule an appointment with him within a week to ten days.

"Then, just before leaving the hospital, a police inspector visited me and again took notes as I described exactly what had happened on the night of my birthday and the following morning. When I asked him about my stepfather, he was polite but quite terse.

'I can only tell you, miss, that we are looking for your step-father, but right now, we don't know where he is. His art store will remain closed until further notice.'"

For a short while, Al sat quietly with a steady flow of tears caressing Lucia's bare shoulders.

Finally, Lucia, in a strong, almost plaintiff tone, whispered, "Al, I love you so much. You are the first person I've ever trusted with my secret. Oh, I've mentioned to Dawn that Michele had raped me, but nothing more. And fortunately, Dawn never pressed me for the details. But she expressed great bitterness for any male who would rape a woman."

Now both lovers were somehow freed of their burdens and in a relaxed mood, Lucia reminded Al that Dawn would arrive the next day, Saturday, about noon. "She'll be driving my car. I expect she will come directly to this house. I've given her directions so she won't have any difficulty."

Al glanced at his watch. "Darling, it's getting toward midnight, shall we turn out the lights and call it a day?"

"The most beautiful day of my life, Master."

"Not Master, darling, but your man, and I hope your husband."

Quickly they rearranged the sheets, blankets and pillows, flicked off the lights, and in a final embrace were soon asleep.

Sometime after seven, Al slipped quietly from the bed and after two minutes in the bathroom, busied himself in the kitchen with orange juice and coffee. Minutes later he placed the tray on the small table next to Lucia. And as he turned to leave, she whispered, "Oh, no you don't. We'll have coffee and juice here and then complete some still unfinished business."

Al almost exploded in joy and laughter. "My loving nymph!" And with that he was in bed beside her, their foreplay was dominated with tender prolonged kisses, now scented with coffee and orange. Almost like a violin and piano duet, they began with a sensuous adagio followed by a playful allegro, which after several measures of melody and counterpoint increased in a rising volume of excitement and modulating pleasure. The allegro ended in a series of explosive chords followed by a coda of legato murmurs.

For a few minutes the instruments were mute, then the piano began a strident atonal introduction which the violin quickly converted to a playful scherzo. But again the piano reasserted its dominance with three powerful chords. After a short pause, both instruments engaged in a lively fugue which ended in a lovely series of E minor questions on the piano, which the violin answered with closing measures of reaffirmation in G major.

Each player was exhausted but surprised by this unexpected transposition. And in a final passionate choral, both voices whispered, "Oh, darling! darling! darling! I love you! I love you!"

The morning sonata over,the lovers lay quiet in hedonistic communion. After several minutes Lucia, noting Al snoring softly, sneaked quietly to the toilet and minutes later began preparing a full breakfast which soon graced the table. Her loving call for her man was answered with a kiss on the cheek. As Al seated his princess, "Time to refill the estrogen and testosterone tanks," he joked.

And with paeans of love, the duo rejoiced and the Saturday morning feast began.

Slowly eating the gorgeous mushroom omelet, they were serene, each absorbed in a silent epiphany of beauty and love. Suddenly they were jolted to reality by a loud, determined pounding on the front door.

"Oh, Damn!" Al murmured, "who can that be at this hour?"

Lucia smiled and almost laughed. "Darling, remember? Who was supposed to arrive around noon? Well, Dawn is early this time."

With that, Al quickly reached the living room as Lucia softly closed the bedroom off. Then Al unlocked the heavy front door. Dawn greeted them warmly. I'd have gotten here sooner, but I missed a turn or two."

Almost embarrassed, Al grinned, "Well, you arrived early anyway. We had expected you about noon. Where's your bag?"

"Oh, it's in the car."

Al, eager to be the gallant host and somewhat hesitant about Dawn's sudden appearance, quickly removed the small expensive "over-nighter" and rejoined the women who were now in a cheerful dialogue.

Before Al could volunteer to show Dawn her room, she teased, "And what kind of games and music did you play last night while I was being bored with an Italian male who wanted something more than food and wine."

"Well," Lucia said, "I don't think we could compete with your social life, but we did enjoy a home-cooked dinner and some piano music. After which, we toddled off to bed."

Nonplused with Lucia's polite and innocent reply, Dawn suggested, "Al, why don't you show me the bathroom and my bedroom? Then we can plan our activities and walk around Greve under more pleasant circumstances. After all, I haven't been in Greve since 'that' night. Also I would like to see Panzano and, if possible, Montefiorale, which according to my map is very near."

Lucia quickly showed Dawn the large bathroom and then guided her to the twin bedrooms at the front of the house. "One of these bedrooms has a small three-quarter size bed and the other bedroom has a small grand piano and a very small cot. I would suggest you take the larger room, Dawn."

Tossing her bag on the bed, Dawn grinned and slyly asked, "So you sleep on that tiny cot, Lucia, and I get the larger bedroom?"

"Of course, Dawn. Why shouldn't I sleep near a piano–it's almost part of my life."

Not wishing to appear too nosey, Dawn laughed, "But you can't make love to a piano!"

"No, but I can try and I do sometimes think that I should try harder."

Both ladies were enjoying their teasing game until Al's presence abruptly ended the conversation.

"Dawn, we're having breakfast. Would you care to join us?"

"I certainly would. I got up fairly early and only had time for coffee and juice, so if you have some solid food, that should hold me until pranzo."

In the large, well-stocked modern kitchen, Dawn noted, "Well, the owner must like to cook. He's got a better kitchen than we do, Lucia."

With the ceremony over, Lucia again quickly prepared another large mushroom and cheese omelet as Al brewed another pot of coffee and prepared the
toast.

The three sat eating and conversing idly. After almost a half-hour, Dawn
raised the guarded conversation, "What's our program for this afternoon? I
recall you mentioning a nearby medieval village, Al. How would that be?"

"Oh, I think that would be wonderful. It's only a short walk from here and
I would like to see it again. How about you, Lucia?"

Relieved of Dawn's possible question about sleeping arrangements, Lucia
eagerly agreed. "I've only seen the village once and that was several years ago.
And this afternoon would be particularly good because the day doesn't seem to
be too cold. Besides, we all need the exercise."

A half-hour later, with all three bundled in jackets, they departed. But
again, Al made certain that the solid and heavy front door was locked. Soon
they were on the narrow, rough road and through the sentinel pines. They
could see the church spire and the outline of several structures.

As they neared the trees, Al pointed to a nearby cemetery. "For a small
town, these people have an impressive burial site," he suggested.

Approaching the small rectangular cemetery guarded by high stone walls,
the trio stopped and peered through the locked iron gate.

"What an impressive bone yard!" Dawn laughed. "And those rows of
decorated graves, that large mausoleum and tiers of tombs."

"Right," Lucia added, "We Italians go overboard to impress society and
descendents with our necromania."

Shortly after departing the cemetery Al pointed out a large impressive
modern house, vine-covered and set back from the narrow road. Both women
were properly impressed. "What a lovely home," Lucia commented, and I
wouldn't expect it here except the owners have a magnificent view."

"And deep pockets," Dawn added.

"I noticed the house only recently when I walked to Montefiorale which,
from my brief visit, indicates that several wealthy people live here rather than in
Greve."

Now they were only a short distance from the medieval village which
was dominated by the church steeple and brick walls. As Al had done only
two weeks earlier, the women quickly approached the facade from the

tiered brick entrance. Dawn quickly tested the front door. "Well, they don't trust us. The door is locked tight."

"So how do we enter this ancient village, Professore?"

"There's a very narrow, deeply worn pathway straight ahead which is the only road I noticed," Al replied.

"But you will see some interesting architecture and a wonderful small slice of antiquity. Furthermore, obviously it isn't occupied by peasants. "

Continuing their stroll, the trio marveled at the skill of the medieval masons who had shaped stone in a curvilinear wall of interlocking dwellings and shops.

"And they did it without mortar," Dawn added.

Occasionally the trio's observations and presence were noted by residents with a polite smile or nod, "Buona sera."

"Quite obviously," Al whispered, "these people aren't locals!"

"Hardly," Dawn added, "and they don't have to worry about cars or trucks."

"Or even wagons," Lucia added.

Already they had noted one small shop which seemed to stock small quantities of food, magazines, and books. But as no one seemed present, the three inched forward and suddenly they were standing in front of the village's only trattoria.

Cautiously they approached the heavy oak door which framed a small square window. They peered in but only a small bulb illuminated the foyer. And the door was locked.

"Well, it's mid-afternoon," Dawn noted, "but maybe they've posted a menu. Oh, here it is," she added.

With three heads close together, they voiced their pleasure and surprise. "For a small place, they have an impressive menu," Lucia noted, "and furthermore, quite obviously they have a larger clientele than the village population."

"I'd love to eat here," Dawn added, "and Al, have you something to write on, I could jot down their telephone number? Sorry, I didn't bring my purse."

With the addresses and numbers recorded, the trio began their walk which revealed almost hidden passages to dwellings or structures at the inner circle of the village. Following the circular pathway they soon reached a brick paved terraced and entrance to the church.

As they descended the staircase from the front entrance, Al noted several expensive cars parked in a row bordering a small park. Then they realized that they had entered the village from a higher pathway and hadn't seen the recently constructed park and area.

Both Dawn and Lucia scrutinized the row of eight or ten expensive cars. Drawing close to Al, Lucia whispered, "Look at that black Mercedes sedan."

"Yes," Al nodded "and a Series 500 model, the only one here, but very much like the Mercedes we both know something about."

At this point Dawn broke the conspiratorial silence. "It's getting chilly, you love birds. Let's head back to the nest."

By silent agreement, they began their rapid descent, which some fifteen minutes later brought them to "Palazzo Pruitt" as Dawn smirked.

After unlocking the heavy oak door, for a few seconds Al hesitated, then pushed it open with a thrust. Both Dawn and Lucia noted Al's strange behavior, but only Lucia understood Al's actions.

The warm interior was a soothing greeting after their afternoon exploration. "Well," Al smiled, "I'm in favor of an appropriate libation. How say you, ladies?"

"Aye, aye, Professore, and what do you propose to offer?" Dawn questioned softly.

"Um, well," Al repeated, "I'm not certain what you have in mind, Dawn? But I believe Lucia will happily share some brandy with me."

"Well, what choice or choices do I have?" Dawn inquired?

"I don't have an extensive bar, but the house has wine, red and white, scotch for those with that desire for iodine, and some gin, vodka and bourbon, plus beer. What's your choice, fair lady from Perth?"

At this Down and Lucia laughed, "You're almost too much! Who's this dame from Perth?"

"Oh, you mean the beautiful blonde from down under, who's flatulence made everyone wonder, whether whisky or wine or a dinner divine, all Aussies were amazed by her thunder."

"What did you say about some blonde from down under, Professor Praitt?" Dawn exploded in laughter. "And all this time, Lucia and I believed you were a scholar and writer of clean prose. We are shocked! Aren't we, Lucia?"

Both Al and Lucia were laughing. "Of course, Dawn. We're shocked and surprised and delighted with Al's new approach."

"Approach?" A scatological approach?" Dawn joked.

"I'm sorry, ladies. I just couldn't resist the chance to be cute." Al offered.

"Shall we forgive him, Lucy? Or should we demand that he wash his mouth out with soap and water as my father did to me when I got too raunchy?"

"No, let's demand that he do penance to Shakespeare. Something noble and beautiful."

If the women were enjoying their teasing game, Al was ready for them.

"But before this prologue must begin, my throat and brain must be lubricated and assuaged," whereupon Al produced a bottle of V.S.O.P. Courvoisier, which drew cheers of delight. With the skill of a professional, Al poured an equal portion of the gold cognac into each of three crystal snifters.

Now feigning great seriousness, he twirled his glass twice, then raising it high, solemnly entoned, "To the glorious wit and charm of Bill Shakespeare, and to the beauty and charm of his supplicants."

With the smooth warmth of the cognac, both women nodded and murmured, "Wonderful!"

"Now something appropriate from the bard, you demand. Yes, perhaps these few lines might be appropriate.

'Libertarians, women and lovers, lend me your ears.

I come to bury the poet, not praise him.

The evil that men do lives after them.

The good is oft interred with their bones.'

So let it be with Praitt.'"

Both women were choking with laughter and cheering. "Crazy! Brilliant! Wonderful!" And with that, first Lucia kissed Al on the cheek as Dawn smothered him with hugs.

"Darling, poet," Lucia whispered in his ear, "you are the joy and love of my life!"

Not to be outdone by Lucia, Dawn suddenly grabbed Al by the shoulders and pressed her mouth against his cheek, "Al, you are Shakespeare, Milton Berle and Olivier all rolled into one."

Extracting himself from his delighted menage, he blurted, "I think it's time for a food break! Besides it's after five and I'm famished. Why don't we try Ristorante Moro, or maybe one of the others in Greve, or maybe that place in Montefiorale. What are your wishes?"

Both women quickly vetoed Moro. "I might like the place later, but not tonight." Lucia offered, "But we might try that place up the hill."

What that, Dawn added, "Yes, that place in the village. I'll call them now. Where's the telephone, Al?"

"It's on the small table in the kitchen."

Within two minutes Dawn had the answer. "They're closed."

As nobody was keen on returning to Greve and taking in a new restaurant, they quickly agreed to "make do here."

Before Al could offer advice or help, both woman agreed, "Professore, you are ordered to sit and play music or read while we perform small miracles. Now don't move, we'll have some finger food and wine or liquor here and then surprise you."

Within minutes Lucia and Dawn were serving salami, cheese, crackers, olives and a large bottle of Chianti.

"This looks wonderful, ladies, are you giving me this generous antipasto?"

"What ever made you think this good food is just for you?" Dawn laughed. "We women slaves don't live only for poetry and love."

Soon the wine was flowing, the food was disappearing, and the conversations turned to Al's teaching and writing.

"Much as I do enjoy poetry and good limericks, I don't teach either or, I should say, I didn't. My literary efforts stemmed from humor, particular American, and I wrote my Ph.D. dissertation on Mark Twain's sense of humor–which was as funny as it was particularly indigenous and original. I won't go into that, but I will add Mark Twain was in a class all by himself. We've had and still have many great comics and several very funny writers: S.J. Perelman, Chaplin, Fred Allen, Jack Benny, The Marx Brothers, particularly Groucho and many others.

"But for variety, originality and form, Samuel Clemens aka Mark Twain, who, for me, is unequaled. And interestingly, like many other humorists, in his private life he was serious and often bitter about life."

"Okay, Professore," Dawn added, "but why don't you give us your ideas for or about humor?"

"It seems to me that I have, Dawn, but I'll expand. But first, what I don't like: stupid, silly, simple, dirty jokes, pointless, ridiculous humor, particularly the kind that TV sitcoms produce. Not that I'm a big TV fan. Most television shows now are dull and silly, but I recall years ago a couple that were marvelously funny. The best was the Fred Allen Show which was a skillfull satire on many of the most mundane and stupid aspects of American life, and another very funny show was Fibber McGee and Molly, and the Jack Benny show. None of these programs or these types are produced any more, I'm afraid."

Both Dawn and Lucia appeared nonplused. "You're right, Professore," Lucia volunteered. "Although we had a couple of television sets in our house, I don't remember seeing my parents watching, but I think my father probably watched football because he had played the game in high school. He had been crazy about sports, but after twenty years in the Air Force, he only played golf and occasionally tennis on our own court."

"And my parents were pretty much the same way," Dawn added. "But I'm certain Dad watched college and professional football games. After all, football got him into and barely through Cal."

"But getting back to your ideas about humor, Al, you mentioned that you are a published author and are writing now," Dawn questioned. "Would you mind revealing any writing secrets?"

Lucia looked apprehensively at Al, as if to suggest that Dawn was threatening his privacy. But before she could move the conversation to an impersonal point, Al had smiled politely. "Dawn, I thought you would never ask."

"First off, much of my writing has been somewhat autobiographical, except for the dreary pedantic junk we English teachers must do to advance our rank and position. The old adage, 'publish or perish' is alive and well and, unfortunately, requires good teachers to become bad writers and poor researchers."

"So how do you handle these professional requirements?" Lucia offered.

"Well, for the first few years I taught as an assistant. I did the usual so-called critical studies. For example, simple correlations between academic success and correct writing skills and theme and variation of that kind of nonsense in thinking and managerial success."

Al stopped, coughed, "These appetizers were good and the wine is gone."

Both women seemed relieved that Al had avoided more professional drudgery. "I think those potatoes and the roast might be ready," Lucia volunteered.

"Right, and I'll finish the salad." Dawn volunteered. "So let's resume your cognitive processes, Professore," Dawn added as she left for the kitchen.

Sitting quietly, Al reflected on his comments, "Silly, stuffy," he thought. "Don't lecture and keep it funny. It's almost the only thing you really have."

With that, Al rose and searched the small library of tapes and CDs. To his surprise, there were several tapes of jazz–Benny Goodman, Artie Shaw, Frank Sinatra, Louis Armstrong, Duke Ellington and several others. For a moment he hesitated, then selected a tape with several important bands.

Turning on the sound equipment, Al popped in the tape and suddenly an explosive riffle from the snare drum introduced the alto clarinet to the first bars of "Begin the Bequine." The exciting music completely struck Al like the sudden appearance of an old friend. Almost transfixed, he was carried back almost fifty years and deep in the musical reverie he remained until both women hovering close by shook him by their words, "Al, what are you playing?" Dawn almost shouted over the clarinet's hypnotic minor notes, "Dinner's on."

Awakened by the arrival of the two women, he smiled, "So you like Artie Shaw and that music? It's called 'Begin the Beguine.'"

For a few minutes they listened as Duke Ellington's "Take The A Train" began. "It's wonderful, but our diner is on the table," Lucia announced.

Now the enticing aromas of roasted lamb, potatoes and vegetables worked their magic and any further discussion of jazz was overwhelmed by the joy of eating and drinking.

"Ladies," Al interrupted, "if I may, a toast to the chefs and their skills."

Dawn and Lucia looked at each other in surprise and managed something between a smile and a frown, then raising their glasses high, "Yes, a toast to us and a toast to our host."

"How do you like this Chianti classico?" Al offered as he emptied his glass. "I think it's okay." Dawn offered.

"Not being much of a wine judge, yes, I think it's quite good," Lucia added.

"This isn't a loaded question, but merely my doubts about a wine that, by all rights, is supposed to be one of Italy's best wines. I really question that generally accepted opinion."

"Why do you raise the question to us neophytes?" Dawn questioned. "I like all kinds of reds and some whites, but I don't particularly know why. Just don't offer me any of the American dago reds which cause instant heartburn."

"I agree with Dawn," Lucia offered. "But having been raised by a wine-drinking family, I never thought much about wine. My father loved wine and was just getting ready to start a winery. He had about fifty acres of vines in and was actually plowing a rather steep hill of vines when his tractor suddenly tipped over and crushed him to death."

Suddenly the light-spirited atmosphere fell silent.

"Oh, forgive me, please," Lucia offered, "I shouldn't have mentioned that personal tragedy, but I think you both know about my father's sudden death. I don't or didn't intend to mention that, and I'm not throwing cold water on the subject of wine. So Al, let's discuss wine. I know that you must be more than just a connoisseur."

Lucia's calm remarks restored the conviviality of the discussion as she added, "Wine is for drinking and good wine is for life, love and. . . ."

Both Al and Dawn were waiting for the last word, "For, for, what Lucy?" Dawn almost laughed, "For lovemaking?"

"Maybe levity? Good conversation?" Al asked.

"Yes, all of those things and spirituality."

For a few seconds, the room was quiet as each weighed a possible conclusion to the subject.

"Yes, wine is all of those things," Al added, "but much more, and I'll just toss this out because when I leave Italy in a few months and return to California, I plan to open a small winery with my two sons and possibly my daughter. And I already have a name and a logo."

Both women were elated. "How wonderful! Really marvelous! But why didn't you tell us sooner? We thought you were here to write and would continue to write when you returned to the states," Dawn added.

"You're right! But the only reason I'm writing another 'potboiler' is to accumulate the considerable amount of money necessary to get 'Cave de Bacchus' started."

"How do you translate 'Cave de Bacchus'," Dawn asked.

"Bacchus Cellars. As you know, Bacchus was the Roman god of wine as Dionysus was the Greek equivalent, but more Americans recognize the Roman deity than the Greek. And my label is a fat Bacchus lying sideways on a marble slab as a nude male nymph pours red wine into Bacchus' flagon and a beautiful reclining nude holds her small goblet for a refill. This is an exciting, full color label which would never be permitted by state authorities, but were I to clothe the male and female, it might get by. But even with full approval, this very elaborate label, framed by a beautifully detailed bordered Greek filigree would be prohibitively expensive."

Both women were thoroughly captivated by Al's enthusiastic description. "Do you have one of your labels here?, Lucia asked?

"Unfortunately, no. I never expected my label or labels would be of interest here. But as soon as I get home and get the necessary funding, I hope to get 'Cave de Bacchus' started."

At this point, Lucia opened another bottle of Chianti, filled each glass and offered, "To Al Praitt and the success of Les Caves de Bacchus!"

As the wine flowed, the conversation drifted to the morrow. "It's getting late," Al added, "so tomorrow, we visit your grandparents in Panzano?"

"Yes," Lucia was somewhat guarded, but assertive. "I think my folks would like to meet both you and Dawn. I've talked to them frequently by phone and they are quite excited about a big Sunday. And they would like us there around noon so we can talk, stroll around Panzano and then have a big dinner around two-thirty. How's that sound?"

"Wonderful," Dawn added. "I'm really thrilled about meeting them, particularly after the important help and information they've given you."

"And I guess that I'm as excited as I am nervous about meeting grandparents as formidable as yours must certainly be," Al added.

"Now let's all turn in. It's almost eleven. You know where the one and only John is, Dawn?" So you get first dibs and as for your bedroom, you have your choice between the cot or bed in the piano room, or if you want real privacy, try the large bedroom at the top of the circular staircase. But take your blankets up. I doubt that the bed is ready."

For a few seconds Dawn and Lucia stared at each other, then Dawn laughed, "Sleep well you two, and wake up refreshed."

Dawn turned and escaped into the nearby bathroom.

With the bedroom door closed behind them, Lucia and Al went fast into each other's arms. "Finally, darling. Are you okay?"

"Of course, dear man. With you, I couldn't be anything but okay. And if Dawn had any questions about us, she doesn't have them anymore."

"And I'm relieved and glad because I sensed that my presence was beginning to become embarrassing for both of you. And I'm really glad that you included her in tomorrow's party."

"Oh, yes. I had to. I like Dawn very much and she has been very good for me. She's helped build my confidence and self-esteem, which I needed and still need, but with you, I'm ready for the world."

Quickly they were in bed and after several tender kisses, Lucia added, "Ill be back in a minute and then it's your turn."

Minutes later they switched places. But before using the bathroom, Al checked and locked the heavy front door. Then as he returned from the bath and quietly closed his bedroom door, he noted the bedroom light reflected below Dawn's door. He hoped she wasn't too upset by her confirmed doubts.

Back in bed together, Lucia squeezed hard against Al until both relaxed into effortless sleep.

Chapter Four

After almost eight hours of deep sleep, Al awakened and slowly realized that Lucia wasn't beside him. For a second he almost panicked then, looking at his watch, he realized that she was probably making breakfast.

Satisfied, he waited for sounds from the kitchen but hearing none, put on his robe and quickly looked into the living room. Empty! Now he visited the bathroom and quickly returned to the kitchen. Nothing. Breakfast hadn't been started yet. He smelled coffee, quickly poured a cup and returned to the living room. Hearing no sounds from Dawn's bedroom, he noted that the door was wide open and the bed unmade.

"Well that little mystery is solved", Al concluded, "they've gone for a walk." Noting the heavy front door ajar, Al felt relieved.

Back in his bedroom, he quickly dressed and considered starting breakfast then, scratching his stubble, he returned to the bathroom and quickly removed the growth.

Back in the kitchen, Al saw that the breakfast table had been set and preparations had been made for breakfast. He paused, "Should I get things started? No, I'd better wait. They should be back soon." As the house had no windows which offered a view of the street, Al decided to take a look, which required descending the stairs and opening the small inner door facing the street. As Al pushed his bulk through the small entrance, he heard the women's voices.

Quickly he closed he door and bounded up the steps and into the house. Hardly had he closed the heavy oak door before he heard Dawn's question, "Do you think he's up yet? Maybe we should be quiet."

"Oh, I think he's probably up," Lucia replied. "But how that man can sleep!" she added.

"So you both had a good, restful night's sleep?" Dawn almost giggled.

"Of course. Why not? We couldn't very well make love all night," Lucia teased.

At this, both women laughed uproariously while pushing the front door open.

Again the room came alive with laughter. "Welcome back, my wandering ladies fair!"

"Hold it right there! No limericks about wandering ladies fair who met their match on the stair."

"Okay, Dawn, I recognize a born poet so I won't attempt to add lines to your rhyme."

"Well, did you enjoy your walk?" Al asked.

"It really wasn't much of a walk," Lucia volunteered. "Only a short distance to that large house on the opposite side of the road."

"Does it seem to be occupied?" Al asked.

"Oh, I'm sure it is, but we didn't see any sign that people are there now," Dawn added. "We walked around the house toward the back where there's a swimming pool—not very large but big enough. And there are lawns or will be, and a large parking area."

"That area has been graded and a small retaining wall seems to enclose the property. Behind that low wall, the hill falls away rather steeply." Dawn added, "If a car went over the wall, it would almost certainly roll all the way to the wooded area some seven or eight hundred feet below, maybe more."

"So that's our Sunday morning report. Now let's have some breakfast," Lucia added.

"May I be of any help?" Al asked.

"You certainly may," Dawn quipped, "by staying out of the kitchen and putting on some music. Just keep us singing and working."

For a minute or two Al studied the rows of plastic boxes, each identified by title and composer. He was tempted by Mozart's Requiem, but as much as he liked he music and never quite thought of it as a mass, he felt this occasion needed something profane and not sacred. So he scanned the shelf until he saw "Some Enchanted Evening" played by the London Pops Orchestra. Scanning the titles, he noted each piece he fondly remembered.

Again he pushed the cassette into position and started the music. Then, adjusting the volume, he waited for a response from the kitchen.

Immediately Dawn responded, "Oh, what beautiful music," to which Lucia added, "Golden oldies. These were my father's favorites. 'Dancing in the Dark,' 'Where or When,' 'Stardust.' My dad must have had this same cassette."

The music flooded Al's memory, and for a few minutes he was completely oblivious to the smells and activities in the kitchen. With his eyes closed he drifted with the beguiling melodies only to be suddenly awakened by a kiss on his forehead. "Breakfast is served, beautiful dreamer!" With that, Lucia grabbed his arm and helped pull him to his feet.

Together they entered the kitchen as Dawn poured the coffee while urging Lucia and Al to be seated.

"Now our piece de resistance, Eggs Benedict," Dawn purred as she skillfully slipped each heated plate into its arranged place.

"Eggs Benedict?" Al exclaimed. "I haven't had this breakfast treat in many years. How in the world did you ladies know about Eggs Benedict?"

"Watch that comment," both women laughed. "Surely you don't seem to appreciate our level of sophistication. We Stanford women were brought up on Eggs Benedict, and on Sundays our family cook always served champagne just before serving the eggs, which was followed with a frothy cappuccino.

"But we Stanford dames were really crude peasants when compared with Lucy's aristocratic family, whose chef was known all over the Piedmontese! Right, Lucy? But since most Italians don't eat eggs for breakfast, didn't your chef produce a divine frittata, something like an omelet with artichoke hearts, asparagus, tomatoes, zucchini flowers and all seasoned with herbs?"

"You must have been reading that from an Italian cookbook, Dawn. It sounds delicious, but I've never had such a frittata. And the fact is my father loved Eggs Benedict and could put together the ham, English muffin, poached eggs and Hollandaise sauce in five or six minutes."

"That's wonderful, ladies, but I'm here to eat while the Eggs Benedict are hot!" But before seating himself, Al deftly slid a chair under Lucia.

Between paeans of chatter and mouthfuls of food, the two demolished the breakfast.

"The only thing missing is the cappuccino." Lucia added.

"Right", Al added. "I should have it on hand because I do prefer it to my regular black coffee."

"Now the only other Sunday necessity," Dawn added, "is the Sunday paper."

"Well," Al added somewhat reluctantly, "I could drive down to Greve and get one, but the Herald-Tribune doesn't publish a regular Sunday paper."

"Not only that," Lucia added, "I suppose we should clean up the kitchen and then consider driving to Panzano. My grandparents had suggested we get there around noon even though we won't eat until much later."

Within minutes, the jobs were done and the only questions were, "What should we wear and should we bring a gift?"

Here Lucia asserted herself, "Let's all dress casually, slacks and sports shirt, Al, and a simple dress or slacks for us and comfortable shoes because my grandfather will insist on showing us around. He loves Panzano and probably owns several buildings."

"I guess we should take two cars?" Al asked.

"Why?" Lucia answered, then realizing the problems that a single car might suggest, she added, "I suppose you're right because Dawn and I should return to Florence today. I have an important lesson at the Conservatory. How about you, Dawn?"

"Well, yes. I have a class or two, but if something better came up, I could stay, I guess," then she laughed. "I was just teasing, of course. I'm going back. I know where my nest is!"

Al cast a knowing smile at Lucia. "Right, Dawn. I have a suggestion. To save time, problems and gasoline, let's take only one car to Panzano. We'll leave my old Fiat or Lucia's Alfa in Greve and ride together to Panzano."

"Good thinking, Professor. We leave your old clunker in the square and take Lucia's car."

By eleven thirty the trio was ready. Each woman had placed her small bag by the door before stopping in the bathroom.

Meanwhile Al quickly straightened the bed covers, turned on a night light and emerged. Dawn and Lucia began descending the awkward staircase with their bags as Al securely locked the ancient, heavy front door.

"What a beautiful day!" Al almost sang. "It's almost a spring day in February."

Without waiting for Al to start the Fiat, Dawn and Lucia began the short descent to Greve. Minutes later he parked beside the Alfa. "Lucy, what might be a nice gift for your grandparents?"

"That's a nice idea, but they wouldn't expect anything, particularly from you. But I think Dawn and I might bring a small offering. It's the Italian way."

Minutes later, both women had disappeared into a small variety shop which miraculously was still open.

"Were you successful?" Al inquired as the women rejoined him in the Alfa.

"Yes, the store had a small box of special Italian cookies. This will please them both."

Lucia slid into the driver's seat as Dawn knowingly took the rear leather seat.

"Well," Al observed, "You are the pilot and the navigator and I'm the observer and not much use, I'm afraid."

"No, dear man, you can take in the countryside. This road, A-22 I think it's called, winds through the Chianti country and takes in a good part of Tuscany. Right now the scenery is rather austere, but in another month it will begin to blossom into spring, and by May becomes a scene of beauty in every sense."

Now the narrow, two-lane road followed the gentle contours of the hills and after ten minutes there, against the moody blue sky, was Panzano, a long continuous silhouette of chimneys, towers and fortresses clinging to the crumbling ridges which snaked their way over the wandering dark Tuscan hills.

Slowly the Alfa rounded the broad, flattened hilltop, which became a circular square with a small fountain and pond forming a traffic hub for pedestrians and vehicles. There were parking spaces against the village's legal offices, bank and principle shops. Here the square bisected the medieval citadel Panzano, once part of the Medici's Florentine defensive system, but now the connective center between the old and newer village.

Thus within the span of a half-century, Panzano was being transformed from a medieval fortification to a beautiful and handsome scene of the future.

"Here we are!" Lucia announced, "Panzano's center. Fortunately not much traffic."

Slowly she sneaked between several illegally-parked cars and managed to turn directly into the main village street, a narrow cobblestone way with only occasional places for a sidewalk. Yet even where the street narrowed to ten feet, small shops hugged the walls. Seemingly this ancient passage was predetermined by the width of the ridge-top. Thus the entire length of the old village was hardly a half-mile.

"How do you like this highway?" Lucia laughed. "As narrow as it is, there are three or four wider places where two-way traffic can pass. Actually, at that space before the church, the road veers to the left and continues on to Castellina. But here on the right is a very narrow one-way road which will take us to the house my grandparents are living in now. Later they may move to a much larger modern villa just beyond the street below the church."

Carefully, Lucia downshifted, allowing the Alfa to miss the holes and safely follow the steep road for about three hundred yards to an open area.

"There's the house! Notice how similar it is to the house you are renting, Al!"

Quickly Lucia parked the car in an open area in front of the house. Before any of the three could emerge from the Alfa, both grandparents were standing nearby. "Benvenuta, Lucia! Velcom amici!"

Both grandparents embraced Lucia and ceremoniously kissed her on each cheek. In turn, Dawn and Al were greeted warmly and minutes later the party of five were seated in the warm living room.

Both Al and Dawn were surprised by grandfather Massimo's height and weight and how slight and very pretty grandmother Justine was.

Before Massimo could say anything, Justine, in almost flawless, unaccented English, suggested, "Are you tired and may I offer you something to drink? Maybe some chocolate or tea or cookies?"

"That would be very nice, Nanna, and here are some cookies we brought," said Lucia extending her package.

For a few seconds Justine and Massimo seemed surprised but soon recovered with an extravagant, "Grazie mille!"

"And our very favorite—almond cookies," Justine added.

Now Massimo rapidly began a short discourse in broken English and Italian. "I hom vari appi to meetu Ms. Dahn and Meester Al. Lucia shi told us about you end Professori. She sai you are femus man. Yu make books. I am veri happi to no yu!"

As they talked and laughed, Al noted how this house and interior was almost exactly like the house he was renting. Somewhat awkwardly Al offered, "Senior Rossi, I'm renting a house very much like this one."

"Si, Professore en Tuscani, dere ar meni houses lika dis. Vari old but gud. Vari stron! I by chees haus lonk go. Mebi feefty ear, but I feex. Now she benissimo."

Soon Lucia, Dawn and Justine returned with a large tray of cookies, tea, chocolate and dates. "Please, let's sit down," Justine suggested. "We may eat and talk and enjoy ourselves."

The room soon became a small amphitheater of laughter and pleasure. Quite obviously the Rossis enjoyed socializing, which seemed to accelerate the passage of time. Sensing the situation and remembering the promise of a walk, Lucia interjected, "Nonna e Nonno, would you like to show us something of Panzano? My friends have never been here and I'm certain they would enjoy walking around the town before it gets too cold."

"Oh, yes, Massimo and I would be very happy."

Bundled in warm coats, Massimo asserted himself. "Thees vay ees bad but vi go up. Hokay?"

Although the narrow, bumpy road was worn with ruts, walking was almost easier than driving. Within minutes the cheerful five arrived at the small junction.

Taking charge as the leader and guide, Justine pointed toward the church. "It's quite old but in very good condition. We were there this morning, but we don't celebrate a big mass, no singing, just the usual prayers. Massimo and me, we are not very good Catholics. My husband is a socialist so he is not religious."

Slowly they trudged along the narrow sidewalk to what seemed to be a school. "And here," Justine said proudly, "is our school for boys and girls. It is very good because we have good teachers."

Lucia and Dawn noted how well-maintained the two buildings were and a playground with swings and some equipment for games.

Pointing, Massimo suggested that they follow the narrow road around the church. "Nih ear es a lateel park. Vi set vor minit, hokay?" The park was a small but groomed grass rectangle with an excellent view of the distant hills.

"Is that a town in the distance?" Al asked.

"Yes, that's Radda," Justine explained. "It's much larger than Panzano and much richer. Many people who work in Firenze live there, but we much prefer Panzano because it is much older and I think much prettier and quieter."

Having hardly spoken, Dawn emerged from a self-imposed silence. "I think we should visit the place when we have more time. After all, neither Al nor I have seen much of Tuscany."

For several minutes the group had a lively exchange of towns in or near the Chianti country, "Well, just as soon as it warms up let's take a couple of days and wander around these places. I'm really interested much more now than ever. Not only is this Chianti in Tuscany, but Tuscany is the center of ancient Etruscan civilization."

"Bravo, Professore," Dawn smiled. "I'll cut a few classes and join you for the Etruscan exploration."

At the mention of Etruscan, Justine became quite animated and in a few, well-chosen words, clearly indicated that she knew Italian and Etruscan history very well.

Massimo seeming bored by the conversation, noted that it was almost four o'clock. With his few chosen words as a strong suggestion, the others heartily agreed that a return to the heated house would be welcome.

Back in the comfort of the warm, old house Justine, without a word, arranged a small round tale and suggested, "Before we have dinner, would you care for some wine and antipasto?"

Within two or three minutes, Justine produced a large plate of thin crackers, salami, gorgonzola and small radishes. "And Massimo will give us wine, both red and white or whatever else you might prefer."

The wine and antipasto quickly produced an animated conversation about Al and Dawn, and somewhat belatedly about Lucia.

"We are very happy that Miss Knight met Lucia and made a living arrangement together. As much as we enjoyed Lucia living here, we knew she must find an apartment in Florence where she could have her piano while still studying at the Conservatory." Justine stopped, then added, "But I forgot how Lucia and Dawn knew each other."

"Well that was a lucky coincidence for me," Dawn volunteered. "I was having lunch in a small restaurant near the Stanford office and classroom building and Lucia came in. As all of the tables were taken, she asked if she might share my table. Well, I was very pleased as I didn't know many Stanford students. And from that first meeting, we became friends and very lucky for me I got out of the dorm and into my own room. And much more importantly, we have similar likes and interests, even though I don't play the piano, at least not anything like Lucia does."

Now restless to become involved, Massimo smiled at Al. "Professore, vat you do in Italia?"

"Well, sir, as Lucia and Dawn know, I am here only for a few months. I am trying to finish writing a book which I couldn't complete in California."

"Vy not? Calefornya es beg plaz, no?"

"Yes, of course, sir. But I have many friends where I live in Berkeley and they are always calling me, and even more importantly, I have three grown children and they, too, frequently telephone or come to my house."

"That's very interesting, Professor Praitt. So you are very busy?" Justine asked. "But where is your wife?"

"That's another part of my problem. My wife died almost five years ago. As much as we worked and helped each other during our thirty-five years together, I needed her even more in recent years. She was everything that I wasn't—a good and loving parent, a wonderful wife, housekeeper, my secretary—everything any man could possibly want." Al almost choked out the last four words.

The room was very quiet. Finally Al added, "I'm sorry. Joan wouldn't have wanted me to talk this way. She was a strong and positive person. But I'm here now not to escape my memories of Joan, but simply to complete this book which I've been paid to write and have ready for the publisher by June 1. It isn't much of a book as Dawn and Lucia know, not that they've read it, but I've told them something about the story. So Senior and Senora Rossi, I'm lucky to have a free house here in beautiful Italy, and here because I met and have come to know two of the most beautiful young women I've ever been privileged to meet—Lucia and Dawn."

Breaking the silence, Dawn lifted her glass of wine. "I'd like to propose a toast to our kind and generous hosts, Massimo and Justine, and to the charm and sincerity of our best friend, Professor Al Praitt."

Now the conversation became a joyful chorus of pleasure and laughter. Quietly, Massimo moved next to Al. Then, gripping Al's free hand, the towering host whispered, "Al, I must talk vit you. Please com ova 'ear."

Somewhat embarrassed by his host's request for something confidential, Al joined him as the three women continued their lively exchange, not that they weren't aware the men's awkward distance.

"I am sorri, Professore, but I vant yu tu no abot Lucia and beeg problem vit vari bad mon, Leone. If I get him, I keel im. Eh rapa Lucia, nough he mussa diah. Youa no theis stori?"

Embarrassed, Al gripped Massimo's hand. "I know almost nothing. Lucia told me that she is afraid of Leone and I think that I know her reasons. Quite by accident on the first night that I met Lucia, I also met Leone, whom I believe was looking for Lucia. This is not a good place for us to talk, but we should get together soon and decide what we or maybe the police should do about Senore Leone." And with that silent agreement, both men happily rejoined the women.

Dawn joked, "Are you gentlemen going to share your secrets with us?"

Before either man could reply, Justine laughed, "We women don't want to hear their secrets or their jokes."

"But now it's time for pranzo. Here we eat in this large room which is also the kitchen and pantry. These very old houses were made that way."

"Yes, I know, signore," Al offered. "The house I am using near Greve is very much like this one, and I like it very much."

"Please, everybody, let's sit down," Justine demanded. "And I would like the Professor and Lucia to sit opposite of me so that I don't miss anything they say."

Almost effortlessly, as the others seated themselves, Justine produced a large bowl of soup which immediately evoked a chorus of oh's and ah's. Quickly Justine distributed the five large bowls of fragrant acquacotta. "This soup is a favorite among us Tuscans. I won't trouble you with how it's made, but it isn't difficult."

For several minutes, the soft murmurs of praise were matched with the joys of tasting and swallowing.

"There's more acquacotta," Justine added, "but we should leave room for my prize cinghiale umido, another Tuscan favorite, boar cooked in wine, herbs and seasoning, and with a side dish of gnocchi which you might add to the boar. They go together."

Quickly, Lucia collected the soup bowls as Dawn distributed large, heated plates. Not to be denied his major contribution, Massimo produced a large bottle of Chianti Classico! "Thees ees vari gout red vino, old, yes—diechi anni. As the women seated themselves, Massimo expertly filled each large wine glass three-quarters full, then lifting his glass, he offered, "To long live and goot helth," followed by "Mangiamo!"

With the tinkling of glasses, the choral symphony of dining, drinking and talking filled the room.

As the bouquet of boar and seasoning engulfed their senses, the vocal quintet, almost in harmony, produced the joys of their food–chewing, talking, slurping, swallowing–a cacophony of dissonance redolent of joy and pleasure. Keeping an erratic beat of the chorus, suddenly Massimo's rich basso would project a large burp which only served to punctuate the merriment of this occasion.

This major course, which could be marked allegro vivace, ended with a chorus of "Wonderful! Magnificent! Glorious!"

Slowly collecting the five empty plates, Justine expressed her satisfaction with her guests' outspoken appreciation of her cooking skills.

"Thank you! Thank you for your kind words–but the meal would not have been complete without a dolci, a dessert for you Americans. So, I've prepared la torta die Fiechi, which owes its fame to Count Opizzo Fiechi of Lavagna, which is near Genoa. To celebrate his wedding to Bianca dei Biachi in 1230, he ordered his cooks to prepare a huge wedding cake, some say ten feet high and weighing some 2,600 pounds, enough for some four-thousand guests.

So here is my small and humble version of that wedding cake. I don't expect any of my charming guests to wed soon, but perhaps the history and attraction of my cake will result in a wedding or maybe two, and without embarrassing the Professor, maybe three weddings."

Everybody joined in the levity of the occasion as Justine expertly cut five large servings from the enticing three-layered cake.

As she deftly served each portion, Massimo suddenly produced a bottle of champagne. "An no I offrire Martini un Rossi, Italian vino spumante." As he spoke, Justine produced five champagne glasses. Again the steady hand of the giant slowly and gently poured the sparking wine into the traditional long-stemmed glasses.

Before anybody else could offer a toast Lucia was on her feet and, raising her glass, she smiled and nodded to the others, "I offer this toast to my good friends, Dawn and Professor Praitt, and above all to my loving and caring grandparents, Justine and Massimo. May you always enjoy good health, enduring love and happiness forever."

Murmurs of joy, affection and kisses were exchanged. For several minutes a quiet sense of elation dominated the atmosphere. Then, sensing the possibility of maudlin sentimentality, Al offered, "Thank you, Signore and Signora Rossi for this magnificent dinner, but lest we insult this beautiful experience by nodding off to sleep, would you forgive my boldness to ask you about your life with Signore Rossi?"

Al's question quickly aroused the others from comfortable lethargy.

Silently pleased by the question, Justine was delighted that somehow she might invigorate the discussion.

"Thank you, Professor, for a chance to talk about myself and my long and wonderful marriage to Massimo."

Suddenly Dawn, Lucia and Massimo were erect in their chairs.

"As most people might guess, not only am I much smaller than my husband—my giant, Il Gigante as he is often called—I am also much younger. Too young, my parents thought in 1945 when I was only fifteen, but the tragedy of the war destroyed any voice they might have expressed for my future. They were both killed just before the war ended and I was left with an old aunt in Volos, Greece, who didn't know what to do with me."

As Justine paused, Massimo added, "For mi, vari lucki I meet theese purte girl, Justine."

Now Al was curious. "What were you doing in Greece in 1945, Massimo?"

"I vas beg man en de docus—longshoreman. I vas der fur tu yar. I see Justine. Shee runway. I teka hur hom. Justine haf no mama, no papa. So she sta wit mi."

"But, Justine," Lucia asked, "weren't you afraid of this giant?"

"Yes, of course I was, but my old aunt didn't know what to do with me, and she was afraid that the partisans would kidnap me and take me to Bulgaria. The civil war was raging and the partisans were taking hostages as they retreated north."

Now Dawn abruptly asked, "So you were only fifteen, without parents, and this older man, who spoke only Italian, and you. What did you speak?"

"Oh, I could speak a little Italian, but most of the time I spoke Greek. But in Egypt, where I was born in 1930, I spoke Arabic most of the time, but in school I spoke English and French."

"That's fantastic. Before we get back to the first part of your meeting with Massimo, I'm sure Al and I, and probably Lucia too, would like to know something about your father and mother, or would that be too personal?"

"Well," Justine spoke softly, "that's a rather long story, but if you wish, I'll try to shorten my life story."

Now both women and men were very attentive.

"As I said, I was born in Egypt–Alexandria, where my father was a partner with a Greek in an import-export business. My father was part Greek and Egyptian and his partner, John Pappadopolous, also spoke several languages. These two men had been partners for a long time and were quite wealthy."

Justine paused then asked for a glass of water.

"So your father and his Greek partner had a shipping business?" Al asked.

"It was more than shipping," Justine explained. "They would buy goods from Greece–fruit, olives, cheese and other Greek delicacies–for sale to the large Greek colony in Egypt. Then they would buy Egyptian cotton, which is very highly prized, some tropical fruits and cloth, and sell most of these products to the Italians."

"And what did they buy from the Italians?" Al asked.

"I'm not sure, but I think they bought–silks and cotton–and probably electric generators, and some Italian foods which they shipped back to Greece and Egypt. So, as I now understand their business, they engaged in a triangular trade business which was very profitable."

Now Massimo added, "Vari gut buezness, tey own mani bots!"

"Well, several boats. I don't know how many, but they weren't all large freighters. Many were small ships, little Greek sailing ships which could only carry ten or fifteen tons, and these vessels carried cargos between the Greek and Turkish and other islands including Rhodes and Crete and Cypress. Their few large freighters could carry much larger cargos which enabled them to transport cars, trucks and heavy equipment to many ports in the Mediterranean."

"That's very interesting, Justine, but now would you just fill us in about your life in Alexandria?"

"Of course. I'll be brief because it's getting late."

Quickly Lucia added, "It isn't too late. Only seven, so there's enough time. As you don't realize Nonona Justine, your story goes back to many years before I was born and I'm very interested in knowing more about my family history."

"As I indicated, my parents were quite wealthy by any standards. We had a beautiful large house in Alexandria and there my parents frequently entertained their English, French and Greek friends. But not many Egyptians, simply because not many Egyptians were wealthy. So we had a so-called nurse who took care of me even though I was an only child. Yes, my parents had a rich social life. We had several maids who did all of the work—cooking, cleaning, gardening, everything. My mother had a wonderful life with many interesting people—diplomats, writers, poets. Alexandria was the social center not only of Egypt, but much of the eastern Mediterranean.

"Fortunately, during the very hot summer months my parents lived in Greece. There they had a large house on Mount Pilion where the climate was cool. I loved that place because we could descend to the sea at Volos or ride horses down trails to the Aegean Sea.

"Ours was a wonderful life which all ended rather suddenly in 1941 when the Germans conquered Greece. And other parts of the German armies were in North Africa and quickly overran the weaker English army. When my father saw that General Rommel would soon be in Egypt we quickly returned secretly to Greece and Mount Pilion. But within a year most of the families on Pilion were captured and often killed. And that is how my parents died. Fortunately, I had been staying with our Greek maid who hid me from the Germans. And not long after that I stayed with my great aunt in Volos.

"And that, dear friends, is a short summary of my life."

"That's an amazing story, Justine, but one final chapter must be told," Al added. "And that part if your life with Massimo."

"It is getting late," Justine added, "but I'll quickly summarize my story. After Massimo, the dear man, took me to his small house, he told me that here he would protect me, but I must stay inside the house all of the time. Nobody must know that I was there. And he also told me that very soon, he would take me to Italy and tell everybody that I was his daughter."

"And," Justine added, "he got his papers proving that I was his daughter to make our escape much easier. The war had ended and now it was possible to leave if Massimo could find a boat going to Italy. Since my dear husband was still in the Italian army, he took me on a small Italian naval vessel which was evacuating many Italians who had been around the port of Volos. And about ten days later he got off the boat at Brindise.

PASSION & DEATH IN TUSCANY

"And that is almost the end of my story. I'll only add this. Two months later we were in Panzano, but not before we were married by priests in Greve."

"What a wonderful short autobiography," Al exclaimed. "A real romantic thriller!"

"Yes," Dawn added, "your life makes my existence a bit of trivia. Thank you so much Justine, if I may use your given name, for telling us about your fascinating life."

"Oh, it wasn't very interesting, but it was somewhat exciting, but nothing to compare with my husband's life story. After all, he was forty-three when we were married in 1945. Now you know that he's almost thirty years older than I am—he's now eighty-four years young and I'm fifty-six years old."

Now Lucia almost pleaded, "Nonna, you haven't mentioned your first and only child, my mother Eleni."

"Yes, I would be glad to, but later, when we have time. Now it's too late and talking about Eleni now would be too much for me. Yes, soon we will have a day together, but now it is late and you and Miss Knight must drive back to Florence."

Nobody contested Justine's decision. Within minutes, the women all pitched in to wash dishes and complete the clean up.

Fond farewells were sealed with kisses. Already Al was in the back seat waiting for Lucia and Dawn who now accepted final directions from Justine and Massimo.

Fortunately Justine had suggested that instead of returning directly to Panzano by the steep narrow trail, she advised them to drive straight ahead and continue with this road which would connect with the main highway, a half-mile before Panzano. Soon they were winding down the well-graded slopes to Greve.

Back in the square, parking next to Al's old Fiat, they exchanged farewells, each promising to phone and make plans for dinner together. And with a final kiss, Lucia released Al and whispered, "Soon, soon, darling, I'll be practicing at your house."

Al watched their car lights fade as they turned out of the square. For a few seconds, Al sat quietly. "Oh, hell," he muttered, "climb the hill and turn in for the night."

Minutes later, Al unlocked the front door, then paused momentarily before entering and quickly flicked on the nearby switch, instantly flooding the room with light. He stared at his closed bedroom, and noting no light from under the door he stepped to the left and pushed the door wide open. Again he paused, reached inside the door frame and snapped on the overhead light. His curiosity satisfied, he entered. Obviously the room was empty. As there was no closet and only a small armoire with drawers, his apprehension faded. He stared at the bed covers–wrinkled. "No," he remembered, "I didn't make the bed."

Returning to the living room, he stepped into the kitchen. Two cupboard doors were slightly ajar, otherwise nothing untoward. Back to the living and the connecting large bathroom, the door was wide open but only the mirrored medical door was ajar. Nothing.

Next he cautiously moved toward the large divided front bedroom–one with a single bed near the small grand piano. Nothing. Now the adjoining bedroom with the large double bed and a large armoire. He hesitated and opened the double door. Except for blankets and sheets, nothing.

He felt relieved, then remembering the spiral staircase to the large upper bedroom, he stealthily moved up the stairway. At the landing he noted the door was wide open. Again, before entering he reached around the door frame and flicked on the overhead light. The room was empty except for the double bed, dresser and chair. As he turned to leave, he heard what seemed like a muted scratching. As the sound seemed under the bed, Al slowly dropped to one knee and peered under the dimly-lit bed springs. Suddenly a large rat dropped from the springs, raced past his outstretched hand and disappeared under the dresser.

Surprised and relieved, Al laughed, "Well, if Mr. Rat is my only visitor, I don't have much to worry about."

Quickly he descended the stairs. Relieved that nobody had probably gotten into this house, he sat. "Yes, probably my imagination about leaving the light on when we left early this afternoon."

Noting that it was now well after ten, he sat quietly for several minutes, then impulsively felt the need for some brandy. In the kitchen he fumbled among the liquor bottles before finding the Courvoisier. As he lifted the bottle to pour the brownish, golden cognac, he noted that it was less than half full.

Slowly he poured a full measure into the sniffer. "Only Lucia and Dawn and I had a small measure which left the bottle at least three-fourths full. God, damn, somebody with a nose for good cognac has sampled my bottle and that bastard must be Leone. So he has been here, that son of a bitch! Sneak into my house and drink my booze!"

Slowly Al returned to the living room, reflecting on what Leone could have been looking for. "Hell, I haven't anything he could have wanted."

Again he sat quietly feeling the warmth and beauty of the cognac. "He must think that Lucia has given me something that he desperately wants. But she gave everything important to her grandfather—everything except the papers and the money which the police took."

Again Al sat comforted by the cognac but vaguely uneasy and nervous. Suddenly without reason, he thought about his story—good, almost finished. Almost impulsively he reached for the manuscript in the large manila folder on the table next to the typewriter. It was gone. For a second he stared at the empty table top then, like a blind man, he began fumbling with other papers, large envelopes, binders. Searching. Hoping. "Could I have misplaced it?"

Slowly, in almost tearful resignation, he accepted reality. Yes, Leone had been there. Nobody else would have taken the manuscript. But how could the bastard have known about the book. How? How? Oh, yes. The professor, here to write. Probably others knew something about his reason for being in Italy. Of course, that must be it. And Leone will be holding my manuscript for a ransom. "Okay, Mr. Leone, you've got me temporarily trapped. But we'll see soon who's the winner when I produce something you desperately want and need. The issue is drawn, you bastard!"

Now fully alert and again certain, Al sipped heavily from the snifter as the telephone rang.

Before a second ring, Al had the phone and before he could say, "Hello, Lucia!" a strong male baritone said, "Professore Praitt, this is Michele Leone. How are you, sir?"

Almost speechless, "Mr. Leone, I'm quite well, but I am quite surprised to hear from you."

"Yes, I thought my call might might be considered upsetting, if that's the appropriate phrase—my English suddenly fails me. But I first wanted to assure that you have nothing to worry about."

For two or three seconds, Al considered his answer, then Leone added, "I am indeed sorry that you seem upset by the inexplicable events of this evening. They upset me, too. As I told the police, I know nothing about either robbery."

"Either robbery?" Al almost exploded. "What in the world are you talking about, Leone?"

"I'm very sorry to be the bearer of bad news, but as I understand the events, my stepdaughter and her pretty roommate, Miss Knight. . . well, somebody robbed their apartment and stole several valuable items, which left both women hysterical."

Now Al was almost too shaken for a quick reply. "Mr. Leone, I know nothing about that and yes, I am very surprised. But exactly why are you telling me? I would expect them to call me."

"Yes, of course. And I am certain that they will when they return from the hospital."

"The hospital!" Al shouted. "Did the robber attack them?"

"No, there was no violence according to the police who called me. But because Lucia was hysterical, the police suggested that both women accompany them to the emergency hospital for appropriate medication. And I suppose they are there now."

"Wait a minute, Leone. Are you suggesting that I robbed Lucia's apartment?"

"Not at all, Professore. You couldn't possibly have committed this heinous crime simply because you were with both women all afternoon and early evening in Panzano, where you were all at the grandparents' house. And upon their return they dropped you off at your car in Greve and they drove back to Florence. Then you returned to the house you have exchanged, which is owned by my good friend, Professor Fagiole."

For several seconds, Al was speechless. Then Leone added, "I'm terribly sorry to upset you. Perhaps you should try to phone Lucia."

"Thank you, Signore Leone. I apologize for being somewhat rude, and thank you for this very important information."

"Not at all, Professor, but there is one other somewhat important message I must convey."

Again Al was confused, "Yes, what more is there?"

"It's simply this, maybe not important, but the police found a large folder and manuscript which they identified as yours. They thought that maybe you had left it at the women's apartment. Anyway, I believe they took the folder with them, or possibly they left it with the women. I would suggest you call them this evening."

Al could hardly talk, then added with a note of finality, "Thank you, Mr. Leone, I did leave my manuscript there a few days ago. So thank you again."

Al waited for a response which came immediately. "Professore, there are several interesting and important things I would like to discuss, and I don't mean right now, but perhaps in a few days after the ladies are settled and you have some free time. Maybe we could have lunch here in Florence. There are several excellent places near my shop, which is quite close by the Ponte Vecchio. Would you come to join me for interesting information and discussion?"

Again Al paused before offering, "Your invitation is accepted right now, but I must have a few days to reclaim my manuscript, which I didn't remember leaving at the women's apartment, but quite obviously I did. So again, thank you. I'll call you at your shop soon. And now good night."

Before Al could pour himself a needed drink or even reflect on Leon's long recital of lies and information, the phone rang.

Al grabbed the worn hand piece, "Hello?"

"Darling, darling. I've been trying to reach you for almost an hour. Something terrible has happened," Lucia's voice was almost a sob.

"Oh, Lucia! I'm terribly sorry because I've been hoping to call you, too. And the reason you couldn't reach me is because Leone has been telling much about your horrible robbery and said the police took you to the hospital."

"What? Lucia added suddenly. "He told you I was taken to the hospital– the trauma center?"

"Yes. He said that's what he remembered the police had told him. He said you were hysterical and needed something to help you with this crisis."

"That lying, rotten son-of-a-bitch!" Al was shocked by Lucia's sudden emotional change. "What happened darling, and please excuse my profanity, but I wasn't hysterical and neither was Dawn. We were both upset, angry and confused. And we had every good reason. Upon our return we found the door open and the entire house ransacked. The place looked like two or three people had broken in and systematically gone from room to room searching for something. And in the process, stealing most of Dawn's and my jewelry.

Fortunately neither of us lost anything of great value and there was less than a hundred dollars in cash in the house."

"Lucia! How are you right now? How can I help you?"

"Darling man, the nicest and most important thing I need now is you. The house is a terrible mess. Dawn and I have been trying to clean up the place, but could you drive down here now? I know it's terribly late, but if you could come down, we can talk a bit and make some plans. Of course you must spend the night with me. Okay?"

"Of course. I'll leave immediately and should be there in forty-five minutes or at the longest an hour. I love you terribly—I'll be there soon."

For only a few seconds Al considered a plan of action. Then, grabbing a small bag and change of clothes, shaving equipment and money, he left several lights glowing and carefully locked the door.

Approaching his car, he noted his neighbor's lights. "Good. I'll mention Leone to Enrico and explain that I believe somebody has been in the house and ask to keep an eye on the place."

Within seconds after Al knocked a voice demanded, "Si chi es la?"

Al replied loudly, "Sono professore."

With that the door popped open and Al in broken Italian and English explained what had happened and that somebody had a key and been in his house.

Enrico was both sympathetic and angry. "No problem, Professore—no worry. I sleep in your house, okay?"

For a moment, Al pondered. "Well, okay. You have the key—chiave?"

"Si, I have chiave, Professore. Fiagiole give key."

And with that Al was relieved, and with a quick molte gracies and buona notte, Al was gone.

As it was almost midnight, there was very little traffic until Al reached the suburbs of Florence. Then, following the route that paralleled the last side of the Arno, he took the large bridge near the ancient library and quickly found himself on the narrow street leading to the women's apartment. There, all the lights ablaze, both Dawn and Lucia stood at the main front window.

As Al reached the apartment stairs, Lucia threw herself into his out-stretched arms. For several seconds they held each other in a tender embrace as Lucia quickly recovered.

Then rapidly Lucia whispered, "Darling, darling, darling. Thank you for coming. I was very frightened, as was Dawn. We didn't know what happened or what to expect. Whoever did this, and we both believe that it had to be Leone, or more probably somebody, possibly more than one person, who tore our place apart looking for something, but also deliberately intending to terrorize us."

Before Al could speak, Dawn was next to him. Quickly he turned and kissed her on the cheek, then the trio quickly entered the house.

All of the furniture was back in place but some drawers remained against the living room wall.

Carefully choosing his words, Al praised both women for their courage and strength to bring a degree of order to the room.

"Thank you for the kind and comforting words," Dawn added almost tearfully. "Both of us have been trying to restore some order, but we still have much more to do. We managed to organize the chaos we encountered in our bedrooms, so we'll have some place to sleep."

"Yes, it's very late," Al countered, "but how can I be of help right now?"

"The best help you can provide right now," Lucia whispered, "is your love and your presence, and I mean that for Dawn as well as myself."

"And now," Dawn added, "I think there may be some coffee and possibly a little something we may have before turning in."

As Al stood up to offer his help, Dawn brushed his cheek with a kiss and patted him on his tail end. "Just sit, Al and comfort Lucia. She needs you more than I do."

For two or three minutes, Al held Lucia tenderly. "God, how I love you and admire you, Lucia. From the brief summary Leone gave me, the thieves almost destroyed this place."

"That's true, but since that S.O.B. never saw the huge mess, he could only imagine it from the police report," Lucia added.

"Maybe he didn't have to imagine it. Maybe he saw it. Maybe he was part of it," Al replied.

Lucia stared at Al in disbelief. "Do you think he had a part in this break-in and destruction?"

"I think it's quite possible, darling, and I'll tell you why. Sometime after ten when I realized that either Leone or possibly one of his employees had been in my house while we were in Panzano, Leone called me. I quickly answered assuming that it was you ringing me to say good night or something even nicer."

Lucia sat up. "Leone called you and described the scene?"

"Not in any detail. He simply said that somebody had broken in and ransacked the apartment–actually he talked at considerable length describing how you called the police who came and investigated and either took you to the trauma center or advised you to go there."

"That's a total lie," Dawn answered from the kitchen. "Neither of us were hysterical. It's true that we were both frightened, and the police didn't do much to relieve our fear when they told us about other violent robberies and one or two cases of beatings and robberies. Then their prize suggestion: pay somebody to guard the apartment!"

Now Lucia quickly recapped the rest of the story, "These carabinieri are hardly more than idiots. I asked them what types of criminals committed robberies like this and what did they want? And their stupid 'answer,' 'All kinds of people.' But why did they empty all the drawers and cabinets and dump the contents on the floor?"

"And what was their answer?" Al asked.

"It was beyond belief, darling. 'They do this because they are poor men looking for valuables, and the fastest and easiest way is to dump everything on the floor.' If that's true, then they must be very stupid."

"My guess," Al suggested "is that whoever did this believed that you and Lucia had something the thief or thrives wanted very desperately and it wasn't jewelry."

"You're probably right, darling. So you're thinking exactly what I've been guessing. Mr. Leone thinks that I still have some, if not all, of his very important papers, which I did have several years ago and are now beyond his reach–at least the ones the police didn't get–which my grandfather now has hidden someplace."

"One more interesting fact I haven't mentioned," Al added.

Now Dawn interrupted, "I've found some chocolate and a few cookies the thieves didn't want. Let's sit here in the kitchen. One chair has been broken plus other things like some dishes."

For the next several minutes, the trio sipped hot chocolate and nibbled.

"Yes, Mr. Leone really filled my ears and told me that the police had found the large folder and my story here in this apartment."

"What?" both women blurted in surprise. "Your 'potboiler' as you call it? The police found it here?"

"That's what Leone said," Al continued. "Now the interesting coincidence about my missing 'potboiler' is that I didn't notice it's absence until about fifteen minutes before Leone called me about your robbery. Finally he added that the police have the folder now.

"Now that's an interesting revelation to us, isn't it?" Dawn added. "They never mentioned finding a large manila folder. But if Leone isn't concocting the whole story about the police finding your story and that they have it now, the necessary conclusion is that Leone himself stole it."

"Right!" Al laughed, "Leone must have stole it shortly after we left for Panzano. Then, after carefully searching my apartment and finding nothing but my bottle of Courvoisier, he and probably his flunky, drank at least six or eight ounces and accidentally saw my folder next to the typewriter. So Leone realized that he had my prized possession and took it as a possible trade for something I might help him recover."

Both women were alert to the possibility of the the value of the "potboiler."

"So," Dawn suggested, "Leone wants you to believe that the police found your folder here and that somehow either Lucia or I stole the folder."

"You've got it, Dawn—good detective work," Al exclaimed.

"Unfortunately, I innocently destroyed his whole story."

"How? Yes, how Al?" Both women demanded.

"I decided to trick him or confuse him. So after he described how the police had found the strange folder among some books and had taken it for evidence, I destroyed his story."

"You did what, darling?"

"I told him that I had shown it to you and had accidentally left it at your apartment."

"What did he say to your tall story?" Dawn almost giggled.

"Well, I'll hand it to Leone, the liar and the thief. He congratulated me and urged me to collect my important work from the police before it was lost."

"Do you believe any part of the ridiculous story?" Lucia asked.

"None, absolutely none. But either he planted the story with the police and book, or he still has the book, and the police know nothing about it."

"So what's your next move, my darling Sherlock Holmes?"

"Simple. After breakfast, in about six hours, the three of us will call on the police about the burglary and their possession of my book. And I imagine that there will be some private discussion with higher-ups while we wait for anything from a half-hour to a few days before the missing book is returned."

"Amazing, darling. So you are confident that the police were in on the robbery or that Leone is using his imporant connections with the police to return the book to you?"

"Right," Al added, "either he had planted my book here after he stole it and conveniently had the police take it to the station as evidence, and that I had something to do with your robbery. But when he learned that we were all together yesterday, his scheme to entrap me went up in smoke."

"So now he or the police must produce your book," Dawn laughed.

"I don't think there's any way he can avoid your conclusion, Dawn, unless he wants to risk a massive 'bruta figura'—if that's the appropriate expression—with the Florentine police department.

"Now the problem is partially solved. I suggest we all turn in. It's almost two a.m."

"Right," Dawn yawned. "We'll have breakfast by nine and head for the police with a big smile. You two sleep well, and I did say sleep!"

Quickly Lucia made certain that the bedroom was ready, then asked, "Darling, did you have a bag in the car? And be sure the car is locked."

Having forgotten his bag and the car, he was momentarily embarrassed. Quickly he bounded down the stairs to the Fiat parked in the driveway. Quickly he recovered the bag locked in the car and was back in the house.

With the house secured, Al cautiously opened the door to find Lucia snuggled under the down quilt. "Hurry, darling! Brush your teeth, your horny princess is waiting."

Wearing only some faded plaid boxing shorts, Al slipped into Lucia's outstretched arms and suddenly they were reveling in the beauty and excitement of the night.

Slowly Al rolled over and Lucia's absence frightened him. Then he heard sounds from the adjoining bathroom and he was vastly relieved. Glancing at his watch, he noted the time, eight-thirty already!

As he bounded from bed Lucia, fully dressed, appeared. "My darling man, the bathroom is all yours. Dawn and I need a few things for breakfast. So take your time and we'll have a wonderful breakfast together about nine, okay?"

"Wonderful!" was all Al could offer.

Within minutes Al had showered and shaved then slowly put on his somewhat wrinkled plaid slacks and tan woolen shirt. Voices drifted from the nearby kitchen. Now rested and ready for two of the most beautiful and charming women he had even known, Al was like a young Aeneas approaching two Roman goddesses.

Some of his demeanor must have been felt as both women radiated their pleasure and confidence while Al greeted and kissed first Lucia and then Dawn.

As Al seated himself, he suggested, "Let's plan our strategy with the police. By that I mean, let's have a prepared list of all your missing valuables, rings, broaches, necklaces, jewelry of any kind, money, clothing, and anything else."

Both women agreed as Dawn added, "Lucia must have had considerably more valuables than I, simply because this is her house and I arrived here a few months ago with hardly more than a few rags from Bloomingdales. As for jewelry, I didn't have any except for a cheap necklace which I seldom wore, a gift from some jerk I slept with once or twice."

"Actually," Lucia explained, "I do have numerous pieces of expensive jewelry–things from mother, gifts from my father. Yes, all together the total value could be several thousand dollars."

Both Dawn and Al expressed surprise which Lucia quickly dismissed, "But everything except for a necklace with a few semi-precious stones and cheap stuff–all of my real treasure is safely locked in a bank vault. So I didn't loose much except my faith and confidence–and to loose these is much worse than most material things."

"Yes, those private and subconscious beliefs are really the forces that guide us and save us, I hope. When we lose these values, we are losing part of ourselves. Oh hell, I'm sounding maudlin and sentimental, " Al was embarrassed.

"Thank you, Al, your words are more important than my losses or the fear which did almost overcome me," Lucia's voice was a soothing tone of love.

Breakfast was soon over and for a few minutes, both women prepared their lists.

"Now," Al suggested, "I think you should phone the police department and ask to speak with Chief Investigator of Home Robberies and, if necessary, request an appointment. Also explain that you were robbed yesterday and that Mr. Michelangelo Leone, who is a relative, suggested you talk with somebody important. Add that your grandfather, Massimo Rossi, who is well-known to the police, is prepared to take whatever action is necessary to capture the criminals and punish them."

Lucia thought about Al's proposal. "Yes, I guess I must do something like that."

"The appointment is very important, Lucia, because you and Dawn together can create considerable anxiety with some department heads, and I'm certain those people know and possibly fear Leone and maybe your grandfather, too."

For a few minutes Dawn and Lucia talked quietly to each other. Then Dawn added, "Mention that I'm a Stanford student here and the university is very concerned about the safety and welfare of its students".

"Okay, but first, do we still have a telephone book?" Lucia asked.

"Here it is. Fortunately the thieves didn't take it."

Scanning the book, Lucia wrote down a number and immediately dialed. Both Dawn and Al could hear the loud ringing and suddenly an almost bellicose, 'Pronto!'"

Quickly Lucia identified herself, also mentioning Leone and Massimo Rossi. Soon another voice forcefully asked a series of questions while Lucia rattled off a volley of answers. Then Lucia, in a very beguiling voice, mentioned Stanford, followed by a series of 'si, si, si, verita, si, grazie!'"

As Lucia hung up, Al quickly asked, "Did they give you an appointment?"

"Yes. The Director asked if we could see him about eleven this morning."

Then Dawn added, "I could hardly understand a word. Everybody talks too fast."

"That's true, but after I managed to get by, somebody named de Putzroso, I talked with Inspector Ruffo who was very polite and added that he knew Mr. Leone very well, and that although he hadn't met my grandfather, he knew all about him because he had knocked out Primo Carnero many years ago."

"Quite obviously you were very impressive, Lucia, and I heard you mention Stanford. What did the man say about Sanford?" Dawn asked.

"Well, that one really tied things together. He said Florence was very proud of its relations with Stanford and that his office would make every effort to apprehend the thieves, and that Signore Leone, who had attended Stanford, would certainly help to find and to prosecute those men who had insulted American women and Stanford University."

Both Dawn and Al hugged Lucia and thanked her profusely.

"Okay, it's almost ten. Let's get there a little early. You know where the police station is?"

"Well, there's a big one on Via della Terme, but I think the most important one is near the Mercato. It's a large building with many offices and two large carabinieri are stationed outside. That's on Via dell'Arento. That's where we should go. But our major problem will be parking. But I do know of a large underground parking garage nearby. So let's get our papers, our passports–yours Al and Dawn's. They may want to see them, but I don't need one."

Within a few minutes Lucia was behind the wheel of her Alfa. Both Al and Dawn were amazed by Lucia's driving skills. Obviously she knew Florence better than most taxi drivers and she seemed to know all of the one-way streets and the short cuts. Soon they neared the central train station.

"There!" Lucia pointed, "is the new underground garage and the main police station should be only two blocks from here."

With the car parked on the second level, Lucia pointed, "We're a little early, so we can take our time walking to the police station."

Soon they arrived at the station where two large carabinieri meticulously groomed in tailored dark blue uniforms outlined in golden braided cuffs and collars stood rigid and erect. Each soldier held a threatening automatic rifle at ready.

As Al, Lucia and Dawn stepped toward the car-width entrance, each officer barked out, "Basta!"

Quickly, as Lucia identified herself and Dawn and Al, the soldier added, "Momento," then calling to another carabiniere, "Visitatori, per Ispettore Ruffo."

Minutes later the trio were shaking hands with Ispectore Ruffo who oozed charm and authority.

"Before I offer my opinion about the stupid and ridiculous robbery of your apartment, Signora Conde and Knight, I must apologize for our police department's failure to protect you women, and all Florentine women, from such stupid but frightening experiences. Furthermore, we will immediately delegate a special force who knows much about the increasing numbers of teenage gangs, which have become quite acute. We call these boys 'crudo dillatante.' Until recently our city never experienced such stupid behaviors."

"Yes," Al volunteered, "You Italians have a much stronger family system, but perhaps your family structure is weakening, as our has."

"I am afraid you are absolutely correct, Professore."

"We have examined your neighbor's apartment," the Inspector continued, "and their place hasn't been touched. Although they seemed to be away, we checked their place and it appears to be okay."

Neither Dawn nor Lucia felt encouraged enough to ask how the Inspector's police entered the locked apartment.

Al, realizing that their discussion was going nowhere, quickly asked the Inspector, "Sir, Mr. Leone suggested to me that you two men are acquainted and that he has great confidence in your professional competence."

"Oh, yes, that's true. I have known Mr. Leone for several years. He is probably the most intelligent and successful businessman in our city. He is widely-respected as an intellectual community leader and important contributor to our police department."

At this disclosure, Dawn smirked, Lucia addled, "Of course," and Al sighed, "how wonderful."

Their obvious subtle, sarcasm confused the Inspector who immediately moved the subject away from Leone and directly toward Al.

"Now back to other important facts. Professor Praitt, I have here your prized manuscript here in its folder. And I'm privileged to know a great American writer."

"How kind of you, Inspector," Al's voice dripped with saccharine gratitude. Have you read any of my novels?"

Somewhat puzzled, the Inspector decided to play it safe and escape with, "No, I haven't had the pleasure, Professor Praitt, but several of my friends have and they tell me that you are one of America's most important writers."

Al could hardly contain himself but managed a broad smile while adding, "That's very kind of you, Inspector and I hope many Italians continue to buy my books, particularly the one you have on your desk."

The Inspector, somewhat confused by Al's jovial attitude, now ceremoniously picked up the folder and handed it to Al.

"Thank you very much, sir. I was quite worried about this manuscript, which is almost finished and must be ready for publication soon."

Sensing that the prolonged interview was a waste of time, Al rose and added, "Sir, you've been very helpful and I believe my young friends also appreciate your professional assistance and the generous allowance of your time."

Not to be outdone, the Inspector put on a mask of bureaucratic conviviality while adding, "I am delighted that you find our humble efforts satisfactory. We Italians have been your most outspoken admirers. Maybe that explains why so many millions of Italians have emigrated to the U.S. and why so many believe that your America is the strongest and most important country in the world."

This outburst of amiable hypocrisy now had both Dawn and Lucia laughing.

Then to extend this extravagant display of exuberant nationalism, the Inspector added, "We Italians have much to brag about—Columbus, Magellan, the great sailors and such scientists as Enrico Fermi, Alessandro Volta and Marconi, and many painters and opera stars, and one world heavyweight boxing Champion, Primo Carnero."

Now between laughter and nonsense, Lucia repeated, "Primo Carnero? What a joke! Even my grandfather knocked him out in Pisa in 1931, and grandfather Massimo had never had fought a professional boxer in his life!"

At once, the Inspector was momentarily speechless, then added, "Yes, I know that's true, but that was before Carnero beat the American Champion Jack Sharkey in the U.S., and later lost his championship to another American, Max Baer. But you're right, Signora Conde, if Massimo has worked and trained as a boxer, nobody could have defeated him."

With that, everybody shook hands as the Inspector wished the trio a ringing, "Buon giorno."

As the three slowly returned to the car, Dawn began the assault, "Have you ever heard a longer and smellier line of bullshit than that? The Inspector should try out as a comedian. He obviously isn't much of a cop."

"And not much of a historian either," Al added. "Magellan happened to have been a Portuguese navigator."

Now Dawn added her bit of Italian history, "I should have reminded him of Verranzano, the navigator and a native of Tuscany for whom the square in Greve is named. Of course, had we wished to embarrass him, we might have mentioned Al Cappone, Lucky Luciano and the many heroes of the Mafia."

"And," Lucia added, "maybe we should have asked him about Benito Mussolini."

"No. That would have been cruel," Dawn added. "So what do we gain by ridiculing him? We still need him on our side because I don't think the question of who really robbed us, and why or for what purpose, has been explained or answered."

"No doubt, you're right." Al nodded. "And I'm sorry that I didn't pressure him about his relationship with Leone. But I think the robbery, Leone and Inspector Ruffo may be closely linked. The Inspector was flattering us because we are Americans."

As the trio approached the underground garage, Al stopped and asked, "Ladies, do either of you have an appointment or a class now or early this afternoon?"

Both Dawn and Lucia hesitated, "No, I don't." Dawn replied.

"Nor do I," Lucia added, "but what do you have in mind, Al?"

"Really not much, but if your stomach is grumbling as mine is, I would like to help assuage any gastronomic needs you ladies might have."

"Oh! You are a gallant, romantic seducer," Lucia teased. "And it just so happens that I know of a fairly good trattoria and others nearby which might satisfy our needs."

Now Dawn offered her sensuous opinion, "I'm impressed with your proposition, even if its only for food, but Lucy and I know that the nicest way to a woman's heart is through her stomach."

"The place I have in mind," Lucia explained, "is the Trattoria Sostanza which is on Via Porcellana just past Piazza Santa Maria Novella. And if Sostanza is closed, which I doubt, another good one several blocks from here is Le Massacce which is also a very old place but with excellent food."

They all immediately agreed to try Sostanza, which they reached in minutes.

As it was early, having just opened, there were several seats available including a small one for three dinners.

Having been escorted to the small table, the waiters quickly produced menus and added in reasonable English, "We have good food—steak, tripe, chicken and fish. When you ready, I come fast, okay?"

Dawn and Al were impressed and enthusiastic.

"Oh this place looks wonderful, 'neat,' as we used to say," Dawn laughed.

For a few minutes, they studied the menu and then Lucia suggested, "Let's each select a different entree, then we can share and have a good idea about the kitchen."

No sooner had they reached their agreement, chicken for Lucia, fish for Dawn and a small steak for Al, the waiter appeared, took their orders and asked, "You like good tortalini? No? Insalata verde, yes? Okay, tre insalata. Ecco, dolce? Okay, later."

"That was very easy," Al added, "and I already like this place."

"Originally this was a working class place, but when the wealthy Florentines recently discovered it, they called it 'troia' which as a proper noun means two very different things: one is a sow or pig and the other is a whore."

Soon the waiter appeared and quickly dispensed the three green salads and the three entrees along with a small serving of bread.

Then as he turned, he asked, "Please, you want vino?"

Al agreed, a bottle of house red.

Now the three gourmands sampled each other's entree while expressing great delight with their collective choices.

"As wonderful as this food is," Al ventured, "we could talk and eat at the same time. And also we could continue our planning strategy. And specifically, what do we do about Inspector Ruffo's and Leone's quite probable involvement in the robbery?"

"Yes, I think we must," Lucia quickly replied. "Furthermore, I am convinced that somehow Leone got Ruffo into the robbery scheme because he not only has given a lot of money to the police department, but also directly to Ruffo. But beyond that, there's something directly that ties these two crooks together."

Al quickly added, "I completely agree with you, Lucia, but what could bind these men together?"

"Well," Dawn interjected, "one obvious force is their animal magnetism."

"Look, you two, as a male, Al, I wouldn't expect you to understand magnetism as a force which would attract some men, but it does. Now if you think about some great leaders like your great hero Franklin Roosevelt, you must agree that some men, and women too, project a force, a kind of magnetism which attracts people to them, and sometimes this magnetism also projects a negative force which works the opposite way."

For a second or two, both Al and Lucia stared at each other. Then Lucia acknowledged, "Yes, I think that's true; it must be true. Why do millions of men and women react positively to many great men–leaders like Roosevelt, Hitler, Mussolini, Churchill? Not by their printed words, but almost personally by their spoken words, the force of their personalities, by convictions, their body language."

"Of course, you're right, both of you. But I'm not convinced that either Leone or Ruffo possesses the magnetism to affect strangers. I'm certainly not affected my either man except in a strong negative way. But I still don't understand how either man personally affects strangers or maybe even friends or acquaintances," Al concluded.

"I'll let you in on a little secret, Al. I find Leone a very attractive man. He's very handsome, has a unusually sensuous and exciting body language which he unknowingly projects in his speech patterns. The man should have been an actor, a movie actor. Women would have loved him as they did Marcello Mastroianni or Clark Gable or Jimmy Stewart, to mention only three of many movie and stage idols, who were not only idolized by women but often greatly admired by most men."

"Okay, Dawn." Lucia agreed somewhat reluctantly. "You know how and why I loathe Leone."

An embarrassed silence followed until Al added, "I agree, but I don't see how Ruffo could or does fit your stereotype."

"You're right about Ruffo's looks, not that he isn't an attractive man, at least to some women, but" Dawn added, "you must admit, he has an excellent gift of gab. He came toward us really fast and smooth, and I have to say, he's a smooth talker. It's just that we could see through him. He didn't know that he was facing a battery of skeptics who weren't willing to accept his glib explanations."

"Again, I must agree with your keen analysis, Dawn. I'm afraid you two women would make a better prosecutor than I."

"But for all our talk, what do we do now? What is our counter strategy?" Al asked.

"Here's what I purpose," Lucia lowered her voice. "Al, you've got to accept Leone's luncheon invitation and make it soon. Try to encourage Leone to reveal his motives. Flatter him. Tell him that Dawn's impressed by him, and subtly suggest he could possibly meet her—maybe the three of you could have lunch together."

Suddenly Dawn began to hum and let the words sing, "Some exciting evening, I will meet a stranger."

"You've got it, Dawn. That's Mary Martin singing, 'Some Enchanted Evening' from the musical comedy 'South Pacific,' circa 1950's."

"Hey, man. You've really got an ear. I saw the movie and loved it, and speaking of sex appeal, that actor who played the French plantation, Emile de Bacques—what a sexy guy!"

"You're absolutely right, Dawn. That actor was the one and only Ezio Pinza, the great Italian basso who had just retired from opera when he was called to play that role in Michner's 'Tales of the South Pacific' in 1957."

"And speaking of sex appeal, Pinzo was the original Don Juan and wherever he lived and sang he left a trail of broken hearts and paternity suits."

Having listened to this prolonged dialogue, Lucia felt somewhat estranged, probably jealous of Dawn's subtle sexuality. Lowering her voice to a sarcastic whisper, Lucia asked, "Dawn, when you have lunch with the monster, Leone, why don't you flatter him and tell him that he reminds you of Pinza, your favorite opera star?"

Sensing a subtle degree of animosity, Al quickly offered a humorous conceit, "Dawn, I believe Lucia's on to something. You could have him eating out of your hand and begging him for more. Just pretend you're a reincarnation of Salome."

Lucia could hardly contain herself as Dawn wasn't sure whether she was being teased or praised. But the twinkle and wink from Al relieved Dawn's apprehension who asked with a laugh, "And who in hell was this broad, Salome?"

Pleased with his reduction of tension, Al asked, "Oh sure, you've heard of that all-time vamp and seducer, Salome, the daughter of sexy Herodias and horny stepfather Herod?" There's only a slight reference to this obscure story of John the Baptist in the Gospel of Mark and Matthew."

"Well," Dawn teased, "At Stanford in a lit. class, I read that Oscar Wilde once considered doing a play about Salome and John the Baptist, but before poor Oscar could write the play, he got tossed in the slammer for being gay."

"Well, Strauss also had a lot of trouble with his opera, which saw only two performances in 1907 at the Met before the moralists got it closed and not performed again until fifty years later. So much for one of the shortest and most shocking plays in the theater today and," Al laughed, "one of the sexiest, particularly if Salome strips all the way as a few divas have done."

Lucia now somewhat subdued, "Can we get passed Salome and return to our original agenda?"

"Right," Dawn snapped. "So Al and I have lunch with Leone as I try to seduce him or use that as bait to learn who wrecked our apartment and why, and what is Leone's connection with Ruffo?"

Quietly the trio finished their lunch and sealed their approval with a handsome tip for their waiter.

"Let's now get back to your place, ladies, and if you're comfortable, I'll return to Greve. I've got a few things to do there and maybe add something more to my celebrated 'potboiler.'

"Then, no later than tomorrow, I'll try to reach Leone and propose a luncheon, which he had suggested. And I'll also ask if he would mind meeting you, Dawn, at this time."

"Sounds good to me," Dawn said.

Throughout the slow drive through heavy traffic Lucia hardly spoke. Then, as her car approached the house, she braked suddenly as a black Mercedes sedan raced through the intersection.

"That S.O.B.!" Al shouted, accompanied by a barrage of curses from the women.

"The car looked familiar," Al grumbled, "bet the driver wasn't Leone."

"No, it wasn't Leone," Lucia confirmed, "but I do feel that the driver may have been connected with that S.O.B."

Back in their apartment, they seemed to have lost their enthusiasm which had dominated the morning and noon. Sensing their frustration and fear, Al quietly began organizing the remaining piles of clothes, dishes and numerous household goods and appliances.

Al's work and somewhat contrived enthusiasm stimulated the women's efforts for organization and order, and soon the apartment appeared normal except for one broken chair.

"Mission accomplished," Al suggested. "Now let's have a drink. Is there anything left?"

After a quick search, a bottle of red wine was found, and further back in the fridge Dawn produced some olives and cheese.

"And here's some crackers," Lucia offered.

Again, the small end table was ready and the three relaxed and nibbled.

"And now a toast." Al lifted his glass, "To the gutsiest and most beautiful women in the world."

Dawn and Lucia drank and laughed.

"You're almost too much," Dawn offered.

"And" Lucia offered, "you're the man who protects and loves us."

"Well, that's a bit strong, but I humbly accept your gratitude. But now, how about some glorious sounds from the piano before I leave?"

With that, Lucia was seated and slowly lifted the keyboard cover. Softly a Chopin nocturne floated. Then suddenly, Lucia stopped playing.

"Is there something wrong?" Al asked.

"I don't know, but a couple of the keys seem sticky." And with that, Lucia lifted the piano lid and elevated it into place. Then Lucia struck a few notes and peered into the exposed strings.

"Well! What do we have here but a necklace!"

Both Dawn and Al instantly had their heads inside the piano.

"Look over there by those hammers," Dawn was excited. "That's the cheap necklace I described and my make-up compact."

Having retrieved their small treasury from the piano, everybody began to laugh.

"Now what do we make of this?" Al asked.

"Superficially, it makes no sense whatsoever," Lucia suggested. "Here is most of the junk we reported missing. So what did the burglars get for their effort? Nothing that I can see except the pleasure of wrecking the place and scaring us."

"You're right, Lucy, but why did they break in, wreck the place and pretend they were after something valuable? And then dump their loot into the piano?" For a few seconds, Al sat silent. "There's much more to this than seems probable," Al added.

"What leads you to that decision, Professore?" Dawn seemed to doubt.

"Okay, this is my analysis. For reasons we don't know, Leone is now desperate to get some of my valuable papers, documents he must recover. So he and some demented accomplice get in, ransack the place and find nothing. The accomplice finds the cheap jewelry and junk, takes the pieces and hides them in the piano. Together they leave empty-handed, but the stupid assailant will return later to reclaim his treasure which he thinks is valuable."

"You may be right, Al," Lucia conceded. "So what do we do now?"

"Yes," Dawn added, "What do we do now? Tell Ruffo that we found all of our junk in the grand piano? That would be a real laugh and we are accused of arranging a phony robbery."

"You're right, ladies. So we don't tell anybody. But I'm afraid we must be alert to the possibility that the accomplice will return to claim his little treasury."

Again both women agreed.

"So what do we do? Stay here in the dark and wait for the bumbler?" Dawn asked.

"No, you don't," Al mumbled, "I'm going to spend the night here with you and with the presence of both cars, I don't believe the burglar would make another effort."

Both women seemed much relieved, then Dawn dropped a small bomb-shell. "Al, you don't have to stay unless you really want to and, quite frankly, I feel safer with you here. But I want to show you something that I have and wouldn't hesitate to use if I were forced. I'll get it. It's in a small bag under a loose board in my closet."

Seconds later, Dawn returned triumphant, holding a small, almost tiny pistol in her right hand.

Both Al and Lucia were speechless.

"This," Dawn almost gloated "is a Velo dog revolver with a folding trigger which I can carry in the palm of my hand. It fires a .22 caliber cartridge and is not accurate at more than twenty-five feet."

Both Lucia and Al were excited and shocked.

Quickly Dawn explained that her father had given it to her not as a joke, but a real weapon whose original purpose was to ward of dogs who were snapping at cyclists' heals.

"Furthermore," Dawn bragged, "before Dad gave me this pistol, he taught me marksmanship and took me hunting for ducks and deer with shot guns and rifles. So when we practiced with the Velo dog pistol, I quickly became accurate at short distances."

"Here," Dawn offered, "take a look at this deadly toy pistol. As I said, it isn't accurate at distances, but close up it could produce a small, nasty wound. And I suppose were its small caliber to penetrate the brain, it could cause death."

Lucia and Al carefully examined the tiny pistol. "It looks more like a toy than a real pistol," Al ventured.

After further scrutiny, Lucia returned it to her roommate with the comment, "I'm really glad you showed us the pistol, but why didn't you mention it sooner?"

"Quite honestly because I forgot about it; not that my carrying it in my purse would have changed anything, and in all probability even now I can't believe any situation would arise when I would want to use it. But just its presence offers a sense of security."

An awkward silence followed which Dawn broke with the surprising comment, "Am I revealing something about myself which you find strange?"

"No, or course not," Al answered, "but because you are a very pretty woman and very feminine, I do find it hard to believe that you could be a 'pistol-packing mama.'"

As Lucia and Al laughed, Dawn added, "You don't know how I was. I've described both of my parents as frivolous pleasure seekers—which they were as teenagers and young adults. But as they really matured, they also developed strong but liberal values. Sure they spoiled me, particularly as a child, but they also helped me to understand the meaning of responsibility, honesty and love."

"I mention these facts because for all of my blase, flippant remarks, I learned a lot from my parents, perhaps more from my father, who hadn't been the spoiled brat that my mother was. Not that mom didn't develop a strong value system after her wild days. She did, and today is more a pillar of Fort Bragg society than Dad. Am I boring you with this confessional?"

"No, of course not, but you are helping me realize your real strength," Lucia spoke softly and sincerely.

"I really appreciate your candor, Dawn, not that you haven't been open and honest. And I mean honest in the sense of revealing your inner self." Al added.

"So in reference to this little pistol which Dad gave me as a small protective device, he also gave me another weapon to ward off overly-aggressive suitors. Here are a couple of perfume bottles I often carry in my purse. One is the real Channel No. 5 and the other is not Caron's Nuit de Noel, but an ounce and a half of the powerful barbiturate, chloral hydrate which, when slipped into somebody's drink, well soon induce peaceful slumber."

Surprised by Dawn's revelation, Al asked, "Do you have a sleeping problem?"

"No, I don't, but any overly-aggressive male who is determined to get in my pants will develop a sleeping problem in a few minutes, particularly if he already has had several drinks."

"Have you ever had to use it?" Al asked.

"Only once. Last year, I dated a big, handsome football jerk in Palo Alto. We were all alone in a booth and this boob came on really strong, so when he got up to take a leak, I dumped about a half-ounce of choral hydrate in his drink. And when he returned, I offered a toast, "Here's to the guy with the best and the most." He quickly tossed it off and order another whisky."

"Yea, and what happened?"

"I was a bit nervous and asked him not to have another drink but he did, and within minutes he was snoring like a drunk."

"Then what?" Lucia asked.

"Not much. I just walked out, got a taxi and went back to my apartment."

Both Al and Lucia were surprised by this unexpected revelation.

"Well," Al observed, "your father really took a protective interest in you."

"Quite!" Dawn suggested. "I'll reveal one other secret, and this will pretty much complete the missing pieces of my short life."

"As I was the only child, I was pretty spoiled and wild. Both of my parents would swim nude as would I if nobody was around. Well, one night when I was about fourteen, my Dad and I were swimming and we had a playful water fight, at least that how things got started. Soon we were grabbing each other, but then he got me from behind and began rubbing my boobs and then he slips his other hand into my crotch. At this, I screamed 'let go of me.'"

Now both Al and Lucia were speechless and only listened in total embarrassment.

"Well, Dad almost immediately let me go and I quickly got out of the pool and put on my clothes. Dad also quickly dressed and tried to talk to me. He kept repeating, 'Please forgive me darling. Please, please forgive me.' Well, I didn't say a word, but ran into the house and my bedroom."

"And your father?" Lucia asked.

"Oh, he stood, tapping on my locked door and whispering, 'Dawn, please let me talk. I didn't mean to frighten you. It was only a game.'"

For several seconds, nobody spoke until Al asked, "How did you resolve this terrible problem?"

"It took a relatively long time, several weeks before I finally relented and we had a long, very private talk. Fortunately, he was very contrite and wept real tears; he was terribly embarrassed. Gradually, over a long period, I always wore a swimsuit and tried to avoid any contact which might be embarrassing."

"Did your mother know anything about your confrontation, or the obvious distance you had created with your father?"

"No, Al. My only solution was to repeat the old female complaint, 'men are real jerks, boy! Guys can really be a pain, et cetera.' But I suspect that Mom had figured out about what happened."

"And how did it end?" Lucia asked.

"Not quickly. I really made my Dad suffer. But the result was that it finally brought us closer together than we had ever been. In the end, or really what became the final resolution, was that Dad taught me about guns and shooting and how to handle myself in difficult times and places. Hence this deadly toy pistol and the choral hydrate and, oh yes, one other thing. He also taught me how to fight and kick—in any male's most vulnerable place—his balls."

Again seconds of silence followed by explosions of laughter from Al and Lucia.

When the laughter dwindled, Al offered appreciation for such an emotional confessional. Then Lucia, emotionally charged, spoke slowly and bitterly about how her stepfather had arranged a wonderful birthday party for her and a few of her best friends at an elegant restaurant. "Then following my fourteenth birthday, he took me to his shop and under a false pretext, he gave me more champagne, laced with choral hydrate, I'm sure, and a Gucci case. When the drug took hold, he raped me. I still have nightmares about the struggle and the pain."

Sobbing convulsively, Lucia continued, "I cannot and will not ever forgive that evil, rotten, son-of-a-bitch who married my mother and then killed her and my baby brother in a car accident."

Following these emotional explosions, the trio sat quietly as Al consoled and alternatively hugged and gently kissed each woman on the cheek.

At last, the tears dried, Dawn and Lucia returned from the bathroom and each hugged Al who hopefully suggested, "Let's all go out to some nearby place and have a light supper. Then return and have some badly needed rest and sleep."

"We don't need to drive," Lucia suggested, "but let's leave the house lights on and the shades drawn. Not that I think we're in danger."

Somehow between their mutual affection and shared agonies, they soon found a quiet trattoria, dined pleasantly and upon return, were almost ready for bed by ten.

"Good night and pleasant dreams, Dawn" Al called, to which Dawn whispered, "Sweet dreams, you love birds."

Chapter Five

Michele Angelo Leone slowly awakened, glanced at the bedside clock, 7:30, paused then slowly but effortlessly raised himself to a sitting position. Reluctantly he moved his athletic body over the smooth blue silk sheets toward the bedside.

Now sitting upright under the scarlet silk brocade canopy Michele waited seconds before answering the tapping on the bedroom door, some fifteen feet distant.

An attractive young maid quickly pushed a small cart toward the imposing bedchamber.

"And what have you prepared for me, dear girl?"

Smiling, Maria, in a beguiling soft voice answered, "For you, Signore, a pot of fresh coffee, cream and sugar, orange juice and two freshly-baked sweet rolls. Is there anything more you might wish?"

"No, dear child, that's fine, you may go."

Quickly Michele eased himself from the bed and visited the large adjoining bathroom, then returned to the bedside cart.

As he poured the coffee and glanced at the Herald Tribune the maid had placed on the cart, his eye caught the words, "Sicilian Mafia."

"So what are my old enemies up to now?"

Quickly he scanned the stories. So they killed the prosecutor and threaten Craxi; U.S. Protests Craxi's Release of Abbas; and what's this? Craxi accepts U.S. Missiles?

Michele seemed amused by the problems the Craxi government was having.

Having completed his breakfast, Michele turned his thoughts directly to his immediate problems: the break-in and the robbery. "Whatever got me to ransack their apartment? Why did I ever listen to Benito and his stupid idea that Lucia might have some of my papers there? Or that the American professor was closely involved with Lucia. Why would a young beautiful woman and her roommate become friends of Praitt?"

Again, Michele reviewed what he knew. "First, what really happened in Ristorante Moro? According to the police, Benito and some other idiot had dated the two women, had something to eat and Benito got drunk, belligerent and was injured. Then he was arrested and held in jail and I got him out and paid his 50,000 Lire fine."

Just reflecting on the problem triggered a barrage of questions: "Why did I ever hire the kid? For a few days he's okay and then he does something really stupid, but this last episode was too much, either he cleans up his act fast or I fire him.

"But that stupid burglary – that was a dumb, real dumb, Italian stunt. No Sicilian would be that dumb. Yes, that's what happened to me when I became a smart Italian businessman!

"Shall I tell him that I know he took the jewelry – mere trinkets, worthless but I saw him slip them in his pocket and then drop them into the piano?

"Damn, of course he intended to return later to get the junk. Okay! that does it. I must talk to him today and threaten him.

"Now, what's my suggestion for lunch with Professor Praitt? He must know a lot about Lucia and that woman, Dawn, who shares her apartment. I must know whether Lucia has told her about my papers and if Lucia could have shared 'the rape' story with her. From the distance, she appeared very beautiful. And from the books in the apartment Miss Dawn Knight is a student here from Stanford – but for the breaks I would have gotten my degree there instead of Rome.

"As for Praitt, he's smart but that story he's writing? From what little I read no publisher would accept it. Still I've got to take him to lunch, find out how much he knows and if he seems to have important information I can use to bribe him or frame him.

"After I see Praitt or should I see Ruffo first? Of course see the Inspector who will see Lucia and the woman Dawn and probably Praitt. As soon as possible I'll take Ruffo out to some expensive hotel restaurant, and find out if he knows anything about the rape charges. But that was six years ago before Ruffo was promoted to Inspector. Well, I've helped him often and sent him several valuable gifts which should be more than enough to have him completely on my side when and if necessary."

Having completed his mental agenda, Michele returned to his ornate marble bathroom and quickly showered and shaved. For several minutes he studied his handsome face – his forehead and cheek bones – then he weighed himself, seventy-five kilos, flexed his muscles and scrutinized his hairy chest and well-proportioned frame. "Can any woman resist me? Not many with my looks and money. But I must first find the right one. I would prefer an Italian, not a Sicilian who are too demanding. Italians are beautiful when they are young but after marriage and one or two kids they put on weight and soon they're domineering fat ladies.

"But not Lucia's mother, Eleni, who was really an Italian-American and absolutely beautiful and very intelligent – smarter than I. And to think that because that stupid peasant was driving his tractor while pulling a loaded wagon on the autostrada caused my darling Eleni to die and my infant son and almost me. Sometimes I wish I had died too."

Having completed his morning ablutions Michele selected a hand-tailored three piece gray worsted wool suit, then carefully selecting a matching tie and polished black loafers, he was the very model of a wealthy Florentine gentleman.

From his study Michele placed a call to the Inspector and left the message to return his call.

Minutes later the Inspector had Michele laughing. "Yes, right Inspector. You would be pleased with the ristorante in the Hotel Excelsior. Fine, yes, about one. See you soon."

It's close, Michele reflected and the Inspector always enjoys expensive places and particularly when I'm picking up the bill.

Now with his self-image and esteem restored, Michele was ready for the world but he never questioned was the world ready for Signore Michele Angelo Leone.

While waiting in the ornate lobby of the hotel, Michele discreetly but carefully studied each female who casually strolled between small shops which contributed to the size and the opulence of the Excelsior.

Within the short period of fifteen minutes before the Inspector arrived, Michele had made eye contact with several beautiful women all of whom responded with smiles and attention. Had the Inspector not arrived a minute sooner, an attractive young woman would have completed her furtive move toward Michele.

With greetings and handshakes the male ritual took them directly to the capo primo who escorted them to a discreet setting where both men could discuss their agendas while feasting their eyes on beautiful women.

After the waiter had brought them menus and poured two glasses of water, he departed.

"It's good to see you again, Inspector. You're looking very well and very handsome in your uniform."

"Please, Michele, we've known each other long enough to skip formalities. You know my name is Giovanni, so let's keep it that way. That Inspector title always bothers me particularly with people I know and like."

"Of course you're right, Giovanni, but in my business I must be circumspect about names and titles. You know how many rich Florentines and Italians in general love titles and uniforms. It gives them pride and prestige and actually keeps unwanted persons from getting too close. And our manners and uniforms also add a certain allure for young women. Don't you agree, Giovanni?"

"Of course, you have no idea how some women flirt and it must be the elegant uniform because I'm not the handsome dandy you are, Michele. Still I do reasonably well but I must be very careful, my wife, you know. If she caught me, well, if she didn't castrate me, she would be very difficult to live with."

"You're absolutely right. No Italian male can stand up to his wife's or his girl friend's rage. Our women are very different from the French, English or American. Their husbands and lovers aren't the jealous bitches that we usually must suffer."

Their conversation was interrupted by the waiter who quickly took their orders and soon returned with an acceptable red wine and a plate of antipasto.

Now lowering his voice, Michele asked, "Giovanni, what do you make of the silly burglary of my step-daughter's apartment? What reason would anybody have to rob the place? I haven't seen it but from my long conversation with Professor Praitt, it's small and attractive and I don't believe that Lucia or Miss Knight had anything valuable there."

"You're absolutely right, Michele. I didn't and won't bother to see the apartment. But it is strange that any skilled burglar would risk detection for whatever valuables he could steal. It's a nice neighborhood but there are no indications of wealth or valuables in any of those small houses or apartments – it's not an expensive neighborhood. And from what the professor and the two women told me, they didn't lose much, nothing of any real value, a coin purse, two cheap necklaces and a few trinkets. Their only real loss was their confidence and several broken things when the burglars ransacked the apartment."

Still affecting a serious mien, Michele continued, "Apparently the three friends were in Greve and Panzano. I believe that's what Lucia had said – not to me because she has refused to speak to me or have anything to do with me for several years ever since the terrible accident in which my wife, Eleni, who was Lucia's mother, was killed as was my infant son; and, I too was seriously injured all because some stupid peasant had gotten his tractor and trailer illegally on to the autostrade. I sometimes wish that I had been killed too. My life has never been the same."

"Yes, Michele, I remember reading about that accident which also resulted in the peasant's death.

"But getting back to the robbery, I tried to assuage the women's pain and fear. Quite probably the robbery was the work of a couple of teenagers who were wandering through the neighborhood looking for something to steal. So they checked Lucia's apartment, somehow got the door open or more likely got in through the unlocked garage. Nervous and with no skills, they didn't bother to look through drawers and closets. They just dumped everything and were angry when there wasn't anything but the necklaces and purse."

"So you think it was probably a couple of boys, obviously not skilled or smart, who did the job?" Michele asked.

"Oh, I'm almost certain. No adult would be that stupid", Giovanni laughed.

"When did you talk to Lucia and the other woman, Dawn, and the Professor?

"Just yesterday, Michele. And while it was necessary that I conduct an investigation, it was rather pointless. I assured them that the burglary division would conduct a very serious investigation if for no other reason than to avoid any criticism from the Stanford University people or possibly some criticism from the Mayor's office."

"And you satisfied them, Giovanni? What is the Knight woman like and what did you think of the professor?"

"Oh, yes. Both women and the professor were satisfied. As for Miss Dawn Knight she is very beautiful and charming and very, very sexy. I didn't listen much to the man but he seemed to be reasonable and intelligent. He is also a very macho man. He reminds me of you but of course you are much younger. My impression was that both women were very interested in the American professor."

At this point Michele could feel twinges of jealously and outrage, "How could either Lucia or Dawn be interested in a man old enough to be their father?"

Rather than display any sign of annoyance Michele abruptly changed the subject to politics. "What do think of Craxi's government, Giovanni?"

Surprised that Michele would switch the subject from women and sex to politics, Giovanni appeared reluctant to answer, not because he wasn't interested in politics but simply because he enjoyed talking about sex and women more than what the Prime Minister was or wasn't doing.

But to avoid any social improprieties Giovanni, the policeman, whispered, "Michele, we public officials aren't supposed to discuss politics on the job. But additionally I don't really know what Mr. Craxi is doing except that the Americans don't seem to like him."

"One final question about the robbery and your talk with the three victims. Did you return the Professor's folder with the unfinished story?"

"Certainly, Michele. It was very important to him."

"Did you read any of it, Giovanni?"

"Yes, I confess that I read some of it but it made no sense to me. But the professor was obviously pleased to get it back."

"Well, I didn't see it but from the brief conversation I had with him about his story, I'm glad he has it." Michele answered with an air of finality.

For a few more minutes the two men exchanged gentlemen's lies then laughing, stood, waiting for the waiter.

"Thank you, an excellent lunch, Michele. You are always a pleasure to talk with. Let's consider the alleged robbery or whatever it was, a closed book."

The two men hugged, shook hands, and agreed to see each other again soon.

Minutes later, Michele strolled through the almost empty lobby. Then, remembering some unfinished business, he called his shop. After repeated rings, he realized that it was now after three. None of his employees were there. Nevertheless he found a taxi and ordered the driver, "The shop of Mr. Leone, Objets d'Art."

Pausing before his distinguished shop Michele felt a certain pride in his achievement noting the small gold lettering: hours 10 to 1 p.m. Tuesday through Saturday or by special appointment. Offices in Rome, Paris New York and San Francisco.

Having enjoyed his quiet reverie, Michele produced two handsome bronze keys. Quickly he inserted one key in a concealed fitting behind decorative door plates. He always took a full measure of satisfaction in the security system – both keys locking the very heavy metal door to the frame while simultaneously disarming or arming the security system.

Closing the door softly, Michele quietly surveyed the elegant interior, a few framed paintings, several bronze castings, two showcases of ivory carvings and various expensive candlesticks and small silver trays.

Passing through this large major showroom, carpeted with heavy oriental rugs, he unlocked the door to his combination office and small living-suite with bedroom and adjoining bath and closet, his own design and the occasional scene of a needed sexual liaison. (He rarely had such exclusive encounters in his large house in Fiesole. This was reserved for large social events or important business-social affairs for friends or occasionally employees.)

Now remembering the importance of knowing and "working" Professor Praitt he prepared to place his call. With the operator's assistance he called Praitt in Greve.

After some five minutes his phone rang and a pleasant operator's voice said, "Signore Leone, Professor Praitt is ready."

Quickly Michele, in an explosive and friendly voice, "Professor Praitt, I'm happy to reach you after these days of turmoil. How are you, sir? Good, I'm glad to hear that. Of course this whole robbery business was a nasty and miserable experience, particularly for Lucia and Miss Knight. Yes, I had a long talk and serious meeting with Inspector Ruffo today. Yes, he's certain that the break-in was the work of two or possibly three teenagers."

For a few minutes the conversation was a medley of deception, lies and laughter. Then Michele suggested a lunch meeting. Again at a handsome ristorante in Florence. "One is the popular Ristorante La Loggia in the Piazzale Michelangelo. Great food and a wonderful view of the city. And another favorite is the Trattoria Cammillo, its food is excellent."

"We need not decide now. Why don't you come to my shop very near the Ponte Vecchio, really the first street across the bridge toward the main side. Yes, it's called the Porta Santa Maria, my shop is 98 and it's very near Ferragamo's wonderful shop. Would about twelve be okay? Yes, that would give us plenty of time to talk, eat and get to know each other a little better. I'm not the monster I've been called on occasion. Good, then noon at my shop and we'll go from there for some excellent food. Thank you very much, Professor. You are a real gentleman."

Having hung up Michele danced a jig and gloated, "I've hooked the fish! Now can I land him?"

Al was equally pleased with the invitation to eat and talk. "Why don't I let him ask the questions? That allows me the opportunity to understand him better and tease him with information which might please but really confuse him."

For several minutes Al sat thinking. "Maybe I should call Lucia and ask for her advice. After all she knows Leone and how he thinks far better than I could possibly imagine."

Minutes later, Lucia answered with the customary soft "Pronto". Then recognizing Al's baritone, she was elated, "Oh, darling! How wonderful ! You read my mind. I was just about ready to call you. Oh, we've cleaned the place up. Actually it's cleaner and neater than it was before the break-in. And we bought a couple of chairs and other unimportant items. So we're perfectly comfortable."

Pleased with everything Lucia offered, Al inquired about the importance of discussing what he should or should not say during his lunch date with Leone.

Embarrassed that he had forgotten to mention the meeting with Leone, Lucia was momentarily stunned then quickly recovered, "Darling, this is an idea. Oh, he proposed it? In a way that's better because you can let him talk all he wants. When are you meeting? Oh yes, both ristorantes are excellent."

Then reflecting on the necessary preparations, Al should plan for the lunch-verbal skirmish, Lucia quietly asked, "Darling, why don't you come here today and we can plan your strategy?'

Al was very pleased with Lucia's attractive invitation. "Of course, dear lady, I'll come. When? Well, as fast as I can put a few things in the car and get there. It's early so I should reach your place about noon. And I'll take you and Dawn to lunch."

Informed that Dawn had a morning class and two afternoon classes, Al was quietly elated.

"You would rather have lunch there, in your apartment? Fine. But I'll bring something good."

As both were overjoyed, Lucia immediately took a shower, splashed on some seductive perfume, carefully remade her bed with clean sheets and then prepared a light lunch. Such was her excited planning that she forgot to put on a bra.

Finally with plans complete she sat quietly as her brain and her body struggled for appropriate responses.

The sound of an approaching car had her on her feet. She rushed to the window just in time to see Al grab his bag and almost run toward the steps.

As he reached the landing, Lucia swung open the door and without a word, embraced her man for seconds while quietly murmuring, "Darling, darling, how wonderful!"

Al managed to release his small bag and returned Lucia's affection with a long, soft kiss. Her smooth lips and sensuous mouth electrified his body and temporarily short-circuited his brain.

Finally both lovers realized that their brazen behavior was a public exhibition and quickly moved into the living room. For several seconds they clung tightly against each other which only increased their passionate energy.

Almost reluctantly they parted and quickly settled together on the couch as Al attempted to conceal his very stiff erection which had aroused Lucia and like a sexual magnet had attracted her firm breasts to pulsate against Al's broad shoulders.

For another brief interlude they sat in a locked embrace unable to speak as their mouths and tongues teased in the language of love.

At last their brains halted the threatening storm and slowly reason was restored.

In embarrassed hushed tones, Lucia offered, "Darling, I didn't mean to get you disturbed but my body just got carried away."

Al was tempted to add something about his body's excited behavior but quickly responded with, "Darling Lucia, our bodies were just greeting each other."

"Well, yes, but first things first, lunch, our battle strategy and if Dawn isn't here maybe we should allow our bodies to get together. After all, it's been a long time for no loving body language."

"You are so wonderful and so intelligent, Lucia. I am ready at your command.

"Food, talk, plans. Can we keep our bodies quiet while other important plans discussed?"

"That will be difficult for me, darling, but if you promise me something, I'll quickly feed you, plot with you and then bed you."

Food was expedient and quickly washed down with a soft Pinot Grigio as they ate and talked. Al explained how Leone had phoned and very skillfully maneuvered him into a conciliatory mood by adding "I know some people think I'm a monster". Actually I was eager to see him, perhaps even more so than he was. So we have much to learn from each other. Now, darling, what are your words of wisdom which will help us win?"

"First, my love, if you can understand but not allow my rage to overpower your reason, first and foremost, what does he want from you? And why do you think he believes you can help him recover his very important and incriminating papers? Even I, who had seen some of those papers only a few hours after that monster, Leone, had raped me, didn't know what was in the large bundle of documents and money. After all I was just fourteen years old and was completely devastated by the events on the night of my so-called birthday party."

"And under the circumstances which you mentioned recently, you hid many of the papers but left the money with the other documents?"

"Yes, I was nervous about the money which the police took along with some official-looking documents. The other papers and pictures, probably of young Asian prostitutes, my grandfather took and still has. And I certainly hope they are hidden where Leone can't possibly retrieve them. These are the papers he desperately wants for they must have all the information which could kill him and probably send him to prison for life."

"But you really don't know the extremely damaging content of those papers, do you, darling?'

"Of course I don't know but I have every reason to believe that those papers contain information about the Mafia which is extremely important to its leaders, the government and probably some important politicians. The reason I believe these papers are extremely important is because on several occasions Michele told me that I should be very careful about any strangers who looked suspicious. He also told me that a Mafia assassin had murdered his father and threatened his mother. The he made a face and pretended that he had slit the assassin's throat."

"Do you believe his story?"

"Yes, I really do if for no other reason than that Leone never went anywhere without a bodyguard for many years. Only recently did he seem relaxed but I believe he still always carries a gun". Lucia seemed elated but morbid by her revelations.

"Do you suppose that his guarded behavior has anything to do with his business?" Al asked.

"Quite possibly." Lucia added, "After all he was dealing in expensive art things, everything from pictures and jewelry to expensive wall hangings and arty things. He knew a great deal about these which accounts for the wealth he accumulated from his shop in Rome – where he started about twenty years ago, also here in Firenze and in Paris, New York and San Francisco."

Al was almost shocked, "I had no idea that he had stores in San Francisco and New York."

"The only reason for his store in San Francisco is because he was there as an exchange student in high school and he came back later and spent his junior year at Stanford, just as Dawn is doing now."

"Well, that does explain many things," Al added, "his apparent affection for the U.S., his perfect English, without the trace of an accent. And perhaps most importantly he is a very smart and a highly educated man."

"Absolutely, darling, and with his good looks and personality, there isn't much that he doesn't know or can't do – except keep his hands off beautiful women ." Again Lucia's voice reeked of scorn.

"After all, darling, he swept my mother off her feet only two years after my father's death and the loss of, first, my uncle in Vietnam , then immediately after Dad's death, my grandfather and then my grandmother either died or committed suicide.

"We were both devastated and could no longer remain in California even with all the support we got from friends and the community. I really loved the Napa Valley and the entire Bay Area, particularly, San Francisco where Dad kept an apartment that where we could stay on our frequent visits. Then suddenly everything ended." Lucia could hardly speak as tears dripped from her cheeks.

For a minute or more Al held her closely stroking her hair and kissing her forehead.

"Yes, I can't imagine a more tragic fate which may explain my anti-religious behavior. True, I don't believe either Mom or Dad were believers, at least they never said grace or attended church but also they almost never criticized religion overtly or ever suggested any beliefs one way or the other. But they did enjoy what many people would call religious music."

"Like what?" Al asked

"Several masses, particularly Mozart's but also Verdi's and I think Faure. But there were other religious pieces. Gounod's Ave Maria and Schubert's. There's a large body of religious music that atheists and non-believers like us can enjoy for its beauty and not its message."

Now aware of the time, Lucia glanced at her watch. "Darling, do you feel prepared for the verbal battle with Signore Leone tomorrow? Now you know much about him and if knowledge is armor you are ready for battle. But, darling, even if you didn't have the facts we've discussed, I know that in the end you will win and therefore I too will win!"

"Are you ready for what is now the most beautiful feast we can share? Let's hurry before Dawn returns and dampens our libidos."

In less than a minute Al and Lucia had disrobed and stood enjoying each other's bodies. "Darling you are the most gorgeous woman I've ever seen clothed but you are more beautiful naked. From your silky dark hair, soft adoring eyes high cheek bones, perfect nose and flaring nostrils and breasts! Oh! such lovely gorgeous rising breasts, tilting toward heaven – beyond description and that lovely flat tummy, enticing and compelling to that dark, satiny covering of love's treasury."

"Darling, lover! Do you really want me? Words! Words! Do you want me to sing paeans of longing and begging for that tall sturdy member now throbbing for love and passion? I could caress your silken hairy chest and kissing the giant's waiting mouth and continue to delay the entrance of the god but for Christ's sake, as Dawn would say, let's fuck".

And so began their love feast a royal banquet of gourmet offerings of firm, ripe, pink cherries quivering atop twin volcanoes of warm tan flesh pressed hard against a chest of soft silken silver threads. As hungry salivating mouths and teasing tongues darted and chased, searching and exploring exotic crevices and marvelous treasures of bouquet and pleasure. Hands and fingers danced in rhythm to a ballet of bodies, arching and plunging to the vocal duet of soprano and baritone harmonizing their voices in songs of passion and ecstasy.

Finally, after a marathon of feasting, their every desire sated and their bodies exhausted, the lovers lay locked together in a dreamland of pleasure.

But suddenly their love tryst was shocked into reality.

"Whoops! I'm sorry" was Dawn's bugle-voiced call as she closed the bedroom door.

Immediately the dreamers were awake and standing in embarrassing nudity. "Damn", Al whispered.

"Oh hell! " Lucy added. Then with a laugh, "I guess we better get dressed before Dawn demands a part in our celebration".

Al laughed, "Well, we haven't been doing anything she hasn't done many times. Besides she knows that we are lovers and always sleep together whenever we get a chance."

Within minutes Lucia had dressed as Al showered and minutes later, fully clothed, they greeted Dawn in the living room.

"Hey, you two bedroom athletes, after that workout you need something to revive you." And with that Dawn handed each a glass of champagne. "I'd say bottoms up but that would be rather redundant so here's to love's greatest competitors! By the way who won and who lost?"

Al and Lucia burst into bawdy laughter. "Don't worry about us, Dawn." Lucia offered, "You're toasting two winners. We always win and never lose!"

Their shared comedy and laughter quickly squelched any embarrassment or annoyance.

"So what compelling interest other than the obvious brought you back to our fair city and apartment?" Dawn snickered.

"A very important appointment with our mutual antagonist, Signore Michele Leone", Al answered, "and yours and Lucia's advice on how I should conduct myself."

"Well, since I don't know this monster I can't offer you much advice, I'm afraid."

"But I think, as a woman, Dawn, you can probably suggest some ploys or advances that neither Al nor I have considered even though we spent considerable time discussing how I, a victim of the monster's lust, might trap or learn motives my one-time stepfather has in asking Al to have lunch with him tomorrow."

For a few seconds nobody spoke until Al explained, "He called me yesterday afternoon and very cordially asked me to have lunch with him tomorrow in an expensive restaurant. At first I was somewhat hesitant which Leone quickly picked up·on and added, 'I'm not the monster some people believe I am', an obvious reference to Lucia. So I went along with his line which was very clever and smooth".

"And what could I suggest or advise you to do, professor?" Dawn asked. "Nothing very specific or direct since I don't know what possible information he hopes to extract from your discussion. But I know as a woman what I would do. I would go along with his game, stroking his ego, admiring him and flattering him and doing anything reasonable to learn what he wants and why?"

"Brava, Dawn," Lucia enthused, "That's pretty much what I suggested and Al too had considered. But I also gave Al a lot of facts and information which I've never discussed with you, Dawn. Not because certain details of my four-year relationship with the son-of-a-bitch were a particular secret – they weren't but neither were they relevant to our friendship."

"But", Al added, "I think Dawn's suggestions particularly from a woman, might be and probably are both challenging and subtle. Obviously I couldn't be as beguiling or as tricky as you could be, Dawn."

For a few seconds nobody spoke. Then, suddenly, Lucia announced, "I've got a tricky idea, a real surprise."

Both Al and Dawn asked simultaneously, "What?"

"I propose, since I know how vulnerable Michele is to women and for that matter how equally or maybe even more so, women are to Michele."

"Yes?" Al asked.

"Simply, this is a calculated risk which won't hamper your style, Al, but without calling Leone, why don't you bring Dawn with you as a good friend you once knew in San Francisco".

Now both Al and Dawn smiled.

"Do you really believe that Leone would accept me or that my presence wouldn't compromise his ideas to the extent that he wouldn't reveal his motives for the meeting?"

Again several seconds of consideration.

"No, I don't, Dawn. As a matter of fact your presence would both please and challenge Michele. Of course he knows that we're roommates and that we have a lot of information. But much more importantly, as an Italian male, Mr. Leone's greatest weakness is beautiful women and particularly charming, intelligent blondes. Your presence, Dawn, would completely blow Leone's mind."

Now Al was excited, "Of course! Your presence and participation will completely change Leone's calculated plans while creating a strong sense of desire and lust."

"This is rapidly developing into an opportunity that I can't turn down. I like it. I really like it!" Dawn almost exploded.

"Okay, we're in total agreement but we must now prepare a short scenario about how and why I invited you to this men-only lunch meeting."

"Why don't you introduce me as your part-time secretary?" Dawn asked.

"No," Lucia quickly added, "He knows that you're here as a Stanford student. Let's not complicate the problem." Then turning directly to Al, she added, "Look, all you need to say is that you had a previous lunch engagement with Dawn so you brought her along to meet Leone because he knew that Dawn and I share this apartment."

"Okay", Al offered. "Of course you're right. And Leone may know more about Dawn than we think. Furthermore I'm certain that Dawn can quickly impress Leone to the point where he will decide to try his luck with her."

"Wait a minute, Professor! Exactly what are you suggesting?" Dawn sounded irritated.

"Of course not sex, Dawn, but what I'm suggesting is that you may very well so excite – if that's the word – Leone, that his efforts to entrap Lucia and probably me will be frustrated by your charm and beauty. Let's face it. Leone's greatest and most glorious weakness is his enchantment with beautiful women."

"So, I'm the selected decoy?" Dawn asked.

"That isn't my word or my intent", Al said apologetically. "But you do possess the charm, wit, intelligence and above all the appeal that could reduce Leone's determination to avenge Lucia's charges against him and further more possibly convince him that none of us knows anything about his important missing papers."

Al's argument eased Dawn's irritation.

"Now," Lucia added, "Neither Al nor I were suggesting that you are sexual bait for Leone's libido. But we all know that your presence would completely confuse Leone and give us the opportunity possibly to know what his plans are. What are his connections to Inspector Ruffo and the police? We all know that Leone and his black Mercedes continue to show up in unexpected places. For example, how did he know we visited my grandparents in Panzano which allowed him to tear this place apart and before that get into Al's house?"

"Good questions." Dawn replied, "but Mr. Leone couldn't collect all of this information without help. He must have an assistant, somebody who works for him. Yes, of course, that Benito guy who was giving us a lot of trouble that night we met you, Al, in that ristorante in Greve."

"Oh, I wasn't aware that Benito worked for Leone", Al offered.

Dawn, somewhat subdued offered, "I guess that I missed the big episode. I seem to recall getting way-laid that night."

"So that's what it was, Dawn. I thought you said something about passing out or sleeping."

"Okay, let's skip that part and focus on Benito. Didn't you date him a few times, Lucy? Or have lunch with him?" Dawn snickered.

"Yes, I did but never a date until that night we met Al when he was celebrating his birthday and Mozart's. I used to swim and still do at the Tuscany Sports Club. He was a swimming instructor and lifeguard and helper for the club owner. But until that night in the restaurant he was a perfect gentleman. **And that first date was the day we went skiing but neither he nor your date, Dawn, skied."**

"Right, and that bozo I was with was Carlo but I didn't know his last name and I would like to forget the entire evening."

"Well", Lucia added, " I most certainly would too except for the fact that was the night we–I met Al. Another strange thing about that night, Carlo kept calling my date, Benito but he used the name Bernardo Rosso. And the handsome young man I knew introduced himself as Bernardo Russo.

"Could they have been twins?" Al asked.

"Maybe, but I wouldn't think so. They looked exactly alike, had the same mannerisms and except for that night, always behaved politely and sincerely."

"Quite probably", Dawn added "when Benito-Bernardo starts drinking his personality changes and his behavior certainly changed that night."

"Wait a minute. We're off the subject. We were suggesting that Leone must have a flunky of some kind. Could this guy you know as a swimming instructor at the Sports Club also work for Leone?"

Both women seemed perplexed, "I suppose that's possible, Al. Sure, Why not? When Benito-Bernardo isn't drinking, he's perfectly okay. Don't you agree, Dawn?"

"I suppose so, Lucy, but I hardly know the guy."

Eager to complete their plans for Dawn's introduction to Leone, Al added, "Let's forget that guy; let's not worry who's Leone's assistant. Now, here's my idea, Dawn. You will accompany me to Leone's shop tomorrow. I'll explain to him that several days ago I had invited you to lunch today and had then forgotten about it. Now you have accepted my necessary change to dine with Signore Leone."

"And you think Leone will accept that story?" Dawn asked. "Suppose he refuses then what do we do?"

"Oh, he won't refuse," Lucia quickly cut in. "He'll fall all over himself with charming agreement. I can't possibly imagine him rejecting Al's proposal. No, he can't if for no other reason than his determination to pick Al's brains. Your appearance, Dawn, may also undermine Leone's plans to trip Al into admitting something that Leone wants or needs".

"Now we're getting somewhere, "Al agreed. "So after introductions and the pleasure of including Dawn to the lunch-chess game, what's next?"

"I think you're getting ahead of the chess game, to use your term, Professor." Lucia smiled. "We must first dress Dawn suitably for the occasion.

"So," Dawn laughed, "Now you're going to tell me what to wear? Perfume? Do my hair? And what else would you two Svengalis advise? Or could you possibly accept the fact that I probably know more about trapping men, tricking men and performing my own enticements for men than both of you amateurs could imagine?"

"Touche, Dawn," Al joked.

"Of course you know far more about how to present yourself than we."

"Good. Now I'll share a few secrets with you. I have a particularly snug-fitting skirt which definitely outlines my well-endowed fanny and it's just an inch below the knee which, while acceptable as a fashion piece creates a magnetic impact on male libidos. And the blouse for that skirt is a loose, low-cut baby blue silk piece with three buttons for lower exposure and without a bra, I can create considerable heat and excitement. Because of the problems this outfit creates, I only wear it on certain occasions."

"Wow!" I can hardly wait," Al laughed.

"Good, glad you agree," Dawn added. "As for shoes and stockings, no problem. Medium high pumps, dark of course, burgundy. And then the jewelry. Nope, don't have any. Oh yes, I've got a small gold cross the thieves didn't get because I always carry it in my purse. That should celebrate my Christian virginity."

"Your what?" Al gushed.

"And for perfume, I've Channel, Joy and maybe Caron. I'll splash a bit of perfume in appropriate places. Then you'll have to help me fight off the amorous Mr. Leone."

"I can hardly wait to see you, Dawn. Maybe you'll have to fight me off before you do Leone," Al joked.

"Seriously, "Dawn added, "Are there any particular questions you think I should ask this monster?"

Both Al and Lucia pondered that question. "I am confident you will know exactly how to flatter him and tease but the only thing I would avoid is my relationship or his marriage. Just avoid it but should the monster touch on his marriage, either cut it short completely or possibly you could risk it with **something like, "Oh, you must have been a wonderful husband and lover"**

"Just play it by ear, Dawn," Al ventured. "I'll wager that Mr. Leone will be eating out of your hand while I only nod my head. Unless I overestimate his attitude toward pretty women, he will largely forget what he wanted from me. And I'll predict right now that he will request or demand a date with you as soon as possible."

"So we've got the scenario pretty well planned?" Lucia asked.

"Why not?" Dawn asked. "Unless Signore Leone concocts something far out, we should be able to play everything by ear."

"But now I'm ready for lunch." Lucia suggested.

With unanimous agreement, Al asked for something nearby, adding, "It's on me," and afterward, "I've got to get back to Greve for several important details. Okay?"

After a few minutes walk from their apartment, Lucia led them into a small cheerful trattoria one block from the river. As it was near closing time and the trio were the only diners, they soon demolished the pasta and cheese, a green salad and some fruit. And in a half-hour they were almost back at the apartment.

Once inside Lucia was subdued and quiet as Al collected his few personal items. Then Dawn reminded Lucia that she had a four o'clock class which triggered Lucia's memory that she too had a two-hour rehearsal at the Conservatory.

· With a flurry of hugs and kisses, Lucia accompanied Al to his car. "Darling, be very careful. I worry about you because you seem to be oblivious to the danger or it certainly doesn't worry you."

"That's not altogether true," Al conceded, "but I've learned to recognize danger and how to evaluate it. My Air Force career did teach me that. But thank you, darling. The only danger I would consider is losing you and that you might find another man."

At that they both laughed and after a long embrace, Al was in the car and then remembered . "Lucia, darling, I'll be here by ten tomorrow."

Although the traffic seemed rather heavy, Al maintained a moderate speed while carefully weighing Lucia's concerns about his safety. When first one speeding Alfa cut directly in front of him Al braked and avoided the second car which seemed ready to force him toward the car in the next lane. "Bastards!" he muttered. "I wonder if either one of those drivers was trying to take me out?" "Hardly," he considered, "there wouldn't be any reason. This is simply the way some of these idiots drive."

Continuing at reduced speed, about five minutes later the traffic stopped completely. For a very short time, with their engines still running, drivers sat quietly. Then suddenly one loud horn blasted which immediately triggered a constant barrage of horns and angry drivers. For a half hour no traffic moved as the motorcycle police twisted between the stalled traffic and waved signs with a large black X through the red outline of a horn. Miraculously the ear-splitting din silenced.

Minutes later the traffic, now directed into a single lane, where soon Al spotted the Alfa and a large Fiat smashed against each other.

Once past the scene of the accident, traffic thinned and shortly after five, Al parked his car near its usual place. It was getting dark as Al approached his house. At the gate his neighbor, Enrico appeared, "Buon Giorno! Professore, come va?"

"Bene, Enrico, e lui, bene?

"Si, buona sera."

With that greeting Al felt better; his apprehension from the accident melted away. Back in the house everything was exactly as he remembered. Still he felt some gnawing anxiety which again triggered a quick room-to-room survey. Then content with the house glowing in light, Al remembered that he had forgotten to ask about his "poste". Well, he questioned, do I really need to check? Do I need anything from the store? He checked his kitchen larder and decided that he had enough for breakfast–no need to drive down to Greve, he concluded.

For a few minutes Al sat quietly, then after reviewing the discussion and plans for spending at least two hours with Leone and considering the remote possibility that some unplanned or unexpected event might occur, Al was satisfied that he had taken every reasonable precaution necessary. Why not some music, piano of course and Beethoven, um, let's start with the Waldstein or the Tempest.

With that Al began flipping through the file of Beethoven CD's all neatly organized on the long shelf just above the radio and CD player. Quicky he found one which included four sonatas no. 21, op. 53 (The Waldstein), no. 17, op 31 (The Tempest) no. 26, op 81a (Les Adieux) and no. 24, op 78, played by Rudolf Buchbinder–what a find but I don't know this pianist.

Seconds later, Al slipped the CD into position and sat back as the silence was broken by a series of rapid chords then quickly repeated. Well, Mr. Buchbinder, you're pushing this allegro con brio. After nine minutes of piano pyrotechnics, Al was relieved by the beautiful slow movement. A short adagio molto. Then just as the final movement began, the telephone rang twice before he could offer a soft, "pronto."

"Oh, darling, I've been trying to reach you for the last half-hour. Have you been out?"

"Oh, no, Lucia, I've been home almost an hour and I was listening to a Beethoven sonata. Yes, the C Major, opus 53, the Waldstein. But I don't understand, you've been trying to reach me for a half-hour and you always get a busy signal?"

"Yes, and once I heard some kind of background noise."

"Were these sounds voices?"

"No, just a couple of clicking sounds much like, well, static, a metallic sound."

"Have you heard anything like this on your telephone before?"

"Yes, come to think of it. I have heard similar sounds and Dawn mentioned this static too."

"Okay, darling. I think the solution is obvious. But first, when did you first notice these sounds?"

"Only recently. I think since the burglary." By now the anxiety in Lucia's voice had waned.

"As I said this static is not anything unusual. Just a matter of static produced by the system itself or more likely by the automatic dialing system. More importantly, darling, you and Dawn are okay? No problem about tomorrow?"

"What in the world are you talking about, darling? " Lucia seemed annoyed or worried.

"Oh, nothing really, lady of my heart. I was just listening to some Beethoven."

Al heard a laugh, "Darling, have you been nipping or something? Say Courvoisier?"

"No but I guess my mind is caught somewhere between the Waldstein and tomorrow's meeting, my lunch with the interesting Mr. Leone. I've been thinking about him. He's really a nice guy. Maybe he isn't the real monster after all. But, darling I have something cooking in the kitchen. One final thing, I'll try to get there a little earlier than our schedule."

Before he could hang up, Lucia asked in a quick apprehensive voice, You don't sound exactly coherent, darling. Are you okay and not drunk?"

With a soft laugh, "No, neither, sweetheart. I'll explain tomorrow. But don't worry." And with that Al gently replaced the receiver only to return it to his ear in time to hear the distinct and familiar sound of phone disconnect.

Immediately he dialed Lucia's number, "Darling,me, No, I'm not crazy–our phone is tapped. Bye".

"Well! So il Signore Leone is listening in but only since setting up our meeting. I wonder if he has tapped Lucia's phone. Probably, because since he has ways of tapping mine, he must also have their phone tapped but I can't call back because any message from this phone will be recorded."

At this point Al turned up the volume on the CD player which by now was producing a different sonata. For a few seconds Al listened intently."Ah, The Tempest, the d minor, opus 32. Good music while I put together some soul food."

After a bowl of soup, a glass of wine and cheese and salami, Al was pleased– the food, the music, his woman and his discovery. "Mr. Leone, you're clever but you aren't really very smart."

With those final words, Professor Praitt visited his bathroom, turned off all the living room lights, except a table lamp and prepared for bed. Then remembering his small bag he removed everything except his folder and the enclosed manuscript. "This potboiler will be kept in a much safer place. Leone might still think it could be of value in a pinch."

Before slipping into bed, again Al roused himself, traversed the small living room, checked and locked the front door and then slipped the safety bolt softly into the ancient oak frame.

Back in his bedroom, Al glanced at a nearby Herald Tribune. "Why bother, it's old stale news." Quickly in bed with a final finger snap, the bedroom was dark and minutes later Al was lost in sleep.

Sometime after seven, Al rolled over, half asleep and reaching for Lucia's soft warm body and enticing smell, he panicked for a second. Then, wide awake, he laughed, "Too bad she isn't". For at least two minutes he basked in the totality of his love, "How could I have ever been so lucky to have found her!"

Quickly he completed his bathroom needs, finished shaving. Then remembering his appointment, he considered , "Suit or slacks? No, this suit, old but still passable. I always looked good in this Harris tweed." Pulling on his warm bathrobe he returned to the kitchen, prepared coffee and found some stale pastry. Now for orange juice and I should be out of here by eight-thirty. Then check for mail in Greve, pick up a Herald and reach the apartment by nine-thirty."

As he sat enjoying the modest breakfast, again he reviewed plans for Leone's Waterloo. "So you think you've got me on your line. Well, Don Juan, you are about to meet your match. Miss Dawn Knight is a rare combination of Aphrodite and Catherine the Great."

As Al dressed, he checked his mental list, remembered his "potboiler", then quickly ascended the spiral staircase but at the top reversed his direction and, folder in hand, descended and went directly to the baby grand. Carefully raising the lid to a fixed position, he checked the entire area under the lid and noted that the keyboard terminated several inches from the rounded tip of the body and here in this small empty area was sufficient space for his "potboiler" which he removed from the heavy manila folder. Quickly he secured the manuscript and lowered the lid to its closed position.

Just before leaving the house, he carefully filled the folder with a file of papers and useless notes. The he returned the folder to its original place next to the typewriter. Wouldn't it be a marvelous joke if Leone should again steal the folder.

Now ready for departure Al grabbed his bag, packed it quickly and locked the door securely. Although the temperature was a cool 10 degrees Celsius, in his top-coat he was comfortable.

Minutes later, Al parked in the almost empty Verrazano Square, accepted several letters from the smiling postmistress, got a Herald-Trib, then found a small box of chocolates for Lucia.

Already the traffic increased before Al reached Impruneta. He took the small bypass road which brought him almost around the west bank of the Arno, past the Bobolino and soon to the apartment. At nine-thirty with bag in hand, he bounded up the steps and into the waiting arms of Lucia.

They embraced and for seconds traded kisses. "Oh, darling, I'm so happy and relieved. After that call last night I was very worried but Dawn kept reassuring me that your mixed message was the only way you could alert us that Leone has our telephone bugged."

"Darling, when I realized what the static sounds were, that immediately alerted me that somebody had put a tap on our line and our conversation was being recorded. Fortunately I didn't blurt out my discovery and my first explanation about the static probably delighted the S.O.B. Well, now we know and he doesn't know that we know."

"So we have him by the short hairs, as you so love to be pubicly quaint."
Lucia laughed. "God, I'm lucky to have a handsome lover and brainy giant!"

"By the way, Lucy, how did your rehearsal go yesterday afternoon?"

"Well, considering all of my problems, plus yours and today's session
with the monster, after a few minutes of warming up, my practice turned out to
be satisfactory. My teacher listened to my first movement of the Appassionata
and praised my technique but offered some good advice on my tendency to
overstate a few passages. It was an excellent session for me. Once I get focused
my other worries vanish. That's the joy of the piano–it's a wonderful escape
mechanism for me."

"Maybe the piano is good therapy, as it is for me." Al volunteered. "How
I wish I could play but now it's too late, much too late."

"Not really, darling. I could teach you a few basic exercises."

"Maybe, Lucia. And if we had the time I would gladly accept your help. But
the facts are you've got a huge event coming up soon. In May, isn't it?

"Yes, it's an annual event , the May-June Maggio Musicale which the city
recently started, to bring in some money. I've been invited to be the principal
soloist because I got the honorable mention at the Tschaikovsky Competition
in Moscow last year."

"How wonderful! But you never mentioned that to me," Al cheered. "So
you really are a world famous pianist!"

"Hardly. You flatterer. I wish I were and I still hope to become an important player but, well, with your love maybe I might win some recognition."

"And whom do you prefer? Beethoven, Brahms, Chopin, Bach, Schubert?"
Al was very interested in her answer.

"All of them and several others too. Even Janacek and Schonberg and
Amy Beach."

"That's an astounding repertoire, darling. Do you play without the score?"

"Not completely, but once I've studied the piece and practiced it repeatedly–and with help–I can memorize it. But there are some composers who are
more difficult than others, for example, both Beethoven and Schubert, yes, and
Janacek. And several others too."

"My favorites, and I have several," Al added, "are the late Beethoven
string quartets 130, 131 and 132 and the last few piano sonatas particularly
106, the Hammerklavier."

"I agree," Lucy offered somewhat hesitantly, "It's very strange really, the only piece of Beethoven which I just can't understand. Oh, I can read the score and study his markings but there's something about the music, particularly the third movement which is very long, complicated and beautiful. But I just can't play it—it almost tears me apart with fear."

"Well, maybe not fear but awe and wonder." Lucy's voice trailed off in a whisper.

Somewhat bewildered by Lucy's melancholy tone, Al sought to comfort her. "Beethoven certainly was a complicated and tragic figure—as was Schubert for that matter. If anything, Schubert had a much worse existence. For all of Beethoven's problems, his hatred of nobility, his loss of hearing at an early age, his failed romances and assorted other family problems, unquestionably he was the musical giant and immediately after his death, funeral masses were held in almost all the European capitals."

"Yet poor Schubert, living in the same city as Beethoven, was hardly known or recognized and was rarely included in any of the social life which Beethoven often scorned. Two composers couldn't have lived and composed in the same city almost unknown to each other and suffered more ignominiously different fates. Beethoven, honored, but arrogant, fairly well-off, while Schubert, humble but known yet seldom recognized, composed some of the most lyrically beautiful music ever written with no hint of his poverty, illness and agony, then dying of syphilis at age thirty-one."

Al's somewhat pedantic lecture interested Lucy and surprised her. She had no idea that her lover was so well-read about music and composers.

Glancing at his watch, Al noted that it was eleven. "Lucy, is Dawn prepared for our noon sin-fest?"

For a second Lucy feigned confusion then laughed . 'Sin-fest?' Is that what you and Dawn are soon to partake?"

"For lack of a better phrase, 'sin-fest' might suggest our lunch date with Signore Leone," Al laughed. "We eat, we tell lies and generally behave like sinners."

Dawn suddenly burst into the room, "Sin-fest? I like your phrase. But how do you like my sin-dress?"

Al's immediate response was, "Wow! Dawn! With that sexy outfit—your makeup, your hair, I think that you may create a sinful response from Signore Leone and many other males nearby."

"So you like it. Is that what you are suggesting, Professor?"

Admitting that she was awed by Dawn's transformation, Lucia added, "I think you have or soon will have given far greater meaning to the phrase 'Clothes make the woman.'"

"Fortunately my skirt and blouse and accessories will be concealed by my light wrap," Dawn explained, " but once in the hotel I'll remove my coat and reveal the concealed weapons."

"Perfect, Dawn. I'll wager that Signore Leone will make certain that you are seated very close together," Al added gleefully.

"How I would like to be there for the unveiling," Lucy offered, then added, "So you're armed and dangerous, Dawn, but don't overplay your role or you might start believing it."

"I doubt that, Lucy. Still he may have more charm than I might realize. After all I've never met him. Anyway, I will soon. So let's get moving."

As Al helped Dawn with her warm long wrap, he asked, "Lucy, would you mind lending us your car? It's a bit chilly and a fairly long walk from here."

"Of course not. Here are the keys. Now while you're gone I'll practice and wonder about your celebrated meeting and victorious sin-fest."

Quickly Dawn and Al were in the car, delighted but apprehensive.

"Al, stay to the left until you reach via Serragli which will take us across the Arno. In that area we should find parking and we're only a short distance from Leone's very classy shop."

Minutes later they spotted the sign,'M. Leone. Objets d'Art'. As they reached the shop, Michele greeted them, first shaking hands with Al who quickly introduced Dawn, explaining her presence and suggesting that she might join them for lunch.

Even as Al spoke Michele made a quick study and could hardly restrain his enthusiasm for Al's request.

With a broad smile and wink toward Al, Michele said, "I knew today would be a lucky one. Not may she, Miss Knight, join us, but will she." Then staring at her cleavage, "Dear lady, you are here with two great admirers of beauty. You are indeed the guest of honor."

As Michele held Dawn's hand and spread his enticing masculine charm, Al was impressed with Michele's prescience even as Dawn was entranced.

Quickly recovering from her enchantment, Dawn squeezed Michele's hand while adding, "After all I've heard about you, Signore Leone, you are indeed a gentleman and a scholar."

"How very kind and generous of you, Miss Knight. But please enter my humble shop. It's quite cool here."

In the warm comfort of the shop, Dawn allowed her wrap to drape open, exposing her silken blouse and inviting cleavage.

Leone was almost speechless while Al too stared in disbelief.

Sensing their embarrassment, Dawn only smiled discreetly while allowing, "What a beautiful shop, Signore Leone. I had no idea you were such a business man."

At this, Leone almost blushed. "Thank you, Miss. . . "

Quickly Dawn added, "I'd feel better if you'd call me by my given name, Dawn, and maybe you wouldn't mind if I called you Michele."

For a few minutes the trio smiled and exchanged small talk. Then Leone excused himself momentarily.

In his absence, Dawn almost purred. "Al, Leone is really a charming and handsome man, much more than I expected."

"Yes, he is indeed a very handsome Italian and no doubt he can turn on the charm. So be careful, Dawn, don't get carried away."

Suddenly Leone returned. "I hope you've been looking around. I have many lovely and beautiful trinkets for the idle rich. But now let's visit my office for a few minutes before we go out for lunch—as you Americans call the mid-day meal, or colazione, as we say."

From the large ornate showroom, with an abundance of expensive art, wall hangings, display cases, Leone took them through the heavy mahogany door identified as "M. Leone, Privato".

Both Dawn and Al were surprised by the space and elaborate design.

"Here," Leone explained, "is my desk and a few office necessities. That nearest wall which is exactly half the width of the showroom, some eight or nine meters, and contains a bathroom, which is available from my office, but also serves the same purpose for the small apartment directly behind us which is also a special resting place when I occasionally must spend the night here. It has a small bedroom closet, kitchen and large area for storage, behind the living quarters."

Both Al and Dawn were impressed by the organization and utility of this arrangement.

"Signore Leone," Al started to ask but Leone quickly added, "Please, Professor, just call me Michele. I feel more comfortable with the more informal first name and would you object if I call you Alfred, or simply Al, as I hear Dawn say, occasionally?"

Al agreed, "First names suggest a friendlier relationship."

"Now before we leave for lunch, shall we have a glass of bubbly, French bubbly—Moet rather than Martini and Rossi which is adequate for Italians but not for Americans or Sicilians." Michele was elated.

As he carefully opened the iced champagne from his cabinet and began to pour, he explained, "I'd like to offer a toast in the form of a very old Sicilian proverb." Then lifting his glass, "Fidarsi va bene, non fidarsi va meglio."

Dawn and Al slowly drank the soft sparkling wine, then asked, "And exactly what does that Sicilian toast mean?"

Michele laughed. "It means 'To trust is good but not to trust is better'.

I only mention this because it was and still is pretty much the code of the Mafia with whom I had some unpleasant dealings and cleverly beat them at their own game."

"Wasn't that dangerous?" Al asked.

"Yes, of course, but as a Sicilian born in Corleoni, a small town not far from Palermo, I managed to trick them by a complicated series of currency exchanges which resulted in them killing one of their own people, who had been cheating them on a similar money deal as I was using.:

"But weren't you afraid they might discover your deception?"

"Not now, Al" Michele gloated. "They cut the tongue out of the poor bastard before he could explain what I had done."

Looking pleased Michele added, But you have the Mafia in America."

"Yes, Michele, we had them in the U.S. and still do but I doubt their influence there." Al added.

"Unfortunately, the Mafia remains powerful here because of its secret leadership and its oath of omerta to the onerata societa—the honored association."

"When we have more time, I'll explain a couple of personal experiences I had with the Mafia several years ago and why I am determined to find many of my private papers which were stolen from my office about the same time that my stepdaughter was allegedly raped here."

Then taking a deep breath, Leone added, "I'm very sorry to have mentioned that subject. Now let us go to lunch and enjoy getting better acquainted."

At the door, Leone again paused, "We have several excellent restaurants nearby. Probably the best are in the Excelsior or the Grand. We could walk there but why bother in this chilly weather?' And with that admonition, Al summoned a nearby parked taxi.

As the taxi approached the Piazza Ognissante Leone mentioned "Grand Hotel" which faced the Excelsior also on Renaissance Square.

Once inside the ornate and massive hotel lobby busy with tourists, Michele quietly ushered Dawn and Al past the salons and elegant shops toward the Winter Garden, an enclosed hall of arches. Soon they were directed to a quiet area of Italian elegance. Nearby a pianist at a large grand piano was playing Chopin.

As the waiter first seated Dawn in her dazzling two-piece décolletage, both Michele and Al could almost feel the shocked stares and murmurs.

The waiter paused as he carefully seated Al and then Michele while softly asking, "Questa tavola conviene, Signor Leone?"

Dawn and Al discreetly feigned indifference as Michele whispered an order to the waiters. Then Michele asked in a clear voice, "How do you like this place? It has a long history dating back to the eighteenth century. This hotel and the Excelsior across the piazza are probably the best hotels in Florence. Whenever I get a client whom I wish to impress I bring him or her here and that usually clinches the sale."

"If you don't mind, Michele, would you share the secret of your success?" Dawn smiled.

"My success is relatively simple. First and foremost you must know all you can about the art objects you're selling, you must be completely honest and guarantee every piece you sell. I promise a one hundred percent return on any item a customer doesn't like but only for a limited time—say, six months and the returned item must be as perfect as the day it was sold."

"That sounds very fair," Al offered.

"Of course but that guarantee requires that all my sales staff must know this business almost as well as I do. In fact I have several employees, usually the managers of each of my five stores, to be experts on jewelry, rugs, everything we sell."

Dawn and Al were amazed. "But where do you buy or acquire your merchandise?" Al asked.

"From many sources. For example, I have a Russian, an expert who frequently comes with modern art, Czarist jewelry, crystal. There are still a lot of very valuable art pieces in the Soviet Union."

"Yes, but how do you get it out of Russia?" Dawn asked very demurely.

"Simple! Bribes, preferably American currency. I always handle this end of any purchase because I speak Russian quite well usually with a Persian accent and only because I speak Arabic and Middle Eastern languages, Aramaic, Persian, some Hebrew and of course Spanish, French and German. These several languages enable me to trade or buy almost anything that would appeal to customers here and in America."

"I'm flabbergasted!" Al then asked, "But how do you buy the art things from South America, Asia and Africa?"

"Almost all of the art pieces are first requested by customers and I have a few representatives in Brazil, Argentina and Chile who usually can find them. But some pre-Columbian genuine pieces, which are often in demand, are hard to find and to authenticate. And the same problems I have with getting Japanese, Chinese and Asian pieces. But here my problem is first getting authentic items for a fair price."

"I am amazed!" Dawn almost exploded. "Your business is so complicated!"

"True but that is why I frequently pick the brains of art and museum people who are only too pleased to help me for a modest fee."

"Thank you, Michele, for your fascinating information." Al was very sincere. "And I suppose there is also the problem of management, salaries, commissions et cetera."

"Of course and those problems require my attention so I must make at least two major trips every year."

"And one final note about my business and then we'll enjoy some wine and delicacies."

From the hushed seriousness of Michele's voice, neither Al nor Dawn was surprised when Michele said "secret, stolen papers". Among my stolen papers were names. Addresses, special documents, photos which were extremely important to my business deals but even more important to some government officials and important to the Mafia too although that secret organization doesn't bother me as much as, say, elements of the secret police–the CIA and FBI plus the Musad and Russian KGB."

"One last word. Please don't mention our conversation to anybody including Lucia."

Both Al and Dawn whispered, "You have my word, Michele."

Fortunately the waiter arrived with champagne and a large plate of antipasto.

Although the trio of conspicuous conspirators didn't realize that most of the elegantly dressed diners were discreet observers from their tables, the quiet atmosphere was broken when Dawn rose and announced she would return in a few minutes.

"Wait a minute Dawn," Michele whispered. "There's a ladies room at the far end of this next arch."

With a polite thank you, Dawn managed a perfect gait as the room erupted into a ripple of excitement.

"Well, Michele," Al asked, "how do you like Dawn's outfit, her costume?"

"She's the most gorgeous woman I've ever seen, Al. Beautiful, marvelous with an athlete's body. She's got every woman in this room green with envy and every male dreaming and lusting. I had no idea that she was so beautiful. By the way how old is she?"

"I'm not sure, Michele, but she's just about twenty-one, the same age as Lucia, I think. But since she's finishing her junior year at Stanford she must be twenty-one although she could pass for a slightly older woman."

"Confidentially, Al, do you think she might accept my invitation for a date? Does she have a male friend?"

"I can't answer either question, Michele, because I don't know. She has mentioned male friends but, from what I know about her relationship with Lucia, she isn't directly involved with anybody here but I do know she attends dances and social affairs here. And in California she is well known if for no other reason than that her mother and her mother's mother are very well known for their beauty and sometimes for their scandalous behavior. Yes, Dawn comes from a long line of handsome and wealthy men and women."

Suddenly the social lull of the room became a magnetic buzz as Dawn managed to transmit exciting and envious messages during he slow calculated return to the table.

Both Al and Michele sat in amiable silence as Dawn reached the table. Before Al could move, Michele almost leaped from his chair in time to slide the cushioned chair under Dawn's ample derriere.

As diners stared Al was afraid the room would erupt in loud cheers from the conspicuously attentive males.

Again the handsome trio resumed their animated conversation, sipping champagne and calmly indifferent to the social spotlight which remained focussed on their every movement.

Determined to discover some incriminating evidence in Michele's confessional biography, Al nudged Dawn's knee, then slyly looked at Dawn. "As an attractive young woman, Dawn, who has heard our friend here relate several fascinating facts and aspects of his life, is Signore the kind of man you would seriously consider as a friend or husband?"

Dawn blushed in confusion. Michele stared at Al and blurted, "Sir, I am embarrassed by your question and I don't believe that Miss Knight should trivialize her reputation with such a personal question."

Again Al signaled Dawn's knee. "Oh, Michele, I'm sorry the professor has been so gauche. He was simply testing your sense of humor. Al is a real joker sometimes, aren't you, Al?"

"I'm afraid you've exposed me, Dawn. Yes, I do have a crazy sense of humor. Something I picked up from some professional friends at the university who frequently teased each other with personal questions about their students."

The answer seemed to assuage Michele's embarrassment. "Thank you, Professor, now I understand. We Italians and I, a Sicilian, only joke about women who are sluts or worse, fat bitches."

"Thank you, Michele, as I am neither a slut nor a fat bitch. My presence and my reputation are secure. But as for Al's question, would I consider Signore Leone as a friend, lover or husband? You bet I would! He's extremely handsome, interesting and caring friend and probably equally good lover or husband. Well, yes, probably a great husband for the right woman and I most certainly could be that right woman."

Now both Michele and Al erupted in laughter which created a pronounced echo across the large room.

Some seconds later, the waiter arrived with a very large gilded multi-page menu printed in Italian, English and German.

The trio studied this culinary guide for several minutes mumbling the language of experienced diners.

"For a first plate or course, the stuffed artichoke hearts are excellent, as are the smoked trout and oysters. But everything is good. And for a second important course, Beef Wellington is always excellent, as is the rack of lamb, sword fish. Any one of the three is always excellent."

"What about salad? " Dawn asked. "Instead of a first course I would like a salad, maybe something with avocado and shrimp, but first rather than after the main course."

Soon the trio had completed their requests as the waiter murmured words of approval and Michele completed the order for a bottle of Domaine de la Romance-Conte and with final dictate perhaps Grand Cru.?

As the hour of two passed quickly and the room silenced to muffled laughter, Al decided to continue his investigation of Signore Leone.

"So you grew up in Sicily but how did you manage to escape the poverty and misery of your childhood?"

Michele was pleased. He enjoyed boasting of his hard life and how he escaped the fate of poor Sicilians.

Having finished his Beef Wellington, Michele was ready to talk. "Indeed we were very poor as my parents frequently told me. But just allow me to establish the time frame of my early youth. I was born December 7, 1936 in my parents very small house in Corleone.

"Somehow with loving care from my mother and also my father I managed to survive. And I might add without heat or running water but usually a mid-wife, some babies survived, but not many which accounts for the small families. Not that the women, young women didn't get pregnant. They certainly did. But under endless poverty and lack of doctors or medicine, it was almost a miracle that some families included several children but many had only one or two and some families had none."

Michele stopped, then added in soft somber tones, "So those were my early years. But about two years before the war started in 1939, my family moved to Palermo where my father became a fisherman which greatly improved our conditions. We had a small house with both heat and running water and a bathroom and more than enough food."

"I had started school and enjoyed learning to read and write. Then when I was about seven the war came to Sicily–the Germans. Almost instantly, I hated them. They were rude, arrogant and bullies who had no respect for Italians, or Sicilians. But there wasn't really anything we could do about it–just try to avoid them."

"But you did survive and become a wealthy man, Michele." Dawn spoke with admiration.

"Yes, that's true but part of my early years were lucky, very lucky. When the Allies invaded Sicily in 1943, the bombing started and increased rapidly, particularly as the Americans advanced. I think the first sight of an American soldier thrilled me more than anything else I've known."

Michele paused, then speaking rapidly, described the constant bombing and terror. "I saw this large group of American soldiers climbing over and around the ruins and then after only one day the Germans began leaving. By this time I had waved and yelled, "America good! Kill Germans! At this point an American, you say G.I., came over and picked me up and said many things I didn't understand. But he smiled and kissed me on the cheek. Then others came over and all of them talked and laughed and then they gave me some candy and chewing gum".

"What a wonderful story, Michele," then Al added, "but what happened?"

"Well, all of the Germans hadn't retreated. I guess they had been ordered to stay in several heavily fortified places and prevent the Americans from advancing. But I knew where most of the strongholds were so I told a few soldiers to follow me and where to hide. And the Americans did then when the Germans were asleep, late at night or just at daybreak, the G.I.'s would throw hand grenades and when the Germans came out the G.I.'s would kill them with machine guns and some small cannon.

"I showed the Americans many places, most were in old buildings and churches in Palermo but I knew of a few in the steep hills and I pointed to them. Then the Americans showed me maps and I pointed to several places where the Germans might be dug in."

"This is amazing, Michele. No wonder you became rich and powerful," Dawn exclaimed.

"Well, that's partly true." Michele added.

"Very quickly, in two or three days, some officers came to see me and they had an Italian translator who made a good conversation possible."

"They said very funny things like, 'Here is the boy general. Here's our leader'. Then suddenly one day this big American officer in riding boots and two big pistols and metal helmet came to where I was standing with several G.I.'s. Immediately all the G.I.'s stood at attention and saluted the man. Then the officer said something and the soldiers all began to talk and laugh.

"And who was that officer, Michele?" Al asked excitedly.

"Believe it or not, that was General Patton!"

"Then what happened?" Dawn was intense.

The translator told me that this was General George Patton, the supreme commander. Then Patton praised me for being a great and brave soldier who had courageously led his soldiers where they were able to take hundreds of prisoners and kill hundreds more, that I, a small boy, had made it possible to chase the Germans out of Sicily."

"Was that really true?" Al asked.

"No, of course not, but the Americans and some British units, did force the Germans to retreat rapidly. It's a long and detailed story about the Allies' invasion."

"You haven't mentioned your parents, Michele. What happened to them?"

"Well, like most Sicilians they tried to hide and avoid all the fighting. And most of them did. My parents' house was in an old section of Palermo which wasn't very close to the actual fighting. So they managed quite well except that they had very little to eat, but not for long."

"How's that, Michele?" Dawn asked.

"Well I skipped the best part about my meeting with and helping the Americans. I mentioned gum and candy and then when I told them about my parents they began giving me cans of food and something they called K-rations which my parents loved. After only three or four days I carried about two or three hundred kilos of food to my parents."

"What a wonderful story, Michele. That makes me proud to be an American".

"But there's one more final point. Just before the Americans pulled out, a small group of G.I.'s and officers came to me with a large package.

"Here this officer, not General Patton, but another general, gave me a badge which had my name on it and said First Sergeant. Then they opened the box and inside were large piles of paper money, bills, ones, fives, tens and a few twenties and large piles of Italian lire."

"The general pinned the medal on my chest, kissed me on each cheek and saluted me. And all of the other men saluted me and called me, Sergeant."

"Michele, that's the best war story I've ever heard. It's almost unbelievable." Al was almost overcome with emotion.

"And what did you do with the money?" Dawn asked.

"Gave it to my parents who counted it and there was over five hundred dollars in American money and just about the same in Italian. And I might add that enabled my parents and me to live very well through the war and added to that I became quite famous as the boy commander."

For several more minutes the trio, now alone in the large room, sat quietly until Al suggested, "I think we should leave before they charge us for a room."

With that they departed. In the lobby again Dawn attracted strong attention as she reclaimed her coat and sexily manipulated the garment over her shoulders.

In the late afternoon chill, Michele hailed a cab and stopped at his shop. He again urged them to stay but Al and Dawn persisted and soon found the Alfa.

"What an afternoon!" Al enthused. "Great fun, didn't you think so Dawn?"

"Of course. Really fantastic and it cost the wealthy Signore Leone a large bundle." She laughed, then added, "But you really threw me several bad signals."

"Oh, you mean the embarrassing question about your opinion of Michele?"

"Exactly, at first I didn't pick up on your knee motions but then I got your message."

"You sure did and within minutes you had him ready to propose."

"Well, not quite but I really enjoyed the game."

"Now what's your next move when he calls you for a date?"

"No problem. I'll accept enthusiastically and I mean that. Hell, he's handsome, rich and horny."

At the word 'horny' Al almost choked. "What would you do if you don't mind my asking?"

Now that's one I'm going to skip, Al, if you don't mind. Right now I would probably say, no way, too risky. But fortunately I won't have to make that decision now or maybe ever."

Minutes later, Al parked the Alfa on the sloping driveway. As the couple prepared to open the door, Al could hear the piano. "That sounds like Beethoven" he suggested as Dawn unlocked the front door.

Hearing the slight noise, Lucia spun around on the stool somewhat apprehensively.

"Oh, it's my celebrants." Lucia laughed. "Well, how did the lunch go? I was beginning to think you would stay on for dinner."

"That wouldn't be too bad if we hadn't pigged out for lunch." Dawn added. "Leone took us to the Grand Hotel and when Italians say 'Grand' they really mean grand, luxurious and opulent. It's everything like that and more and the food is out of this world."

For almost a half hour Dawn and Al entertained and delighted Lucia.

"So you learned everything you hoped to discover?"

"Probably not, darling, but we fed the gullible Mr. Leone a lot of baloney which he seemed to have enjoyed."

"Good, but how much baloney did the clever Mr. Leone feed you?"

"That's really hard to know because he did most of the talking–about his shop in great detail and about his childhood in Sicily during World War II."

"Do you believe his long war story?" Al asked.

"Well, I guess I do. He certainly must have been there and his description of what happened is probably true."

"I agree but I know of ways to evaluate his stories and I intend to check them out. You know what an effective liar he can be." Al added.

"I'm not so sure." Dawn replied. "He pretty much convinced me and until I learn otherwise, I'll go along with him. And Lucia should know, I'm going to see him again soon."

At this announcement, Lucia appeared surprised but she offered no comments.

As it was now almost dark, Al felt uneasy. He knew that he should return to Greve but now he equivocated. "I really should be getting home,." Al offered lamely.

"Why?" both women interjected. "You don't really have to leave now, particularly at this late hour. The traffic is still bad and I would feel very nervous with you dealing with all those crazy Italian drivers."

For a minute Al struggled then quickly succumbed. "Of course you're right. I am only too delighted to accept your wonderful hospitality."

Both women looked pleased and Dawn added, "All we have to do is prepare dinner for Lucia."

"Maybe," Al laughed, "we should describe in detail our extraordinary noon meal."

"Not every course, not the entire meal. By the time we could finish Lucy would be starved to death."

"Look, you two gourmands, either we fix up a light meal or we again visit that trattoria where we had lunch yesterday."

With a collective veto Al and Dawn agreed to whip together "something". Then, as the self-appointed chefs prepared the meal, Lucia returned to her piano.

Quickly al surveyed the well-stocked kitchen and suggested spaghetti a la carbonara and a mixed green salad and ice cream.

Dawn dismissed the carbonara, "Sure we all love that pasta but it's rather tricky to put it together just right. Besides I doubt if we have bacon and basil."

"You're right, Dawn, No bacon or basil. O how about some simple spaghetti–garlic, onions, tomato sauce?"

And Dawn added, "Thyme, salt and pepper and some ground meat, if we have any."

"I didn't see any hamburger, so let's get the water on and start the sauce. Would you make the salad, Dawn?"

Within twenty minutes the two efficient chefs had served the spaghetti feast and compelled the engrossed pianist to sit down at the table.

Before Al could speak, Dawn was on her feet, "We forgot the parmigiano and the wine."

As the three slurped and smacked the spaghetti while washing it down with a chianti, Lucy was ecstatic, "This is wonderful and the best meal I've had in a years. I propose that Al move in and share cooking with Dawn while I sweep and clean and practice."

At this proposal Al lifted his glass in a toast, "To the two most beautiful and talented ladies in the world, I pledge my life, love and devotion."

For a few more minutes the laughter continued. Then Lucy noticed the chianti bottle was empty. "Oh, waiter. Another chianti , please."

Quickly Al responded and filled each glass. "Now," Lucy solemnly added, "And to the two best friends in my world, Dawn and my future husband."

Al, a bit embarrassed but smiling, nodded as Dawn stood, "And to my two best friends, my confident and my music teacher, Lucia and to my mentor and advisor and pal, Al Praitt."

To complete the ceremony the trio exchanged hugs and kisses, then finished the second bottle of wine with the remaining bits of salad.

"One last dinner delight," Dawn added. "We have some wonderful chocolate ice cream."

Soon the meal was a sweet memory as Al suggested, "Let's review our memorable afternoon with Signore Leone and with Lucy's most important input and advice, try to organize a strategy and plan."

"Good!" Lucy then asked, "What did you learn today that we didn't already know? And by that I mean something important."

Al glanced at Dawn. "We soon learned that Dawn has already found a serious breach in Leone's armor. But how we may exploit his weakness is yet to be planned and developed."

"Well," I hope this weakness is much more serious than I might believe," Lucia added.

"Oh, it's very serious, I'm certain," Dawn Added, "and if I see him a few more times, I should be able to determine what he intends to do to obtain secret papers which he maintains were stolen by you, Lucy, and your grandfather. And additionally what important papers and documents the police may have."

"No doubt the large bundle of papers, photos and cash which I accidentally discovered are very important. So the logical question is what will he do to obtain those precious papers? Would he attempt to buy them? Steal Them? Use violence to get them? We don't know."

"So how do we find out exactly what he wants and what he might do, particularly as his efforts will probably involve us. Would he try to bribe us? Try to enlist our efforts? Or might he use violence or threats of violence to get what he wants?" Dawn appeared worried.

"Well" Al added, "you've certainly summarized his problem and ours. So first and foremost we must learn more about those papers and then we must decide how much we may seem to be cooperating with him. This is really a very elaborate cat and mouse game."

"Or," Lucy commented, "a lion and a lamb game and I think we all know who the lion is which makes me a bit uneasy to be a lamb."

Dawn laughed, "Very good and since I seem to be the first and self-appointed lamb, I'll be pleased to play that role. Is that acceptable to both of you?"

"Of course," Lucy agreed which Al seconded. "Yes, Dawn and I hope you are not endangered because should the wily Leone discover that we are baiting a trap for him, that could be extremely dangerous for you, Dawn."

Collectively the three seemed pleased and relaxed with their plan.

"Okay," Lucy smiled." Let's all get a good night's rest before we begin operation 'Discovery.'"

At her bedroom door dawn paused and offered a sensuous smile and wink as Al quickly followed Lucia into their bedroom.

Quickly Al disrobed as Lucy carelessly stepped from her silk panties. For seconds they stood motionless caught in the erotic magnetism of their bodies. Slowly they tightened hard against each other as their bodies began a ritual ballet of teasing and caressing.

Then effortlessly Al, in a sweeping motion, gently lowered Lucy into their bed.

In the darkened security of their room their bodies instantly united in an introduction to passion and music. Slowly they began the caressing motion of a ballet lasting several minutes before Lucy climaxed in a coda of soft cries of exultation, Oh darling! Darling! Darling! I love you! Oh! How I love you!"

And Al, quivering in a final thrust replied with a series of tender kisses and whispers of passion and exultation.

As the security of the night enveloped them, they lay wedded in their vows of courage, devotion and love.

Chapter Six

Reluctantly Al returned to Greve Wednesday morning. After three days with Lucy in Florence neither the security of a small Tuscany town nor the quiet ambiance of his ancient house could dispel an ominous threat to his existence. "Why," he asked himself, "do I feel this nervous condition? I should feel well confident and ready."

Before leaving Greve, he visited the post office and was given several letters by the smiling Postmistress, then as he traversed Verrazano Square, he was greeted several times by smiling faces, "Buon giorno, professore." He visited all of the necessary shops for bread, meat, wine, butter–all of the necessities that he would need for the next several days. And, of course, the Herald-Tribune, his only source of news, except for the difficult FM stations of BBC and the Armed Services Radio.

Feeling somewhat comforted by his friendly reception, as he left the square, Al absentmindedly forgot to turn left and soon found himself directly in front of the town cinema. He had never been there but suddenly he became curious. With the car stopped almost directly in front of the teatro, Al noticed several advertisements for coming attractions. One poster attracted his attention for a film starring an attractive female, Princesslina, Venerdi Marzo 6. "Well," Al thought, "why not." If Lucy doesn't visit me, maybe I'll see what Princesslina looks like Friday night.

Minutes later Al returned to his hillside fortress, carefully unlocked his car and quickly entered the house. His hasty, survey revealed no change, so he quickly stored his purchases and sat down to read his mail.

First Virginia's letter, "Dearest Dad, Greetings, good news, etc., etc. I'm bulging, baby due in May. Everything excellent." Then several paragraphs about the firm and her work. "Oh, one final positive note, this should surprise you, Steve and Alan are working and have enrolled in wine making classes through U.C. Extension U.C. Davis, which you know offers a full program of enology."

"Well," Al considered, "so they're finally going to take me up on the winery deal."

Carefully Al opened the next letter from his agent. A few polite sentences about the book, "As soon as you get me the manuscript, the presses will roll and so will the cash. Oh, enclosed is a piece from Herb Caen."

Quickly Al scanned the column which ended with the final short comment, "The word is that U.C Berkeley's favorite humorist and traveler is exciting Florentine ladies with his charm and wit."

At that disclosure, Al laughed, "Caen, you bastard. You must have been really hard-up to print that silly piece. But why and who tipped you off that I was here, oh sure, my agent, that's it. Well, maybe it helps to sell books!"

For a few minutes longer Al sat quietly reflecting on the plan to catch Leone. First Dawn must learn more about his past, his secret agenda—assuming that he has one—but of course he does. But he must not know that we are baiting the trap for him.

As it was now well past noon, Al considered a light lunch—soup, bread, salami, and canned fruit. Quickly his inner suggestion became a reality as he sat down to a large bowl of vegetable soup, then remembering the Herald-Tribune, he began reading as he slowly sipped the hot soup.

"Hell!" Al uttered. "Reagan warning Qaddafi, and what the hell is Craxi doing refusing to hand over the hijackers of the Achille Lauro?" Having skimmed most of the news, Al had just started the crossword puzzle when the phone rang.

Pleased by the interruption and expecting a female voice, Al cheerfully answered, "Pronto!" There was a pause then Leone's questioning reply, "Professore Praitt, please."

Recognizing, Leone's voice, Al offered pleasantly "Hello, Michele, how are you?"

After the usual small talk, Leone became, serious, "Al, I know you are a friend and a man I admire for your intelligence and wit. Now I have a request for your advice."

"Yes, how may I help you, Michele?"

"I'd appreciate your assistance in helping me to become better acquainted with Miss Knight—Dawn Knight."

"What do you have in mind, Michele?"

"Well, I really like her. I'm quite attracted to her and from our recent conversation, I think that she finds me attractive. Would you agree that we seemed to be attracted to each other?"

Al was inwardly delighted and could hardly conceal his pleasure. "Well Michele, from her remarks which were he answers to my really rude questions, I'd say she's very interested in getting to know you better. So why don't you just call and ask for a date? I think she would be pleased to accept."

"Thank you, thank you very much Al, for your encouragement and advice. But I'm somewhat concerned because I've called her number three or four times recently and either get a busy signal or Lucia curtly says, 'Miss Knight is not here,' and hangs up."

"Well, I don't know what the problem is, Michele. I'm certain that she and Lucia are still living together. But I'll call back and try to talk with Dawn. But also Dawn maybe studying for examinations. You know she takes her studies here very seriously even as I am certain you did during your junior year at Stanford."

For a second or two Michele didn't reply. "Yes, of course Al. She's probably studying. But, by the way, how did you know I went to Stanford?"

"Oh either you or Dawn told me."

"Yes, of course, I must have mentioned it during our wonderful lunch recently. Good, I'll hope to hear form her soon. Goodbye."

"Well," Al laughed, "so Dawn is really beginning the cat and mouse game with him. She and Lucy are really baiting the trap."

As Al resumed reading the paper and eating, the phone rang again.

Suddenly Lucia's excited voice, "Al, darling, our apartment has been robbed again, not trashed, but again the same routine. Somebody, obviously the same idiot or maybe two idiots broke in through the garage door maybe, but more likely they had a key. And they were fast and quiet because the Rossi's who rent my other apartment said that they didn't hear any noise."

"But Lucy, are you okay and Dawn is taking it okay?"

"Oh sure, but I have phoned the police and they promised to investigate. But I'm really fed up, so is Dawn and I will immediately search for another place."

"Damn!" Al Offered. "What may I do to help? But perhaps more importantly, how can you continue to practice and what about Dawn's classes?

"Yes, this stupid burglary problem is important only because it creates several problems for us—all of us, and you too, darling."

"Of course. With your permission I'll start looking for another apartment. I've seen places advertised in the Herald-Tribune and in the New York Review of Books. Now, another problem, not really problem but only minutes ago I got a call form Leone, who is worried about his relationship with Dawn. He hasn't heard form her for a few days and is afraid that she isn't interested."

"Good, Al, that's really good. Dawn and I decided to well, oh you know, it's like the weather. We're always interested in the weather."

For a second or two Al was nonplused, then remembering their "telephone code" Al added, "Oh yes, the damned weather, miserable. We need spring which should be arriving soon."

Then continuing to relate Leone's conversation and knowing that their conversation was being taped, Al added, "I don't think Michele has anything to worry about. Why don't you talk with Dawn about Michele's problem? She will understand."

"Well, yes, of course. I'll see Dawn later this afternoon and mention Signore Leone's problem."

"Before hanging up, you're emotionally all right, darling or should I drive down in an hour or so?"

Receiving a firm "No,' Al added, "I have a few other suggestions regarding the burglary which we can discuss tomorrow. In the meantime, I'll check several of the ads I've seen in the Tribune and the New York Review."

For several minutes Al sat quietly reflecting on the burglary and the problems that it had created. "First, I think Inspector Ruffo should be alerted to this second burglary. He might know that Leone planned it and maybe I should inform the Inspector why I think Leone had a serious reason to ransack the place—his papers! Quite possible the Inspector knows nothing about Leone's secret private life. Okay, I pursue that line tomorrow and urge Lucy to demand an immediate appointment with the Inspector.

With that detail taken care of, Al picked up the classified ad section of the Herald. For a few minutes he scanned two pages with numerous rentals offered in Italy, France and Spain. Having exhausted the Trib, he now turned to the New York Review. Quickly he scanned the classifies: "Real Estate–Rentals: Italy, lovely sections in Tuscany, Umbria; Charming House, Todi 4 bedroom etc. Orvieto, Florence, Nine Miles South." "Too far," Al muttered. "Florence, Piazza Santa Croce. 2 BR large kitchen, living room, 2 bathrooms, fully equipped $1600/month, call/fax.: Al reread the ad. "That's fantastic! I'd better phone that number right away–that's too good to be true!"

Before dialing, Al considered the problem of talking about the advertised rental if the agent or the owner only spoke Italian. Then concluded somebody must speak English or it wouldn't be advertised in English. Momentarily he considered the problem of his phone being tapped. That could be a problem for Lucy and Dawn. "No, I'd better not risk it. I'll go down to Greve and use the phone in the bus station."

Quickly Al put the dishes in the sink, carefully noted the telephone number, struggled with his top coat, closed and locked the door and was gone.

As it was now almost four p.m., Verrazano Square was slowly coming alive. Quickly Al bounded into the combination bus station and variety store. Near the front, Al spotted the telephone, then realizing that he didn't know how to reach the operator, he asked the smiling clerk who had seen and talked to him several times, "I wish to call Florence and here is the number and my money."

"So, professore momentino." Quickly she deposited the coins and almost heard the polite "Pronto." She mentioned something about an Americano professore and handed Al the phone.

"Hello, this is Paulo Procci's office. How may I help you?"

"Thank you sir, my name is Alfred Praitt, and I'm calling about your rental which I found in the New York Review. Is the apartment still available?

Assured that it was, Al explained the reason for his call, pointing out that his friends weren't looking for a permanent rental, but simply until June if that would be acceptable. Apparently Mi Procci who spoke without an accent was pleased when Al identified Dawn and Lucia, who were young American women. Apparently Procci was an enthusiastic as Al was. Al satisfied all of Croci's questions, who gave him an exact description of the apartment and a time the following day when he and the women could see the apartment. Then as a final question, Al inquired about the piano, which Procci answered simply, "She may have her piano moved in but that probably would be expensive as this apartment is on the second floor."

Again there was total agreement as Al reconfirmed the time and the place, Number 11, Via San Giuseppi, across the narrow street from the church.

"This is my lucky day! Wait until the girls hear my news. I can't believe it, only $1600 a month and a perfect location! And if she doesn't need the piano there, she can always practice at the conservatory."

Al was absolutely elated as he profusely thanked the young lady who had helped him make the call. Suddenly he considered calling Lucia there but then decided against it, preferring to surprise her the following morning.

Back at his house, Al again reviewed his plans. Phone Lucy, be at her place by ten and with Dawn they would meet Mr. Procci at the apartment at 11am. Pleased with his accomplishments, Al quickly found the Courvoisier and poured himself a copious measure of the "Brandy of Napoleon."

For several minutes he sat in blissful solitude only to be awakened by the telephone ring.

"This must be Lucy," Al was certain, and as he lifted the receiver he was delighted with Lucy's voice.

"Darling, darling I've some good news about the burglary, but the weather isn't particularly good. Are you ready for some good news?

Al could hardly believe his ears. "Oh to hell with the weather, I've got some absolutely fantastic news for you."

For a few seconds the lovers were ready to exchange their news but Al calmly reassured Lucy that he would prefer to meet her and Dawn at their apartment about ten a.m. Then as a final goodnight they caressed each other with love sounds for a few minutes before remembering that Leone could replay their tender romantic words.

Again, Al returned to the sofa and continued to sip Napoleon's brandy. As he reveled in his good fortune he began to feel slightly nauseous and dizzy. For two or three minutes he sat quietly trying to determine the course and source of his confusion. Finally he took his pulse and was surprised that his heart was pounding rapidly. Carefully he checked the count against his watch's second hand. "Well 102, that's about 30 beats faster than normal. No wonder I feel strange and dizzy. Damn! I've never had a heart problem. Maybe it was the brandy, but I doubt it.

For several more minutes, he sat quietly then decided some music might slow his pulse and quiet his nerves. Slowly he stood up, still a bit dizzy and then played a Beethoven Sonata, "The Appassionate." The music was a marvelous soporific and soon Al was resting comfortable. Sometime later Al awakened to a darkened room then found a nearby lamp and soon felt surprisingly rested and a bit hungry.

Again he prepared some soup and cheese and a glass of wine. Slowly he consumed his modest dinner and now fully recovered from his nervous condition. He cautiously took his pulse. "Well, that's better, down to 70.

Within minutes Al was ready for bed then suddenly remembered to lock the front door. Back in bed he again almost rejoiced about the day's events and "Now, tomorrow it's going to get better." His thoughts trailed off in a pleasant series of dreams.

The night past, swiftly and just after dawn, about seven, the continuous ringing from the phone brought him to his feet. Just as he picked up the receiver, the ringing stopped and when he repeated, "Hello! Hello! Pronto!" He heard no reply. "Obviously Lucy must have called and then given up. But why would she call so early? Could there be an emergency?"

Somewhat confused and nervous, Al hastily dialed Lucy's number, who finally answered after almost two minutes of continuous rings. "Hello," she blurted and was surprised to hear Al's voice.

Quickly she reassured him that she hadn't called and they agreed it must have been a wrong number, then with a few words of affection and Al's reminder that he would see her no later than ten, they whispered "bye."

For the next two hours Al relaxed in a hot tub, shaved and completed his preparations with a solid breakfast.

Anxious to see Lucy and exchange information and meet Paulo Procci at his apartment, Al left his house again making certain that the door was securely locked. Carefully Al descended the steep hill into Greve. Once on the narrow highway, Al passed several cars and soon arrived at Lucy's just before ten.

As he bound up the steps, Lucy and Dawn were waiting. Once inside Al asked, "Has something unexpected happened?"

"We aren't certain, both of us thought we heard somebody trying to steal the Alfa."

"Was it locked?" Al asked.

"Yes, but only because I leave it here, not that I really have any choice." Lucy was calm but worried.

"Did you see anybody?"

"Yes, I did but as it was dark I could only see somebody running down the street." Lucy added.

"That's frightening, but soon you won't have any more worries about break-ins and robberies," Al's voice was excited." I've found an apartment, fully furnished and ready for you. We're scheduled to meet the owner at the apartment building at eleven."

Dawn and Lucy were surprised and elated. "Wonderful. Where's the apartment and how much is the rent?"

"You won't believe this but it's only $1600 a month, fully equipped and with two bedrooms.

"I hope you aren't teasing us, Al. A fully equipped, two bedroom apartment in Florence for only $1600 a month? That's hard to believe!" Then Dawn surprised Al with a quick kisss on his cheek.

For a few minutes Al explained how he found the place and his conversation with the owner who sounded like an American. Again they questioned how and why a large apartment in the center of Florence could be rented for so little.

"Well," Al concluded, "if the apartment is the way Mr. Procci, the owner described, it's a real steal and I think I may know why."

"Okay, professore, tell us because it's a mystery to me."

As you probably know and I'm certain that Lucy knows, the city of Florence has strict rent control laws which applies only to Italian renters. So if a landlord rents to an Italian, he can't force him to move or to pay more rent. But this law doesn't apply to foreigners, and I suspect that Mr. Procci is very happy to rent it now in the low season. He might get more when the tourists arrive. Furthermore if for whatever reason he wished to remove a foreign tenant, he would have no problem but were he to rent to an Italian, he couldn't kick him out or raise the rent."

"Wonderful, now let's get moving. He'll be waiting for us at Number 11 San Guiseppi. It's across the narrow one-way street from Santa Croce."

Quickly the two were in the car, and with Lucy driving, they reached their destination at eleven. And standing next to the door at number eleven was a handsome, youthful appearing male who could hnave been anybody but a stereotyped Italian landlord.

Quickly Lucy parked the car and together the two approached the stranger. Simultaneously Al and the stranger cautiously greeted each other. After firm hand-shakes, Al introduced Lucy and Dawn. With formalities over, the owner, P. Procci said, "Let's take a look at the apartment. It should be clean and ready for rental. It's been empty for a couple of months. Oh yes, one other important fact, I own the entire building, but there are only three apartments, one on each floor. The rental I've advertised on the second floor is the one we lived in shortly after our marriage.

"This is a very ancient building which accounts for the rather high risers, wide treads and square landings, all quite necessary to move large boxes and containers to the second and third floors. At the second floor, Procci produced a large key and opened the door and switched on the overhead light. "Here we are in the hallway and on the right is a large bedroom which also has its own bathroom." Dawn, Lucy and Al entered the room and were pleased by its size, the furniture (a double bed) and two large windows opening on a small garden some twenty feet below.

Dawn and Lucy were very enthusiastic, "I really dig this bedroom," Dawn enthused.

Together the two descended two steps to the principal level. "On your right is a smaller bedroom and bath which our daughter used until she went away to the university."

Dawn and Lucy scrutinized the smaller bedroom with its two smaller single beds and separate toilet and shower. This bedroom also contained two large windows, exposing part of the lower garden and roof of the adjoining building. Both Dawn and Lucy were sparing in praise but agreed that it was a good practical bedroom.

Now, Mr. Procci explained, "here is the central room of the kitchen, which as you can see is also a dining room with a small laundry. That closet contains space for brooms, mops and the ironing board. It's adequate and utilitarian."

"It looks practical and adequate," Lucy said as she quickly pulled open drawers and cabinets which revealed a variety of modern cooking and cleaning devices.

"Now," Procci added, "here is the living room, a sofa which can be converted to a double bed, and there's a TV and a wall heater. And these two large windows look directly to part of Santa Croce and the narrow street below."

Both Dawn and Lucy were ecstatic and generously shared there enthusiasm with Al as Mr. Procci smiled attentively.

"One additional point," the owner added, "I pay all of the utility bills and pay the costs of repairs whenever necessary. I have a man who takes care of the building for me. But as he completely cleans and repairs each apartment whenever a tenant leaves, I seldom have any unexpected problems. Now have you any questions?"

"Where can I park my car? I notice that permanent street parking is illegal," Lucy asked.

"Yes, parking is a problem and although signs clearly indicate this is a tow away zone, people do have their cars towed frequently. But in this immediate area there are several garages where for a reasonable rental, your car is protected."

Dawn and Lucy were all smiles and excitement. "Oh, about my piano, it's a small grand piano. Do you think it could be moved into the front room?"

"Yes, I would guess you could but it would be a problem."

After a long studied statement, Lucy added, "Well, it isn't terribly important. I'm a graduate student at the Conservatory and I can use their pianos whenever I wish. So, no I agree. I'll put my piano in storage. Also, as neither Dawn nor I expect to remain in Florence longer than the middle of June at the latest, my piano is no problem."

"Now one last question, Mr. Procci," Al asked, "when can the ladies move in?"

"Whenever they wish, the sooner the better," was the pleased reply.

At this point Lucy took out her checkbook and asked, "So shall I write you a check right now?"

"That's fine with me, Miss Conde or when you actually move in."

"Well, Dawn and I hope to move in today or tomorrow if we can find somebody to help us, not that we have much. Most of the furniture and otherwise necessary items we can store or I can leave in the apartment I own near the Boboli Gardens."

With all of the details completed, Lucy handed Procci her check for $1600. The ceremony was brief and pleasing.

"And here's your receipt Miss Conde, and the standard rental contract which I guess you've seen and understand."

"Yes, I do as I also have a connecting apartment in my building which is rented to an Italian couple."

"So you know about our laws which completely protect Italian tenants?"

"Oh yes, but I'm not concerned so long as the people take care of the apartment.

With the ceremony over, Procci gave each girl a relatively large brass key, and quickly explained any questions about the apartment's electrical and plumbing equipment.

"Oh, one important point," Procci added, "the telephone, it's listed under my name because were it changed for each new tenant, it would create an impossible problem. So the number will remain the same as it was when we last lived here about twelve years ago. As for the telephone company bill, I'll send it to you next month."

There was total agreement as the ceremonial hand shaking procedure was completed.

Just before leaving, Procci gave Dawn, Lucy and Al his card. "As I live only a short distance from here, you should feel free to call or visit my large house whenever you wish. As I'm teaching at the University here this semester, I'm usually available."

At this point, Al's interest quickened, "I gather you teach elsewhere, Sir?"

"Yes," Procci added, "I also teach one semester at Harvard where I got my Ph.D in economics about fifteen years ago and sometimes I teach for a semester at the London School of Economics. But frankly I prefer to live and work here. I much prefer being with my wife and family and friends here in Florence."

As Procci turned to leave, Al added, "I too am a professor, now retired. Maybe we can get together before I return to Berkeley."

"I would like that Professor Praitt. Just give me a call." And with that Professor Procci quickly departed.

For several more minutes, the trio wandered about the spacious apartment. Dawn was particularly exuberant as was Lucy.

"Al, I owe you a tremendous debt. No wonder I love you so much. You are a miracle worker. This apartment is perfect for Dawn and me and for you too Al. What would I do without you? And now it's official, you can sleep here whenever you wish. For all practical purposes we've moved in already, the apartment is completely furnished, blankets, sheets, even toilet paper. And best of all the telephone. That bastard, Leone, can never reach us unless one of us gives him this number. And none of us will. Right? Dawn and Al?"

"So we're in total agreement, shall we sleep here tonight?" Dawn said hopefully.

"I'd like to," Lucy answered, "but I've got a closet full of clothes and other necessities at our apartment and so do you, Dawn. So, we've got to get moving right now."

"What may I do to help you move?" Al offered.

"Nothing, you darling man, but you could try to see the Inspector this afternoon, if possible and that would save Dawn and me the struggle to convince him to get off his big fat Italian ass!"

"Okay, so let's go." Al suggested.

Soon they were on the street and were relieved to see the car in the same place and without a windshield warning tag.

"We'll go back to the apartment, have a snack then you call or I'll try to reach the Inspector. And as we pack, you talk to the head cop."

"What about tonight?" Al inquired.

"I, we would love to have you stay with us this last night, but maybe you've got your own work in Greve."

"Yes, I have some rewriting to complete, but that isn't immediately necessary, so if you can use my help, I'll stay. Besides, if I see the Inspector, I must let you know right away."

"Okay, let's get back to the apartment, eat and get packing while Al talks to the head cop." Dawn suggested.

Back at the apartment, before either woman got too busy, Lucy called the Inspector's office and asked to speak to Inspector Ruffo. "Yes, this is Signorina Lucia Conde." "Momento" was the reply. Soon the Inspector's booming voice could be heard by Al and Dawn. After several rapid sentences, Lucia hung up. "Well, we've got the Inspector excited and will see you, Al, at 3:30."

"Good, that will give us time for a fast lunch, pack our personal items and bring anything else we don't want to leave." Lucy concluded with an air of finality.

Within minutes, the lunch was ready and consumed. Then both women hastily packed four suitcases with clothing and accessories.

Al was impressed with their speed and efficiency. "From what I see," he offered, "we'll need both cars. So if you put your bags in the Alfa, I should have sufficient room for any other things you may not want to leave here, like your small TV and radio, and the tape deck."

"Why do you think we should take them to the new place? Lucy asked.

"Since I won't be returning to this apartment," Dawn added with a note of finality, "I'll bring all of my junk, which isn't much."

With Al's help, most of the bags and a few items in cardboard boxes were loaded in the Alfa and the rest of the baggage was piled into the back seat of the Fiat.

Their immediate plan was to unload everything, including the large box of groceries and wine—which they almost forgot—and now jammed it into the Fiat.

"Now let's drive directly to your new apartment, leave everything there and then all of us can put some heat on the Inspector."

By two-thirty, the mission was complete and Dawn quickly suggested that, "We celebrate our new home with some wine—too bad we don't have champagne." As Lucia opened the refrigerator, there was a bottle of champagne and a short welcoming note from Paulo Procci.

"Wow! Look at this, our landlord left us a bottle of good French champagne and chilled glasses in the fridge."

Quickly Al skillfully uncorked the bottle and, without spilling a drop, filled each glass to the requisite three-quarters. "Now a toast," Lucy offered, "to the generosity and consideration of our landlord and to the diligence and help to our leader and mentor, we drink."

As they sipped the sparkling champagne, Dawn added, "Can you imagine that only twenty-four hours ago we were desperate, at least I was. I really didn't want to spend another night in that apartment."

They all agreed that this had to be a day they would never forget.

"But," Al observed, "it isn't over yet. In a few minutes we have an appointment with Inspector Ruffo. And here's what I suggest, that you two women lay it on thick. You are very angry and very frightened. Dawn, you bring in the Stanford pressure and Lucy, well you know how to intimidate the Inspector.

And I, and here's the most important point, because your lives are at stake, you are moving immediately to Greve and will share my large house even if this move will force you both to commute almost daily from Greve to Florence."

"Great!" Dawn cheered.

"Perfect pressure, Al!" Lucy added.

"Were I to confront him myself," Al added, "he could weasel around with bureaucratic threats and baloney."

All agreed as they walked toward the car. "Let's put on all the pressure and then suggest that Signore Leone will be grievously concerned and demand immediate action. And you, Lucy, add that for all of your despising of this man who robbed you and raped you, expect complete police support. And the Inspector should search the police files for the event which almost destroyed your life only seven years ago. And now you wander if the men who have twice broken into your house, and seriously threatened and robbed you and Dawn might just possibly be related to Signore Leone."

Both Lucy and Dawn seemed perplexed by Al's suggestion. "I agree," Lucy added, "but don't forget Leone is a good friend of the Inspector."

"Right, Lucy," Dawn added, "and since I'm not related to Leone, maybe I should make those charges while you turn on the water works."

"Brilliant suggestion." Al exclaimed. "Yes, that's the way to mitigate any threat of prejudice toward Leone by Lucy and allow Dawn to play up rape as the most heinous crime any woman can suffer. You could very well force the Inspector to distrust Leone and perhaps reveal some incriminating information which he would otherwise keep secret. And I'm confident that the Inspector does know something about Leone."

As it was now two-forty-five, the three eager combatants first moved the Fiat to a safe zone and then Lucy drove them to the police headquarters and parked in a special zone for official visitors.

At exactly three, the two entered the headquarters and were immediately confronted by an armed carabiniere. Quickly Lucy confronted the Carabiniere who was soon reduced to a polite, but very nervous policeman who welcomed the two to seats in a large, impressive office.

Apologetically the policeman explained, "Most of the staff won't return until three-thirty, but the Inspector usually gets back sooner, but I'll check his office now."

Dawn and Al almost laughed, "What did you say to that poor man, Lucy? You almost reduced him to tears."

"Oh, I didn't say much, just the words that we are important friends of the Inspector who had requested that we see him at three."

"Maybe it was the tone of your voice, Lucy, but you really intimidated that cop."

Both Al and Dawn put on their best Cheshire cat smiles, which would have confused the Pope.

Suddenly Inspector Ruffo arrived, and with exceptional hospitality, greeted the trio. Once in his inner office, the Inspector put on his bureaucratic face and began with an apology for this latest report of vandalism and thievery.

Quickly Lucy corrected him, "Inspector, as you know, only a few days ago we were vandalized, but no thievery that we know about, but last night we had an attempt to steal my car, an Alpha Romeo sedan. Fortunately our screams frightened the thief and he escaped. Now we have had three or more attempts on our property and more importantly our safety and our lives."

For seconds the Inspector pursed his lips, stared at the ceiling and then softly replied, "Before offering my plan of action, again please accept my most sincere regrets for this shocking and unusual series of criminal behavior. This city and our people will not tolerate gangsters, whether they represent the Mafia or the gypsies, or some of the latest arrivals from Africa. We will not allow our citizens or visitors to be robbed or violated. Now having said that, I am immediately assigning a small squad of investigators to review the information we have in our files for any other reported crimes similar to your experience. And furthermore, I will personally appoint a selected force to patrol your immediate neighborhood and apprehend any suspicious characters."

Having heard enough, Al interrupted the Inspector's monologue, "Sir, we appreciate your sincere efforts, but we would like to provide you with information which could possibly offer a solution to this serious criminal behavior."

"Thank you, Professor, as you Americans say, 'I'm all ears.'"

Al coughed then quickly asked, "I assume you know Signore Michele Angelo Leone."

The Inspector offered a shocked response, "Of course I know Signore Leone, he's a friend I've known for several years. But why do you ask?"

"Well, Sir, I ask because are you aware that the honorable Signore Leone was, for a few years, the stepfather of Miss Lucia Conde?"

Again the Inspector wavered and nervously tapped his pencil on his desk, "Well, yes, I guess I might have known that, but only because six or seven years ago Signore Leone was married to Miss Conde's mother, who was killed in a terrible accident on the autostrada. Yes, his wife and son were killed and the Signore, fortunately survived, but only after a long time in the hospital. So I should say yes. Signore Leone was and maybe still is Miss Lucia's stepfather."

At this response, Lucy erupted, "That bastard is not and never was my accepted step-father."

The Inspector seemed to slip lower in his leather chair but before he could comment, Lucy added, "But most importantly, he raped me!" Then she slowly repeated her accusation. "On the night of my fourteenth birthday, he raped me. And furthermore, after raping me, he departed for Rome and mistakenly took a Gucci bag, my Gucci bag, a birthday present from him. When I awakened early the next morning, covered with my blood, here I found the Gucci bag–Leone's bag, full of money, his passport and many, many papers and some lewd photographs." I could go over that horrible scene in detail simply because I could never forget the pain, sickness and terror I experienced."

In the shocked silence Lucy began to weep and sob and finally blurted out, "Your police department got the money and everything in the Gucci bag and took me to the trauma center at Santa Maria Nuova where all of the incriminating evidence of rape was proven. And the doctor who examined me is Dr. Georgo Valentino, whom I know and respect. And I'm certain Dr. Valentino is still practicing in that hospital."

Again the weight of Lucy's impassioned remarks left the Inspector speechless. He sat staring at the wall.

The short silence was broken by Dawn's quiet remarks, "Now, Inspector, you can better understand the fear and terror Lucia suffered from these violent break-ins of her property. Was Leone returning again to rape her or maybe me? Don't think that my fear of rape or a brutal physical attack is not real. It is probably the single greatest fear that women sometimes experience."

Again the Inspector sat rigid and reserved and was relieved when Al offered his unexpected comment, "I am sorry that Miss Conde and Miss Knight were compelled to reveal this private information. But under the circumstances which have terrorized them, they had to share their painful fears with you. But there is possibly more factual information to the two outrageous break-ins and now the attempted car theft. There is quite possibly information that you do have as to the identity of the assailant or assailants."

Now the Inspector sat straight up and asked in a sharp interrogative voice, "Are you charging or alleging that Signore Leone who has never been charged with rape by anybody, whom I know or have ever heard about, is now the suggested criminal who burglarized your house and terrorized you, Miss Conde and Miss Knight?"

"You bet I am Inspector. And all you have to do is examine your own police department files and request the hospital files on my rape charge. Are you prepared to do that, Sir?" Lucy's eyes were blazing as she leaned forward and added, "Inspector, if you refuse to examine your police records for proof of the charges that not only I made, but also the charges that my grandfather made, I am prepared to risk my money and my reputation before a grand jury to let the public know that Leone was a rapist and a thief who was once involved with some very serious national and international scandals and crimes."

Again a pall of silence hung over the room until the Inspector cautiously replied, "I am shocked and almost silenced by the comments and charges I have heard in the last half-hour. Trust me, as a friend, a good friend of Signore Michele Angelo Leone, as much as I don't want to believe these charges, I will investigate them thoroughly, But remember I was not even an Inspector seven years ago. I was only a carabiniere. At the time of the alleged criminal behavior, I never saw it in the newspaper and I never heard any of my colleagues or friends talk about it. But having said that, I personally will make an immediate investigation and I will personally inform you of what I find. Is that fair enough?"

"That sounds reasonably fair," Lucy answered.

"Yes," Dawn answered "I'll be ready for your report."

"And I too will be looking for your report Inspector, but I have a serious question. Do you intend to question your good friend about these charges?"

The Inspector sat straight up, "Sir, of course I will not question my friend. That would be a direct violation of the law. Every Inspector must take an oath not to reveal the scope or importance of any investigation of serious criminal behavior. Trust me, but now having said what my oath of office requires, don't expect me to provide you with any information which I may find incriminating."

Are you telling us, Inspector, you won't give us any kind of report about your investigation?"

"No sir, that is not what I meant to say. What I can say and will promise you is that if I find there is no legal evidence to support the charges that Miss Conde has made, I will so inform you, but if there are charges sufficient to order a criminal investigation and probably a grand jury, I will not be allowed to inform you or anybody except those officials who were or will be involved in the case."

For a few minutes Al and the two women huddled together then Lucy addressed the Inspector.

"Thank you, Inspector Ruffo, for your information and your honesty, and I hope you will keep us involved in this to the full extent of your promise and your oath."

As the conference prepared to be over, everybody shook hands and generously thanked each other for the important meeting.

Then in closing, the Inspector added, "I want you to know that the promises I made about guarding and protecting your house and property will be vigorously pursued."

"Oh yes, one final note, Sir, considering the severity of the threats to Miss Conde and Miss Knight, you should know that both of these women will temporarily share my quarters in Greve. But as both women have academic and performance responsibilities here in Florence Conservatory of Music where Miss Conde is practicing for her public concert in May at the Teatro Comunale. There she will be the principal artist at the Maggio Musicale."

Having finalized their meeting with Inspector Ruffo, they rapidly breached the crowds of people in the inner courtyard and soon were able to talk as they reached Lucy's parked car.

"How do you think we performed?" Al asked.

"Quickly Dawn replied, "Very well, we came, we saw, we conquered."

To which Lucy added, "I hope so but I'm not sure we've conquered, at least not now."

"But," Al added, "we've really put the Inspector on the spot. He's got to make several very serious moves immediately and depending on how he handles your charges, Lucy, and Dawn's implied threats, will determine his future as an Inspector. Should he make any serious mistakes, his career will be over."

"I agree completely," Lucy added as she started the engine.

"Yes, let's get back to our new apartment and decide on how we share space, who gets which bedroom, but more importantly, what should we do to make certain the Inspector is responding to our threats."

Within a few minutes Lucy found a safe parking place and again the trio were in their new "home." As Al sat in the small living room, Dawn and Lucy quickly agreed that Lucy should have the slightly larger bedroom. "Besides," Dawn added, "you probably will be here much longer than I. Once this spring term ends, I'm back to California.

For a few minutes both women quickly unpacked their bags, checked the two bathrooms and then joined Al, who had turned on the TV.

"Greetings, Pops!" Dawn quipped. "Any good programs on the boob tube?"

"Can't way. I've been changing channels which seem to be limited but reception and color are quite good. Anyway, let's have a snack or should I get started and prepare a first class Italian dinner?"

As Lucy was standing nearby, she quickly responded to Al's offer, "Listen, Pops darling, you aren't going to prepare anything. I'm the chef who knows how to prepare a first class Italian dinner or maybe a good second class Florentine dinner. But first, what would you like me to cook?"

"Anything you enjoy, I'll enjoy just so long as it isn't tripe or pig's feet."

"Okay, that gives me the option to serve my lord and master a delicious meal." And with that, Lucy joined Dawn who now together began their own specialties. "First," opens one, "carbonara." Lucy whispered, "One of Al's favorites." "And I'll toss together a large insalata mista." Dawn replied.

Then heads together, as in a conspiracy, they prepared a costoletta di Vitello Milanese which Lucy whispered, "We don't dare put this cutlet in a hot frying pan until he's finished his carbonara."

"And what about dessert?" Dawn asked.

"I'd love to give him Tiramisu, but we don't have all of the ingredients. But I noticed a bakery shop on the other side of the Piazza. While I find this treasure, you keep him entertained. Give him a glass of wine."

As Al continued to channel surf, a new experience for an American who placed television high on the list of idiot's delight, he took a quiet pleasure in the absence of Italian commercials. Nevertheless, so intense was his concentration, he was quite unaware of Lucy's epicurean mission.

Within minutes of her return Lucy signaled Dawn that everything was ready. Together they confronted Al with the announcement, "Our lord and master, dinner is ready"

Surprised and pleased, Al was soon seated at the small table in the kitchen.

"And now the chef's first course." Dawn announced loudly.

But even before the carbonara appeared, Al detected the mouth-watering aroma of his favorite Italian pasta. Still he refrained form plunging his fork into his serving, as both women teased him with calculated smiles.

After the first bite, Al became effusive, "This is the best carbonara I've ever had. Fantastic, just the right amount of pesto and garlic and with bacon instead of ham, and the parmigiano. Perfect, and which one of you talented chef's prepared this delicacy?"

Quickly Dawn replied, "Lucy, of course. I'm not an Italian and unable to master these humble but difficult delights, but I will offer you an excellent green salad for your added pleasure, sir!"

AS they talked and laughed and ate, suddenly Lucy caught the scent of the very hot iron frying pan.

Quickly she removed the hot pan and opened a nearby window. "That was a close call," she explained. "When the pan cools, we'll have the second course in a few minutes.

Now as Dawn and Al resumed their cheerful conversation, Lucy carefully cooked the veal cutlet. Within minutes, the cutlet was ready, which Lucy served on the nearby hot plates.

Soon the cutlet was consumed and washed down with a gray Riesling. Now the conversation became a guessing game. "We haven't come to any conclusion about our question and answer game with the Inspector, have we?" Al asked.

"I'm not sure that we can draw any conclusions from the Inspector's answers," Lucy replied, but I am very certain that we probably have him very worried."

"Well, let's leave it that way." Al added.

"And we have our own problems," Dawn added.

"Yes, we do. But first things first. You'll spend the night here, won't you, dear man?"

"Thank you, I accept your hospitality and your excellent cuisine."

"But we haven't finished our dinner." which brought Lucy to her feet with an apology.

"And now for a surprise!" Dawn produced the Tiramisu.

Al was elated, "You gals take the cake!"

"No," Dawn joked, "You take the cake, we got the cake."

Quickly, most of the elegant desert disappeared as they all proclaimed their pleasure.

"Before we turn in, let's finalize our plans for the immediate future. Tomorrow, I drive back to Greve and I suggest that you join me there Friday afternoon, early. Together we'll walk around making certain that we're seen."

"But why are you making such an obvious move?" Dawn asked.

"Because," Al explained, "we told the Inspector that you were moving to Greve to escape the threats on your lives. And when we're seen together Sigore Leone will be told."

"Yes, I suppose that's true, but don't you think that the Inspector probably called Leone soon after we left?" Lucy questioned.

"Of course he did," Dawn emphasized, "but by our appearance with you in Greve, the whole town will be gossiping about it."

"So you spend Thursday night at my pad, as you might say, and Friday morning you return here."

With a few more cursory comments, Lucy and Al took the larger bedroom as Dawn turned out the lights.

Quickly Lucy and Al were in bed whispering their language of love, but slowly nervous exhaustion overcame erotic pleasure, and they drifted quietly asleep.

Hours later, Al was aroused by the changing church bells and noticed that Lucy had arisen. "Damn! Those church bells. It's only six-thirty. So I might as well get up now." As Al quickly showered and shaved, he heard sounds of activity in the kitchen which encouraged him to dress and make an early departure.

Both Dawn and Lucy greeted Al with teasing questions, "How did you like the church's alarm clock? Are you ready to recite your Matins? Shall we all cross the street for the early morning mass?"

"I'm glad you ladies are so enthusiastic about our neighbor, Santa Croce. I'll join if you do too. Then we may all become saints."

"And if we're canonized, maybe we might take our place with Michelangelo and other religious do-gooders, but for your two saints, there aren't any in Santa Croce. Nope, all males. So I guess we'll just have to take our chances in the atheist's hall of fame–where, at least we'll be among friends."

"Well, dear ladies, darling women, you've wined me, dined me and pleased me, so now it's time to leave me. And there's no need to lead me to the door."

"No, we'll show you to the door, but lead you to your car. We're not the clinging vine types."

Minutes later they kissed and hugged and parted with Lucy's final injunction, "Drive carefully, it's very foggy this morning."

Soon Al was on his way, but almost immediately got lost in the fog. Driving slowly and searching for familiar signs, he finally found himself in Imprunetta. Well, he mused, at least I know where I am and it shouldn't be much more than twenty miles to Greve. Although he couldn't drive more than twenty miles an hour, he finally reached Greve shortly after eleven.

Briefly he considered stopping in Greve then decided to climb the hill to what he called home. Energetically he bound up the stairs and almost expectantly unlocked the front door. Again he was relieved, safe, out of the fog.

For several minutes, he sat quietly reviewing the last two days and now began projecting his plans for Friday. He was pleased, "I think that we may have Signore Leone trapped," then he was suddenly aware of a sudden pain in his chest. "Maybe I'm just nervous." then standing, he became dizzy and quickly sat down. "Damn! What is happening? Why do I feel this way?"

Slowly he reached the kitchen and drank a glass of water. Struggling to retain his balance, he collapsed in a nearby chair. "Could I be having a heart attack? Maybe, but this is the third time I've felt this way." Again he took his pulse which was almost throbbing. "Must be over a hundred and twenty. Well, there isn't much I can do about it now but wait."

Slowly Al returned to the living room and lay down and quickly fell asleep. Soon his sleep was broken by the telephone's repeated rings.

Al managed to reach the phone, but before he could respond, Lucy's excited voice called, "Hello darling! Hello darling, are you there?"

At which point Al quickly replied, "Yes, yes Lucy, I'm here. I've been napping on the sofa."

Now relieved, "Darling are you okay? Good, I sometimes worry when you don't answer. Anyway, I just want to clarify a few questions. But I guess what I'm really calling about is our arrival tomorrow. We would like to be there by noon so that together we can all walk around the square. That was our agreed plan, wasn't it?"

Al quickly reassured her that was the plan then suddenly remembering that their conversation was being recorded, he added, "Well as you know, everything depends on the weather." He paused waiting for Lucy's reply, then she added, "Oh yes, of course, if it's too bad, we'll not come."

"Okay Al, I'll talk to you later." then added, "If it weren't for our problem with Inspector Ruffo, I would love to stay with your forever."

"Oh yes, the other question I had really concerned me about the weather, darling man, since we've been having fog for several days, did you have any problem with the fog this morning?"

"Not really," Al lied, "I managed to get back before eleven."

"Well," Lucy added, "we've still got some fog here but it should lift by tomorrow morning. I guess I'd better let you get back to work and I've got to practice at least two hours at the Conservatory. Her's a big smooch for my man." and after the sound of an exaggerated kiss, she hung up.

For several minutes, Al sat in a glow of joy. Again he silently repeated his mantra, "Lucy, you are my love and my life."

Soon, he recovered from his spell and realized that by suddenly mentioning the weather code, he had not only confused Lucy, but certainly confused Leone.

But upon further reflection, he concluded that Lucy had picked up the code and tossed in the comment about the Inspector which would add further confusion to Leone's understanding of the entire conversation.

Sitting in the almost dark room, Al turned on the lights and noting that it was seven, he quickly prepared a light supper which he slowly consumed, as his mind continued a restless analysis of the day's events.

Soon he was ready for bed, but picked up a day-old copy of the Herald-Tribune and glanced at the front page: "Reagan refuses to see Gorbachev;

Senate votes to support 'Contras'; House Democrats reject Reagan's budget." Then turning to a page 2 news summary, Al noted a few lines that Reagan ordered an investigation of criminal abuse of drubs in labor unions.

"Well," Al observed, "it seems that Ronnie is hell-bent on destroying any cooperation with mainstream Democrats.

Had Al been a bit more prescient, he would have been ready for Reagan's blustering behavior with Africa and with Lybia's Quaddafi.

Slowly Al dropped the paper and drifted away.

Some eight hours later, Al aroused himself, turned on the bedroom light and glanced out the window.

"Damn!" he muttered, "more fog and thicker than a bucket of cold bean soup. Well, I hope Lucy and Dawn can cut through this slop."

"I'd better phone and remember the code."

Quickly he dialed and after two rings he was greeted with Dawn's cheery "Hello."

When asked about the fog and their travel plans, Dawn cheerfully answered, "The fog isn't too bad here. Of course we're driving and will be there no later than eleven."

Al took a deep breath. "I'm glad to hear that, but why don't you drive directly here and then we can decide our next move."

"Sounds good to me Pops. See you at your pad. Bye."

Dawn's confident assurance always impressed Al. "She's smart, beautiful and sexy, and real catch for the right guy."

With details out of the way, Al prepared himself a hungry man's breakfast, juice, bacon and eggs over-easy, and a stack of whole wheat toast, and a large mug of black coffee.

His apprehensions of the night had been cast aside by Dawn's brilliance and wit.

"She really is an unusual woman. Were it not for Lucy, I could have gotten involved with Dawn, but that relationship would never have worked out. We're much too different, and much more importantly, I'm too old for her and really for Lucy too. But Lucy and I are very much alike in so many ways—music, art, tolerance, generosity, trusting—too much, affectionate, liberal. Somehow we've been cheated. I'm too old and she's too young.

"To be fair I should seriously discuss our age differences with her. I'm forty-five years older than she and should we marry, at age eighty, if by some miracle, I'm still alive, she would be only thirty-five—an old man and a young woman in her prime.

"Furthermore, if my heart condition is as serious as I'm afraid it is, I'll never live to eighty. In all fairness, I must somehow let her know about my heart. But what happens when I do? She would probably give up her first major piano concert of the city's Maggio musical series. No, I can't do that. Furthermore, maybe my heart problems aren't as serious as I believe they are. The only thing left for me is to see a cardiologist, have an examination, hope that my condition isn't too serious and maybe there's medication. Yes, that's the answer. See a heart doctor as soon as possible."

Casually glancing at his watch, Al was surprised by the time, ten-thirty. "Well, the ladies might be here by eleven, but I doubt it, if the fog is as bad as it was yesterday." Quickly he shaved, dressed quickly but appropriately, and suddenly he heard pounding on the front door.

Lucy and Dawn burst into the room and immediately greeted Al with unusual spirit and affection.

"Well, Pops, have you completed our grand strategy?" Dawn questioned.

"Hardly, but I've given it plenty of speculation. But let's drive down to Greve and make our presence known. But how did you manage to get here early? Wasn't the fog a serious problem?"

"That it was, but we left early fortunately," Lucy explained, "because we couldn't drive over fifteen miles an hour and since we were coming this way, the traffic in our lane was very light."

"Before we make our appearance in Greve, would you ladies like some coffee, or use my bathroom facilities?" Al joked.

"Thank you sir. I'll accept your hospitality." Dawn smiled as she left the room.

"Al, you merry prankster, you almost confused me with your coded weather reports. And I'm certain that Leone will be even more confused if he listens to his own tapes."

"You're right, darling. I did confuse the message, but then I detected a pause in your answer, which was very effective, because it almost confused me too."

Dawn had returned and suggested they all descend on Greve's citizens and "maybe we'll see that handsome evil art dealer, our friend and enemy, Signore Michele Leone."

Outside a few rays of sun seemed to be cutting the fog, but the steep switch-backs demanded slow, careful driving.

Soon, Lucy parked the Alpha in the half-filled square and the trio began their nonchalant stroll around the square. At several small, but interesting shops, they entered and were always greeted with polite enthusiasm.

Quite obviously every shop owners recognized Al and possibly Lucy and Dawn.

"Buon giorno, Professore e Signorne" many shop owners and towns-people offered.

Appropriately the trio found several small items of interest which they purchased along with bread and pastry, which Al suggested and then added some chicken and vegetables.

"I hope you're not planning a meal for us," Lucy questioned.

"No darling, just a few items for my larder."

"You're dispensa, Al, my lover and chef."

"Oh, so that's what it's called. Good, at my rate of learning, I should be speaking reasonably good Italian in fifteen or twenty years."

After almost an hour of browsing and idling in shops, Al startled Dawn and Lucy with the suggestion that they have lunch "on me" in the Restorante Moro.

Almost nonplused Lucy and Dawn appeared confused, "You said the Moro, Al? Lucy asked.

"Sure, why not?" Al answered.

No both women laughed. "Of course, why not. Besides, it's probably the best trattoria in town."

Once in the narrow confines of Moro, the three quickly settled at a table near the kitchen and soon the same friendly waiter, Dino, approached them with a big smile, "Buongiorno, Professore e Signorne Dawn e Lucia."

Leaving them with menus, Dino returned to three other tables, each with a middle-aged couple quietly dining and talking.

Before Al could comment, both Dawn and Lucy giggled, "that night, what a surprise and what a shock!"

"It's one that I will never forget." Al added.

"Nor will probably few of the diners who stayed around to take in the action." Dawn laughed.

"You got off lucky, Dawn. You escaped before the violence got heavy."

"And I went there to celebrate a couple of birthdays and had to defend myself from your drunken boyfriend, Lucy."

"I'm still almost too embarrassed to think about it. As for that boyfriend, he turned out to be a wolf in sheep's clothing. I can't believe that his drunken behavior came from my friendly and helpful coach and swimming teacher at the Club Sport."

Have you gone back since?" Al asked.

"Yes, but only once. He was giving a woman a swimming lesson."

"Did you wave to him? And did he see you or recognize you?" Dawn asked.

"No, I didn't wave to him and I pretended not to see him when he waved to me."

By now Dino had returned and waited patiently as the trio ordered a few dishes: salads, pasta, soup and wine. "And gelato later." Al added.

The historic night wads soon charged with questions and answers about Signore Leone, then suddenly Al nudged Lucy who quickly responded "So there the bastard is."

At this point Leone was talking with Dino. Seated at a point almost opposite the entrance, he obviously hadn't seen the trio until Dino whispered the message.

Abruptly Leone, obviously surprised, stared hard, then managing a smile, he arose and somewhat cautiously approached the trio.

Before Leone reached earshot, Al whispered, "Let's be friendly, cool but surprised."

At the table with Al and Michele standing, and vigorously shaking hands, Lucy and Dawn smiled and awaited recognition.

Quickly, Michele, all confidence and aplomb, offered, "What an absolutely marvelous coincidence that I should be so fortunate to meet the two most charming and beautiful women I've ever known."

But neither woman quickly accepted Michele's easy charm, which was all the handsome womanizer needed to accept the chair Dino had ready.

After appropriate small talk, including orders for wine and more dishes,

Michele became casually inquisitive, "How do you happen to be in our fair town? I thought you were both very busy with your studies in Florence?"

"Yes, of course, we are Michele. As you know Lucia is practicing harder than ever for her piano recital as the guest artist at Maggio Musicale and I'm studying for several mid-term examinations. I'm sure you remember these exams form your year at Stanford."

"Oh, indeed I do, but I also remember how difficult they were particularly for this poor Italian student."

"Oh, come now, Michele," Al added, "I'll bet you had no real academic challenge at Stanford."

Lucia almost commented, but Michele accepted Al's compliment with a smile. "Thank you, Professore, you are very generous. But it's true the examinations were difficult, and the only reason I made the Dean's list was because I had learned to study very hard in high school, particularly at Lowell High in my junior year where I had the good fortune to have been accepted as an Italian exchange student."

Dawn was quick with a winning smile and approval, "Michele, you always were a smart and challenging winner."

As Michele reveled in the pleasure of Dawn's extravagance, Al nodded while Lucia faked a weak smile.

For several minutes the conversation was strained as each diner sought a topic to break the impasse.

Finally Al seized the initiative with a question to Michele, "I suppose you know that Dawn and Lucia have moved form their house in Florence to stay at my place until Inspector Ruffo completes his important investigation of the very serious problem concerning the several robberies which have threatened Lucia and Miss Knight?"

The question appeared to take Michele by surprise, who was temporarily at a loss for words. "No, no, I was not aware of that serious problem or the investigation. I hardly know what to say."

Sensing Michele's confusion, Al added, "As you know, some unknown person or persons broke into Lucia's house about ten days ago."

"Oh, yes, I knew about that, but did you tell me or was it Inspector Ruffo?"

"Of course Lucia told you, Michele, and maybe the Inspector did too."

"But now the situation has become much more important particularly so since Lucia and Dawn and I had a long and very serious discussion with Inspector Ruffo, who promised that he would conduct a very thorough investigation and submit his findings to the Chief of Police."

For several seconds, Michele sat quietly, obviously very nervous, his brow furrowed. Finally he asked, "Did, did, the Inspector name anybody whom he thought might be involved in these crimes?"

"No, of course he didn't. He couldn't without risking his reputation and his job."

Al's answer drew a deep sigh of relief form Michele, who cautiously answered, "Exactly. I know the Inspector fairly well as a personal friend and I am confident of his integrity and honesty." Michele smiled. "Did the Inspector suggest or indicate how long his investigation would last and would his report be released to the press?

Both Dawn and Lucia had remained silent as Al continued to pressure Michele to break. But now Dawn saw a possible opening in Michele's question. "As you probably know, Michele, the laws in the United States are very different regarding police investigations. In the 'States criminal investigations and related reports concerning specific individuals may only be reported publicly at the risk of a counter-suit by the individual who was named."

Then Lucia added, "but here in Italy, the law is just the opposite, In the 'States, one is always innocent until proven guilty, while here the reverse is true. One is guilty until proven innocent."

"So by that line of reasoning," Al added, "when the Inspector's report is made public and certain persons are charged then that person or persons may be found guilty unless they can be found innocent by a judge. I believe this is the way the judicial systems differ in the United States and not only Italy, but all of Europe."

Again Michele's nervous body language betrayed his confidence. "Yes, I understand your explanation, Professor, and you are correct. But in such a specific case, as Inspector Ruffo's report, I cannot believe that any really serious legal action would follow unless the Inspector digs up something far more important than a couple of robberies."

Smiling broadly, Dawn added, "Well, Michele, you don't have anything to worry about. Obviously you had nothing to do with the robberies and the implied danger to Lucia or to me. And I believe that the Inspector's report will not implicate you in any way, manner or form."

With that subtle bit of sophistry, Michele replied with a benign smile of gratitude. "Thank you, Miss Knight, for your generous and important words of support and I hope that Lucia and the Professor share your opinion."

For seconds Lucia and Al frowned then recognizing Dawn's calculated ploy, they added their words of approval: "Of course, no big deal. Nothing to worry about, Michele."

Not wishing to prolong their teasing game, the trio terminated their fortuitous meeting with a mutual excuse for study, practice and writing.

"Of course, I understand you have more important things to do, as indeed I do too, but I certainly appreciate your advise and opinions."

Now on their feet, the trio shook hands with Leone, who quickly paid the bill and departed.

As Al and Lucia and Dawn left Ristorante Moro, Michele's Mercedes sped quickly out of sight.

"Well, Dawn gloated, "we really had the lion growling, didn't we?"

"You certainly did, Dawn. But for a couple of seconds I didn't grasp your sarcasm," Lucia added.

Now Al offered his words of praise, but wondered, "Leone, the growling lion. That's good, but I'm afraid he is also a wounded lion, and a growling, wounded lion can be very dangerous."

As they soon reached Lucia's Alpha, the trio suddenly were aware of swirling wisps of cold damp fog.

"Damn!" Al muttered. "I thought the fog would life by now."

"Well," Lucia offered, "I don't want to drive back to Florence now. It would be too dangerous."

"Right, let's get back to Al's house and if the fog begins to lift, we leave. But I'm in no hurry, besides, I don't have a date or anything to do tonight in Florence. Let's go to Al's and celebrate."

Al was quietly pleased with their decision and added, "I've plenty of good food and drink and maybe we could take in a movie."

"A movie?" Dawn asked.

"Yes, a cinema, there's one here in Greve, and they are showing a comedy tonight."

Without further comment, they slowly ascended the fog-bound switch-backs to Al's house. Once in the comfort of the warm, spacious old structure, Al deposited his purchases in his dispensa as Lucia produced several bottles of Al's wines and liquors.

Then both women gently pushed Al out of the kitchen. "Sorry, Pops, but we're in charge now." Dawn laughed. "Read the paper or put on some music."

Minutes later Dawn produced three martinis as Lucia placed a large plate of antipasto on the small end table.

"Before we imbibe, "I propose a toast, here's to the three lion-tamers who teased the lion while twisting his tail!"

"That's a wonderful toast, Dawn. I'll gladly drink to that." Al added.

"But," Lucia suggested, "let's tie a knot in his tail."

"And," Dawn joked, "may be never get another piece of tail."

Now the conversation became bawdy with several old limericks and concluded with Dawn's winner:

An enterprising young lady named Gale
Was working her way through Yale
For the sake of the blind on her behind
Was the price of her tail in braille.

After several more feeble efforts at levity, all agreed that dinner should be prepared and later they should investigate the local cinema.

Again, Al was relegated to his "work" while Dawn and Lucy prepared a gorgeous dinner of roast chicken, pasta and vegetables, and concluded with chocolate sundaes.

Some forty-five minutes later, Al was awakened from a nap and escorted to the feast.

"You ladies are too much, too wonderful. What did I ever do to deserve this treatment?"

"Good sire," Dawn solemnly intoned, "you are the Knight and our Master. Now sit down, pour some wine and regale us with your charm and wit."

The elegant meal and coffee ended with several witty proclamations about bearding the Lion of Judea.

"Now before we descend to Cinema Boito, I'll wash the dishes." Al ordered.

With only token protests, Dawn and Lucia vanished and reappeared some ten minutes later as Al had just finished his kitchen assignment.

"We're ready for a good movie whenever you are, Pop!"

Turning and facing them, Al was pleasantly surprised how chic and stunning both women were. "Wow! I didn't know you two women had so many beautiful clothes."

"We don't, at least I don't have any dresses here. These are Lucy's dresses. We frequently wear each other's clothes."

"These, I forgot when I was here the last time." Lucy explained.

"Well, you are both smashing. I'll put on a tie and jacket."

Minutes later they were in the Alpha, which Lucia carefully negotiated safely down the foggy switch-backs into Greve.

At the first and only intersection, Lucy asked, "Which, darling?"

"It's the next intersection, and turn left."

As the fog seemed thicker than ever, "Lucia slowly moved forward until she saw car headlights form the connecting street.

"The theater is about two hundred meters straight ahead and just beyond the little bridge over the creek."

As they approached the theater, numerous cars slowly searched for parking spaces.

"Now what, Pops?"

"Why don't you two park the car while I buy the tickets. I'll meet you near the box office."

Al carefully dodged the few cars still caught in the fog. At the box office, Al waited until his turn, "Tre biglietti, per piacere."

"Scusa, signore, il teatro e completo."

Al was confused and asked, "No biglietti?"

"Si, professore, ma per voi—in leetul balcony okay?"

"Si tre." Al stammered.

The very polite attendent produced tickets adding, twenty-one tousand lire, puleese."

"Mille graze! Signore."

Soon Lucia and Dawn appeared, "This place must be filled, but we finally found a place to park."

At the door, the attendant studied the three Americans, then explained to Lucia that all of the seats were sold, but they could sit in the small balcony near the projectionist.

Lucy quickly explained. "Since you have already bought the tickets and there are no more seats on the main floor, we must sit in the small balcony, okay?"

Quickly they noticed a small entry with stairs, which soon brought them to a tiny balcony with several chairs next to a light operator who hardly noticed them.

"This isn't much of a a theater." Lucia questioned Al, "but it's completely sold out."

Then Dawn asked, "Al, are you sure this is a cinema or a theater with live entertainment?"

"I don't know, but we'll soon find out."

Seconds later, the house lights slowly dimmed and soft strains of Liszt's "Hungarian Rhapsody" filled the small theater. Simultaneously, the stage curtains parted on a scene of a small house and square and two or three painted buildings.

Suddenly the music ascended to a crashing coda, as the theater darkened, then as the stage lights brightened, an almost totally nude beautiful blonde playing a violin, repeated two or three bars of Liszt's "Rhapsody".

The theater was very quiet as the nude violinist who wore only a thin silk net wrap over her shoulders, played several bars before the announcer introduced her Princesslina, to a cheering audience of about three hundred or more males and possibly twenty-five women.

Al, seated between Dawn and Lucia, was at a loss for words as the women repeated in his ears, "What have you gotten us into? This isn't a movie! Who is this naked bitch?"

Al could only struggle a plaintiff response, "I thought it was a movie. I'm terribly sorry. Shall we leave?"

Lucy started to rise, but Dawn whispered, "Oh sit down. This might be interesting."

Quickly Princesslina played a series of popular pieces, snatches of Chopin, Tschaikovsky, Brahms, and several Italian songs, which evoked an immediate and loud enthusiastic response.

Then removing her see-through wrap, she bowed and threw kisses to the cheering audience. As the cheers subsided, Princesslina began a series of dances, bumps and grinds, accompanied by canned music. Her sensual hip and breast movements–her breasts were large and firm–produced loud cheers, whistles and clapping.

Lucy turned to Al and whispered, "She's quite pretty, very sexy and can play the violin. How do you like her?"

Embarrassed and flustered, Al could only reply, "Yes, she's pretty and can play the fiddle."

Then Dawn whispered in Al's ear, "You sly devil. You heard about Princesslina, didn't you? And you must admit, she's really a very sexy lady!"

After several more variations of her dance and violin accompaniment, she handed her violin to a stage hand and said something. Whatever she said to the cheering crowd, produced a standing ovation.

Then responding to their requests, she began a slow sensuous maneuver as to suggest fornication. Her rhythmic grinding, twisting and thrusting pelvis brought most of the males to their feet in a chorus of yelling and whistling.

Finally, she indicated a three minute respite only to return with her violin for several short pieces, which clearly proved that she could indeed play the violin professionally.

Next she announced something to the audience, which immediately evoked cheers and whistles and increased as three males quickly climbed onto the stage.

Both Dawn and Lucy were as amused as Al was embarrassed.

Now Princesslina questioned each male and rewarded each with a kiss. Then to searing canned music, she danced and teased each male while pushing her firm and ample breasts against them while teasing them by grinding and arching her pelvis against each male who alternately pushed and shoved to gain body contact.

Al could hardly contain himself, "I'm sorry, Dawn and Lucia. I had no idea this was a sex show."

But the women only laughed and whispered, "Stop worrying, Al. Besides, look whose in the second row. It's our sexy lion!" Somehow the unexpected appearance of their enemy seemed to vindicate Al and offer him some solace.

For another half-hour Princesslina encouraged males to join her, which seemed to suggest a series of sexual behaviors, but nothing explicit could be seen.

Finally, in a grand finale, after the last male had departed, Princesslina began a slow rhythmic dance, sensuously moving circularly as she dipped low while projecting her hips forward with her torso and breasts sloping back. As her lithe motions carried her forward toward the stage apron, she slowly stopped, then bending far back on her heels, her pelvis arched and projecting upward, her legs spread wide, she suddenly spurted a golden stream over the stage lights and beyond the screaming males in the front row.

The entire house erupted in an explosion of laughter, clapping, whistles and shouts.

Quickly, Al pushed Dawn and Lucy toward the stairs and out the front door.

They were well beyond the theater as both women laughed and teased Al with taunts. "So you took us to a tits and ass show, Al, and now you're embarrassed." Lucy was secretly delighted.

Then Dawn added her evaluation, "Al, we're not embarrassed, so why should you protest? We both loved it. That lady sure has the equipment to drive males crazy!"

"And that climax! I wouldn't believe it if I hadn't seen it. That woman peed at least twelve or fifteen feet and several guys got a golden shower!"

By now they reached Lucy's car and soon they slowly climbed through the dense fog to their welcomed fortress.

Once inside the warm house, Dawn and Lucia again teased Al only long enough to receive a gently scolding. "Please, dear friends, enough is enough. I've apologized. I was stupid. Now let's have a nightcap and get some needed sleep."

Quickly, Lucia embraced Al and with a loving kiss added, "We know that you misunderstood the situation, but Al, darling, Dawn and I were amused and educated by Princesslina's performance. I'm glad that I saw the show."

"Me too," Dawn added. "I wouldn't believe that anybody could really pee that far, and more importantly, several hundred males would be sexually aroused."

"I'm not sure that the men were aroused as they were amazed. Anyway, let's have some brandy and call it a night."

For a few more minutes, they sat enjoying the soothing brandy, while discussing their immediate plans,

"I suppose you will return to Florence tomorrow morning?" Al asked.

"Yes, of course, fog or not. I've missed too many hours and days of practice."

"And I hope none of my professor's have noticed my absence. But that one guy, Leo Biagge, who teaches Italian art history, probably noticed my absence because he frequently has asked me to see him in his office."

"Has he made any moves?" Lucy asked.

"Oh, not directly, but he has come on pretty strong, like suggesting he take me on a personal tour of the Uffizi. I'd have to be stupid not to understand his motives."

Al noted his watch, "Well, it's almost eleven, so I'm turning in. But ladies, you have first call on the bathroom."

Soon the lights were out and Lucy and Al were close together in bed. Holding each other passionately, Lucy whispered, "Al, you're such a lover, so intense and giving and yet you acted like an old prude at the theater."

"Yes, I did. And I suppose that I am something of a Puritan, insofar as overt public sexual behavior is demonstrated. And I guess that maybe I was really embarrassed because I was afraid you and Dawn might think I was really a dirty old man."

Lucy only laughed and teased Al with luscious French kisses. Al quickly responded with nimble dancing fingers playing Lucy's body like a keyboard as she responded with sighs and low moans, followed by gasps, hard breathing and a climax of pleasure which radiated throughout her entire body.

As they lay quietly, Lucy now rhythmically positioned her body around and over Al's always caressing, teasing with fingers, mouth and tongue, until he exploded into spasms of ecstasy.

Slowly they were engulfed in a deep, dreamless sleep.

Arising shortly after seven, the trio shared a simple breakfast and quickly reviewed their plans.

"When can I expect to see you again?" Al inquired. "During your absence, I expect to complete my book and what about the future?"

"I suppose that between your plotting and my studies at the conservatory, we must try to determine what the lion is doing."

"Right," Dawn added, "and I am the designated sheep bait for the lion, right?"

Now they are agreed to keep each other fully informed, but also agreed they should plan to visit Lucia's grandparents on or before Easter.

Soon their discussions were complete and Al reluctantly kissed first Dawn and then Lucy in almost a tearful farewell.

"And if necessary, call me," Al added, "but don't forget our weather code prefix."

At the car, an additional sound of hugs and kisses and then they were gone.

Back in the house, Al sat quietly, reflecting on everything from Leone's surprise meeting at Ristorante Moro and then his own gaucherie during and following Princesslina's sexually explicit act. "Maybe it was okay for me to be embarrassed. Had I not been, both women would probably have been embarrassed. As it turned out, maybe I lucked out. And in bed, Lucy was so quickly responsive, she must have climaxed ten or fifteen times. And I think Dawn too was very aroused. I would never believe that such explicit sexual behavior by one woman could so thoroughly arouse another who was simply watching. Strange. And that leads me to conclude that Dawn might pursue Leone. He's bound to find her and ask for a date and then the heavy fireworks will really begin."

Finally to break his critical soliloquy, Al poured himself some coffee and attempted to resume the final short chapter of his "potboiler." It didn't stimulate him and he was aware of a nervous reaction in his chest. Quickly he took his pulse, which was quite rapid. "Damn!" he uttered loudly, "Well, I must see a doctor in Florence. Someone at the consulate must have a list of doctors."

Then checking the weather, he was surprised by the clear sky and sunshine.

Minutes later, after again carefully locking the heavy door, he was again on the road to Florence. For a few seconds, he considering stopping by the "new" apartment and calling the consulate for a heart doctor's number, but he quickly dismissed the idea as too dangerous for Lucia.

Finally, parking near the Piazza Sante Croce,, he quickly found a telephone and book which eventually led him to the name of a medical doctor and address. Now remembering that he had tossed a city map into the glove compartment, he was delighted to note the doctor's office was near the cathedral.

Within ten minutes, he had located the street and number of Dr, Sprandoli's office. Ascending the narrow stairway, he soon entered the doctor's office and requested to see the doctor. Soon the middle-aged doctor appeared, and in excellent, but accented English, greeted Al–who introduced himself as Professor Praitt.

Once in the inner office, the Doctor asked several routine medical questions, which Al hesitantly answered.

"So you think you have had a series of heart attacks, Professor? Could you describe where you feel the pain and how long did it last, and please explain if you had any other symptoms of pain or nervousness."

Slowly, Al described the pain–the center, near his heart and maybe some degree of nauseousness.

For a moment, the doctor stared at the ceiling and then tentatively replied, "I don't think that you had a real heart attack, Professore. But I will give you an EKG test. But first, please take off your shirt and undershirt and I will listen with my stethoscope. That will give me some idea about the strength and regularity of your heartbeat. Then I'll place a few electric wires on your chest and hook these up to my recording device, which should give me an accurate measure of the frequency and strength of your heartbeat. This is a painless procedure, which will take only a few minutes."

As Al removed his shirt and tee-shirt, the Doctor quickly took a series of readings on and all around the heart. Then removing his stethoscope, he quietly said, "Well, sir you have no symptoms of a heart attack. But now let me attach these small suction cups to several places around your chest and to those places where major arteries would indicate irregular heart pumping activity.

Again, the procedure was simple and seemingly easy. For two or three minutes, the Doctor watched a graph with an electric needle indicator of the specific strength and regularity of the heartbeat.

Soon, Dr. Sprandoli removed the equipment and turned off the recording device.

"Now, Professor, I do have some important information. Periodically, you have had a series of arrhythmias. They usually subside after a few minutes, leaving you feeling tired and weak."

"Are these life-threatening, Doctor?"

"Not usually, but if they persist untreated over a few years, they are very serious. Also there are several types of arrhythmias. The atrial and ventricular, which refer to upper and lower areas of your heart, and are caused by the irregular heartbeat between these areas. In effect, they are caused by a kind of electric short-circuit between the upper or lower parts of your heart. I've given you an over-simplification of how your heart functions. It's very complicated, and I'm not fully qualified to advise you about further heart treatment. I could prescribe a drug called Wayfarin or Coumadin, which is a blood thinner and anti-coagulant, which will prevent blood clots. These clots are very dangerous, because unless properly eliminated, they can break off and travel into the circulatory system and cause serious damage.

"Also, I've given you a prescription for Verapamil, which helps to prevent arrhythmias."

The doctor's examination and prescriptions almost instantly eased Al's fears.

"One final word, Professor, when do you expect to return to America? Although I believe the medications I've suggested should take care of your heart problems for a few months, you should consult your doctor soon after your return home. And I am confident he will help you recover completely. Actually, you seem to be in good health. Obviously you've taken good care of yourself, which mitigates any serious problems for now."

"Thank you very much, Dr. Sprandoli. You've relieved my fears."

Having written the two prescriptions, the doctor added any pharmacy would fill them quickly.

"And now my bill, Doctor?"

"Yes, my secretary has prepared one. This is my usual fee for the examination and tests. It works out to $125 American."

With that, Al produced the exact sum and with further words of gratitude, Al quickly departed.

Chapter Seven

Relieved by Dr. Sprandoli's tests and advise, Al soon found a pharmacy, and with his medications returned quickly to his car.

Although he had intended to return directly to Greve, he now decided to share his good news with Lucy and Dawn. "But," he warned himself, "don't make too much about it."

After several repeated rings at the girls' apartment, Al heard Dawn's voice coming from an open window on the second floor.

Suddenly there was Dawn, smiling and exuberant. "Welcome, Pop. Come in. What brings you to our new apartment?"

As they ascended the wide staircase, Al casually mentioned that he had just had a physical exam and hoped he might see his "girlfriends" before driving back to Greve.

"Well, how nice you're here, Al. Lucy is at the Conservatory and I have a class at two. But it's lunch time, so I'll fix something fast and easy. But why did you have a physical?"

"Oh, it wasn't necessary, but I've occasionally felt uneasy so I saw a doctor who said I was in good shape, but gave me prescriptions for medications which will relieve my occasional anxiety attacks."

Dawn laughed, "So your bedroom athletics have worn you out."

"Please, Dawn, don't embarrass me. Maybe last night's porn show was too much for me."

"I seriously doubt that, you horny old fox. It wasn't Princesslina's show, it was yours and Lucy's later. I heard you guys groaning and moaning and I was almost tempted to join in. But I guess that you and Lucy are too straight for a frolicsome threesome."

"Dawn, I appreciate your humor, but really, I'm too old for multiple partners and I'm certain Lucy shares my feelings."

"Of course, Al. Please forgive my libidinous suggestion. But in all candor, Al, I must admit that women last night really turned me on. If Lucy hadn't been here, you would have been raped."

Blushing and embarrassed, Al could only add, "Well, Dawn, you surely know several available men."

"Right! But when I or any other male or female is in heat, we need quick satisfaction, capisce?"

"Yes, of course. Now, may I change the subject?"

"Of course, Al. Have a sandwich and some wine."

Relieved, Al asked, "Have you considered when you might make a move on Signore Leone?"

"Yes I have, and I plan to call him later this afternoon, and if he responds as I expect he will, I'll have an expensive dinner with him tonight."

"Good, but do you feel strong enough—no—confident enough that you can control his amorous behavior?"

"Of course I do. I wouldn't put myself in such a vulnerable position if I didn't think that I could handle it."

"Having finished eating, Al thanked Dawn and wished her well. Then added, "Please don't mention my doctor's visit, but please ask her to call me around seven."

Upon reaching Greve Al stopped for a Herald Tribune, checked his mail and exchanged greetings with several shopkeepers. Without realizing it, Al was rapidly becoming the town's celebrated Professore.

Once in his medieval stronghold, Al scanned the paper, then remembering his medication, he washed down the Verapamil with bottled water, which seemed to ease his anxiety.

"Well," he reflected, "back to this piece of junk." Having reread the last twenty pages, he was quietly satisfied.

For several minutes he sat silently reflecting on the confused pattern of his life. Suddenly he was aroused from a deep sleep by the telephone's repeated rings.

"Hello, hello! How wonderful to hear your voice, darling. How did your practice go?"

As Lucia began to answer, suddenly he heard the clicking sound of the recorder. "Because of the weather I needed things in Florence which aren't available here."

Almost mesmerized by the sounds of each other's voice, both Al and Lucy struggled for words which would make sense, but confuse Leone.

"You asked about Dawn, Al? I saw her just as she was leaving. She was all dressed up so she must have a date."

"Yes, but I think she probably has a date with Michele because he had asked me about arranging a date. We needn't worry about them. They're made for each other.

Then in a whisper Al added, "I must see you soon. Maybe next week when we plan to visit your grandparents in Panzano?"

Reluctantly Lucy agreed. "I know that I've got to practice every day and my teacher is very supportive. Yes, she has suggested a wonderful program. There's music for everybody."

"Of course my program isn't a secret. It will be a short program beginning with Bach's Chromatic Fantasy and Fugue. Then Mozart's Rondo in A minor, followed by Beethoven's Apassionata. Then following a fifteen-minute break, I'll complete my program with Beethoven's last Sonata in C major, number 32, opus 111. Some of this is very tragic, much like the Hammerklavier 106, which we've discussed, but this C major piece doesn't bother me as much as 106. It seems to fit my tragic sense."

"What about encores, darling? The theater is certain to be sold out."

"Yes, I hope so. But as long as they clap, I'll play. The encores? Probably Beethoven's Romance opus 50, then maybe some Ravel, Debussy and Janacek's October 1905–a very tragic piece–it's part of a longer sonata he had planned. This will prepare the crowd for my final encore, Lizst's Consultation, number 3–a real tear-jerker."

"After that very long program, darling, may I take you out for a late-night dinner?"

"Not may you," Lucy laughed, "but will you?" Then she added, "Since I can't eat before playing, I'll be famished after playing. But your invitation does suggest a problem. I mean, who will join us?"

"Oh, let's not worry too much. But Dawn, of course, and your grandparents, and who knows, maybe Leone."

At this Lucy almost answered, "I don't think so."

"But we don't have to finalize our plans now, do we?"

"Of course not, darling. But we'll see each other soon at your grandparents in Panzano."

Very reluctantly they said good night.

For several minutes Al sat reflecting on the interesting complexities of the immediate future. Probably Dawn is with Leone right now. Between my encouraging him to see Dawn and her self-admitted sexual appetite, this would be an interesting evening for a voyeur. But the more important effect of their meeting is who will win and who will loose. I would bet on Dawn, but how much verbal teasing can she risk without letting herself go? I'm afraid that unless she holds him off she will give in, which for our side, could be a serious defeat.

Then mentally shrugging off the fantasy, Al had a light supper and was off to bed.

Either the medication worked like a soporific or Al was ready for a good night's sleep, nevertheless, by seven a.m. he was alert and ready for action.

After a hearty breakfast Al was restless. Briefly he reviewed the fantasy event with Leone. Then dismissing that, he decided to mail his potboiler. Quickly he produced a self-prepared manila envelope, and with a short note to his agent he squeezed in his manuscript and muttered, "Good riddance."

Soon he was ready to deliver the small but weighty package to the post office. And with that out of the way he decided to call Dawn on the nearby public telephone and ask about her meeting.

After several repeated rings he heard Dawn's grumpy, "Hello."

"Good morning, Dawn! This is Al."

"I might have known! So now you want a report on last night's ten-round championship!"

"Really? Was it that bad?"

"Without abusing the truth, it was awful!"

"Oh! I'm really sorry, I had hoped everything would have been satisfying."

"Yes, the first part was, an excellent dinner and plenty of good wine.

But when we returned to his apartment, the action quickly became a wrestling match. That bastard was all over me. Fortunately I'm almost as strong as he is or I wouldn't be talking to you now!"

"So it was really bad? I'm terribly sorry Dawn. I had no idea that he would come on so strong."

"It isn't your fault, Al. I volunteered to be lion meat, which I wasn't, but I sure as hell wasn't a lion tamer."

"I really feel awful, Dawn. I should have known better, particularly after Lucy's long and bitter experience."

"Oh, don't worry, Al. This was only the first round, which was pretty much even. And now if I see him again, he won't know what hit him. I know how to play dirty. I've done battle with other guys who thought they were going to have an easy lay."

Surprised by Dawn's bitter but strong language, Al asked, "You mean you're going to see Leone again?"

"Hell, yes I am! And soon, and he asked for it."

"Really, you are willing to risk you life a second time? Please don't, Dawn. Not for Lucy or me. He may have something worse if you risk meeting him again."

"Look, Pops, you know I can handle myself. My dad taught me how to fight and how to shoot. Not that I intend killing the bastard, but a few well-placed kicks in his pride and joy and he'll be screaming for mercy."

Almost embarrassed by Dawn's violent threats, Al soon begged off. "Well, aside from the violence, I guess the evening was anything but pleasant."

"Oh, it was okay, Pop. Don't sweat it. I've got to get started. I have a class at nine. Now take care. I'll see you soon."

After hanging up, Al slowly walked back to the Fiat. Clearly he was confused and angry with himself. "I should have known better than to risk our plans, but Dawn is really risking everything to see Leone again."

Finally he wandered into the nearby coffee shop, bought the *Herald Tribune* and scanned the news. "Um, so Reagan is again threatening Quadaffi. Stupid! There are still thousands of Italians working in Libya." But his mind continued to dwell on last night's fiasco. Unable to dispel his concern, he decided to phone Leone.

Again he solicited help from the obliging young woman who accepted

Al's money and asked, "You want Signore in Greve or Firenze? Is better in Firenze." Al nodded approval and soon he heard Leone's voice.

"Michele, this is Al Praitt. I've been thinking about Dawn."

"You must have read my mind, Professore, and I was just about to call you again. I tried to reach you about an hour ago but you didn't answer."

"You liar," Al thought, "I was still home."

"Well, that's interesting. Michele. I'd like to talk to you about Dawn. She said you had a date last night and seemed to be upset about the evening."

"Really, Al, I'm surprised because I thought we had a good time. But if you would like to see me this afternoon, I'm free. Or if you wish, I could meet you in Greve."

"No, I think your office would be better because I have a doctor's appointment about noon in Florence."

"Good, I'll be waiting for you in my shop. It will be closed but just tap on the door."

As they hung up each man gloated considering that each might dig up some important information.

Even driving reasonably fast Al reached Florence by ten-thirty. Now for a parking place near Piazza Santa Croce. After a few minutes Al found a public parking lot and soon paid the attendant a mandatory five thousand lire–good for three hours.

With a couple of hours to kill, Al wandered toward Piazza dalla Repubblica, had a cappuccino and for the first time since his arrival in Italy, he became an active "people watcher." He was very impressed by how well-dressed everybody was and the absence of vehicle noise and traffic pleased him. For almost on hour he sat comfortably soaking in the color, the beautiful women, and their small thoroughbred dogs. Reluctantly Al stood, left a tip, and wandered off towards Il Duomo, pausing here and there to enjoy the handsome shops. "Funny," he thought, "I've been here for three months and I've never taken the time to really see this beautiful city."

Somehow the bustle and activity of the city captivated his imagination–the smart shops, the well-dressed people, nobody in a hurry. Almost unexpectedly he found himself at the Arno, which he slowly followed toward the Ponte Vecchio. This scene, he mused, could be a painting by a Caravaggio or a Leonardo, not that I know much about each painter. Slowly Al realized that for the first time since his arrival in January, he was intoxicated by the beauty and ambiance of Italy's most beautiful city.

Whether by luck or magic, suddenly Al found himself almost in front of Leone's shop.

For three or four minutes he marveled at the shops, Ferragamo's, Gucci's and, finally, the much smaller was M. Leone, Objects d'Art.

Approaching the door, his euphoria dissolved at the sight of Leone smiling at him—a welcome which seemed to dampen his inner security.

Quickly Michele had Al by the shoulder and in what Al realized was a heartfelt friendship. Leone proclaimed, Professore Praitt, my good friend and comrade in arms, welcome! Together they squeezed easily through the heavy bronze and glass door.

"You're here exactly on time, at least for me," Michele bragged.

"And for me too, Michele. I parked my car somewhere near the Piazza dalla Repubblica and have been strolling around this beautiful city for an hour or more. For the first time since my arrival, I'm seeing and feeling the real Italy, the beauty and pleasure of Florence has suddenly captured and intoxicated me!"

Michele could hardly believe his ears. "This American, this stuffy professor, I can't believe it. He talks and sounds like an Italian."

Al's unexpected and ebullient enthusiasm confused but delighted Michele who completely forgot his plan to impress Al with his several important art pieces.

Quickly Leone swept Al into the plush inner office, which even by Italian standards was a bit overwhelming. "Now Al, first, if you don't mind, I would like to pour a bit of Dom Perignon for us. It's good for our senses as well as our souls."

With the tinkle of crystal as their glasses touched, Al offered, "To my good friend, Michele Leone."

Leone glowed and added, "And to your continued good health, charm and wit."

Obviously both men were combining easily forgotten lies with a naturally shared unexpected camaraderie.

Again Michele deftly filled their glasses and again their dialogue waxed eloquent until each man realized they did have some important self-interest questions and statements to make.

"This wine is absolutely beautiful, Michele, but lest it confuse our thoughts, perhaps we should move on to our shared agenda."

Michele smiled, "You mean our concern about the welfare and well-being of the beautiful Miss Dawn Knight?"

"Quite. She talked to me this morning about your dinner last night, which she much enjoyed."

"As indeed I did too, Al–if you don't mind my familiarity with shortened given names."

"Not at all, Michele, but maybe you could give me a short summary of how you felt about the evening. But before you do, Michele, please accept me as a friend who is inquiring about a young and beautiful mutual friend. Furthermore, if you feel your relationship with Dawn is none of my business, I will accept it and offer no other reason to intrude into yours and Dawn's privacy."

"Thank you for your candor and understanding. I don't think you are intruding and I do welcome your interest in Dawn and our relationship, which I gather is your concern."

"Well, yes, I suppose I am concerned, but only because I like her as a friend and as a good friend of Lucy's. Anyway, to be blunt, for whatever reason, when I asked her how her date with you was, she gave several somewhat confusing answers."

For a second Michele seemed to blanch slightly and coughed, "Well, yes. I think that I probably did confuse her, not that she didn't set me straight. I'll be honest with you, Al. We had a lot to drink and a wonderful dinner, and afterward I invited her here to my office, which she seemed to accept. Then, once here in the privacy of this comfortable room, we began to make out, if that's the correct American term for kissing and feeling each other. I seem to remember a phrase like that from my days at Lowell and Stanford."

"They haven't changed, Michele, and my own feelings are and were, if your date seems to like making out, you do, and if she doesn't she should let you know. I think that I understand the confusion here, Michele."

"The confusion, Al? There wasn't any confusion in our mutual behavior. We were both pretty damned sexually excited and maybe I did come on too strong, but she soon let me know that she didn't like some of my overly strong Italian love-making tactics."

Al was almost nonplussed by Michele's candor. "Well, Michele, what you've just told me is almost exactly what she told me, which hardly leaves me much to say. I know that Dawn is quite capable of handling herself and I, as a father of a once and probably still very sexy daughter, quickly learned that my daughter had to be and also became a very responsible woman."

Michele was secretly overjoyed with Al's encouraging response. "Thank you very much for your understanding words, Al. I really am crazy about Dawn and I do mean love. She would be a wonderful wife and lover, but I suppose for many reasons our relationship would never end in marriage, as is frequently the case in opera."

"In opera? Are you an opera fan, Michele?"

"Very much so. I really enjoy opera, particularly Italian and specifically Mascagni's Cavalleria Rusticana."

"I do too. But what do you like about it?"

"Everything! It's a perfect opera in every respect. It's really a perfect Sicilian story. As a Sicilian, I completely understand and relate to it and it was based on a true Italian story. What could be better or more dramatic than a tragically violent love story sung and acted on an Easter Sunday morning in a small Sicilian town?"

"Yes, and a story of adultery, betrayal and violent death," Al added.

"That opera sometimes seems too real. I could very well have been the Alfio or the Turiddu in that story."

Al was delighted with Michele's revelation. "Might I ask how?"

"Why not? It was many years ago in a small town near Palermo. I was very much in love with a pretty young woman, Alicia, but I left to serve my two years in the army, and when I returned she had already married a slightly older man, Don Riccardo, whom I knew. Well, Alicia and I did see each other and made love, but when her husband found out, he was going to kill me, but I escaped and went to live with my aunt in Catania. There I enrolled at the university, which was really the beginning of my academic life."

"So you really were a Turiddu, Michele?" Al laughed.

"Or an Alfio. Since I haven't married, I couldn't be the jealous husband. But I can understand Alfio perfectly because jealousy is probably the strongest and most violent passions we Italians share. We really are very passionate people, but that is generally true of all Mediterranean people. Not that we're equally violent. We leave the violence to the Germans and Slavs; their histories are written in blood-thirsty brutality. That's why I have little interest in the Krauts or Russkies."

Al was amused and not surprised by Michele's candor.

Suddenly both men noticed the time. "Michele, I suggest that we have something to eat. Nothing elaborate or time consuming. I do have a doctor's appointment, just a check up. Would that be okay with you?"

"Of course, I know a small fast service trattoria nearby. Maybe we could continue our discussion there or later. Better later because I don't like important discussions in public places."

"That's fine with me, Michele, and I, too, don't and won't talk about important or personal affairs in a public place."

Quickly they departed for a small quiet place across the Arno. As they quickly finished some pasta and salad, Michele picked up the check and in a conspiratorial tone suggested, "If you're free tomorrow about this same time, we could discuss one other important problem I had hoped to get to today, but I let the opera get in the way. Tomorrow, Al, Tuesday, at my office."

As Al slowly and carefully retraced his way back to his parked car, he was confronted by the parking attendant who demanded Al's ticket. Fortunately Al produced the ticket and backed from the lot. Then it occurred to him that he should see Dawn or Lucy, whose apartment was nearby, so he backed into the lot and again repeated the toll charge.

At the apartment Al repeatedly rang the bell and finally Dawn leaned out their front window. "Oh, it's you, Pops. I'll be right down."

Escorting him quickly up the stairs, Dawn laughed, "You handsome devil. Have you been out chasing women again?"

"No, but before I met Leone, I did see many beautiful women as I was having coffee in the Piazzo dalla Repubblica."

"Well, you better not tell Lucy that you're suddenly discovering other women."

"I stopped by, Dawn, to discuss several things, i.e. you."

Before Al could complete his sentence Dawn asked coldly, "Me? Why me?"

"Well, after your description of Michele's behavior last night, I thought maybe I should learn what we, you and Lucy, and I should do."

"Okay, I suppose that's a fair answer. But what did the sex master say about last night?"

"You won't believe it, but he said almost the same thing you told me."

"What? I can't believe it. He told you that he came after me like a freight train?"

Al laughed, "Your metaphor seems strong, but he did say he really went after you but that you were too strong. He admitted he got too amorous, which he blamed on too much wine. But he also added that he loves you and hopes that maybe you'll agree."

With a smile Dawn asked, "So he admitted that he really came on strong and that I held him off?"

"Those were almost his very words. And he hopes that you'll forgive him and see him soon."

"Well, Al, that doesn't surprise me, but I am amazed that he told you the truth. But I'll bet he didn't say anything about my bra slipping loose and one boob almost hitting him in the face."

Al burst into laughter. "No, he never mentioned anything like that. Did that really happen?"

"Yes, it really did, Al, and I was terribly embarrassed. It wasn't Michele's fault. He was, shall we say, trying to fondle my breasts?"

"Well, of course he was, what date doesn't?"

"But as I jerked sideways, my bra strap broke and I was wearing that low-cut blouse, which allowed my left boob to almost hit him in the face."

Between laughter and embarrassment, Al was speechless. Then, recovering, he asked, "What did you do then, Dawn?"

"Well, I turned around, found the john, and put myself back together."

Then quickly getting serious, Dawn asked, "So what important news did you get?"

"Not anything really. I had intended to mention the Inspector but Michele, too, had something important to say, so we agreed to meet tomorrow at the same time."

"So you two horny old guys got your jollies talking about my boobs and how sexy I am?"

"Of course not, Dawn. As a matter of fact, we spent most of the time talking about opera and specifically Cavalleria Rusticana, which is Michele's favorite opera.

Then he explained that he, like Turiddu the jilted lover, had been jilted too while he was doing his military service. Then, just like the opera's jilted lover who had married, he resumed his sexual liaison with the guy's wife. And that the guy was going to kill him but he escaped."

"An interesting story," Dawn added, "but do you believe it?"

"Why not? As he confessed, Italians are very jealous lovers and can and do become violent."

"So you're going to see Turiddu-Michele tomorrow? But stay away from opera, let's get some important information. Like his so-called very important papers which he believes you or Dawn or I have or maybe the grandparents."

"Right, Al added, "these papers must exist. Lucy once had her hands on them, but the cops took most of them and the others must be with her grand-parents."

"By the way, Dawn, when do you expect Lucy back?"

"Well, any time soon. Maybe an hour. She's practicing harder than ever. She leaves here by eight and stays at the Conservatory until at least four."

"Does she return at night?"

"Of course but she's become so determined, I wouldn't be surprised if she slept there."

"I ask because I really need to see her. Not anything really important. But since I will see Michele at his office tomorrow at noon, I would like to spend the night here."

Dawn laughed sarcastically, "Of course, Pops, you know we've plenty of bed space and you're welcome in either bedroom."

"Oh, Dawn, don't tease. The three of us are all very dear friends and we're certainly tied together with this interesting character, Michele Leone."

"I'm sorry, Al, I'm not challenging anybody except possibly Don Juan, whom I believe is a big fish that we will soon net."

"Now why don't you sit down, read your paper or watch the Italian boob tube. Or fix yourself a drink. Lucy should be back soon."

"Thank you, Dawn, I'll do as you advise, and if there is anything I can do to help, just give me a growl."

"Give you a what?"

"Call and I'm ready." And with that Al moved into the small living room and soon fell asleep.

Sometime later Al awakened to whispers and quiet laughter. Then he recognized the women's voices, but he couldn't eaves-drop on their soft whispers, so quickly he tip-toed several feet to where they were rapidly conversing.

"Boo! Surprise!"

"Al! You devil! Scare us, will you! We'll make you sing for your supper."

"Lucy, darling, Dawn says you're practicing day and night. But tonight, I hope not!"

"With you here, sweetheart, nobody would pull me back to the Conservatory. Besides, I practiced almost eight hours today and my teacher suggested I take a break."

"Dinner's ready!" Dawn announced.

"Now, maybe we can eat and talk and decide what to do with our alleged friend and sworn enemy. Again, I'm meeting him for lunch tomorrow, which will probably be our last," Al spoke in a low, cautious tone.

"Why do you say that?" Lucy asked.

"Because he clearly stated that he had something very important to discuss."

"There's only one important issue to Leone," Lucy added, "and that is my parents' final deed and will, which he believes will give him all the property and wealth which are mine or my grandparents. I know all about those documents as do my grandparents.

"I don't quite follow, darling. How can Leone claim title to property which has been yours ever since the death of your mother?"

"Well," in a low ominous tone, Lucy almost whispered, "should anything happen to me or my grandparents, then Leone could claim the property and the wealth."

"So you're suggesting that anything happening to you really means should you die, Leone gets the property?"

"Yes, Dawn, that's what I mean. In other words, that rotten bastard could hire an assassin or arsonist—a murderer to kill me and my grandparents."

For seconds nobody spoke, then Al added, "Is that really possible here in Italy?"

"Yes, it really is. That's one of the nice jobs the Mafia has performed many times, and if not the Mafia, there are plenty of men and even women who would gladly perform this service for a large fee. But least I criticize Italy unfairly, there are probably just as many "guns for hire" in the States."

Again a thoughtful silence until Al spoke. "Before we can offer any protective action I believe we must learn how and when Leone intends to get hold of these very important papers. As I am having lunch with him tomorrow, I believe that he will press me to help him get these papers."

At this Dawn added, "And as Al knows but Lucy hasn't heard, I, too, am having a date with him tomorrow night."

"What happened last night, Dawn?"

"I'll be brief. We had a sexual wrestling match."

"Yes, but what happened?"

"Nothing really, because I held him off and I think that he won't be ready to wrestle me again, but should be try, his 'family jewels' may be smashed to pieces." Both Lucy and Al roared, "His family jewels?"

Dawn was very pleased with herself.

"Before we say good night," Lucy offered quietly, "now don't anybody get too excited, but I've some good news."

Both Dawn and Al smiled and waited.

After a thirty-second pause Lucy smiled, "Yes, some good news. I'm three months pregnant."

Cautiously Dawn asked, "You're really sure?"

Before Lucy could reply, Al held her while smothering her with kisses. "Darling, darling, how wonderful, but why didn't you tell me sooner?"

"Simply because I wanted to be certain that my body wasn't playing a trick on me. Well, my body isn't lying. I saw a gynecologist this afternoon who confirmed what I suspected when I missed my first period in February, then again last month and now today, the eleventh, so that all adds up to three months."

When Al released her, Dawn held Lucy quietly. "How wonderful for you and Al." Between tears and laughter the celebration continued for a few minutes with the usual pleasantries, then Al added, "I'd say let's break out the champagne, but not unless Lucy agrees."

There was no champagne and soon Lucy and Al were together. "Shall we darling?" Al replied with tender loving kisses. "I think we might celebrate later when we're not caught up in a storm of uncertainty."

By seven a.m. the next day Santa Croce's clanging calls to worship had the two fully alert.

"That damn church should tone down that early morning racket," Dawn's comment brought silent agreement. Soon breakfast was finished and by eight both women kissed Al, who silently noted that Dawn's usual wet kiss was now a dry peck.

"I don't suppose either of you will return until this afternoon," Al asked.

"Not likely, darling, now that I've got another reason to practice."

"I expect to study for a final mid-term but I should be back by four, maybe five."

"Excellent, Dawn. I'll see Leone around noon and should be back here by three. And I hope to be able to bring you good and interesting news."

Again, quick kisses and both women were gone.

Al sat pensively reviewing Lucia's shocker. His mentality and emotions almost brought him to tears. "So I am again to be a father—and at my age! Won't that bring my children to total unbelieving bewilderment—a new bride and a baby brother or sister! And won't my friends rave and laugh about me. But when they see and meet Lucia, that should register a loud seven degree shocker.

Then silently he tried not to think about it. I should never have let it come to this—I'll be seventy when the baby is born and Lucia will only be twenty-one.

In resignation Al comforted himself, "I'm the luckiest man in the world, a beautiful young wife who adores me and a beautiful baby."

For a minute or two he reveled in his good fortune only to be jolted to reality that in two hours he should see the man who might try to kill his bride to be.

Again his anger raged until he scolded himself. "You have no proof that Leone might try to kill Lucia or even use violence in his attempt to obtain the deed or whatever the legal paper is."

For over an hour Al agonized about his new role as husband, father and protector. Then another strange idea floated forth. Suppose I tell Michele that Lucia and I are planning to marry very soon and hint that she's pregnant. What would that do to his plan to use violence to get the papers? Then maybe I should first ask him about an engagement and marriage ring—before I say anything else. Then, if he offers a positive response I'll toss in our forth-coming marriage. That should really confuse him more so than ever because I think he really did love Lucia as a step-daughter until his stupid testosterone got him in bad trouble.

Soon Al had dressed somewhat formally for the occasion. As he descended the darkened staircase he prepared a short list: first the rings, then the marriage, but don't mention the pregnancy. Then, depending on his reply, bring up the possibility of the Inspector's report. Then when Leone gets to the secret papers, I'll bring up the threat of the Inspector's report.

Confident and cheerful Al soon presented himself to the smiling Leone.

"Professor, you are indeed a punctual man. It's just now twelve and a time for celebration."

Al was puzzled by Leone's ebullient behavior.

Once in Michele's inner office, before Al could speak of wedding rings and marriage, Leone exclaimed, "Al, Professore Praitt! I have the best news possible. It will change my life! My search is over!"

Shocked by Leone's almost child-like enthusiasm Al could only demand, "What are you talking about, Michele?"

"My papers, the precious document, the property deed that somehow got in the wrong hands, the deed which will legally entitle me to my rights should Lucia die, which I hope and trust will never happen."

"Wait a minute, Michele. Did you ever see this deed or whatever this document is? Have you actually seen it?"

"Well no, not exactly. But when I was married to Eleni, Lucia's mother, she told me just before she died that she had deeded all of her property to me as trustee for Lucia."

"But Michele, if that's true, that doesn't mean you are the legal inheritor of the Conde property. At least I wouldn't guess that you get the property before Lucia."

Those words suddenly were a glass of cold water in Leone's face. "Al, Professore, in Italy, I become the protector and administrator of the property, and only when I die does it pass on to Lucia. In the eyes of Italian law I am still her stepfather—no matter what she says or wants. Really, she's hardly more than a very gifted child."

Al was shocked and angered by Leone's blithe and exuberant behavior. As Al listened and Leone raved while filling two champagne glasses, Al suddenly considered a sobering rebuttal to Leone's enthusiasm. Then he reconsidered as Michele handed Al the champagne. "Al, here's to our friendship and good luck."

Smiling, Al sipped the champagne as he decided to hit Leone first with his marriage to Lucia then the rings, and after Leone had accepted that with enthusiasm, I'll frighten him with the shocker that Inspector Ruffo had called me with the same information and that I and Lucia could see them.

As Leone began refilling the champagne glasses Al quietly said, "Well, I hope your good news is as good as mine, Michele."

"What good news, Al?"

"Lucy and I are now engaged and expect to marry in mid-June."

For a few seconds Michele was speechless then managed to blurt out, "Really? That's very interesting. I had no idea that you and Lucia were. . . were in love. You are much older than she. But why would such a young woman want to marry a much older man? Please, Professore, I don't wish to offend you, but she is really too young for you."

"Now Michele, you are becoming judgmental about a very important relationship about which you know nothing. Yes, you were her stepfather for a few years, which she remembers fondly until your role as her stepfather became something less than it should have been."

At this Leone stood and in complete confusion groped for words. "Al, you are mistaken. I always loved Lucia and I still do, but I refuse to believe that I ever abused Lucia. Yes, I had been drinking, celebrating her birthday on the very night before I was to obtain the release of many American hostages in Iran. I had, with the help of Colonel Donovan and the American Embassy in Rome, a plan which would have had a major impact on international relations. But I failed because I had been drinking champagne with Lucia and fell asleep. Then I soon awakened, took my attache case, the money, about a quarter of a million dollars, my passport, and a letter to the Ayatollah Khomeini, whom I had known several years before during the rule of the Shah, who also was a sometime friend of mine. I realize, Professore, that you might not believe what I am saying, but it's absolutely true. I am fluent in Farsi and Arabic and once had a very lucrative business there."

"That's all very interesting, Michele, but has absolutely nothing to do with your strange relationship with Lucia, who will become my wife in two months."

Embarrassed and speechless, Michele could only stutter.

To ease his pain Al added, "Since I am soon to marry, perhaps I could buy the appropriate rings from you, or am I asking too much of our friendship?"

Vastly relieved by Al's request, Michele almost gushed. What type of rings? Gold with jewels? I have a very large collection here in my store. Or if you wish, I could have one of my craftsmen make the rings to your's and Lucia's specifications. This would not be difficult because I have Lucia's ring finger size, which probably hasn't changed much. About how much would you care to spend for two rings with a few appropriate stones?"

"Well, I'm in no position to spend a large amount, but I suppose somewhere between two fifty and five hundred dollars."

"Very good, and for even the smaller sum I could make or show you lovely rings in that range and higher, should you wish to really impress your bride. Since I wouldn't expect Lucia to drop by for a fitting or a selection, I could lend you a few samples, or you could have one of my catalogue which shows a large variety with suggested prices."

"Excellent, Michele. I expect to see Lucia later today and she will make her decision."

Before leaving Al decided to withhold any further discussion of the deed, which only would complicate if not completely destroy their relationship.

As Al prepared to leave, Michele quickly produced a brochure. Here's a good guide to ring selections, Professore, and whichever you and your bride select, I will give you a large discount–really my cost price–just a small bridal gift I would like to offer."

Al accepted the multi-colored brochure and stepped toward the door. "Again, thank you very much for your advice and help. Oh, by the way, how are things going with Miss Knight?"

"Very well, I hope and believe we will have dinner together tonight."

With generous Italian flourishes, Al quickly departed leaving Leone caught in a quagmire of emotional and financial confusion.

Before Al had walked a few blocks he suddenly remembered that the "lunch with Leone" had been replaced with a long and complicated, unpleasant discussion of Leone's lost deed.

Minutes later Al's hunger symptoms were dispelled by a salad and pizza and a glass of excellent Italian beer.

Hoping that Lucy would return early from the conservatory, within minutes Al crossed the Piazza Santa Croce and produced his key to the "new apartment." He quickly bounded up the ancient stairs and was delighted to find both women home.

Surprised and delighted, both women were lavish in their greetings. "Well, big daddy, have you confused and humbled my gallant date?"

"Perhaps I have, Dawn. This was a long and confusing lunch meeting that was forgotten in our prolonged discussion, which was much more a verbal duel."

"Darling man," Lucy asked, "what happened?"

"A lot. I had a plan, but before I could say anything Michele announced that the missing deed to the Conde property had been found, which would now allow him to resume his legal rights."

Lucy could hardly believe her ears, but became alternately angry and amused by Al's detailed report.

"But does Leone have this so-called deed?" Dawn asked.

"No, he doesn't, nor did he explain where he saw or learned about the deed, but I'm almost certain that the Inspector has it and so informed Leone."

"So, what's your next move, my dearest husband?"

"I intend to call the Inspector today, but before, let me summarize the more important part of my unexpectedly long meeting. After I had pretty much disabused him of his right to Lucy's property, I shocked him out of his shoes when I told him that we are getting married. He couldn't believe it, but soon I had won him over, particularly when I mentioned that I would like to buy an engagement and wedding ring."

"Darling husband, I don't need an engagement ring, and we don't really need wedding rings unless you wish to maintain society's marital rules. But I don't care one way or the other. You are my husband whether we wear rings or you put a ring through my nose and I keep you chained to me."

"What do you think, Dawn?"

"In most cases I would probably agree with Lucy, but you two don't fit the pattern, and I think rings are appropriate and nice. So it's an engagement ring and two wedding rings," Dawn laughed.

"That's fine with me, and to prove my good intentions I have here a brochure of all kinds of rings that Leone sells or will make, and at a fifty percent discount."

Now both women reacted as Al handed Lucy the brochure. For several minutes the conversation was animated, and after a half hour Lucy, with Dawn's approval, had selected the appropriate rings.

Somewhat apprehensively, Al approved of Lucy's selection. "But what about ring size, Lucy? Michele said that he had your ring finger size from sometime when you were thirteen. Is that possible?"

"Oh, I suppose. He used to give me a lot of junk jewelry. And I suppose my finger size hasn't really changed much."

"Well, darling wife-soon-to-be, would you object if I took up Leone's offer?"

"No, I guess not, just so long as I don't have to meet him."

"Well, you two love birds, why don't we celebrate? This is certainly the time for it."

"But we don't have champagne, do we?" Al asked. "If not, I'll pick up a bottle in one of the nearby shops."

"No, we don't need champagne. Some regular white or red will do. Besides, the doctor told me to go easy on wine and liquor, a glass is okay he said, and also he suggested that I watch my weight and my diet."

"Nevertheless," Dawn demanded, "I want to tie this knot with the appropriate beverage. You two rest from your labors. You've made your point, but I'm going to celebrate your numerous efforts to reach your goal. I'll be back in five minutes."

For a few minutes Lucy and Al smiled and joked. "So you see what happened when we began sleeping together, darling? You hit a home run."

"That's a good metaphor, better than saying I struck out."

The embarrassed banter abated when they considered where and when they should marry. For convenience purposes Lucy suggested, "I would prefer to marry here, which would be very important to my grandparents."

"Of course, darling. In every respect we must have the wedding here. My children would approve. In fact, they may want to fly over."

Then Al asked about the wedding service, to which Lucy quickly replied, "No church, darling, even my grandparents would prefer a civil ceremony."

As they sealed their plans with a long, passionate kiss, Dawn burst into the room.

"Caught you at it again! And now we seal that kiss with a little bubbly."

Neither Al nor Lucy protested as Dawn proposed a toast. "To the greatest lovers I've ever known."

After a convivial period Dawn excused herself. "I've got to dress for my date, but I won't wear that same floppy blouse again."

Shortly after seven Dawn appeared, now in a tight skirt and cashmere sweater. "How do I look now?"

"You look great," Al offered. "Are the sweater and skirt adequate for your self-defense?"

"Well, they're better than what I was wearing the last time."

With further warnings and advice, Dawn started to leave. "Just a minute, Dawn, would you like me to drive you to Leone's shop, or maybe I should call a taxi?"

"Neither, Al. It's only a short distance and there's no danger."

After Dawn left and the excitement had subsided, Al reminded Lucy that neither had eaten anything for several hours. "Maybe we should go out for a bite," Al suggested.

"Let's not, darling. I'll fix something and then I'd like to go to bed."

Between the excitement of the last twenty-four hours and the prolonged discussion of their plans and hopes, they were exhausted. Minutes later they were in bed asleep.

About the same time as Lucy and Al had escaped to bed, Dawn had met Michele who again greeted her with great affection. "How wonderful of you, Dawn, to meet me here. Did you drive here from Greve?"

"No, dear man, I stopped by a friend's apartment where I had a chance to shower and change clothes. As you know, I do have classes here almost every day."

"Oh yes. I keep forgetting that you are a Stanford student. Well, shall we have some bubbly before having dinner?"

"Why not? But where are we having dinner, at the Grand or maybe some other secluded restaurant?"

Michele paused before answering, "No, darling, I hope you don't mind, but I've called to have our dinner served here."

Surprised and annoyed, Dawn could only reply, "Michele, are you up to another surprise tonight? I thought you invited me for a dinner date."

"Yes, yes, of course I did, but I thought we could enjoy dinner together in the privacy of my office."

Before answering, Dawn was quickly calculating several alternatives. "Look, Michele, I accepted your invitation for a dinner date and what you're telling me now is certainly not a dinner date. Maybe I should leave now before you make a fool of yourself trying to seduce me."

Dawn's heated response confused Leone who tried to apologize, but finally agreed. "I'm sorry, Dawn, I really am. I'll call and cancel the catering service."

Having won her point, Dawn played her next card. "Before you call, Michele, let's have some of your champagne."

Relieved but still confused, Michele quickly produced the wine and glasses. Then, with a professional touch, he poured, "Now, dearest lady, I wish to offer a toast. To the most beautiful and wisest woman I've ever known."

As they touched glasses Dawn added, "And to a handsome man who likes to gamble."

In a confused state Michele sipped the wine then finally asked, "Do you really think I'm a gambler?"

"Well, aren't you, Michele? You invite me for a dinner date, then gamble that I'll accept your trick or whatever substitution you had in mind. And you gambled on our last date that you could seduce me. Right?"

Now Michele was not only flustered and embarrassed, he was angry. "Of course, part of what you say, Dawn, is true, but my intentions were honest. And I confess, because you are very beautiful and well, yes, you are also very sexy, I thought and hoped that we might enjoy each other."

"Enjoy each other, Michele? Exactly how and where were we going to enjoy each other? In your office here as you did the other night?"

Again, Leone was confused. "Well, Dawn, having sex in Italy is quite different from the way it is in America. Here we must be very private about where we make love."

"Maybe, Michele, but my experience tells me that where and when two people decide to make out is not very different in Italy than it is in the States."

"Well, maybe it is. I guess you're right because I think Italians are more passionate than Americans. When we become sexually aroused we do take chances, many chances. We can't just stop as you Americans do."

"So now you're really agreeing with what I said, you're a gambler, you'll make out wherever and with whomever is possible."

Before Michele could reply both Dawn and Michele responded to a polite knocking on the show room door.

Michele quickly answered and ushered in a waiter with a large tray of sealed dishes, which he arranged on the small table in the small office-apartment.

With appropriate bowing and behavior, the waiter quickly departed.

Before savoring the enticing odors of their dinner, Dawn again teased Michele. "So the gambler won again. You really are a smart giocatore or speculatore, Michele."

So you do know some Italian, Dawn. I might have guessed that you know far more Italian than you practice. Yes, I'm a gambler and a speculator. In my business I must be or I wouldn't have any money. But I don't cheat. I am an honest man."

"Okay, Michele, you won. Now let's see what smells so enticing." Quickly the pewter lids revealed a garnished duck in wine sauce, a smaller platter of loin lamb ribs, a small bowl of gnocchi, a single bowl of assorted vegetables and a dessert of chocolate truffles.

"Congratulations! Signore gambler, you've won again."

Michele beamed satisfaction and contentment. "Now, if the food is as good as it looks, I'll be pleased."

Quickly Dawn spread the plates and dishes. Then noting that all was in order she reached for a chair even as Michele carefully seated her.

Then, removing a bottle of Burgundy from a nearly cabinet, Michele served the wine. "So you see, my darling Dawn, our catered dinner isn't as disappointing as you suggested."

"Yes, Michele, I'll hand it to you, the food looks and smells great. You seem to know that the way to a woman's heart is through her mouth."

"No, I didn't know that. I always heard that said about a male, but maybe food and wine are the great equalizers. Maybe both sexes respond to wine and good food."

"I won't suggest how women respond, but it takes more than just good food and wine."

After a prolonged dinner of rich food and wine Dawn was soon relaxed. Quietly Michele removed the dishes and placed them in the small kitchen.

Returning quickly he noticed that Dawn was on the verge of sleep. Very carefully he moved her chair, which immediately aroused Dawn.

"Let's sit over here on this sofa, it's much more comfortable."

Now Michele was alarmed that Dawn would soon fall asleep and would defeat any chance of a seduction or winning her assistance in obtaining the necessary papers which he now realized were necessary for his legal claim to the Conde fortune.

Before Dawn slumped sleepily, Michele offered her coffee. But Dawn's only response was a sleepy, "Thanks, Michele, not now."

"But Dawn darling, you can't fall asleep here. It's getting late and I had hoped we might discuss an important plan I have."

Dawn feigned drowsiness.

"Please, darling woman, talk to me."

Slowly Dawn pulled herself together. "Okay, Michele, what's bothering you? You want another sexy wresting match? So you're horny and want to fuck? Is that it? Well forget it! I'm not in the mood."

Michele was really shaken by Dawn's outburst.

"Please, Dawn. Really, I'm not suggesting sex. I just wanted to talk about something very important which would be as rewarding for you as for me."

Sensing that Michele was about to reveal his real motive for dinner, Dawn continued to feign drowsiness while remaining fully alert.

"Okay, Michele, what's really bothering you?"

"You know about the legal documents which will prove that I am the legal beneficiary of the Conde property?"

"Yes, I've heard you mention them, but I thought you had them."

"No, the papers I have are only copies and I must have the original documents. Will you please help me? I will make it well worth your efforts. Please help me!"

"Okay, Buster, what do you want me to do?"

"It's very simple, find where those papers are, who has them, and when I get them I'll reward you with fifty thousand dollars."

"Really, Michele, now how in the hell would I know where they are, who's got them, and how could I possibly get them and then give them to you? You must be crazy, Michele."

"So you won't help me? So that's what you're saying? God damn you! You'll damn well give me what I want!"

Suddenly Michele lunged for Dawn's waist and tried to rip her short shirt. But as he lunged he started to slip to one knee. At that point Dawn managed to spring her right knee forward and catch Michele directly in the testicles.

Falling sideways to the floor he attempted to cover his genitals while moaning. "Stop! You're killing me!"

Dawn's immediate response was a swift kick at his clutching hands followed by another kick in his face.

Momentarily she watched the blood flow from his nose as he muttered, "Please, please, no more!"

"So you've had enough you lying rotten son of a bitch!"

Quickly she recovered her wrap, straightened her skirt, found her purse and noting that Leone was still lying, almost crying, she quietly and carefully let herself out the front door.

Noting that the street was entirely empty, she quickly walked the short distance to their apartment.

Again noting that nobody had been following her, she opened the ground-floor entrance and let herself into the darkened apartment.

There she moved into her darkened bedroom and then turned on the light. For a few minutes she sat quietly reviewing what had happened. Then she felt a rather sharp pain in her right toe. "Damn! I hope I didn't break my toe on his face, not that it wouldn't be worth it."

Slowly she disrobed and slipped into her nightie, popped in an aspirin and was soon sound asleep.

Suddenly, about seven hours after falling asleep, the mighty Santa Croce bells alerted her as did her swollen big toe. Cursing and almost crying she pulled herself from the bed and stared at her right toe, now swollen and very red.

"Oh hell! What do I do now? No doctor around at this god-forsaken hour. Struggling to stand on her left foot, she tried to remember what to do. A hot shower? No, not on that toe. Oh yes, ice! That's it. Dulls the pain and slows the swelling.

Carefully she hopped to the nearby closet, found her bathrobe and managed to get it on just as Lucy knocked and entered.

"I'm sorry to have wakened you, Lucy, but I may have broken my big toe last night when I kicked Leone first in his genitals and then in his face. But the pain in my toe couldn't compare with the great pain he has in his family jewels and in his big nose."

As Lucy tried not to laugh, Al quietly entered the room and having heard what had happened, he immediately rushed to get some ice. Within two minutes he had emptied two trays of ice cubes into a basin and returned with his prescribed treatment.

"Here, Dawn, put your foot in the basin and keep it there for as long as you can, then remove it and repeat while Lucy and I get you some juice and coffee."

"Thank you, Al, you're just what the doctor ordered."

"Al, you help Dawn while I get the juice and coffee, and I will fix us breakfast."

Now Al directed his full inquiry to Dawn who was making certain that the cubes covered her toes but not her heel and arch.

"Are you okay, Dawn? You seem to know more about the treatment than I do."

"Not necessarily, dear man. But having skied a lot and stubbed my toe a few times when running, I learned quickly about the ice treatment."

"I overheard your comments about Leone and how you damaged his "family jewels." So your dinner with the amorous Michele was something less than a pleasant dining experience."

"Well said, Professore, but that is a bit terse, not that a full recital of the evening's events isn't interesting."

"I'm eager to hear a blow-by-blow account, but first, maybe I can help you hobble into the kitchen, and while you soak you toes we can eat and listen."

Al quickly helped Dawn hop on one foot while gripping her shoulder. Seated comfortably Lucy asked, "Is that chair okay? Now here's the juice and coffee, and have some breakfast pastry."

"Thank you both so much. Already I'm feeling better."

"I'm dying to hear your story, Dawn. So my alleged stepfather was not his reputed gracious host?" Lucy's voice dripped irony.

"Hardly, but let me give you a summary of my dinner date. Leone greeted me warmly and quickly broke out a bottle of champagne. Then he tells me that instead of having dinner in an elegant restaurant, he's having our dinner catered in his office. That immediately sounded my red alarm. I became very nasty and threatened to leave. He apologized and while I sulked he continued to pour champagne, which finally weakened my resolution. He continued to babble while I napped."

"Yes, but what about the dinner?" Lucy asked.

"The caterer showed up soon and produced a very elegant dinner. It really was outstanding, as was the wine. Then, after eating I sat on the sofa and fell asleep."

"But how did Leone react to that?" Lucy asked.

"He aroused me and talked about his god-damned papers, his so-called deed to your property, then he offered me fifty thousand dollars if I could produce them."

"Really! He thought that you could deliver the deed, which would be worthless, even if you could. Then what happened?" Al was eager for an answer.

"When I told him that he was crazy and I wouldn't help him, he became violent."

Shocked, Lucy almost shouted, "Yes and what did you do then?"

"As he tried to grab my skirt, he slipped and fell to one knee, just as I jammed my right knee into his genitals. Then as he fell sideways to the floor, I kicked again in the balls and again in the nose, which left him sobbing on the floor and crying, 'Please! No more.'"

Both Al and Lucy were almost cheering. You really did all of that, Dawn?"

"I most certainly did! I think he was badly injured as was my right toe!"

"That's fantastic, Dawn. And after that?"

"I quickly left. Nobody was around and I got back here as fast as possible. My toe hurt so I took two aspirins and hopped into bed."

Al and Lucy were stunned. "I'm sure glad you're on our side, Dawn. You really are a champion."

As they continued to bask in the glow of Dawn's victory, Al questioned, "Now that we've temporarily got Leone on the ropes, what might we expect next? I ask because we all know that he will make at least one more effort to get his so-called papers and probably exact some kind of revenge."

"Of course he will," Lucy offered, "and he will probably be violent or more probably hire somebody to do the job. And since that is the logical thing for him to do, we must be extremely careful about where we go and what we do."

They were unanimous and decided that Al should always be with either Lucy or Dawn.

"And that brings up another question," Al asked.

"What about your grandparents? Do we warn them?"

"Oh yes, I must," Lucy offered. "My grandfather will arm himself and I must convince my grandmother not to let Massimo go looking for Leone. He swore that he would kill him after he raped me."

"And one additional defensive action for us is Dr. Valentine and possibly Inspector Ruffo. We should alert both of them to Leone's rage and violence and clearly indicate that he plans revenge in one way or the other."

"Are we certain that he doesn't know about our new apartment?" Al asked.

"I'm reasonably certain that he doesn't. He believes that Dawn and I commute from Greve."

"Well, he knows all about me and the house and I think that somehow he has a key. But I have asked Enrico, the man who fixed the car, to watch the house when I had reason to believe that Leone was getting in."

Having finished breakfast, Al asked, "Is today Wednesday or is it Thursday?"

Assured by both women that today was Thursday, Al apprehensively asked, "And do both of you have classes?"

"We both do, but how do you expect to protect both of us when I'm at an art class near the Uffizi where I'll spend the entire morning in the museum and in the afternoon I'm free, so I'll return here. No, Al, you can't protect both of us at the same time."

"How about you, Lucy?"

"I'll be at the Conservatory practicing, which is quite private, but my teacher wouldn't mind if you sat in an adjoining small room."

"Fine, we'll walk together to the Conservatory and I'll bring something to read."

"One final idea. Let's all walk the trail from Greve to Panzano. We can see my grandparents, and since Sunday is Easter, we could plan to spend the Friday with them."

"I hope the weather will cooperate. If not we'll plan something else. And while we're in Greve I can check out my house."

"Wait a minute," Dawn added, "let's check my toe."

As most of the ice had melted, Dawn's big toe appeared almost normal. "I think it's almost ready to walk."

Then, standing on the injured foot, Dawn was enthusiastic. "Only a bit of pain. Maybe all three of us could walk together, drop me off at the galleria and I'll have lunch with a friend and return sometime after one."

Soon the threesome were moving together easily. Traffic was light but Al constantly studied all foot traffic and vehicles. At the Uffizi, Dawn exchanged a few words before Lucy and Al rapidly advanced towards the Conservatory where Al stopped momentarily to buy the *Herald Tribune*. At their destination Lucia urged him to follow, and soon she would introduce him to her instructor. "I think that I'll introduce you as my American uncle. Let's keep my pregnancy and our plans secret, at least for now."

"Here we are in this ancient building. I don't know what it was before it became the Conservatory, but in this immediate area are the university, the art school and our music school." Lucy was obviously proud of the Conservatory.

Once in the relatively small practice room Lucy suggested that Al might wait in an adjoining empty room. Soon Lucy introduced Al to her teacher, Signora Maria Fonzi, who seemed pleased that Al should take an interest in his niece. Following a brief conversation in Italian, Lucy began practicing as her teacher sat nearby.

Between reading and listening to Lucia playing, the morning passed quickly. As much as Al enjoyed listening to Lucia practice, he was disappointed by the sudden interruptions as the teacher and Lucia talked and frequently replayed several bars.

Finally, the almost four-hour session ended, and Lucy greeted Al warmly. "Could you hear the music through the window and wall separating us?"

"Yes, of course, darling, although the sounds were muffled. But I thoroughly enjoyed listening to you practice."

"Shall we stop for lunch on our way back to the apartment?" Obviously Al would prefer sitting in a small trattoria while enjoying the afternoon sun.

Sensing Al's preference Lucia gladly agreed adding, "This is better for both of us because four hours of practice tires me and this saves us both from fixing a noon meal in the apartment."

Returning to the apartment after three they were greeted by Dawn who admitted that her toe was still sore. "But that was a cheap price to pay for the pleasure I had in kicking Leone in the balls and face."

"Yes," Al offered, "and I don't think he will ever forget your aim and your power. But he will also be determined to seek revenge."

Soon the conversation drifted to their weekend plans. "I've been thinking about hiking from Greve to Panzano on Saturday, but it just occurred to me that tomorrow is Good Friday. Will either of you ladies have classes tomorrow?"

"Not being much of a Christian, I don't know much about Easter, but here I would guess that Good Friday and Easter are observed as a good reason to celebrate and to include Saturday so that everybody is off from Thursday through Monday."

"You're right, Lucy. Stanford wouldn't dare break with the Italian tradition," Dawn added.

"That being the case," Al offered, "why don't we go to my house tomorrow and spend the entire weekend there? Then we could return here late Sunday."

Plans were soon completed for food, drink and clothes. "Since we'll see your grandparents Sunday, should we offer to bring an Easter dinner?"

"No, Al, my grandparents would consider that a 'bruta figura.'"

Al laughed, "There we go again with a 'bruta figura,' which I gather is a serious social mistake."

"Yes, of course, we Italians have an unwritten code for all kinds of social behavior."

"Oh, so do we Americans," Dawn added, "but only a few people seem to observe them."

Al glanced at his watch and noting that it was well after five suggested, "I think that it's only appropriate that we get a start on this Easter holiday."

"I'll vote for that," Dawn answered, "but I doubt that we have anything here to drink. Just a bit of heart-burn red. I'll go out and get a few bottles. What would you like, Professor?"

"Why don't we both go out while Lucy fixes up a plate of antipasto. Oh yes, Lucy is there anything else we need or something you might especially want?"

"No, I just want you two to get whatever is good, but don't break the family bank."

With that injunction they found a nearby wine shop and realized that the shop didn't sell gin or other hard liquors. So Al bought three bottles of red without realizing that these weren't cheap Chiantis, but he soon was shocked that the three cost almost fifty dollars. However, he accepted his mistake without a murmur.

"So now you know, Al, but I'll buy some gin and vermouth and whatever else we may want."

But Dawn plunged deeper than Al and soon had a bottle of Four Roses, which Al knew was not much, but then got a bottle of Courvoisier and visited a third shop for a bottle of Italian champagne–Martini and Rossi. Then she capped the entire bill with a wedge of Gorgonzola and Swiss cheese. She never flinched when her total bill amounted to almost two hundred dollars.

Her only comment to Al, whose face registered some concern, was, "What the hell, Al, it's only money. And there's a hellava lot more where this came from. Don't worry, my dad has very deep pockets."

Soon they were back in the apartment where Lucy had put together a beautiful platter of antipasto.

Looking over the large collection of wines, booze and cheese, Lucy's only reply was, "It's like you two are preparing for a long party!"

"Nope, we're just planning to help celebrate our version of Easter and maybe the Fourth of July."

Quickly Al assembled a dry martini, a whisky sour for Dawn, and a champagne cocktail for Lucy.

Soon they were drinking, eating and reveling in pleasure and dirty jokes. After a second round of drinks, Lucy, who was the reasonably sober survivor, announced, "Okay, you two clowns, the bar's closed. Besides, we've got to take the rest of these goodies with us tomorrow."

Somehow Lucy and Al managed a modest dinner before tumbling into bed.

Again their deep slumber was rudely awakened by Santa Croce's bells which seemed louder and longer than ever.

"Jesus H. Christ!" Dawn shouted, "can't those god-damned bells give us a break!"

"No," Al laughed, "We're being punished for last night."

Slightly hung over, but eager to leave the tumult of Florence by nine, Al had the necessities loaded into the Fiat while Lucy and Dawn escaped with two suitcases in the Alpha.

Fortunately the traffic was very light all the way to Greve, where the trio stopped in Verranzano Square. The place was almost completely empty and even the bus station shop was closed.

"Well, we might as well drive up to my house," Al suggested. "This place is about as empty as it gets."

Having been away for almost a week, Al was apprehensive about the house. But after cautiously entering, he began unpacking as Dawn and Lucy appeared.

"Well, the place is still here," Dawn noted.

"And I hope that bastard Leone has vanished for good," Lucy added.

"Why don't' we take a walk around just to work up an appetite?"

"Good idea, Al. Should we try for Montefiorale?"

"We can, but that's a bit much. I just want some exercise. Might do us all some good when we hike all the way to Panzano tomorrow."

A pale spring sun and light breeze offered some encouragement as the trio again stopped at the cemetery. "For a small town, Greve really maintains an attractive bone yard," Dawn noted. And they all agreed that cemeteries were no place for the unfaithful.

After a few minutes, Lucy suggested that she was tiring and would like to return to the house.

Quickly Al realized her problems as did Dawn, and soon they were comfortably settled.

Although Lucy hadn't mentioned her condition, Al belatedly understood that Lucy shouldn't really challenge her physical problem again. And now he was quietly apprehensive about their planned hike to Panzano.

As they later sat sipping wine, Al cautiously kissed Lucy while asking, "Do you think you are strong enough to hike tomorrow?"

"Why not? The trail isn't steep and the distance is only about three miles. Actually the walk would be good for me. The doctor advised me to walk as much as I wanted or felt comfortable doing–that was his advice."

For a half hour the two continued to discuss the nearby hills and their plans. But they each avoided the name of Leone, a curse that now confronted them.

Quickly Dawn and Al served a light dinner which ended with a fruit compote.

Al felt expansive and pleased. "Hasn't this been a really good Friday?" Al smirked. "We had the best of a religious holiday without suffering the pains of Christianity."

"Be careful, you heathen," Dawn laughed, "the Church doesn't like anti-Christian ridicule."

"Oh, let's not get into the Easter dogma, we'll feel enough of it on Sunday, and not from my grandparents. They won't attend mass, but the entire town of Panzano will. And also Greve. Anyway, I'm going to bed."

Quickly Al rose, wished Dawn a pleasant night, and with Lucy completed their nightly ablutions.

Soon the loving couple were locked in each other's arms, passionately kissing, teasing and whispering love songs. Slowly their bodies began a rhythmical ballet, rising and falling, then suddenly climaxing in a harmony of ecstasy. As they slowly relaxed from the frenzy of passion, still united in love, they slowly drifted to sleep.

Rested and ready for the day, Al arose in the quiet house only to be surprised by Dawn preparing breakfast.

"What a pleasant surprise!" Al exclaimed. "A beautiful day and two beautiful women. What more could a man want?"

"Maybe a harem, if you were a sultan or a caliph," Dawn joked. "And did you and your beloved survive a night of revelry with Aphrodite and Adonis and assorted gods of the temples and the bedroom?"

"Oh yes! Indeed we slept well. In fact, Lucy is still sleeping."

"Not anymore, my handsome god. I'm up and ready for the day's pleasure."

Quickly they dispensed with breakfast and prepared for their hike.

"I found a small backpack here which is large enough for sandwiches, water and any small items you ladies wish me to carry."

Before leaving, Al again made a mental security check then joined Lucy and Dawn at the car.

"Is the plan to leave the car in the square or do we drive directly to the trail head?"

"Darling husband, the trail head is about a half mile or so from the Greve outskirts and as I recall, there is a parking area there. I know that because hunters still look for quail and even deer in those hills."

The day's outing soon became a reality as Lucy parked her Alpha in the empty hillside parking area.

As the trail was clearly marked, the two had no difficulty in moving casually over the broken rock and tangled vines. Nearby were grapevines, dry and seemingly dead, but as Lucy observed, "They're not dead even though this has been a dreadful winter. But this year wasn't as bad as last when thousands of large, old olive trees died."

As they followed the wandering trail now through several cleared acres, they came on small mounds of bottles and cans. Nearby was a posted a sign waring that hunting was prohibited in this forest. To emphasize the point, the metal sign already riven with bullet holes was nailed to an old oak tree.

Al laughed, "Well, if you can't hunt, you can always shoot at warning signs."

"Or we can throw the cans in the air and try to hit them" Dawn added.

For several minutes Lucy lobbed cans as high as she could while Al and Dawn threw rocks, but seldom ever came close.

Then, as Lucy lobbed a medium-sized rusty can, Al threw a rock simultaneously as a ping sounded sending the can rumbling sideways.

Shocked Al shouted, "What was that? I didn't hit the can."

Dawn burst into laughter, "Nope you didn't hit the can, Al, but I did!"

"Wait a minute, Dawn, I didn't see you throw a rock."

"Of course you didn't because I didn't throw a rock, but I did hit the can," Dawn quickly recovered the can and handed it to Lucy.

After noting the small hole almost in the center of the can, Lucy asked, "Did you hit the can with your tiny pistol?"

Dawn was laughing hard, "What tiny pistol?"

Now both Al and Lucy were close to Dawn who suddenly opened her right hand, "Is this what you are suggesting? My tiny dog pistol?"

"That's amazing and I wouldn't believe it if I hadn't seen it," Al said shaking his head.

For a few minutes they continued their banter, then Lucy challenged Dawn to try again.

"Why not? But first I must reload. These very small bullets are the same caliber as the American twenty-two short, once more commonly used in a long barrel twenty-two rifle to hunt small game, mostly rabbits."

"Okay, Dawn, are you ready to fire? I'll throw this same can and see if you can hit it again."

Al lobbed the rusty can about twenty feet and, at the snap of the pistol, again the can spun sideways as it fell to the ground.

Quickly Lucy recovered the can, studied it for a second, and yelled, "Dawn, you hit it again!"

"You didn't expect me to miss it after my first shot," Dawn joked.

Al was amazed, "You really are an Annie Oakley!"

"Nope, I'm not nearly as good as she really was," Dawn explained. "I've read that she could shoot a lighted cigarette from the mouth of her husband at thirty paces. She was world famous and traveled with the Buffalo Bill Wild West Show. But I'm certain she wasn't using a tiny Vela dog pistol."

"Well, I guess we should get going. As I recall, the trail gets a bit steeper for the next half mile. After that we follow a trail which soon meets a small dirt road that will take us to my grandparents house."

Not long after the trail steepened, Lucy abruptly sat down. "I'm sorry, but either the trail is steeper or I'm carrying a heavier load."

Immediately Al was sitting beside her, "Darling, here's some water. Now rest as long as you wish."

After a short discussion Dawn suggested that they return to the car and then drive to Panzano.

"That isn't necessary, Dawn. I'm really okay. But I guess we should walk slower."

"Do you really insist on hiking to your grandparents?" Al asked sympathetically.

"At this point, yes. We're not far from their house. But I have a good idea. Dawn, why don't you return to the car and then drive to Panzano. We could meet you at the small parking area in the town square."

"But wouldn't that complicate our problem of meeting Dawn?" Al asked.

"Well, I suppose it would. But," Lucy added, "I know another small road which joins the highway just before it ends at the parking lot."

Having solved the problem the two split, pleased by their decision.

As Lucy and Al resumed their climb, Dawn quickly covered the two miles to the parking lot. As she emerged from a thicket she noticed another car parked very near the Alpha. Cautiously she approached the Alpha and soon saw a man trying to open the door on the driver's side.

Apparently the stranger, oblivious to Dawn's presence, continued with his efforts.

Silently Dawn closed in on the stranger. "What the hell are you doing?" she shouted.

Startled, the stranger stood then started to move.

"Basta! Mascalzone!" Dawn shouted. Then raising her walking stick in a threatening manner, she demanded, "Come si chiamo?"

Cowered by Dawn's threatening stance, the frightened young man shouted, "Benito, mi chiamo Benito."

Pleased with her violent behavior, Dawn demanded, "Chi e il suo Padrone?"

For a few seconds Benito didn't answer.

Again, Dawn, now enraged and raising her stick even higher, demanded, "Benito lui gran bastardo, chi e il suo Padrone?"

Slowly Benito replied, "Il mio Padrone e Signor Leone."

Pleased and very surprised, Dawn motioned for Benito to leave, which he did as fast as possible.

As Benito sped rapidly from the lot, Dawn laughed. "And now the plot thickens! Won't Al and Lucy be surprised."

After parking the Alpha in Panzano, Dawn suddenly uttered, "Benito, you SOB! Now I remember you. That night last January in the Moro. You were with my date who made an ass of himself. And you work for Leone."

Soon Al and Lucy arrived just in time to see Dawn talking to herself.

Unaware that she had been seen talking to herself, she blushed when Al greeted her.

"Hi, Dawn. Who are you talking to?"

"Nobody really, but I have some news that might surprise you."

"Like what?" Lucy asked.

"Like Benito, who works for Leone."

"You mean that bastard who dated me on January 27—my birthday! Whom I thought was a nice guy until that night!"

Al had been quiet but now asked, "But what happened for you to bring up Benito, the night, and the present."

"Right. I should have described what I saw when I reached the parking lot. There was Benito trying to break into the Alpha. I caught him by surprise and threatened him with my walking stick."

Quickly Dawn summarized the event as the trio questioned Benito's motives.

Soon Lucy suggested they drive to her grandparents and after an hour return to Greve.

Carefully Lucy edged the car slowly along the very narrow street, then reaching a small, steep connecting unpaved road, the Alpha bounced down the rutted passage to a wide clearing in front of an ancient stronghold, almost exactly like the house Al now occupied.

As they discussed the house, suddenly the grandparents opened the heavy front gate and embraced the trio.

Once in the comfortable house Dawn and Al were surprised how different the interior was from Al's house.

There Lucy asked grandmother Justine about Easter plans which were quickly completed as Massimo gave Al and Dawn a quick tour while explaining the many changes he had made since acquiring the house some thirty years earlier.

"So now you have complete central heating and those two small bedrooms have been changed to one large bedroom with its own bath."

"Si, si, et vas nesisary." Massimo was delighted.

Soon, the tour over, the trio gathered in a spacious dining room where Justine served warm drinks and a variety of almond pastries.

Although it was only four, Al suggested that they leave soon, which met considerable protest from Justine and Massimo.

"Please stay for dinner. I can have a nice warm meal soon."

"Thank you, Nonna Justine," Lucy begged, "but we must leave very soon. Something very important, I can't discuss now, but I will tomorrow when we are here for Easter."

The grandparents were definitely sorry that the short visit was terminated and insisted on an Italian goodbye at the car.

Soon Lucy had the car on the alternate road, which brought them back to the town square.

"That was wonderful," Al noted. "But I know that we must return to my house soon."

"I agree," Lucy added.

"And I do too. I just hope that Leone and Benito haven't already gotten into the house," Dawn seemed more apprehensive then Al or Lucy.

Together the two questioned and sought reasons and answers why Benito was trying to break into the Alpha.

"Steal it? Wreck it? But why? Oh, Leone must have ordered Benito to damage or maybe steal the car," Al offered.

Soon Lucy parked the car in its usual place. "Al, would you lead the way and we will wait here for your signal."

"Of course!" Al slowly and cautiously entered through the heavy gate, stopped, listened for any possible warning then, confident at the door, he paused before inserting the key and pushing the door open with his foot. Quickly he flicked on the room switch and was relieved by the light and silence. Confidently he noted each room for any changes.

Finally convinced that the house was secure he called to the women who quickly bounded up the staircase.

For all of Al's confidence both women scrutinized every room, every space where a person could possibly hide.

Only when they were collectively satisfied did Al bring out the brandy.

"Now," Al pronounced, "we're safe but we don't know how or why Benito was trying to get into the Alpha."

Prolonged speculation brought no positive answers. Let's go over the entire scenario and begin with Dawn practically destroying Leone only four days ago."

"Three," Dawn corrected Al. "And so now he's hot for revenge so he calls on his fool to steal Lucy's car or to sabotage it."

"Then what, Dawn?" Lucy asked.

"Then, when Lucy's car won't start, Leone and Benito suddenly appear and try to take us hostage."

"That would be too risky under the circumstances. No, I think that quite possibly Benito did this on his own. Either to steal the car, hide nearby and return to get his car. Then later win some praise from Leone."

"Maybe, but not likely," Al added. "But I do think that we're making too much out of what was really a stupid idea."

Finally, after over an hour of speculation, they all agreed that Leone probably didn't have anything to do with the stupid plan.

Soon dinner was in readiness and just as they sat down to eat the sound of banging on the front door jolted them into a state of alarm.

With the outside light on Al quickly demanded an identity from the outsider.

"Sono Enrico, Professore!"

Quickly Al opened the door and then introduced Lucy and Dawn.

Al tried to speak Italian but quickly Lucy asked the appropriate questions and repeated Enrico's answers in English.

"About three this afternoon Enrico says two men tried to enter your house, but he quickly stopped them and asked what they were doing. The older man, whom he has seen in Greve, and a younger man, whom he had never seen, refused to answer.

"Enrico says both men seemed to be trying to get into your house. He warned them that he was the custodian of this property for the Italian professor who was in America who had asked the police to help me guard the property."

"And," Lucy added from the last translation, "when he mentioned the police both men got back in a big black Mercedes and left."

Al and the women almost broke into cheers and both women hugged the delighted Enrico.

As Enrico turned to leave, Al slipped a 20,000 lire note in his hand while thanking him profusely.

Amid laughter and almost tears of relief, the two returned to their dinner.

"So now we know. Leone and his fool were here and planning something important."

"Okay, Mr. Leone, now it's our turn to put the heat on you."

"What's your plan, my loving husband and protector?"

"Tomorrow, no Monday, tomorrow's Easter, but the first thing Monday we demand to see the Inspector and local police and charge Leone and Benito with attempted burglary."

Both women agreed, but Dawn quickly pointed out, "How can we prove that Leone and Benito were trying to break in?"

"We can't, but we can again press the Inspector to go after Leone for the earlier burglaries and his determination to obtain his 'stolen papers.'"

As they continued their arguments between food and wine, they soon tired.

By nine their energies spent, they toppled into bed.

The early morning echoed with church bells but this Easter was damp and cold. Slowly the trio emerged and complained, "Here it is Easter Sunday and the first day of Spring."

"So this is what Christians get! It's enough to make one switch," Lucy snapped.

"What time are we expected at your grandparents?" Dawn seemed less affected by the weather.

"Grandmother wasn't specific, but I think we should get there after twelve, but don't expect to eat before three because my grandfather will be roasting a small lamb on a spit, which must be turned frequently over a glowing bank of charcoal."

"How big is the lamb?" Al asked.

"Well, that depends on my grandparents' decision. If there will be only the five of us, he will get a small lamb, maybe twenty pounds. But if he has invited friends, he will get maybe a thirty or thirty-five pound lamb."

Dawn had never seen an Easter like this and Al could only vaguely remember this ritual when his children were young, but the memory evoked a flood of pleasure from his childhood.

"Long ago," Al recalled, "Easter was the second most celebrated Christian holiday. As I knew nothing about Christian dogma, nor did any of my friends, when we became adolescents we loved Easter as a time for Easter eggs and new clothes. It really was a wonderful holiday—we always got off a week from school."

After almost two hours of bathing, dressing and speculation, Lucy, Dawn and Al were ready to leave."Do you women realize," Al almost whispered, "the three of us all look like wealthy Christians on a pilgrimage?"

"Al, you jokester," Dawn laughed, "that's almost one of your dirty jokes."

Less than an hour later Lucy parked her Alpha next to three other cars. "Well, that answers our question if there will be several other people here today."

At the heavy gate Nonna Justine welcomed them with appropriate Italian greetings.

"Welcome, all of you! As you see from the cars, we are having a large Easter celebration."

Once inside some eight or ten guests were already sampling cookies and a rich variety of Easter breads and finger foods. Quickly Justine introduced the trio to the well-dressed neighbors and friends, then she explained that Massimo and others were roasting the Easter lambs on a spit in the backyard.

Approaching the small coterie of males who were alternately slowly turning two spits, Massimo, greeting Al with a bear hug, introduced him to Guiseppi Tosso, Antonio Peri and Nicolo Pacini. Soon the four men were joking and laughing in Italian and broken English. At the mention of Michele Leone all of the men cursed his name and spat.

When Al inquired about the size and age of the two lambs, Massimo answered, "Piccioli, sette, otto kilo."

After taking his appropriate number of turns of the spit, Al excused himself and returned to the center of discussion. Quickly he attached himself to his beloved Lucy, who seemed to be the main attraction. Not that anybody would have guessed that she was three months pregnant—even Justine wouldn't have guessed, although she was very aware that her granddaughter was deeply in love with the professor.

Finally, about three, tables were organized and some fifteen chairs were positioned. With only a few words of prayer, the barbecued lamb appeared on large trays along with plates of crostini de polenta ai funghi, asparaga di campe scarpacci vianeggina, and a separate table of breads—panettone—and then desserts.

The din of eating, laughing and toasting was being repeated all over Italy.

Although Lucy, Dawn and Al were anxious to leave, they waited for an appropriated time to thank Massimo and Justine. Waving goodbye to the several friends and neighbors, they soon were on the road back to Greve and "home."

At Al's ancient dwelling they cautiously ascended the staircase as Al slowly inserted the key and switched on a nearby light.

Soon their anxiety was dispelled and within a half hour they were in bed.

Monday came as a welcome relief from the long Easter holiday. Soon everybody was packed and on the road by eight-thirty.

"In spite of the trouble Leone and his clown created, we did have a good time, didn't we?" Al asked.

Dawn and Lucy agreed. "But Al, you must see the Inspector as soon as possible."

"I'll call for an appointment from your apartment, and when I fill him in about Leone's threats and his large reward for his so-called papers, I think the Inspector will change his mind about Leone."

Back in their apartment, Lucy and Dawn changed clothes and soon were ready for their Monday classes. Meanwhile Al managed to schedule an eleven o'clock meeting with the Inspector.

Together they walked quickly as Al continued his guarded presence. Soon Dawn noted that her Monday morning classes were in a nearby teacher's college. Then Al guarded Lucy all the way to the Conservatory.

Just before eleven Al entered the heavily guarded central police station where he was ushered into an inner office. Again Al reviewed the complaints he intended to relate.

Soon Inspector Ruffo greeted him in a friendly but somewhat guarded manner. Before Al could speak the Inspector cautiously asked, "I hope you enjoyed a pleasant Easter holiday, but I gather that something serious brings you here."

"Thank you, Inspector, we did have a, well, an interesting Easter holiday. We had gone to Panzano to be with Miss Conde's grandparents and that experience was really a beautiful holiday. But the Eastern weekend was disturbed by several unexpected events."

"I'm very sorry to hear that. Would you please explain, Professore?"

"Before I relate the two explicit events which I don't fully understand, Miss Knight, who couldn't be here this morning, asked me to describe to you what happened last Thursday night when she had a dinner date with Michele Leone."

Now the Inspector leaned forward in great anticipation. "So my friend Michele had a date with the beautiful Miss Knight? But what happened?"

According to Miss Knight, when she met Michele at his shop he soon told her that instead of having dinner at a restaurant, he was having their dinner catered. Surprised, Dawn—I'll use her given name—was angry. But as their catered dinner soon arrived, Dawn accepted the dinner. Then after dining, Michele demanded that Dawn reveal any knowledge she might have about his papers."

"His so-called 'inheritance papers'?" the Inspector asked.

"Yes, Inspector, but from everything I've heard about those papers, they're worthless."

"You're absolutely right, Professore, he's asked me about them, implying that we have them, that we 'stole' them along with a large sum of money when we received a telephone call form Miss Conde's grandparents that their granddaughter had been raped in Michele's office. And that was about seven years ago. And," the Inspector added, "when the police arrived at the store about seven a.m. only Miss Conde was there in a hysterical state, and maybe her grandparents were too. I don't know much about the case because I wasn't there and I wasn't the Inspector. So I really know very little about the case or Michele's papers and money."

"Well," Al added, "getting back to Dawn's dinner date, after dining, Michele offered Dawn fifty thousand dollars if she would delivery his papers to him. That irritated Miss Knight who refused Michele's offer and said that she was leaving. At this point Dawn claims that Michele attacked her, threatening 'I always get what I want.'"

"Then what happened?"

"As he lunged at her, he slipped on a rug and fell to his knees as Dawn swiftly kicked hard, hitting him in his face. Then she repeatedly kicked him in the face and genitals until he screamed for mercy."

The Inspector's face grimaced as he laughed, "Well, Michele got what he deserved. Yes, he does have a record of getting what he wants from a woman he's trying to seduce."

"Unfortunately, Inspector, there's much more to the story than that."

"I'm not surprised, Professor. Has Michele gotten himself in more trouble?"

"Possibly, Inspector. This is what happened during the Easter holiday, which worries Lucy, her grandparents and all of us. First, on Friday we decided to hike to Panzano from a small parking area at the trail head. The three of us began walking when Lucy became tired and was afraid that she wouldn't be able to walk to Panzano and back to the car lot. So Dawn returned to the parked car where she discovered Michele's helper, Benito Bosso, apparently trying to steal Lucy's car."

"What a stupid thing to do," the Inspector offered. "I know about that man. He's been in trouble many times. I don't understand why Michele defends him."

"Well, Dawn threatened him with a heavy walking stick and demanded his name and for whom he worked. Frightened by Dawn's aggressive threats he identified himself by name, and Leone as his employer."

"Yes. Then what happened?"

"Dawn let him go and he left in his own car."

"Well, that's very interesting, but I don't believe you can press charges against Michele on the basis of the alleged rape or the car robbery. If Miss Knight wishes to do so, we most certainly will take appropriate action."

"I understand that, Inspector, as does Dawn, but there is still more to the story."

"More?" the Inspector asked.

"Yes. Late yesterday afternoon, as we were returning from the Easter holiday with the grandparents, we were met at my house by Enrico Costello, who lives in the adjoining house owned by Professore Fagiuolo. Enrico was very agitated and told us that Michele and Benito were trying to break into the house."

Surprised the Inspector asked, "Does this man, Enrico, know Michele and Benito were trying to break in?"

"I'm not certain, but the way Enrico tells the story I believe it's true. He said that he has seen Michele and a younger man here before, but now they were trying to force open the front door."

"Now that report does require an important investigation and I can promise you that we will carefully include everything you have told us, and I will call you in Greve or you may call me here, Professore."

"I much appreciate your help and advice, Inspector. Before this latest series of events, I trusted and believed that Michele was okay, even though there was good reason not to trust or to believe him."

"With a firm handshake Al quickly departed and now was thoroughly convinced that Leone was a very dangerous man.

Satisfied with his specific evidence about Leone, Al returned to the girls' apartment.

Over a quiet dinner the trio were pleased with Al's report. But Dawn pointed out, "We really don't know what the wounded Leone will do next, do we?"

"No, of course not," Al offered, "but I am confident that the Inspector will demand many explanations from Leone."

"But," Lucy asked, "suppose the Inspector's police can't find the bastards? Then what?"

"Well, I suppose the beat and the heat goes on."

Satisfied that the future was securely in their favor, the trio resumed their demanding routine.

Fortunately the weather had improved—warm, sunny days but cold, clear nights. When Al decided to return to Greve Lucy and Dawn quietly agreed.

"But will you return this weekend, my devoted lover?" Lucy pleaded.

"Of course. I'll be here for dinner Friday."

After three days of killing time in Greve and exchanging greetings with most of the shoppers, Al's only refuge was reading the *Herald Tribune* and learning that Reagan really seemed ready to attack Muammar Quadaffi for a long list of crimes against the U.S.

"Damn!" Al thought, "if he does, the Italians will be very upset. That boob doesn't seem to know that Libya was an Italian colony and that many Italians still live and work there. I hope that these people won't take their wrath out on us."

Finally by Friday Al was only too happy to return to Florence.

Al's welcoming appearance raised his spirits and he quickly forgot Reagan and Quaddafi, and even the spirit of Leone.

For all three the weekend had been a continuous party, not excessive drinking or eating, but an ambience of mutual enjoyment. Dawn was able to get Lucy and Al into the Uffizi and the Pitti Palace. Later Lucy became Al's tour guide of Giotto's Bell Tower and Il Duomo.

But Al's quiet exuberance troubled him and his pleasure was tinged with quiet. I shouldn't be interfering with Lucy's practicing or Dawn's studies. Soon will be the Maggio Musicsale festival and Lucy's big chance, and Dawn will be tied down with final exams.

Quickly Al broke the news that he must return to Greve.

"But why? Why Al? You aren't interfering with our routine. In fact, we love it, don't we, Dawn?"

"Of course, I think your old man is on a witch hunt, or more likely a lion hunt. Right, Professore? I can't understand what draws you back to Greve when we need you here."

For seconds Al waivered then suddenly remembering his sons and daughter and the importance of maintaining an appearance in Greve, he ended the discussion with a firm short reply. "I'm sorry, but I must leave tomorrow."

Al's firm decision cast a pall over the apartment and even the dinner was a somber contrast to the trio's cheerful social life.

As Lucy and Al lay quietly, Lucy again offered a final plea. "Darling, I don't understand why you are leaving me for five long days."

"Well, my darling, as much as I may belong here with you and of course Dawn, the reality of my short absence is to collect my mail, particularly letters from my daughter and maybe my sons. But quite possibly I'll have other important letters. I'm afraid my absence will be noted. Then, too, there's always the problem of the empty house. I can't believe that anybody, including Leone, would attempt to break in, but it is a possibility."

"Yes, those are important reasons and I agree, but before we do what I love to do, I want to discuss, briefly, one small but important question."

"Of course, darling."

"A wedding ring. Now that Mr. Leone and his rings are completely out of the question, what do we do?"

"Why don't' we visit one of the many other jewelry shops and you select one and an engagement ring too."

"Yes, that's okay, but over Easter my grandmother showed me a beautiful, large gold ring that Massimo had given her when they married."

"But why would Justine want you to have her wedding ring?"

"I don't know for sure, but I think that she wants to make sure we get married soon. But she also added that the ring no longer fits her arthritic finger."

Al was quietly very pleased, but only added, "I think that's as generous as it is beautiful. So the ring that bound them together will do the same for us."

So radiant was Lucy's love and passion that she couldn't conceal her sexual arousal any longer. Now her loving, subdued demeanor suddenly erupted into an intense explosion of vibrant motion and sound. The waves of passion rose and fell until exhaustion left them silently bound in a world of love and sleep.

With the clanging church robbing their slumber, Lucy and Al were soon together with Dawn.

Again the immediate departure of Al silenced their usual cheerful banter over the breakfast table.

As Al held Lucy tightly, then finalizing their separation with a series of tender kisses, he slowly kissed Dawn on the forehead, and with bag in hand he quickly disappeared into the damp, gray fog.

For several minutes both women sat quietly.

Then Dawn, eager to break their shared melancholy offered, "I'd better pull myself together and get ready. I have a class at nine in that damn high school. I really wish Stanford could get its act together with buildings of its own."

Lucy could only add, "Yes, I'm afraid that's the price you pay for a year in Italy."

Chapter Eight

Although the heavy fog tended to exacerbate Al's melancholy, it also forced him to drive very carefully. Finally, after two hours of slow traffic, Al reached Greve.

By now the fog had lifted and the slight change improved his feelings. At the post office, the post mistress handed him several letters with a terse, "Buon giorno." Quietly he visited several shops for a few needed items. Again the greetings were a cool, reserved exchange. "Well," Al observed, "so that's what I get for Reagan's bombing Quadaffi."

Finally, stopping at the small variety store for the *Herald Tribune*, the usually smiling clerk stared and coldly said, "No American paper today."

Surprised by her attitude, Al suddenly remembered the *Herald Tribune* wasn't published on Sunday.

Soon Al was again in his lonely, old house. Indifferent to any possible dangers, he boldly entered and immediately turned up the thermostat. Then he sifted through the several letters and quickly opened his daughter's letter. After the usual greetings she detailed the important events and questioned how the Italians were reacting to the Reagan threats to bomb Libya, adding that most Americans were opposed to any attack on Quadaffi. She closed with a positive note about her pregnancy and that, "Dad, maybe you'll be back just as my baby arrives. And one further note, Herb Caen suggests you may return with a beautiful brunette?

"What in the world is Caen writing about? Please explain that one soon. I'm confused and your sons are making silly jokes."

Before opening other letters, Al was dismayed and could only ask, "Who could have possibly told Caen about Lucia?"

Glancing through the other letters, his agent scribbled, "Great satire, everybody will love it. But you didn't include the title, but *Lust and Sex in Academia* wouldn't be bad, or maybe *Tales from the Phallic Towers: Cal and Stanford.* The book will be going to the printers next week, so please respond with a title.

Without glancing at several other letters, Al scribbled a note to his agent. "Thanks. Use the first: *Lust and Sex in Academia.*"

Quickly Al scanned the other two letters, then tossed them into the wastebasket.

For several minutes Al sat reflecting on some way to explain to his children his impending marriage. Finally he concluded that anything he might write now wouldn't mitigate the problems which would arise when he introduced Lucia to his children, all of whom are several years older than she.

But to satisfy his daughter, he dashed off a short note. "Darling daughter, don't believe everything you read in Caen's column. He's probably got me mixed up with somebody else."

Content that he had solved that problem for now, he soon put together a large salami sandwich, which he washed down with beer.

Sitting quietly, Al couldn't control his mind from raising a series of questions and answers. Nothing seemed to relieve his anxiety. "Maybe I should listen to some good music. No, that won't solve any of these problems."

Reluctantly he turned on a small radio, and after tuning in several Italian stations and endless static, he finally found BBC, whose signal was clear and strong. For several minutes he heard a series of reports strongly criticizing the U.S. for bombing Tripoli and Benghazi and reports of severe damage and fires. Other reports stated that Quadaffi had been killed.

Perplexed by the reports and angered that "our government should attack Libya," Al cursed Reagan and turned off the radio.

For several minutes he continued to sit in silence as darkness engulfed the room.

Finally, turning on the lights, Al noted that it was after six. Between the news reports and his loneliness, he felt trapped in the vice of his own despair.

"Too early to go to bed. Maybe I should call Lucy. No, that might upset her. Hell, I'll take the flashlight and go for a short walk."

Soon he stepped through the small, heavy, outside gate. The air was cold and the quiet atmosphere was bathed in the last rays of light. Almost immediately his spirit was raised and with each step his anxiety quickly disappeared. At the main road he was pleased by the silence and waning light only punctuated by a few distant street and house lights. Turning to the large house nearby he noted its darkness and loneliness then, as he approached the property, he saw the headlights of a distant car. Quickly he concealed himself behind a nearby shed.

At the junction of the house, driveway and the road, the car slowed before continuing to an area behind the house. Al, recognizing what could be Leone's Mercedes, quickly returned to his house.

Once in his warm living room, Al was relieved but also concerned. "So Mr. Leone has come home, assuming that was Leone." With that thought, Al quickly descended the staircase to the small oak door which he secured with the large metal block.

Back inside, Al felt relieved, but decided he needed a night cap to sleep well. Again, the Napoleon cognac was a powerful soporific. Pleased, Al quickly fell into bed, sleepy and confident.

Having slept well, Al quickly dressed while noting that a cold haze obscured the sun. As he was preparing breakfast the phone rang, which Al answered with a cheery "Pronto."

"Darling, I'm so happy to hear your voice. I tried to reach you last night, but you must have been out."

"Yes, I was, but not for long."

"Now I am calling because everybody's very upset about America's bombing Libya. Already several of my friends have made rude remarks."

"Yes, I have had that experience here too, but I don't believe our friends or neighbors will blame us. The most important thing for you, sweetheart, is to practice and concentrate on your work."

"Yes, you're right, but I have some other unexpected information. Dawn walked past Leone's shop yesterday and a posted sign said, 'Closed Temporarily.'"

"Now that is important. Apparently Leone is in serious trouble. I'll call Inspector Ruffo. No, I won't, because I don't have his office number or probably know enough Italian to cut through the bureaucracy. Maybe you should call the Inspector. Would you sweetheart?"

Lucy readily agreed, and with several words of love she hung up.

Having finished breakfast, Al questioned the information about Leone's shop and connected it with the possibility that Leone was now living hardly more than a hundred meters from this house.

Suddenly the phone rang and Al was greeted with the Inspector's booming voice.

"Professore, this is the Inspector. I have some important news. Michele Leone has closed his shop."

"Really, Inspector. Closed permanently?"

"Probably not, but it is closed."

Then Al socked the Inspector with the fact that Leone could possibly be living in the house across the street. Pressed for details, Al described what he had seen the previous evening.

As the Inspector expressed surprise, Al quickly interjected, "Inspector, I must tell you this. Mr. Leone is taping our conversation right now. He put a tap on this telephone almost a month ago."

Suddenly, seething with rage, the Inspector demanded, "How do you know this?"

"Quite simply, sir. Shortly after he had put a tap on this phone, I could detect the sound of the tape recorder. Now listen. I hear it clicking."

For a few seconds only the low clicking sound of the recorder could be heard.

Quickly the Inspector exploded, "You are right, Professore. Now we must find Leone as soon as possible. Taping telephones is a serious crime and I will have a special police unit after Leone right now."

Following that interesting exchange, Al poured himself a second cup of coffee and gloated, "Well, Mr. Leone, the police net is closing in on you fast."

Finally Al decided to investigate the house which must be rented or owned by Senior Leone.

The early morning haze had dissipated as Al cautiously approached the interesting but unkempt modern structure. While maintaining a discrete distance, Al managed to circle the entire house. As there appeared to be no garage and no parked car, Al warily approached the house while searching the windows for any sign of life or occupancy. Emboldened and encouraged he approached the rear area where the Mercedes must have been parked. Here deep tire marks on the grass clearly indicated that a car had recently occupied that area near the back entrance to the house. Additional ruts in the grass where the car had turned clearly indicated that it had recently departed.

Pleased with his sleuthing skills, Al soon returned to his fortress. For a few minutes he sat evaluating his information and investigation. Satisfied that he was secure he decided that a walk to Greve would be beneficial. Again properly dressed for this modest occasion, he soon reached the busy Verrazano Square. As he mingled with the numerous strangers his presence attracted few stares or comments.

With the Tuesday Herald in his pocket, and a few purchases to placate his needs for something special, Al plodded up the winding, narrow road. Just as he had completed the last switch-back, he heard a car skidding around the turns only some hundred meters or so behind him. Quickly he slipped behind a high, hilly slope just as the Mercedes raced past.

"Wow! That was close!" Then watching the car accelerate and abruptly turn into the driveway of the nearby house, Al offered a cautious note, "You bastard, Leone!"

Just as Al reached his destination, Enrico drove in and stopped next to Al who greeted him warmly. For a minute or two they spoke in broken Italian and English. Then Al shocked Enrico with news that Leone was living in the nearby house. Enrico shook his head and swore violently.

"You call polizia, Signore. Presto. Okay?"

"Si, Si Enrico!" And with that Al bounded up the stairs.

Sitting quietly Al debated the question of immediately trying to inform the police of Leone's presence, but he quickly dismissed that demand by his realization that if he could possibly reach the Inspector, the call would have been monitored and Leone would have escaped.

"Well, it's too late to do anything but cause unnecessary alarm even were I to drive to Florence right now."

Then, realizing that should Leone and Benito make an effort to assault his house, Al quickly locked the gate securely.

Satisfied with his effort, he directed his skills to a modest but satisfying dinner, complete with a small creme cake.

After his gourmet meal, Al indulged himself with his favorite brandy while enjoying a Beethoven sonata and reading the Herald-Tribune. But hardly had he gotten comfortable than the phone rang twice before he could reach it.

"Pronto," Al offered softly.

"Darling! Is that you?"

"Oh, Lucy, dear lady, yes that voice is mine."

"Your voice sounded too soft, but anyway I've got some important news."

"Yes, yes! What?"

"The police think they know where Leone is hiding."

"How do you know, Lucy darling?"

"Well, about an hour ago the Inspector called me to say that they are about ready to arrest Leone and probably Benito too."

"Now wait a minute, darling. In this weather? You know this weather, well I don't believe that the Inspector would tell you anything like that."

For a few seconds Lucy didn't respond, then she laughed, "Of course not, what a silly idea. I was kidding you about the Inspector calling me. I haven't talked to him since last week."

"Good," Al laughed. "Maybe I should drive down to see you tomorrow."

As Lucy replied softly, Al heard the recorder stop its clicking.

"Darling, did you hear the recorder stop?"

"Yes, I certainly did, and I'm glad that you confused my message. Now is it true that you will be here tomorrow?"

"It certainly is, not because I can't stand living here without you, but because of several important things I've seen yesterday and today demand that I see you."

"Oh, how wonderful! I'll be waiting anxiously. But what time, darling husband?"

"Well, how about mid-morning?"

"Perfect. I'll be waiting impatiently, but please drive carefully."

With that wonderful surprise, Al could hardly wait for Wednesday morning to arrive.

Pleased with the probability that he would stay with Lucy and Dawn through the weekend, Al packed a small bag, locked the heavy door, and soon reached the Fiat.

Quickly he inserted the ignition key then hesitated, as the smell of gasoline surprised him. He got out and examined the rear gasoline cap, then opened the engine hood and there, balanced on the engine, was a quart-sized container of gasoline with a wire running from a spark plug directly into the container.

Shocked, for seconds Al stared in disbelief at the simple but deadly device. Carefully he removed the electric detonator then decided that Enrico should share his discovery.

After knocking at his neighbor's door, Enrico arrived. With only a few words Al lifted the hood and with the wire indicated the home-made bomb. Enrico exploded in a rage, "Leone, criminale bastardo!

Al patted Enrico on the back, "Grazie, Enrico. Adesso polizia!" Then Al handed the container of gasoline and the wire to the surprised Enrico, "You keep these. Okay?"

For a second Enrico was confused then, understanding Al's wish, took the container and wire.

"Ora," Al added, "the police!"

As Al seated himself in the Fiat, Enrico said something about Leone and pointing to the house across the street added, "I look to Leone." With a final handshake Al backed the car toward the street.

As the car slowly descended the steep, hilly road, Al pondered the question of reporting the bomb to the Greve police. Then, realizing that he still didn't know where the police station was, and his problem of explaining the bomb, he decided to wait until he could see the Inspector. "This should excite him."

Driving rapidly but carefully, Al parked the Fiat in a nearby lot, carefully folded the time card into his wallet, and soon reached the apartment.

There, Lucy threw her arms around Al's neck and kissed him repeatedly. "I'm so glad you're here, darling man! I was beginning to worry."

"I'm really sorry, dearest. I would have arrived sooner but I was detained by a rather unexpected and shocking experience."

As Al quickly related the bombing threat Lucy grimaced and almost cried. For several minutes they held each other tightly before Lucy recovered.

"Well, darling, after that terrible experience, before we call the Inspector, let me pour you some coffee and warm up this pastry."

While Al enjoyed his second breakfast, Lucy talked rapidly on the phone to the Inspector.

"Darling, Inspector Ruffo wants to see us, but is tied up until about one thirty. Is that okay?"

"That's excellent because it will give us plenty of time to piece together the entire story."

Quickly Lucy confirmed their appointment with the Inspector's secretary then sat down facing Al. "Now, what is the rest of the story, my guardian angel?"

Broken only by Lucy's frequent questions and punctuated by sighs and groans, Al gave a detailed description of Leone's frequent visits to the house. "But I don't understand what he is doing there or why, other than to spy on me.?

Then suddenly Al almost shouted, "Of course!"

"What?" Lucy demanded.

"That house is where he is recording our messages and that explains why he drives in and soon leaves. I should have noticed that our telephone line is connected to the same pole which serves Leone's house."

"Darling guardian, you are a real Sherlock Holmes, only smarter and more handsome and, well, you know how much better you really are than any other man."

"Oops! Lady Eve, let's stick to our detective work and your report to the Inspector."

"Of course, you're right. First things first and then, well, piano music," Lucy whispered.

As they sat holding hands, suddenly Dawn popped in. "Well! Our guardian angel!" And with that she planted a wet, juicy kiss hard on Al's mouth. "There. That's a reward for your protective service!"

Quickly Lucy summarized Al's account of the car bomb attempt and his discovery of the telephone recorder adding, "And now we all have an appointment with the Inspector at one thirty."

"Okay, let's have something to eat now," Dawn added as she produced some canned soup. "What else do we have, Lucy?"

Minutes later the soup was ready along with a plate of pasta and a green salad.

Before Al could suggest some red wine, Lucy poured three glasses of Chianti Classico, which immediately brought Al's glass to a toasting stance.

"To the extirpation of Michele Leone and his fool!"

As they continued to eat and to revel in their excitement, only a Cassandra might have offered a cautionary prayer.

Noting the time, the trio moved quickly through the crowded streets and reached the police headquarters minutes before their appointment.

With his usual friendly but bureaucratic welcome, the Inspector shook hands as he explained the importance of their cooperative efforts.

"Although I have known Michele Leone for several years, I now realize that this man was exploiting our friendly relationship for activities that were as illegal as they were immoral and had we, the four of us, not suddenly realized some of Leone's lies and deceptions, he might well have succeeded at our serious expense."

"Now, having said that, would each of you, or an appointed speaker, tell me of any new or otherwise important developments which have occurred since our meeting a week ago?"

Both women quickly urged Al to speak.

"I'll try to be brief, Inspector, but the ways and behavior of Leone are clever and complex, probably because he knows far more about Italy, this area, these people, and how the system works than we could even imagine. Obviously he's a very smart businessman who speaks many languages and is very highly educated.

"Now he finds himself in serious trouble over two very important issues—women and money."

"Don't forget the law, Professore. Michele is now very seriously in trouble because he either doesn't know or understand the law, or maybe because he believes he can evade our laws. I have just learned that several people, some once his best customers, are suing him for overcharging them, lying, and misrepresenting the quality and value of expensive jewelry and art pieces. I am amazed at the many serious swindles Leone has committed.

"But please, Professore, I interrupted your important charges. Please continue."

"Fine, and I'll be brief. You have heard about Leone's tapping my telephone and recording the messages?"

"Yes, you mentioned it during our telephone call yesterday."

"Well, I can now tell you that he has that recording device in the house just across the road from where I live. And I believe if we get there before he does, we or you can take the machine. I became aware of this because almost every day that I've been in Greve during the last two weeks or more, I've frequently seen Leone's black Mercedes drive onto that property.

"Now a second important fact. This morning, about eight, as I prepared to leave my house, just before I tried to start the car, I smelled gasoline. When I opened the engine hood there on the engine head was a container full of gasoline with a wire immersed in the fuel and the end attached to a spark plug. Had I tried to start the engine in all probability the gasoline would have been ignited, or more probably exploded, since the engine compartment reeked of gasoline fumes."

"So now we have attempted murder, Professore. I must say that you were very quick to detect the problem and save your life. Do you have that device here?"

"No, I showed it to our caretaker, Enrico, who has the device now. Enrico Castillo is the man who last week stopped Leone and his employee, Benito, from breaking into my house."

"Your information is very important and I will immediately order a police watch on your property, Leone's house, and especially around Enrico. Unfortunately we don't know where Leone is. He has been missing from his house in Fiesole, his store and office here, and we just learned that his store in Rome is closed. But I don't believe for a minute that Michele has left this area because there are two very important things or forces that will keep him here—revenge and money. I must warn all of you, Michele is extremely dangerous and he will be looking for all of you."

"Thank you very much, Inspector. We will take your warning very seriously."

"But one other interesting fact about Leone that I meant to share with you about his money problems. Do you have a few minutes? I'll be right back."

Al and both women were amused but quite nervous. "What do you suppose the Inspector intends to show us?"

Soon Inspector Ruffo returned with a large grey canvas bag which he opened, and dumped four large piles of American currency on the table.

"Do you remember Leone charging this police department with stealing some $225,000 dollars in American bills which belonged to him? These large bills are the ransom money he was taking to Iran to ransom the Americans who were being held hostage there in 1981—I believe that was the year. Well, I was only a lowly carabiniere at that time and until recently I had never heard of the story.

"Well, after Michele's personal plea to me, I investigated his claim and learned that this department did have the money. Take a look at it—brand new American hundred dollar bills. Wouldn't you love to have them?"

Quickly the trio examined the bills. "Well, these look like real American bills, don't they? Lucy? Dawn?"

Both women scrutinized the bills. "They sure look real and they feel real, they aren't counterfeits, are they Inspector?"

Smiling, the Inspector explained, "They're not real, but they are very good counterfeits, except for one serious problem."

"What's wrong?" Dawn demanded.

"Well, Miss Knight. Whose picture is on this bill?"

Carefully examining the bill, Dawn said well, that's President Grant, isn't it?"

"Yes it is, and that's the principal reason Leone had them."

"But what does that prove?" Lucy smiled.

"I guess you Americans don't know that the real hundred dollar bill has the face of Benjamin Franklin on it—the fifty has Grant on it. Isn't that interesting? Now we don't know how Leone got these bills or whether he knew that they were skillfully made counterfeits, but with the wrong person on the bill."

"That's a marvelous joke that somebody played on Leone and he never realized that the bills were very seriously flawed. Furthermore, had he taken them to the Ayotollah Khomeini, he would probably have been seized and still been in jail."

After that they all thanked the Inspector who again warned them about their safety. "Please be very careful wherever you go. We will alert all Italian police agencies as well as your CIA and FBI to be on the alert."

Again a round of handshakes and the trio emerged into the bright sunlight of this late afternoon.

Quickly they returned to their apartment, cheerful but cautious. "Well, that was a damn interesting hour and a half session," Al offered.

For the next several days Dawn spent most of her time studying at their apartment and only venturing forth for a class. But Lucy realized that with her Maggio Musicale concert only three weeks away, she had to practice at the Conservatory. Frequently she and Al would discuss the program, which she now thought might be too long.

"Much as I like the Schubert, it runs to about forty-one minutes, which throws the entire program out of balance, so I've replaced the Schubert with Beethoven's last piano sonata, the C major, opus 111. As I explained, it's tragic, which may over balance the program, but I can't risk changing the program a third time."

For the next four days the trio maintained a quiet, disciplined schedule only leaving the apartment when necessary. As Dawn felt more secure than Lucy and Al, she did the necessary shopping while Al carefully guarded Lucy while she practiced.

As much as Al loved to hear Lucy play, the strain of his protective role bothered him, but more importantly, his limited wardrobe annoyed him and he was anxious to pick up his mail.

After dinner on Tuesday Al struggled to bring up the problem of leaving the women alone for the few hours necessary to satisfy his needs.

Quickly Dawn resolved the problem. "Look Al, why don't the three of us go together tomorrow morning?"

"No," Lucy explained, "I've got an important lesson with my teacher tomorrow and I couldn't get away before noon."

"Well, I'm restless here so why don't I drive to Greve a little earlier and then meet at Al's writer's retreat about three."

Al was very pleased with Dawn's suggestion but added, "There may be traffic, so let's make it for a bit later, maybe four."

Pleased with the idea of escaping from Florence for a few hours, they soon returned.

With breakfast over Al reviewed their plans, then he and Lucy left for the Conservatory. Dawn dawdled, wondering whether she should take a change of clothing, then quickly dismissed the idea, but before leaving she checked her purse for money and the usual assortment of "junk." Finally, about noon, she decided to leave, then jotted a note that she was taking Al's Fiat.

After an hour and a half of slow driving, Dawn was pleased to park the old car in Verrazano Square, which was virtually empty. Somewhat surprised she reluctantly drove the short distance and parked in front of Ristorante Moro.

The place was almost empty, which allowed the few diners to feast their eyes on the nonchalant Dawn who savored their attention.

Suddenly a smiling Dino appeared with a menu while welcoming Dawn with a cheerful "Buona sera, Signorina."

Dawn impetuously flashed a sexy a smile while accepting a nearby chair. For a few minutes she studied the menu before ordering a salad, veal cutlet and spumone. As she started her salad Dino reappeared with a large glass of red wine.

"For you, Signorina, courtesy of the house."

"Well," Dawn thought, "you've come a long way, Dino."

Some forty-five minutes later, Dawn paid her check and left Dino with a handsome tip.

As it was now after three, Dawn was eager to see Al's familiar fortress. It seemed a long time since she had eagerly visited the place. Now, with the car parked, she slowly approached the house wondering if by chance the front door would be unlocked. "Maybe I should wait here in the car." Then, dismissing the idea, she quickly ascended the stairs.

At the door she paused, then quickly pushed the door wide open. As she entered the dimly-lit room, a familiar voice ordered, "Come in and close the door behind you!"

Shocked by the voice Dawn swiftly turned, "I'm sorry. I got the wrong house."

As she moved to leave, the explosion of a pistol shot exploded above her head sending fragments of rock cascading on to her shoulders.

"I'm sorry, Miss Knight, to greet you with such an unfriendly welcome, but you really surprised me. I had no idea that you might attend the little party I've planned for my ungrateful step-daughter and her fiance."

"Well, Michele, again we meet under less-than-friendly circumstances."

"Yes, I'm afraid that's true, Dawn. Until you tried to kill me on our last date, I had believed that we might become lovers."

"Yes, that's true, Michele, but when you became too aggressive, I had to fight you off. You were determined to rape me."

For a few seconds Michele only stared at Dawn then, waving the pistol he ordered, "Please sit down in that chair facing me. We've got to talk."

"What do we have to talk about, Michele?"

Again a long pause. "Well, first, and I ask you again, what do you know about my legal papers, the deed to the property I will own when Lucia and her grandparents expire?"

"Michele, you asked that question before and I told you that I know nothing. And my answer is the same, I don't know." Dawn paused, then looking directly at Leone she added, "I wish that I did, if only to prevent you from becoming violent."

Smiling, Leone added, "That's a good answer, but until you offer something better, you must remain my hostage. If you comply with my request, you will be perfectly safe."

"Your request, Michele? What do you want from me?"

"Not much, darling lady, I just want what I always wanted from the day I first met you."

"Yes, and what is that, Michele?"

"Simple, beautiful one, take off all of your clothes."

Dawn knew that Leone would probably demand a nude show, so she had a ready answer.

"Okay, Michele, why not? But before I undress, may I use the bathroom?"

Michele weighed his response, "Is it really necessary?"

"It is. I must use the John before I pee in my pants. Then after, I'll take off my clothes there and emerge as naked as the day I was born."

Again Michele paused, then standing, "Let's visit the bathroom together. I just want to make sure there isn't any way you might escape."

Still guarding his prey with the pistol, Michele entered with Dawn now beside him. Quickly he surveyed the small bathroom, "Well, there's only that small, narrow window, so you couldn't possibly escape. Then, glancing at the tub, old but quite large, Michele suggested, "Maybe we could take a shower and bathe together?"

Weighing her reply, Dawn agreed, "That might be a real blast, Michele. Good, clean fun!" But before we do, I must use the toilet."

Very pleased with Dawn's cooperation, Michele sat down just as Dawn called, "Michele, would you please bring me my purse? I need some deodorant."

As Michele began to comply, he quickly ransacked her purse noting that her bag contained all of the usual women's toiletries–powder, lipsticks, three different perfumes, etc.

Leaving the door ajar, "Here's your bag, Dawn."

As Michele returned to his chair, Dawn opened the small window, then taking the large roll of toilet paper, she quickly printed, "No! Don't come! Danger!" Each word printed on each connecting piece of tissue. Now with the long printed warning, she fastened it between the outside base of the window and the frame.

Pleased with her effort she urinated, flushed the noisy toilet twice, then quickly disrobed.

"Michele," she called, "are you ready for a naked Venus?"

Before he could answer, Dawn opened the door wide and quickly stood directly in front of the shocked Michele.

For several seconds Michele could only stare in amazed delight. Then, rising quickly, he threw his arms around her ample bosom and bending, he kissed each breast tenderly. Then fully erect he clutched her bottom while kissing her hard on her mouth.

Dawn responded quickly by returning his kisses with her own version of a French kiss. Within seconds she could feel his very stiff erection hard against her thighs. For another two minutes their erotic teasing continued until Michele almost ripped off his clothes.

Michele, now naked, pressed his hairy chest against Dawn's firm breasts. As the thoroughly aroused Sicilian gently massaged Dawn's quivering body, she gripped his large rigid penis and suddenly kissed it while continuing to stroke it with a delicate teasing motion. Suddenly he groaned as spurts of semen covered Dawn's teasing hand and fingers. Michele's whole body quivered as he muttered, "Oh! God! Jesus! Oh! God!"

Dawn, still aroused, seductively summoned Michele to the sofa. He wedged himself hard against Dawn's nude body, but Michele now realized that he couldn't quickly match her sexual performance. For several minutes he teased her with erotic kisses then gently cradled her into the bathroom.

"Are you suggesting we shower, Don Juan?"

"I think maybe we should," Michele agreed.

Quickly Dawn adjusted the fine spray, then as the almost hot water caressed their bodies, again their libidos rose, and in a standing position they performed their erotic tricks which soon brought them to climax simultaneously.

While the tub drained, they sat facing each other as the fresh hot water again invited them to excite each other with erotic sparring of fingers and toes. These ploys, heightened by oral manipulations, slowly increased the sexual tension toward an explosion. But Dawn, wishing to prolong her pleasure, slowly reduced her gentle foreplay as Michele also slowed his movements.

Hardly moving, they managed to readjust their bodies to a prone position with shoulders now resting side-by-side against the tub's slope. With just enough water to cover their legs, they resumed subtle splashing as they kissed and fondled.

Suddenly, as their sexual energies threatened, Dawn reacted, realizing that they must complete their marathon soon because she feared that Lucy and Al might arrive.

Desperately Dawn sat directly on Michele's erect penis. Rhythmically she gently moved in an exciting, circular motion while squeezing hard with her powerful vaginal vice. Suddenly they both climaxed in a loud chorus of gasps and groans.

With appropriate kisses, Dawn stepped out of the tub and quickly grabbed a towel. Now aware that the love feast was over, Michele stood as Dawn handed him a large towel.

"Darling lover," Dawn cooed, "I'll get dressed and find some champagne."

Michele, thoroughly exhausted, could only grunt his agreement.

Quickly Dawn found the champagne she hoped would be in the fridge. Then she carefully filled one glass before pouring about an ounce of chloral hydrate in the second, to which she added about three ounces of champagne. Slowly she tasted the potent sedative and could detect no difference between the two. Then on a tray she placed a few cookies between the two glasses.

As she carried the tray to the small living room, Michele, now dressed, greeted her with a passionate smile and darting tongue. Comfortably seated, Dawn raised her glass in a toast, "To the most fantastic lover I've ever known."

Then Michele lifted his glass and repeated her toast. Lifting his glass to drink, he paused and suggested that they switch glasses.

Dawn quickly assented then asked, "Lover man, why did you wish to switch glasses? Did you think that maybe I had poisoned you?"

"No, of course not. Switching glasses is just an old Sicilian custom. Now, bottoms up!"

Dawn gloated, then quickly snuggled up to the unwary man. "Are you worn out Michele? Did I satisfy your inner-most pleasure?"

"Dawn, you are the most amazing lover I could ever imagine. You did things that I never dreamed about. Please darling, marry me and we'll escape right now. I don't give a damn about the property or the money. I just want you!"

Eager and enthusiastic, Dawn squeezed the soft bulge in his pants while whispering, "Lover-boy, you've got the largest, most beautiful dick I've ever kissed and loved, and now it's going to sleep for a long time."

"As she gently touched him, he slumped backwards on the sofa. Pleased, she pushed him, then slapped him very hard. He never moved. Dawn watched him breathe quietly.

Then Dawn triumphantly opened the door to the surprise of Al and Lucy, now standing expectantly on the lower stair.

Quickly the trio examined the silent Leone. "You didn't kill him, did you?"

"No, but he's out cold on chloral hydrate and, unless he's unusual, he won't wake up for at least eight hours."

"So now what's your plan, Al?" Dawn asked.

"Well, I think we should give him one last ride in his Mercedes, which is parked behind the house across the street."

"But how are we going to carry him that far?" Lucy asked.

"We're not," Al noted. "He should have the car keys in his pocket, which I'll now find. Then I'll bring the car to our gate. We'll put Mr. Leone in the front seat while I drive him to his last resting place."

Quickly Al found the keys and left to return with the Mercedes. Soon he returned, but not before Dawn and Lucy became very worried.

As Al parked the car to point it towards the street, suddenly Enrico appeared, then recognizing his friends, he greeted them quite unaware that his hated enemy would be riding in his Mercedes for the last time.

Immediately Al and his helpers relieved Leone of any identification papers and his wallet, then they dragged him carefully down the stairs.

Slowly they were able to push and pull the totally limp victim and place him in the passenger's seat.

Now Al ordered the women to follow the car as he drove it slowly to a final point just above the steepest section of the hill where Leone, now seated behind the wheel, would take his final plunge.

With Dawn and Lucy standing away from the doomed car, Al released the parking brake, which allowed the car to coast forward. Suddenly the black Mercedes, caught in the gravitational pull of the steep hill, rapidly accelerated. At the bottom, the car crashed through a small grove of trees and exploded violently in a ball of fire.

Quietly Dawn called out, "Good night, sweet Prince, and may flights of angels sing thee to thy rest!"

Shocked by Dawn's soliloquy, Al and Lucy added, "Hell yes!"

Quickly they returned to the house satisfied but not in a celebratory way. When pressed to describe how she had managed to best Leone, Dawn was reluctant.

"Just believe that I tricked him into forgetting what he planned to do to all of us."

Without much discussion Al collected some clothes and soon the two were driving through a pleasing sunset bound for freedom and success in Florence.

The first few days were measured by their studies and passion: Lucy, long hours at the Conservatory concentrating on the Beethoven C minor sonata, a haunting piece of music; and Dawn, very serious about her final in Art History and studies of Modern Art. Now they all felt exhausted and confused–the weight of their disposal of Leone gnawed at their collective conscience, particularly Dawn, who struggled to assuage her guilt with secret visits to Santa Croce where she sat in quiet resignation.

Still, none of their collective efforts to rid themselves of guilt prevailed until suddenly they and all of Italy were threatened with nuclear radiation from the Russians' Chernobyl explosion. Caught between the confusing reports of radiation poisoning of foods and atmospheric threats to their health, Dawn, Lucy and Al mentally huddled together in fear and loathing as did much of Europe.

But after three days of suffocating lies and nonsense, first Al, then Lucy, and finally Dawn came to their senses.

Seated around their small kitchen table quietly absorbed in their pasta, salad and wine, suddenly Al erupted, "Ladies, we are now free. No more self-persecution and no more fears of radiation." Then, filling his glass and topping Lucy's and Dawn's, "Here's to freedom from guilt and freedom from fear!"

Startled by Al's pronouncement, both women suddenly smiled and drank. Then Lucy proclaimed, "You're damn right! We only did to Leone what he was waiting to do to us!"

Relieved, Dawn quickly added, "I beat Michele at his best game!"

Both Lucy and Al, confused with Dawn's remark, asked, "What?"

With a sneering laugh Dawn answered, "Michele demanded what I had to do. I gave him more than he could handle, then I gave him my final gift, a real Mickey Finn—a champagne cocktail made with chloral hydrate!"

"So now we're all free, thanks to you, Dawn!" Lucy exclaimed.

"Leone didn't win and neither will the Russians," Al added.

Freed of guilt and fear, Al, Lucy and Dawn all kissed and embraced each other. Now they were more firmly bonded by their mutual love and strength than they were with shared living.

For another hour they continued laughing, joking and drinking wine. Finally Lucy quietly ended the celebration with a few words, "Good night, dear ones, but I need some rest and my baby needs some rest because I've got only three more days to study and to practice before my May first performance."

With that Lucy said good night, then kissed Al softly as she whispered, "You will join me soon, darling?"

"Of course, but I should help Dawn clean up our dinner mess."

Quickly the two cleaned, rinsed, and within minutes the dishes were in the washer and the kitchen was spotless.

Turning to enter their bedroom, Al paused, then quietly kissed Dawn on the forehead. "Neither Lucy nor I can ever thank you enough for what you did, Dawn. You really saved our lives. I know now that Leone hadn't included you in his plans. He was waiting for us. Dawn, you had more courage than I could ever imagine!"

"Thanks, Al, but I was also saving my own life! Now get some rest with your beloved!"

The next three days were filled with periods of excitement tempered with a cloud of anxiety. Lucy's practice sessions were relaxed as she had now settled on her announced program: "First the Bach Chromantic Fantasy, then Mozart's A minor Rondo and ending the first half with Schuman's Nine Forest Scenes, opus 82. Then, after the fifteen-minute intermission, I'll come back with a late Beethoven sonata no. 32 in C minor and end with Debussy's Afternoon of a Fawn. For encores I'll play the Ravel Toccata, two Chopins, the Prelude no. 15, and the Fantasy Improntus, and finally end with Jancek's 1905 sonata, a real tear jerker."

Dawn was pleased with her finals, telling Al and Lucy she "cooled" them and would be flying home after the concert. Then smiling, she asked, "I hope you don't mind because I've been seeing that guy from our first double date–that night we all met.

"That idiot I slugged?" Al asked.

"I wasn't there when you cooled Lucy's date, Benito, but the guy I'm seeing is a swimming coach and his name is Bernardo. I asked him about Benito and he explained because they look alike people mistake him for Benito. So anyway, they aren't related and don't know each other. And just to answer ahead of time, 'No, we haven't made out yet,' Bernardo is a bit slow!"

"So your concert is tomorrow night? You do have a ticket for me?"

"Of course, Dawn, you and Al and my grandparents all in the first row of the grand tier at the City Theater. It's really big and I hope will be full."

"What do you plan to wear, Lucy? If you wish, choose anything from my wardrobe–not that you don't have your own large collection."

"Thanks, Dawn, but I'm going to keep it simple, something practical, loose and pretty, but probably cut full to give me enough room to play and breathe. But please come to my dressing room and make certain I look presentable."

"Of course, after all, we are almost sisters. No, more than sisters, after what we've been through."

"What about the dinner party at Villa Medici near Panzano?"

"All taken care of," Al offered. "We have reservations–dinner reservations for seven."

"How do you get seven, Professor?"

"Well, there's the two grandparents, you and Bernardo, Lucy and me, and a surprise. I invited the Inspector, but he gave his ticket to Dr. Valentine."

The last two days before Lucy's concert were an exhausting pleasure. Finally, on the big day, May first, after a light breakfast Lucy, with Al at her side, they soon reached the Conservatory for a final run-through. Her teacher, Signora Fonzi, shook hands with Al and suggested he should seat himself outside the practice room.

Finally, after almost two hours, Lucy and her teacher appeared smiling. "It went very well, dear man, I hope you weren't too bored."

"By no means, darling. I could hear most of your program and I loved it."

As they prepared to leave, Signora Fonzi spoke briefly, "Lucia, very good, no problem!"

With formal best wishes and goodbyes, Lucy and Al hurried to their apartment where Lucy had a sandwich and glass of milk. Then she folded her "performance" gown into a small hanger bag, and together they drove to the Teatro Comunale. At the stage entrance she was stopped momentarily for identification before the stage manager greeted her warmly, showed her the dressing room, and then escorted her to the stage and the nine-foot-long Steinway. As the stage curtain was closed, Lucy seated herself and ran through a series of exercises.

Finally, turning to Al, she spoke softly, "Darling, it's still some two hours before my recital begins, why don't you return to the apartment, pick up Dawn and my grandparents, and return here about seven thirty. You should be able to park in one of the nearby guarded parking lots. And here are five tickets."

Al marveled at her efficiency, that she could think of everything when the most important night of her life was only two hours away.

Quickly they embraced and whispered words of courage, success and love.

At the apartment Dawn was cool but anxious. For a half hour they talked while preparing a light meal. Suddenly the doorbell rang and Al quickly descended two floors to greet Justine and Massimo, who quickly shared Al's enthusiasm.

After an hour of talking and eating, with Dawn leading the way, the poked their way through traffic to the parking lot.

With Lucy's performance only some twenty minutes away, the towering Massimo cleared a path through the foot traffic. Soon they were seated first row center of the balcony.

Finally, at eight o'clock the stage curtains slowly opened as the crowd cheered. Then Lucia, looking radiant, approached the piano, took the mandatory bow, seated herself, and with her hands on the keyboard paused, she gracefully and

precisely began Bach's toccata and fugue. For seven minutes her fingers produced Bach's glorious music.

After the last note she waited as the applause reached a crescendo of
appreciation, then Lucia stood and bowed again. Following more formal applause she seated herself, slowly placed both hands on the keyboard, and began
Mozart's A minor Rondo.

For almost ten minutes the huge audience sat transfixed by Mozart's glorious music. And in the balcony first row center, Lucia's greatest fans glowed in
the beauty of her performance. Again the great hall erupted in appreciation as
Lucia again stood erect, smiling, and a low bow before leaving the stage for a few
moments.

At Lucia's unexpected departure, Al, Dawn and Justine exchanged quizzi-
cal glances only to be reassured as Lucia quietly returned.

Again accepting polite applause, Lucia ceremoniously raised her hands
and quickly produced the first introductory chords of Schumann's Nine Forest
Scenes, opus 82. Each of the nine short pieces beginning with "Entrance"
elicited polite applause, which continued to increase in volume and excitement
until, at the final quiet, reflective "Farewell" the audience clapped and cheered.

For three or four minutes the great hall reverberated in clapping and vocal
appreciation. Again Lucia stood in appreciation then, in a generous, deep bow,
she walked quickly from the stage.

The capacity crowd stood, talking, staring, enthralled with Lucia's performance. And her lover-fiance and relatives marveled at her technique and passion. For a few seconds Al and Dawn considered the possibility of visiting
Lucia, but quickly abandoned the idea with a shrug.

After ten minutes the house lights blinked in a rapid warning sequence
that the second half of the program would soon begin.

With most of the crowd in their seats, the great curtain opened and seconds
later Lucia quickly entered, faced the crowd and bowed, then seated herself, dra-
matically raised her hands, and quickly the first chords of Beethoven's C minor
Sonata No. 32 began questioning. For the next twenty-three minutes or more
Beethoven's haunting music, melancholy, teasing and ultimately tragic strains
brought tears of sympathy and beauty to most of the appreciative audience.

As the great crowd stood, clapping slowly, Lucia bowed and quickly left
the stage for a half-minute.

Soon she returned and, bowing formally, she smiled and waited for the audience silence.

With hands raised to shoulder level she began the last piece of her formal program, Debussy's Afternoon of a Fawn. The quiet, reflective moods of the music, slow, questioning, enchanting, captured the audience, and after almost ten minutes left them between tears and joy.

Suddenly, the crowd burst into a rhythmic pattern of clapping. Finally Lucia, who quickly left the stage after the Debussy piece, returned, stood poised, and as the audience listened, Lucia announced for an encore she would play a short piece of Liszt's Liebestraum No. 3. Again the huge audience in rapt attention listened to the short, tragic piece then, at the conclusion, clapped enthusiastically. Lucia acknowledged their praise and departed and returned. The crowd continued to applaud.

Standing beside the piano Lucia now offered, "Two final pieces by Chopin, Prelude No. 15, the so-called Raindrop, and following that I'll end with his Fantasy Impromptu."

The crowd reveled in the beauty and melancholy of Chopin, and after ten minutes of intoxicating beauty, the audience refused to stop clapping and cheering.

Finally Lucia returned to the stage. "Thank you very much. You are a wonderful audience. But I'm now weary and hungry. At this the crowd cheered, "One more, one more!"

Lucia stood silently, then turning to the piano she seated herself, and in a loud voice said, "As my final encore I'll play you a very tragic sonata called Nov 1905 by Leo Janacek.

As Lucia again raised her hands slowly, the crowd silenced, seeming not to breath as the very slow minor chords of the sonata began their tragic story. For almost ten minutes of the second part, the huge audience was trapped near tears as Janacek told them the story of the Bohemian student's demonstration against the German soldiers' occupation of their university, and how the student leader was bayoneted and killed by a German.

At the conclusion the clapping was slow and soon ended almost in a funeral atmosphere.

Lucia took one final, slow bow as sounds of appreciation followed her from the stage.

Seconds after Lucia reached her small dressing room, Al and Dawn and her grandparents crowded her room, kissing her, praising her, and soon exhausting her.

Justine and Massimo again praised her and agreed to join her family and friends at Villa Medici for dinner the following night. After they left, Al and Dawn bolted the door against uninvited guests. While Lucy changed clothes and the threesome praised and commented, they were ready to leave. Al announced that he had reserved a table for three at the Grand Hotel.

Comfortably seated in a small dining room at the Grand, Dawn almost mentioned that the last time she was in the hotel was with Michele Leone. Catching her blunder, she raved about the concert as Al seemed determined to praise Lucy for everything until she quietly protested.

"Of course I'm pleased, but I would rather talk about something else, something much more important to me."

"What's more important?" Dawn asked.

"First, tomorrow night's dinner. And my only real concern is that there will be many people there whom we don't know."

"Yes, but we are a group of seven," Al protested.

"You are right, darling fiance-husband. It's just that I always feel somewhat shy around strangers, but in a large concert crowd I'm perfectly at ease.

"But I also have one other concern," Lucy added.

"And what is that?" Dawn asked.

"Our marriage and a wedding ring."

Quickly Al answered, "Darling, we can get married any time you wish, and the sooner the better is my hope and wish." Then adding, "But you also mentioned the wedding ring, your grandmother Justine's wedding ring, right?"

"Darling Al, you're right. Would you like to see it?"

Quickly Lucy retrieved the large, plain gold band from her purse and handed the ring to Al.

For a minute Al examined the heavy ring. "It's quite heavy, darling. Could it be pure gold?"

"No, I don't think so, but it must be at least ten karats or more."

Now Dawn asked to see the ring which she seemed to weigh in her hand, then brazenly fitted it on her ring finger. It's very pretty, simple but pretty." Then she returned the ring to Lucy, who quickly slipped it on her ring finger.

"It's a little large, but I really like it. And Al, if you don't object, I would like to wear it tomorrow night."

As they quietly dined several people walked by obviously noting Dawn's decolletage, but few, if any, recognizing Lucy.

Embarrassed by the frequent stares, the trio quickly finished their dinner and left.

"Well," Al laughed, "I guess the people must have thought you were the piano player tonight."

"Oh, Al darling, don't tease. You're embarrassing Dawn and me."

Without further comment they reclaimed the car and soon were back in the apartment.

As it was now almost midnight Lucy and Al quickly slipped into bed while Dawn lay quietly wondering when her new boyfriend would make his first pass.

Monday came as a lazy day. Only well after ten were Lucy and Al aroused by Dawn's kitchen performance, but the smell of fresh coffee really pulled them into the kitchen-dining room.

Well rested, they shared a leisurely breakfast while again reviewing Lucy's concert. Then they slowly turned their attention to speculation about the dinner party. Did everybody in their group understand that they should meet there about seven thirty? To relieve her doubts Lucy called her grandparents. Justine quickly reassured her that she and Massimo would be there on time. But she hesitated about calling Dr. Valentine or Dawn's new boyfriend, Bernardo.

"He knows all about it," Dawn reassured Lucy.

Time seemed to drag until the three decided to get dressed for the occasion. But first they took turns in the shower—Lucy and Al's shower seemed temporarily too slow. Finally by six they were ready. Just before leaving, Dawn again checked her purse, and noted to her surprise that the very small "dog" pistol still occupied a small inside pocket in the large purse. She considered leaving it, but quickly snapped the large purse closed.

As the three left Florence, the late afternoon sun warmed them through Greve and all the way to Panzano. Here they stopped before getting directions for Villa Medici.

Finally, at seven-thirty they arrived only to spend several minutes finding a parking space.

At the door to the dining room they stopped, waiting for directions to their table. Then, peeking through the small window, they noted Justine and Massimo seated next to Dr. Valentine. Without waiting for a waiter they cheerfully greeted their friends and were in a lively discussion before a waiter appeared to ask if they wished to order a drink.

Al immediately replied by ordering a bottle of champagne. Soon the wine and champagne glasses arrived interrupted only by Lucy's request for two additional glasses.

With the dining room almost filled, only a few chairs indicated less than a capacity house. As the waiter began to pour the wine, Al noticed that the long, rectangular room had tables set for two, four or six settings arranged in spaces between the outer walls and small marble dance floor. Then it occurred to him that this large room must have been a carriage house and wasn't a direct part of the original villa.

Curious about the room, Al noticed a small divider between the dance floor and an entrance to the kitchen. Quickly waiters began appearing with plates and dishes and bottles. And now Al noted that several women guests also entered that divided area from both sides. "So," he mused, "there must be rest room there also."

With the champagne poured the six friends quickly touched their glasses and began a salubrious evening of drinking, dining and pleasure.

From their table setting in the center section of the room, their party of six could easily witness the snobbery and affectations of Tuscany's beautiful people as they gossiped, drank and snidely evaluated each other. Even as they frequently table-hopped they greeted each other with exaggerated congeniality.

But for Lucy's and Al's party of six they were transparent isolates until one aging, elegantly coiffured dowager recognized Lucy. With calculated gentility, she boldly stopped at Lucy's table and smiling broadly said, "How wonderful to see you here, Miss Conde. Your concert last night was divine! Now you've proved to all of Italy and the world that we Florentines encourage and cultivate the arts." Before Lucy could replay, the grand old dame rejoined her party of eight.

Minutes later Lucy and all of their table became a shrine which was as humorous as it was annoying–particularly when bottles of Dom Perignon and Moet Chandon would suddenly appear as the donor would rise and applaud.

Thus the center table, with Massimo and Justine seated next to Al and Lucy, and Dawn and Dr. Valentine at opposite ends, became the focus of attention.

For several minutes the embarrassed sextet sat awkwardly and uneasily. Finally Al stood very erect and with a champagne glass offered, "A toast to the generous and beautiful people of Tuscany."

Al's words broke the crowd's pretensions and sophistry, and for two hours the Villa Medici became a scene of exaggerated pleasure–the small marble dance floor crowded with "beautiful people" exuberant in their rediscovered youth.

Finally about ten the management, now wallowing in their unexpected revenues, feared that dangers were too threatening by the diner's exuberance, and disconnected the sound system, which had the immediate effect of dousing the crowd with ice water.

As the guests sat drinking and grousing, Dawn stood and whispered that she was going to the John.

Suddenly the celebrants were shocked into silence as two armed men, their heads concealed by ski masks, demanded silence.

Standing in the center of the room from the marble floor, one loud, grating voice announced, "This is a hold-up. My partner and I need money and you are all obviously very rich. Please do as we demand and nobody will be hurt."

At this point the silent robber produced a laundry bag. "All that we ask of you is your wallet, your wrist watch, and the ladies' jewelry. I want you to remove your jewelry and money–wallets and watches–and drop these in the bag my partner will pass around. Do this quickly and quietly, don't talk! With your cooperation we'll be out of here in five minutes and nobody will be hurt."

At this point a woman fainted as several nearby friends began to shout.

Immediately the blast of a pistol shell shocked the terrified crowd.

"Leave that woman on the floor and put your donations in the bag!"

Now the confederate quickly confronted each person as he held the bag with one hand and belligerently threatened with the pistol in his right hand. Terrified, each man and woman quickly complied, and within five minutes the heavy bag was half-filled.

"Take the bag to the front door, Benito," the leader shouted. Then, confronting the center table, the leader shouted, "You two–the old man and young woman–come with me!"

Neither Al nor Lucy moved. Then suddenly the bandit grabbed Lucy by the arm and shouted, "Bitch, I said come!"

"No! No! You bastard Michele Leone!"

· At the sound of "Michele Leone" a wave of shock shattered the silence.

As the furious bandit, Leone, struggled to grab Lucy's high, stretched left hand, he fired, the bullet glancing off the heavy gold wedding ring and smashing the joint of her index finger. As Lucy fell sideways a second bullet blasted through her bulging uterus as it spewed blood, tissue and fluid. Screaming, Lucy slipped to the floor.

Suddenly Al and Massimo lunged over the table towards the bandit, who rapidly fired at both men, but only stopped Al's forward thrust. Simultaneously two rapid shots from the confederate's pistol hit the shocked Leone in his shoulder as Al hurled a champagne bottle that smashed Leone's skull and simultaneously ripped off his mask. As he slowly slumped, a barely audible bullet pellet punctured his head while shouts of "Leone" reverberated from the terrified crowd.

Bleeding profusely from his chest, Massimo threw himself on the prone Leone and repeatedly smashed his head against the marble floor.

While screams and confusion filled the room with terror, the confederate dropped the bag and raced toward Dawn who was still cowering behind the plant-like arras. Reaching the terrified Dawn, he grabbed her while repeating, "It's me, Dawn, Bernardo! Come quickly with me!" But Dawn held back until Bernardo, pointing his pistol toward the terrified and confused woman, quickly went with him. In the excitement and confusion nobody saw Bernardo and Dawn dart out a nearby front door.

Once outside, Bernardo ripped off his mask to the shocked woman who couldn't believe what she had seen and heard.

Quickly Bernardo pushed her into a black Mercedes. "I've got Leone's car and we both must get away from here fast."

"But why? Why?" Dawn blurted.

"Because I saw you fire that single shot from your little pistol, and that was the shot that killed him. Oh I hit him twice, once in the shoulder and the second in the chest. If I got his heart that might have killed him too. But regardless, that old man smashed his head to a pulp."

"But why do we have to escape, Bernardo?"

"Simple, because the police will try to hold and question everybody connected with this shooting."

"But why did you get involved? How did you know Leone?"

"Because I have a half-brother who looks almost like me and he, Benito, worked for Leone for the last few years. He was Leone's flunky. Leone ordered Benito to help him with this crime, which meant taking Lucy and that man, the Professore, and then later killing both of them."

"But, why didn't you warn me about this horrible crime before it happened?"

"Because I didn't find out about it until Benito got drunk on poisoned wine this afternoon and told me. He said that Leone would kill him if he didn't help, so I decided to take his place. And if Leone hadn't gone off crazy and started something, I would have killed him tonight."

"Okay, I guess, your story makes sense. But what do we do now?"

"Now, we'll dump this car minus our finger prints in Florence and hole up in an apartment that I have in Pisa. Nobody there knows who I am. They might think I am Benito who, if he isn't dead from that wine, will soon be. He got some of that junk made with wood alcohol, which has already killed several people."

While Dawn and Bernardo were rapidly fleeing the murderous scene, Dr. Valentine had called for medical help and police as he worked to stanch the bleeding in Lucy and Al. Lucy's left finger was severely smashed but saved only by the large gold ring. The bullet in her uterus had killed the fetus and created severe blood loss. And Massimo, with a massive wound in his heart, died within minutes after smashing Leone's head to a bloody pulp of bone, blood and hair. Lucy and Al were raced to the trauma center in Florence while first aid was given to numerous diners at the Villa Medici.

For several days Lucy remained in a comatose state barely clinging to life. Dr. Valentine and a group of specialists monitored her every movement. After several blood transfusions she finally recovered consciousness and asked where she was being treated. Dr. Valentine explained what had happened, which suddenly stimulated her memory. In a terrified scream she cried, "Al! Al! Where are you?" Quickly Dr. Valentine tried to soothe her, "Lucy, Professore Praitt is recovering and has been transferred to another hospital."

For a few seconds Lucy seemed placated, but suddenly she again screamed, "But Professor Praitt is my husband and I must see him."

Again Dr. Valentine tried to soothe her, but now she was hysterical, repeatedly calling, "Al, Al, darling! I need you!"

Quickly he was given a powerful sedative, which soon allowed her to sleep.

As the stricken woman lay breathing rapidly, Dr. Valentine and his four colleagues quickly agreed that Al Praitt should be returned from the General Hospital, Santa Maria Nuova immediately.

Within minutes Dr. Valentine was talking to a head nurse at the General Hospital. She reassured the doctor that Professore Praitt was still in critical condition, but was improving. Then she added that Professore Praitt was being held in protective custody by the police.

Shocked by this information, the doctor demanded an explanation, only to be informed that he should talk to Inspector Ruffo who had ordered a twenty-four-hour guard be posted outside the Professor's room.

When Dr. Valentine informed his colleagues of this inexplicable order, they all agreed that this information should be withheld from Miss Conde-Praitt until she was strong enough to accept it without another hysterical outbreak.

As Dr. Valentine racked his brain for some other positive force he might use to alleviate Lucy's fear, he suddenly remembered Dawn Knight, and it now occurred to him that he hadn't seen her since "that" night. Immediately he called the central police office and demanded to speak to Inspector Ruffo. After almost ten minutes the Inspector answered.

Dr. Valentine identified himself and almost at once was told the reason for guarding Professore Praitt. "We know that Leone and his partner, whoever that might have been, escaped and the man we believed was Leone's confederate, Benito Bosso, died of alcohol poisoning in the hospital here just about the time the robbery was taking place. Now we think that Leone's partner was a Mafia member who had been paid to kill either Praitt or the woman, Lucy Conde. We also know that Leone had very strong reasons to kill both Praitt and Conde."

"For these reasons you believe that Leone's partner might be trying to kill the Professor?"

"Yes, we think it's possible. Furthermore there are two other unexplained facts about the robbery. Several shots were fired, not only six by Leone who had emptied his pistol, but by his confederate, who had shot at least twice."

"How do you know that, Inspector?"

"From the autopsy we discovered two nine millimeter bullets in Leone's body, one creased his heart and exited in his right side, and the other creased his skull but only grazed his brain. But neither of these bullets killed Leone."

"But what did?" Dr. Valentine almost shouted.

"You won't believe it. The deadly projectile which killed Leone before Massimo smashed the back of his head to a pulp, that tiny lead pellet was fired by somebody who is an expert with this pistol. They are still sold in Italy."

"That's hard to believe. Was this small lead bullet powerful enough to kill?"

"Oh yes, doctor. That tiny ball almost exploded in his brain tearing pieces of tissue for four or five centimeters."

"And you don't know who fired that tiny pistol?" Dr. Valentine asked.

"And you mentioned some other unexplained fact," the doctor added.

"Yes, Leone's confederate escaped, but left the large bag of money and jewels at the door as he escaped."

"But I have another unanswered question that has me worried, Inspector."

"Yes, what is that?"

"Certainly you remember that beautiful blonde woman, Dawn Knight?"

"Of course, she is the most beautiful woman I've ever seen or met. But what about her?"

"Simply this. Nobody has seen her since the big party at the Villa. Nobody saw her leave and now the only surprising information I got was from the man who rents his apartment to Lucy and Dawn. The landlord is a professor named Dr. Procci, who said that she collected her clothes three days ago and told him that she couldn't stand the tragedy that almost killed her two best friends, and she was leaving for the U.S."

"That is very strange, Dr. Valentine, but I believe it. She must have been almost out of her mind and now probably hates Italy."

"Thank you, Inspector, for all your important information. But is there any way that I or my colleagues can arrange to have Lucia Conde and her fiance, Professor Praitt, see each other. I'm certain that Praitt is just as determined to see his woman as she is to see him. Really, I've never seen a man and a woman so totally in love with each other. I know both of them very well, and even though the man is much older, he loves her with as great a passion as she loves him. If there were ever a couple made for each other, it must be Lucia and Al.

"Please, Inspector, use all of the force possible to unite these two people. Either or perhaps both will die if they aren't united soon. I really believe that, as a medical doctor who has treated both of them."

"Dr. Valentine, I wish that I could promise you something positive, but I can't because I'm afraid there is somebody with a lot of power who demanded the protection for the Professore, and now I have a feeling that this same person or power will demand that he be returned to the U.S."

"But Inspector, what you must be suggesting is that either the Italian government or the American government is now handling this case. Could that be true, Inspector?"

"Yes, of course it could be true. But I would not be allowed to know or make any serious effort to find out. And now I feel that I am the jailer without any reason for my assignment."

With a flourish of formalities the two men said goodbye.

For the next few weeks Dr. Valentine, assisted by two special nurses, maintained a constant vigil frequently changing bandages and administering drugs to fight infection. A bone specialist examined Lucy's ring and index fingers and would whisper guarded opinions to Dr. Valentine.

Lucy never smiled and only whispered when asking about her fingers or pleading for somebody to "Find my loving husband and bring him to me."

But Justine was almost as ready to die as Lucy. Following Massimo's murder, Justine's grief was constant and terrible. Only a few close friends could prevent her suicide, which they gladly did twenty-four hours every day, which finally terminated when she was taken to see Lucia. Their unplanned joyful reunion was Dr. Valentine's insistence that Justine must come to the hospital for a check-up.

Until that day Justine blamed herself for her husband's death and for Lucia's tragedy. "I know this was my fault," she would weep to her friends. "I knew how evil Leone was and somehow I should have known that he was waiting to kill all of us."

But finally, when Justine was directed into Lucia's bedroom, both women stared at each other as if each were a ghost, then both women almost screamed their joy as they held each other tightly, crying and laughing.

Medicine and Dr. Valentine had kept Lucia living, as medicine and friends had held Justine from the final plunge. But now this unity of their blood revived them and they were ready to live.

A week later Lucy was released from the hospital and, with Justine, they returned to Panzano. For several days their friends and neighbors provided the spirit and comfort to strengthen both women's need for a new life. And the tonic worked, encouraging both women to return to Florence, and first and foremost demand to know what had happened.

So on a Thursday, later in the month of July, they called Dr. Valentine, who joyfully welcomed them to his office. And after an hour of preparation they called the U.S. Consulate who agreed to see them within the hour.

Both women agreed that the question of Al Praitt's presence or disappearance must be foremost. With Dr. Valentine offering advice as physician and friend, the trio was ushered in to see the Counsel, a Mr. Arnold Herrington. The Counsel affected a friendly, diplomatic demeanor, but quickly disqualified himself as an authority on the strange disappearance of Professor Al Praitt.

"We were told by Inspector Ruffo that Mr. Praitt was being held in the hospital here for treatment and protective custody. Now we learn that Praitt has returned to the United States for additional medical treatment?"

"Yes, that's exactly what I'm told," the Counsel replied.

"But why was he held in so-called 'protective custody?'" Lucy demanded.

"That I can't say because I don't know. When this office was first notified that Professor Praitt was being treated and held by a twenty-four-hour police guard, we assumed that very serious threats had been made on his life."

"By whom and why?" Justine demanded.

"Again, I repeat. I don't know whether this guard was ordered by the hospital, the police, or perhaps our government."

Annoyed by the Counsel's bureaucratic defense, Lucia finally demanded, "Well, sir, do you know or have any idea what happened to my fiance?"

"Yes, I can answer that question. At the Professor's request, and with the U.S. Embassy's support. Professor Praitt was returned by a U.S. Air Force transport about ten days ago."

"What? By a military aircraft?" Dr. Valentine demanded.

"That's what I said, doctor. And now, if you will excuse me, I have other important affairs that require my attention."

Disgusted and angry, the two women and the doctor left the Consulate.

"What are your plans now, ladies?"

"I suppose we will go back to Panzano. We have no reason to stay in Florence." Justine sounded depressed.

"Yes, that's true, but I must return to the apartment and collect the few things I left there but, more importantly, I must see Dr. Procci and pay the outstanding rent and anything else I have or perhaps Dawn owed before leaving."

As the two had walked the considerable distance to the apartment, they were tired. Fortunately Lucy found the key to the apartment, but as Dr. Valentine said goodbye, he added that he would immediately call the U.S. Embassy in Rome and request information about Dr. Praitt's strange departure by the U.S. Air Force.

Then he asked, "How long do you ladies think you might stay here? I ask, because if I get any good information I'll call. Do you have a telephone?"

With all the details completed, Dr. Valentine returned to the trauma center.

Back in the empty apartment, Lucy almost wept as she slowly visited each room which she last saw on June 2. Then she remembered her responsibilities and called Dr. Procci's office.

At the sound of his cheerful voice she felt encouraged as she explained the chaotic sequence of events. "But now, Signore Procci, I must pay our rent and any other outstanding charges.'"

Quickly Procci reassured her that whatever rent was unpaid, the charge would be minimal. Then he added, "I could drop by now and take care of anything you might consider."

Lucy agreed and then explained everything to Justine.

Soon the telephone rang and Dr. Valentine quickly related his information. "Miss Conde? Yes, Dr. Valentine here. I have all or almost all the information about Professor Praitt."

"Yes! Yes! Please tell me."

"The reason he was under protective custody was because the police and the hospital were informed that the Mafia was going to kill him. Added to this, the doctors were afraid that Professor Praitt was too weak to endure the long and detailed surgery to repair the shattered bones in his leg.

"Fortunately, Professor Praitt was a retired Major in the U.S. Air Force, and since he couldn't fly back to the U.S. in a commercial airline, he demanded that the U.S. Embassy should arrange his return by the Air Force.

"That was accomplished and I was told that reconstructive surgery was successful at the university hospital in San Francisco."

"Thank you for this wonderful news," Dr. Valentine.

As the two women were quietly celebrating the good news, Professor Procci arrived.

Procci, a debonair, handsome Italian was anything but the stereotypical absent-minded professor. Lucy related the information she had acquired, which Procci acknowledged with sympathy. Quickly he dismissed any outstanding charges for rent, telephone or cleaning as "nothing."

"As for me," he explained, "I am terribly sorry that you were subjected to such misery. I hope that you will return here with your husband. The apartment will be yours whenever possible."

With that, Procci departed.

"Shall we stay for one final night in this place where my man, my lover and my husband-to-be lived and loved. One final night of dreams, Justine?"

"Of course! Your man, Al, was the most handsome, considerate, loving man I ever knew–except one."

"Yes, I know, your husband, Massimo, a giant among giants."

With that emotional outburst, Lucy searched the kitchen shelves and a bottle of Martini and Rossi magically appeared.

"Shall we celebrate our men, Justine? I feel awkward calling you grand-mother when you are barely old enough to be my mother, but that's how I see you, a mother and my best friend."

The two women closeted with their memories soon were slightly drunk. Then Justine, aware of their sentimental weakness, demanded that they go out for dinner.

As Justine and Lucy slowly satisfied their tastes in an expensive restaurant, Lucy asked Justine about how she should get information about Al. "The only information that seems possible to me is that Al almost lost a leg and that he had reconstructive surgery."

"But you don't know if the surgery was successful and you don't know where he is now."

At this point, Lucy almost wept. "And what is worse, Justine, I don't know where Al lives, his address–nothing! I know that he has three children and that he retired five years ago after teaching at the University of California in Berkeley."

"Don't give up, Lucy. There must be ways to find Al." Justine was adamant and determined. "Well, you could wait. Surely he must be as determined to find you as you are him. He has your address at the apartment."

"Yes, but nothing else. Maybe I should wait. Oh Justine! I'm so desperate that I can't think straight."

For the next few weeks Lucy stayed in Panzano with Justine–waiting, hoping and almost praying. Like a cancer her despair grew until Justine called Dr. Valentine for sympathy and advice.

Again Dr. Valentine became a doctor, a psychiatrist, and ultimately a loving friend. Quietly and slowly Lucy accepted the doctor as a surrogate companion and lover, but only after her unopened letters to Professor Praitt were returned from the University of California.

And her efforts to find her friend, Dawn, were returned stamped "Addressee Unknown."

With only Justine and the doctor to comfort her, Lucy became a recluse until Justine and the doctor demanded that she return to the piano.

At first Lucy could hardly finger the keyboard with her left hand. But gradually she discovered that by allowing her index finger to remain slightly bent she could reach the left position. And soon she began playing from memory snatches of Schubert and Chopin and Mozart. When Justine asked what she was playing Lucy smiled, "I don't know."

Nevertheless, after about two weeks of playing, first only for a half hour, but finally for two or three hours, she became an aware, almost assertive personality. Quietly and unobtrusively sheet music appeared and within a month she was a transformed personality–much as she had been a year earlier.

Now Dr. Valentine, too, was transformed as was Justine. Soon the doctor's spacious apartment became the social center for recitals, pianos, string trios and quartets. Music had become Lucy's salvation and love–now greater, deeper and intense. She resumed playing the Beethoven sonatas, particularly the late ones. And finally she began studying her greatest challenge, the Hammerklavier, opus 106. Again she studied the score over and over before she suddenly understood.

Finally, her confidence in command, with only Dr. Valentine and Justine in the apartment, Lucy's fingers began to explore and to search the puzzling, strange and difficult score for the meaning of Beethoven's longest and most difficult piano sonata.

For hours she poured over the score, striking notes and chords, then shaking her head in disbelief, "No! No! That can't be it. It doesn't make sense. Then, quite suddenly, her fingers began finding answers. The mystery was solved. Lucia smiled!

As her life with Dr. Valentine and his friends continued to grow, Lucy's memories and nightmares of the past year receded. Yet, occasionally, something would remind her of Al and she would quietly weep. Finally she lost all hope of finding "her man" and when Dr. Valentine proposed marriage, Lucy passively agreed.

A month later they were married with only Justine and a few close friends of Dr. Valentine's invited to the private civil ceremony.

Upon their return from a two-week honeymoon in Egypt, Lucy found two letters, one addressed Miss Lucia Conde from Mrs. Robert Edwards, and the other from Dawn Rossi.

Quickly she ripped open Dawn's letter, which began with a long apology for not writing sooner and a series of sympathetic questions about Lucy's health. Then she gave a detailed account of what had happened to her on the "fatal night." She described how Leone's confederate had kidnapped her, and only after the escape in Leone's Mercedes did he reveal himself as Bernardo. "The same guy I had been dating." Then she detailed why Bernardo had killed Leone, ". . . because he was a Mafia member and had intended to kill Lucy and Al and probably me, whom he thought was his flunky, Benito. More importantly, Leone owed the Mafia a lot of money, which they were demanding."

Then Dawn added that they hid in Bernardo's apartment in Pisa before escaping to Switzerland. After about six months there, "We returned to San Francisco where we plan to open an art shop."

"Now I'm trying to find Al, whom I'm sure is still alive. I'll write again soon."

Then Lucy, curious about the other letter, opened it and was shocked that the writer was Al's daughter, Virginia.

Elated and nervous she read and reread the letter: "I'm certain you are the lady who is or was my father's fiance. He is still recovering from severe wounds he suffered that night. And he still frequently mentions your name, but he is now resigned that you died soon after that night.

"Please, if you are the Lucia Conde whom my father desperately loved, write to me. I will break the good news to Dad who has almost recovered after having his left leg amputated. Your survival could really insure Dad's survival."

Lucy's hands were shaking as tears fell on the letter. For minutes she sat trembling and thinking. Finally she considered her immediate action: "First, tell my darling Georgio and make certain that he understands I will not leave him for Al, not that I don't still love Al, but now it's too late. Georgio will understand and agree that we must go to Berkeley or wherever to find Al and meet his children."

Soon she informed Georgio of the good news from Virginia Edwards and Dawn. And Georgio responded as she hoped and expected. With only a hint of sadness in his voice, he completely agreed that they should fly to California. Also, before leaving, they should try to reach Al by telephone. Then he added, "And we should be able to meet Dawn and her husband at the same time. Maybe we can have a magnificent reunion party."

Within a month, Lucy first talked briefly with Virginia and then Al, who seemed hesitant but cheerful. For several minutes they whispered and laughed before Dr. Valentine was handed the telephone. Soon the doctor was his animated, enthusiastic self, and between the two men plans for a reunion were discussed in great detail as Virginia in Berkeley, and Lucy, next to the doctor, listened on connecting telephones.

Between frequent letters and telephone calls, all of the friends and close relatives of Lucy's immediate family and Al's children, plus Dawn and her new husband, Bernardo, participated and planned for a January reunion first in Berkeley, and then at the Conde family house near Napa.

As the multi-planned celebration grew and expanded, Lucia diplomatically suggested to Georgio, as she now referred to her husband, that she would like to give all of the land and property that she inherited to Al and his family. "We know that he has already started a small winery, but unless he is extremely lucky he will need a lot of money and good luck to become successful."

Without a moment's hesitation, Georgio agreed, adding, "Darling Lucia, that is your property. Of course you can give it away. Even if I were to legally own half, which I don't, I completely agree with your plan. It would be a practical and wonderful gift for them and for us. We don't need the relatively small income the property generates.

"But my darling, we must immediately hire a lawyer to advise us and make all the legal decisions for both us and them."

Now with the holiday season rapidly approaching, Lucia and Georgio managed to understand the problem of transferring the American property while planning a few small family affairs.

As she had done a few years before the disaster, she reestablished the American tradition of a Christmas tree and a few parties for family friends and Georgio's professional colleagues. Then she complicated her life by sending Christmas packages to Al and his family and Dawn and Bernardo. She really enjoyed the entire responsibility except for the long lines at the post office.

Somehow the Christmas celebration generated an explosion of excitement, jubilation and surprise as she and Georgio, Justine, plus the doctor's relatives, all celebrated, sang, ate and drank too much.

With New Years finally over, Lucia and Georgio completed their travel plans.

Epilogue

As the Alitalia 747 neared San Francisco International Airport, Dr. Valentine, Lucy and Justine rejoiced. Traveling first class, they agreed, is the only way to fly: excellent food and service. Noting his watch, Georgio commented, "Well, we're almost on time and the weather is good."

When the plane finally rolled to a stop, the few first class passengers were invited to depart first. Within minutes there was a small crowd of friends and relatives with Al limping along in the lead.

Quickly the two families and friends exchanged greetings. As they headed for Berkeley, Virginia explained, "I've made reservations for you at the Hotel Durant. It's small but comfortable and, more importantly, it will be easy to leave from the hotel when we drive to Napa."

Before the baggage was delivered to their respective rooms, Lucy, Justine and Georgio joined Al and his family who were proudly introduced. Again, as greetings were exchanged, Lucia was surprised how attractive and alike Al's sons and daughter resembled him. She also noted now much Al had aged even as Al was noting Lucy's small worry lines.

When the waiter suggested a beverage, everyone but Virginia ordered. Within minutes the cocktails arrived and soon Lucy began describing her family house in Napa.

"Much as I love returning to the Bay Area, which I once considered part of my life and home, I would like to see our house in the hills soon." Lucy's request was echoed by everybody.

"Well," Al added, "since the weather is quite good, I would suggest that we leave Wednesday, day after tomorrow."

"What about Dawn and her husband?" Lucy asked.

"I'll call tonight. She lives in San Francisco."

As the eight friends agreed, they should discuss their departure time Wednesday and know how many would travel together and in which cars.

Now Dr. Valentine asserted himself, "The car problem seems simple. All five of you Praitts could possibly ride in one car and Lucy and Justine and I will have a rental car."

"But what about Dawn and her husband?" Then quickly answering herself, Lucy said, "Of course Dawn and Bernardo will ride with us."

"Now that we've solved that simple problem," Al added, "what about time of departure and return? What highway do we take? Do we eat there and do we return Wednesday night?"

Here Lucy quickly answered most of the questions. "As we plan to travel in only two cars, Georgio will drive and follow my directions as I'm the only one who knows where our family house is, and it would be difficult to find for anybody who hasn't seen it. As for food, we can buy what we want in Napa. Also I would suggest that we all sleep at our house, which is quite large and has at least five bedrooms. As for the return, any of you are free to leave whenever you wish, but I must spend at least two days there to complete some outstanding tax and legal problems."

With that final and almost flip comment, everybody but Lucy looked confused.

"I'm sorry," Lucy explained, "I'm just feeling giddy and silly about seeing the house I dearly loved, a place where I feel I was born. But that isn't true because I was born in Verona, Italy on January 27, 1966, which was only a few weeks after my father resigned from the Air Force and immediately returned to the town of Napa where he was born and grew up.

"But our house, the one you will see, wasn't built until about a year later when my paternal grandfather hired an architect and contractor and told my father that he was building this house for himself and my grandmother. But even before the house was finished, he told my father that the house was really for him and my mother, Eleni."

"Your grandfather must have been very wealthy," Bob Edwards suggested.

STON

"Maybe not rich, but he certainly had many large pieces of land which became vineyards. I inherited several large parcels which are now in production."

Having finished their drinks, an almost embarrassing silence signaled a change.

"What about dinner tonight?" Al asked.

"If you don't mind, dear Al, or Pops, as I sometimes like to call you, I think that Georgio and Justine are just as tired as I am. So, if possible, we'll eat here."

With that resolution, Al and his family said good night with a promise to call the following morning.

The trio agreed that the Praitt family were a handsome, intelligent five. "Really six," Lucy explained, "if you count Virginia's baby."

Georgio was almost as excited to see Berkeley as was Lucy who suggested that they first stop at the University museum which was almost across from the street from the hotel.

"From here, it's only a short distance to Memorial Stadium, and beyond the football stadium are many important science buildings in the hills, but they are really too far to walk. From the stadium, we can visit the Greek Amphitheater and then slowly wander all the way to Edwards Field at the very bottom of the campus."

Having no idea how an American university would compare with an Italian, Georgio was flabbergasted by the size of the buildings. Standing some distance from the football stadium, he was amazed that such a large structure was used for only one sport. But Lucy corrected him by including rugby. "It's a very rough kind of English football," she explained.

Slowly they strolled around the Greek Theater and followed the narrow paths which took them around and between several large science buildings, and finally past the large library and ultimately to Edwards Field.

"My father had many classes in these buildings, but several of the large science buildings were built after Dad graduated."

"But did you ever have classes, Lucy?"

"No, I didn't, but I would like to have had some of my music classes. But I was much too young. Really I was only a small child. So I studied at the San Francisco Conservatory of Music for several years. There I studied history, theory and composition plus two or three hours of practice every day."

As Georgio knew almost everything about his wife's early life, Lucy quickly changed the subject to their plans for Wednesday, while reminding her husband that they had agreed to meet Dawn and Bernardo at the Durant.

Shortly after twelve, Dawn and her husband arrived as they had planned. Soon they were seated in the dining room and immediately became the focal point of attraction as the husbands began an animated Italian discussion while the two beautiful woman whispered and laughed like Cal students.

Later Al and his sons arrived with the announcement, "Tomorrow evening I'm inviting everybody to the best restaurant I've ever known, Chez Panisse. It's not only a local institution, but now a monument to cuisine artistry."

The next night promptly at six, the party of ten arrived. Fortunately they had reservations in the dining room, but as they were escorted to the second floor none of the Italians were particularly impressed. After a prolonged study of the elaborate menu, they each selected separate entrees and a variety of soups and salads.

Quietly they dined and marveled and compared. They agreed that they had never experienced such a delicious variety of meats, fowl and fish and vegetables plus several side dishes. And everything was beautifully served but also "very fresh."

"You have to agree," Al added, "Alice Waters has put Berkeley on the map for something more than crazy students and losing football teams."

Before leaving the small, crowed restaurant, Lucy explained the program for Wednesday. "We will check out of the hotel tomorrow morning about nine and travel in the two cars close together, Al and his family in his car and the five of us in the rental.

"But there are a few important considerations: We must stay together. If you must stop, I'll pull over and leave room for you, but if you have any problems, blow your horn. We must stay together. The total distance from here is only about 35 miles but the traffic will probably be heavy. I'll stay in the right lane except when passing and I'll cruise about sixty except when the limit is lower.

"Now, Al, you follow me, and at the bottom of University Avenue, I'll turn on to I-80 which will take us across the Carquenez Bridge. About five miles from there, we bypass Vallejo and take Highway 29 to Napa where we will shop for food.

"Okay? Any questions? Remember, we must stay together."

With Lucy driving and Dr. Valentine sitting next to her, nobody spoke for several minutes. Once safely on I-80, Dawn hesitated and nervously broke the tension, "Well, isn't it wonderful that after two years, we're finally back together again? But I do sense a change."

"In what way?" Justine suggested.

Now Dawn's answer was firm and positive. "I feel that we've lost our sense of humor and fortunately our almost teenage lack of personal responsibility. Certainly Bernardo and I have finally grown up and are now really enjoying life."

"I'm not surprised to hear that, Dawn, but considering that night of absolute horror and the following year of fear and agony—Justine and I—not knowing where Al had gone and fearing that he had died; and what had happened to you and Bernardo? The only reason I'm alive and happy is because of my husband and Justine."

"No doubt that you and Al and Justine, who lost her husband, suffered the worst."

"Well, I often blame myself," Bernardo admitted, "but considering the violence of that night and the fact that I would have been arrested as an accomplice of Leone, which I wasn't, and only became a substitute for Benito who begged me to take his place after he had become violently sick on poisoned wine. But by switching places with Benito, I was able to learn about the phony robbery and to let Dawn know that Leone was planning something. I was told that this was to be a robbery, but when Leone began firing, I had to defend myself from Leone. So I shot the S.O.B. twice."

Now Dr. Valentine added, "But your shots didn't actually kill Leone nor did Al's champagne bottle, which smashed his skull, and not even Massimo's choking and smashing his head into the marble floor. Actually, Leone was dead by that time."

"Well, what or who actually killed Leone?"

"Dr. Valentine almost laughed, "You did, Dawn, with that single-shot dog pistol. I know because I was the surgeon at the inquest. Only later did I learn from Lucy that you were deadly accurate with it at short distances. She told me how you hit a tin can in the air."

"Now, I'll give you my story. Fortunately I had gone to the women's john and I had just come out and was standing behind that green arras when Leone started shooting. That's when I fired but I couldn't tell if I had hit him."

Now Bernardo explained, "I grabbed Dawn and forced her to escape with me through the front door. I've often wondered whether I should have forced Dawn to come with me."

"I really didn't have any choice. Everything happened so fast. At the exact time of the shooting I wanted to escape, but you grabbed me. And I was afraid that you were Leone's partner and would kill me if I resisted. Remember, you were wearing a blue ski mask and I was terrified and didn't recognize your voice."

To avoid any further embarrassing questions, Lucy cheerfully added, "Why don't we look at the positive outcome of the tragedy? I'm married and happy. Let's bury the past since we can't change it."

With the tension dissipated, Dawn explained. "Upon our return to San Francisco, both of us were very depressed and frightened. We had no idea where any of you were. Actually I feared that everybody was dead."

"So what did you do?" Justine asked.

"First we sought psychiatric help, but the doctor didn't seem to understand our problem or offer any real help. Then we found another doctor who recommended that we join an EPIC encounter group."

"An EPIC group? I've heard about them." Georgio sounded doubtful.

"Yes, these are self-help groups which offer non-threatening cooperative support for victims who have experienced severe fear and trauma and are desperate and often suicidal."

"EPIC stands for Empathy, Patience, Intelligence and Courage—four simple words which form the strength and structure of every group, which is limited to twelve members. A professionally trained leader helps get the group started then, after four or five sessions, the group functions on its own strength."

"This is self-help, non-threatening therapy by one's peers. It saved our lives and our marriage, didn't it, Dawn?"

"It certainly did. Fortunately we were invited into a group who were very supportive and always positive. It was the best thing that ever happened to us. Not only were we saved, but we still belong and have helped others, some who were in worse shape than we had been."

"That really sounds good," Justine added, "I'm in fairly good shape, but I still get depressed."

Now Georgio added his endorsement, "As a medical doctor, I know that some forms of cooperative therapy work wonders, but I feel that Lucy and I are in good mental health."

That seemed to end the conversation as the two cars were nearing a supermarket. Before entering the large market, Lucy assembled a small group from Al's family: Virginia, Robert and two brothers, Allan and Stephen. Let's decide before we go in—we'll need food for two days and possibly longer. Allan, you and Steve get breakfast foods, Virginia, you and Bob take care of lunch, and I'll take care of dinner. Oh, one other fact, I'm paying the entire bill. Here's a hundred for starters; if it's more, that's okay. I'll wait for you at the checkout stand."

Soon the group reassembled with two large shopping carts fully loaded, which the clerk quickly checked as the men carefully packed everything into four cardboard boxes.

Casually looking over the boxes, Lucy asked, "Champagne, wine? I don't see any."

As the men quickly packed their purchases into the trunks of the two cars, again Lucy took charge. "Now, this is important. Please follow me closely. Soon we'll be on the Silverado Trail, then after about five or six miles, we'll turn onto Highway 128. Then after about five miles, on the left, you will see a large house on the top of a small hill. But we must stop and hope that Mr. Williams, the caretaker, will be there to let us in. The narrow road will circle to the right, past a parking lot for guests, and after about three hundred feet we ascend to the back of our house where we'll park and unload."

Soon they arrived at the gate where the caretaker had the gate open. Quickly Lucy exchanged greetings and comments. As both cars slowly approached the house, Lucy wept as memories overcame her. Quickly Al consoled her and Dr. Valentine maintained a discreet silence.

With all the ten adults surprised and elated, the homecoming celebration began. Quickly Lucy introduced the caretaker's wife, Mary, who, with her husband, followed Lucy as she began showing the back of the large house and grounds.

"As you can see from where we've parked, this is the back and there, between the two wings, is the swimming pool where I learned to swim. This the east side of the property with the various buildings for equipment and storage, and there is the cottage where Sam and Mary have lived since the house was built almost twenty years ago."

Then Lucy slowly led the group just past the pool where she stopped to explain. This house is essentially a large rectangle with the swimming pool as the divider between the south and north wings. All of the sleeping quarters are on the north side and all the storage and kitchen and dining rooms are on the south side. We can enter the house from either side of the double doors directly in front of us. But the formal entrance is from the front of the house. We'll see that later."

Anxious to see the house interior, everybody followed Lucy through the double doors. To everybody's surprise, they were now standing in a long hallway which over-looked the very large living room which could be reached by wide semi-spiral staircases at each end of the hallway.

At this point, Lucy encouraged everybody to explore the house and premises and to select a bedroom "that you plan to use while you're here. And now, while you're browsing and wandering, perhaps Al and my husband will help me prepare a few 'goodies' which might keep us going until dinner."

As the caretaker and his wife had already unloaded the boxes of food and delivered them to the large pantry, Lucy put two bottles of champagne in the freezer, "Just for twenty minutes," she muttered. Quickly the two men prepared several small platters of pate, cheeses, salami and crackers.

"This is the most elaborate and elegant house I could ever imagine," Al offered. To which Georgio added, "This must be an Italian-American house with all of the space, utility and beauty."

"Of course. What would you expect from poor Italian-Americans," Lucy laughed.

Soon the appetizers were completed and Lucy removed the champagne and found twelve appropriate glasses. "We can't overlook the Williamses; after all, they've taken care of the property for many years."

With the food ready on a large serving table in the dining room, soon the hungry guests arrived. Making certain that everybody, including Mary and John Williams were present, Al quickly transformed himself from the aging retiree to the genial, ebullient toastmaster whom Lucy had loved and admired.

"Good friends, dear friends, I would like to offer a toast to our generous and wonderful friends, Lucy and her husband, Dr. Valentine, two people I've known and loved through the good and the bad. Without their affection and help, I wouldn't be here now. So, I say to you and everybody present: Lucia and Georgio, to you. May your courage, strength and beauty be our hope and promise for the future."

For several seconds, the sound of tinkling glasses and cheerful voices filled the room. But before the toasting had ended, Lucy added, "I would like to offer one final toast to the man I loved and will always admire, Professor Al Praitt. He gave me courage and hope, which I will never forget."

The joy and pleasure were infectious as the wine flowed and everybody celebrated for an hour or more. Slowly rooms were selected and everybody was comfortably settled.

As the dinner hour approached, Virginia Edwards suggested that she and her two brothers should prepare dinner. Quickly they agreed and asked Al if he had any suggestions for the meal.

"No, I wouldn't dare after our feast last night at Chez Panisse, but you are all good cooks so fix something tasty."

Accepting the challenge, the trio decided on a pasta, "Maybe some carbonara," Stephen suggested.

"And some lamb chops," Allan added.

"But don't forget a salad and dessert," Virginia demanded.

As their cooperative efforts progressed, they all agreed that the carbonara should be served with a good cabernet. "Right, Steve. Too bad we didn't buy a few of Dad's bottles at the supermarket."

While carefully preparing the meal and setting the table, the trio spoke hopefully of enlarging their small winery. "Imagine having a place like this," Allan said. "I wonder if Lucy's father ever got beyond just growing and selling grapes. He certainly had the space and the land."

"Forget that, you guys," Virginia concluded, "I think that Dad, with your help, will be able to get a small winery started."

With the pasta just about ready, Virginia encouraged everybody to the dining room. Then remembering her baby, who had been left with her mother-in-law, Virginia called her house in Berkeley. Satisfied that Jill, her year-old daughter, was in good hands, Virginia returned to the noisy dining room.

Everybody was talking, their voices a chorus of pleasure and surprise which would have given Lucy's father, Robert and his brother, Charles Conde, great pleasure. Nobody in the Napa Valley loved parties more than the famous Conde brothers.

Finally, with the elaborate dinner over, the group settled around the living room. A roaring blaze of heat and fire helped to celebrate the family reunion. Soon the conversation lagged. Lucy sat quietly at the large Steinway, then suddenly alerted everybody with a series of Chopin waltzes. Each piece suggested more until suddenly Lucy produced music nobody suggested: Duke Ellington, Fats Waller and several others only Al remembered.

After a half hour Lucy closed the piano lid and announced, "Sorry, friends, but I'm tired. Maybe tomorrow I'll surprise you with some really good music."

And with that suggestion, everybody soon found their way to their bedrooms.

When it became apparent that all of the pairs occupied the four bedrooms, leaving only one, Al suggested Justine should have it.

"Are you afraid to share a bedroom with me? In case you're worried, it has twin beds and I promise not to seduce you."

Quickly Al accepted Justine's suggestion and soon a blissful silence radiated throughout the large house.

Following breakfast, Lucy confided to Al that she, Georgio, Justine and Virginia would be gone most of the morning. "It's just some business that I must take care of in Napa. But we should be back for lunch."

"If you feel up to it, Al, why don't you and your sons walk around the place? I think that it's pretty much as it was when I left here twelve years ago. I'm sure the Williamses would be pleased to show you around. He's our very capable maintenance man who also makes certain that the contractor and the crews who manage the vineyards are efficient and, above all, are honest."

Pleased with Virginia's suggestion, Al questioned Virginia's husband, Robert, who politely begged off, but Stephen and Allan were enthusiastic. As his sons bundled up in warm clothing, Al excused himself, "I'm afraid my bum leg couldn't take me far."

No sooner were the brothers near one of the several equipment buildings than the caretaker greeted them. "Would you like to see the property? It's a bit chilly but you're dressed for it. What would you like to see?"

"Maybe you could give us some idea about the size of the property and the kinds of grapes the Conde family grew?"

"Sure. As you can see from these buildings, the Conde family had a lot of equipment: plows, discs, tractors, trucks—enough for the hundred and sixty acres."

"How long have you worked here, Mr. Williams?"

"About twenty-two years with the Conde family. The Colonel hired me in 1968, but I have been in the valley since the war. Actually, I knew and worked for the Conde grandparents since about nineteen fifty. And I'll tell you something, the Condes, all of them, were and still are the best people in this valley. The older Mr. Conde was an Italian from northern Italy and came to California in the early nineteen twenties, worked for the Giannini family in the old bank of Italy, and managed to buy a lot of property during the depression."

"What happened to his two sons?" Allan asked.

"That was terrible, unbelievable. The older son, Robert, was a war hero who won the Medal of Honor, but opposed the Vietnam War and resigned when he was a Colonel. His younger brother was also an Air Force officer who either got shot down or was killed during the Vietnam War. That terrible bad luck happened just after Robert was killed when his tractor flipped over on him as he was plowing a steep hillside."

Both Allan and Stephen were shocked and quickly changed the subject to questions about the property and what varieties of grapes were grown.

"I'm not certain about the exact acreage of the vineyards, but I think there's sixty acres in Cabernet Sauvignon, about twenty in Zinfandel, and about the same number in Merlot. Then there's about twenty in Chardonnay and maybe twenty in Sauvignon Blanc."

Both Allan and Stephen expressed surprise. "That's really pretty big, isn't it? About one hundred and fifty acres in grapes?"

"Well," the old man explained, "it's fairly big, but nothing like some of the major growers, the Mondavis, or the Canales who are just getting started here."

After some two hours of talking and wandering around in the cold air, the brothers thanked the old man and returned to the house.

During his wife's unexpected absence, Robert had been busy calling Berkeley about his daughter, Jill. Satisfied, he quickly cleared the breakfast dishes and set the table for lunch—a minor rule of the marriage vow that he and Virginia cheerfully observed.

Now the placidity of this tranquil rural scene was about to change. The sounds of two large cars arriving together into the small parking lot and the cheerful voices of Lucy, Virginia and Dr. Valentine were doubled by the laughter of two men and one woman who emerged from a large Cadillac sedan.

The cheerful voices and sounds were a serendipity of speech, laughter and joy, which immediately alerted the sleepy sextet of Dawn and Bernardo and the Praitt family to arousal.

Suddenly Lucia opened the patio doors wide open and called, "Anybody home?"

The response was immediate as Lucy and Virginia directed the group to the lower quarters. Here to the surprise of Al and his two sons, Virginia introduced the three strangers as law partners in the firm of Bingle, Houston and Roberts—George Bingle, Harold Houston and Sally Roberts.

"Before we all become confused about the presence of this law firm," Lucy explained, "my husband and I and my grandmother, Justine, have decided that we should divest ourselves of this house, vineyards and all the buildings and the equipment."

For a few seconds, there was silence before Justine spoke, "What my granddaughter is saying is simple. We, really only Lucy and Georgio, are giving all of this property to the Praitt family."

Now a burst of confused laughter and questions erupted as Al stepped forward, "Please, please, Lucy. Are you telling me that you and your husband are giving this property to my family and me? If so, why?"

Again Lucy, now supremely proud and confident, explained, "Al you've talked to me many times about your desire to start a winery and how you were writing a book, 'a potboiler' you called it, to raise money to start a winery. Well, here's your 'potboiler' and you've really earned it."

At this point, Virginia stepped forward, "Dad, before you or my brothers become confused, I'll fill you in on the details of Lucy's, Justine's and Dr. Valentine's generosity. It's quite simple. They no longer want to maintain this large property and all of the problems that go with these holdings. Additionally, Lucy still owns other vineyards in the valley and in Sonoma, which provide more than enough income for her family."

Now, Lucy again interrupted, "Unless you or your family, Al, absolutely refuse to accept this property as a gift, the property will be deeded to you immediately. That's the reason our lawyers are here and why Virginia, Justine and I have been with them all morning."

"Perhaps you would like one of the lawyers to explain briefly what is necessary, important and legal about this contract?" Lucy asked.

"Please do," Al added.

At this point, the female lawyer, Sally Roberts, stood. "Since property transfers are my speciality, I'll speak for my partners. Although this property may be transferred as a gift, there are several important problems, taxation and legal matters that must be resolved. To make this transfer as easy as possible, we have converted this property from a private holding to a family corporation which will greatly reduce the taxation while adding the small burden of corporate law."

Now Al interrupted, "What is that burden?"

"Actually it isn't much of a burden because it protects you, the owners of the new corporation, from silly nuisance lawsuits. And there are many small legal requirements which are simple but necessary."

At this point, Virginia interrupted, "Please, if you, the lawyers and nobody else objects, I would like to talk very briefly with my father, my husband and my brothers."

Quickly the Praitts gathered in a nearby room. "Dad," Virginia said, "please don't quibble about this contract or this gift. As a lawyer, I fully understand what this law firm is saying. It's very simple. They are saving us a lot of money in the form of transfer taxes and operating the winery as a family. Please let's sign the papers and avoid any embarrassment or possible conflict."

Soon the Praitts returned to the larger room where Al explained, "I'm sorry to be such a pain in the neck. I just didn't understand completely what Miss Roberts was talking about."

Again Lucy became the chief speaker, "I believe that all of the important questions have been answered but one. Al, we need a name for your family corporation. Have you one?"

"Yes, it's a name I've cherished for years, 'Les Caves de Bacchus' or 'Bacchus Cellars' and my motto is, 'Wine for drinking.'"

The large room erupted in cheers.

With all the questions and answers complete, the trio of lawyers arranged the all legal papers in order and suggested that the signing should be clear and exact.

"Before we begin this complicated process," Dr. Valentine asked. "Maybe we should first have something to eat. It's now after two and I'm hungry. Furthermore, I've ordered a lot of food which just arrived."

The three lawyers were surprised but pleased with the break in a legal procedure, which could be timely.

After an hour of eating and drinking wine moderately while discussing the problems of starting a small family-owned winery, the papers were signed and the lawyers departed.

Tired but elated, everybody exchanged hugs and kisses.

"Now that you are the new owners of this beautiful house and everything that's in it," Lucy asked, "may I play a piece which the first time you asked me about it, Al, I was confused and frightened?"

Al nodded, "Yes, Lucy, and that was Beethoven's sonata, opus 106, the Hammerklavier."

Turning to relatives and friends, Lucy quietly explained, "All of the late Beethoven sonatas are difficult but not like 106 in B flat major. Furthermore, it's the longest of his sonatas, it's anywhere from forty-two minutes to forty-six depending on how many repeats the pianist decides to take. But its difficulty is the score itself. For me, this is Beethoven's personal autobiography–his complete loss of hearing, his many frustrations, his unrequited loves, his health, his angers and I suppose other fears and hates."

Quietly, Lucy raised her hands and began the Allegro, a dramatic introduction that seemed to be a challenging statement followed by a series of questions and responses, and concluding after about ten minutes with a recapitulation and finale.

With hardly a pause, Lucy almost skipped into the short scherzo, a brief and lively series of short statements which abruptly ended in two and a half minutes.

The third movement, the adagio sostenuto began with a quiet, sustained passage of strong passions and feelings. Repeatedly, Beethoven asked his questions tenderly and angrily. Now, as the very long movement delved even deeper, Al's eyes watered and he almost wept. With his emotions and composure exposed, he noted that Lucy, too, was struggling with small beads of tears falling toward the keyboard.

Quietly Lucy continued slowly and deliberately and everybody seemed to be caught up in the emotional struggle which only ended after almost twenty minutes.

Pausing for several seconds, Lucy began the fourth and final movement, the largo. Written as a fugue, the tempo increased as expressive responses to questions sacred and profane. For several minutes, the arguments were sustained before a final resolution, positive and strong.

For about thirty seconds, the small audience sat in stunned silence, then rising quickly, they burst into clapping and cheering. Slowly Lucy responded with a bow and wistful smile just as Al, holding her tenderly, kissed her softly.